Emily Hein grew up in Victoria, British Columbia, with her parents and four sisters. She attended the University of Victoria where she graduated with a Bachelor of Science, majoring in Biology. It was in the summer of 2018 that Emily decided to dedicate her time to writing a novel, which has become one of her greatest passions.

Dedicated to the parents of America who have lost a loved one to a bullet that never should have been fired.

Emily Hein

DEAR MR. PRESIDENT

AUSTIN MACAULEY PUBLISHERS™

LONDON • CAMBRIDGE • NEW YORK • SHARJAH

Ordering Information:
Quantity sales: special discounts are available on quantity purchases by corporations, associations, and others. For details, contact the publisher at the address below.

Publisher's Cataloging-in-Publication data
Hein, Emily
Dear Mr. President

ISBN 9781643786285 (Paperback)
ISBN 9781643786292 (Hardback)
ISBN 9781645368373 (ePub e-book)

Library of Congress Control Number: 2019911787

www.austinmacauley.com/us

First Published (2020)
Austin Macauley Publishers LLC
40 Wall Street, 28th Floor
New York, NY 10005
USA

mail-usa@austinmacauley.com
+1 (646) 5125767

Chapter 1

Dear Mr. President,

It has been 91 days since the Pandora High School Shooting.

To think how the summer has flown by, but not a single whistle has been heard from the government on changing any laws or regulations for the selling of firearms.

I wish that you could look at the parents from across the country, the people who have had to face many challenges and burdens after losing one or maybe even several children from school shootings.

There have also been a number of cases reported from witnesses attending the schools who are experiencing symptoms of PTSD.

Please make a change; it could be as simple as a mandatory mental health check before anyone is allowed to purchase an automatic rifle, handgun, or anything that can cause life-threatening damages to our children.

Sincerely,
Scarlett Smith

Scarlett read over her message, making sure there were no spelling mistakes. She was nervous that after ninety-one emails, she was beginning to sound redundant, always ending with a plea for change. Yet, she also found it necessary that some people who got their hands on the email may need to have every single word spelled out for them, which was exactly what Scarlett was trying to do. With a final glimpse, she clicked the send icon on the *whitehouse.gov* contact page.

Chapter 2

It was the first day of grade one. Rosie Smith's first day of elementary school was today and her mother, Scarlett, was running around like a chicken with her head chopped off. She was not used to having no help prepare breakfast and lunch in the morning for Rosie. She was on her own, trying to decide what would sustain her daughter till 2PM when she had to pick her up, what would be the most nutritious option. When Scarlett realized that it was five minutes past the time they were supposed to leave, she crammed Rosie's bright pink lunchbox into her matching Dora the Explorer backpack, grabbed her daughter's hand, and raced to the car, nearly forgetting to lock the white door to her middle-class suburban California home.

"I cannot believe my little Rosie is going off to school today," Scarlett said out loud to no one in particular, turning onto West Pandora Boulevard.

As Scarlett tried to swallow back her whimpering sobs, she could hear her daughter giggling in the back seat. "Mommy, you're so silly! I was in school last year."

"But this is your first day at the big kids' school, sweetie," Scarlett replied.

"I am a big kid, I am seven!" retorted Rosie with an upturned smile.

It was Rosie's birthday last week and she was determined she could do anything now because she was seven, which seemed to be much older than six.

Scarlett was taking Rosie to Pandora Elementary School. Every second that passed in the seventeen-minute car ride, she glimpsed at her rearview mirror to see how Rosie was doing. Scarlett needed to know if she was frowning, smiling, giggling, or crying. She was amazed how bravely her little girl was handling everything that happened this summer. It made her happy to think that Rosie could still have a normal childhood, or at least as normal as possible considering the circumstances.

Scarlett turned her blinker on as she pulled up to the familiar school in her black 2009 Ford Escape, which seemed so spacious now with only her sitting in the front seat, and tiny little Rosie bobbing her blonde head up and down in the back. The hot California sun shined, blinding Scarlett while she scurried out of the car to help her daughter get her backpack from the trunk; she had forgotten her

Ray-Ban knockoffs at home. As the two made their way to the main entrance, Rosie noticed the colorful painting of a bear along one of the walls. "Look, Mommy! Aren't the bears so pretty?"

"Yes, sweetie. Someone once told me that it looks like a mother and her cub walking on red, blue, green, purple, and yellow clouds," answered Scarlett, looking at her watch, content that they had made it on time.

"I see it! I see it," Rosie rejoiced.

With the short attention span of child, Rosie dropped her gaze from the bears and began to search the crowd of children for her two best friends, Delany and Jackson. Delany always stuck out of the crowd with her fiery curly hair, pasty skin, and thousands of adorable freckles that scattered her face and shoulders. Her beautiful hair resembled her mother's, Martha, but no one seemed to know which family member contributed to her large assortment of freckles.

Jackson was also easily recognized in the herd of tiny children, towering over the other grade one students; it must be due to the one-year age difference. His mother, Alex, decided to hold him back another year when his kindergarten teacher had suggested this arrangement. He ended up doing two years of preschool; it was not until after his first year that he was placed in a class with Delany and Rosie. Alex would tell Martha and Scarlett that Jackson was kind as can be, but had one hell of a thick skull.

Rosie, Delany, and Jackson have been referred to as the three musketeers over the past year, since they met in kindergarten. During the first week of school, Delany and Rosie had become friends almost immediately. With Delany's bossy and extremely loud personality, she took an immediate liking to Rosie, who was more of a happy follower. One afternoon the two girls were playing in the sandbox making mud cakes. A bigger boy in the class walked over to Delany and Rosie, destroying their decorative cakes "with his big stinky foot," Rosie told her mother. Jackson happened to be watching the girls making their desserts and wanted to join them, but was too shy to ask, so he sat by himself struggling to make his own mud cake look as perfect as Delany and Rosie's. When Jackson saw what the boy had done, he stormed over and put him in a headlock until he apologized.

Scarlett remembered how amazed Rosie was that this boy, who was almost twice their size, was sticking up for her and her new friend. Jackson had told the two girls that he learned that move from his older sisters, who also taught him to always stand up to bullies and if you wanted to get anywhere in life, you had to be a gentleman. Scarlett could picture Jackson, looking all big and bully-like, talking with a lisp, explaining how girls should be treated; she thought it was the cutest thing. Since then, the three of them had been inseparable.

"ROSIE, ROSIE, ROSIE," Scarlett and Rosie turned around towards Delany's excited shouting. She was standing in front of the main doors to enter the school.

"Bye, Mommy," Rosie said as she was about to scamper off before Scarlett swept her little girl up into her arms, cocooning her before she left Rosie for the rest of the morning and afternoon.

"Bye, sweetie. I love you so very much," Scarlett murmured as she petted her daughter's hair.

"I love you too," Rosie whispered back.

With a quick, tight squeeze, Scarlett let her little girl go. She watched as Rosie ascended the two steps quickly to where Delany was now standing beside Jackson, who was holding the door open for the two tiny girls. In a flash, Rosie's blonde bobbing head disappeared behind the school doors.

"They are so adorable," Martha sniffled; she had snuck up quietly behind Scarlett, causing her to jump a little when she spoke.

"They really are," agreed Scarlett, turning to give her friend a side embrace with her left arm.

Scarlett knew how hard it must have been for Martha to drop off her only child at elementary school for the very first time. After seven years, they had finally made it into the big leagues, or at least that is how Martha felt.

"Good riddance, I say," joked Alex as she approached Martha and Scarlett. Alex had more of a busy household with her two older daughters Chloe and Eliza.

Since the three women's children had been conjoined at the hip, so had Alex, Martha, and Scarlett. The three mothers made a very unique-looking group of middle-aged women.

Alex had the most beautiful complexion, resembling the late and remarkable Whitney Houston. With her high prominent cheekbones and petite figure, she looked more like a model than an upper-class mother of three. Although she was in her early forties, she dressed like a rich, young, thirty-year-old, whose clothing and accessories were made by Gucci, Jimmy Choo, and Vera Wang. She could pull off the young look more than anyone else Scarlett had met, most likely because she did not have a single wrinkle marking her elegant face.

In contrast, Martha was one of the palest and least fashionable person you would ever meet. She represented her Celtic ancestry through her scarlet locks that bounced with every tiny step she took. Martha always blamed her dirty clothes on working at Pete's Bakery. She also always liked to chirp in how hard it was being a single mother and that she rarely found enough time to wash her own clothes. Yet, no one ever really seemed to care about her flour-marked clothing, probably because she always smelled like freshly baked pie, cinnamon buns, donuts, or something in between. She also had the kind of beauty that could pull off any look, including the modern hobo chick.

Then there was Scarlett, the oldest and shortest of the two, standing at 5 feet and 2 inches, give or take a couple of centimeters. Her brown hair was often drawn back in a tight professional manner, and she was usually found wearing a blazer paired with matching tailored pants. But over the past three months, she had been dressing more on the comfy side.

The three women bonded just as quickly as their children after meeting for the first time. With Martha's loud personality, Alex's witty attitude, and Scarlett's more reserved demeanor, their personalities complement each other nicely, making their friendship fun and light-hearted.

After saying their hellos, Martha, Scarlett, and Alex headed to Pete's to grab a pastry and coffee before Martha started her shift.

When Scarlett stepped through the door, she heard the bell ring, letting Pete know that he had customers. The smell of freshly made cinnamon buns washed over her, making her mouth water instantly.

"Yum," Scarlett murmured quickly and quietly, without acknowledging she spoke out loud.

"I know, right? I am definitely getting me one of those," replied Alex.

Martha agreed with a quick nod and headed over to the counter to order. Pete greeted Martha with his adorable grin, specifically reserved for her, "What can I getcha', love?"

Martha returned the smile, gushing over the way Pete called her 'love' with his strong Scottish accent.

In response, she did a quick giddy little jump and procrastinated her reply, trying to start up a brief conversation so she can look into his ocean blue eyes for a moment longer.

Pete only stood a couple inches taller than Martha and had a husky brown beard that hid his well-constructed jawline. Scarlett admired Pete for his good looks, it would be hard not to, he was masculine without being overpoweringly so. He had brown, short, curly hair, dusted with gray, even though he couldn't be older than thirty-five. He was undeniably gorgeous, getting hit on by nearly all of his customers. However, Scarlett found herself more attracted to men with not such overpowering features, which was probably why she fell for her husband, Jonathan, therefore she was able to retain herself from getting lost in the mixture of his beautiful eyes and Scottish accent.

After ordering, Scarlett wandered around the small space of the bakery to peer into the enclosed pastry cases. She glanced from one freshly baked assortment to the next, licking her lips when she noticed how crisp the butter croissants looked. Her mouth began to water again at the thought of getting another treat. She began to wonder if she had made the right decision on the cinnamon bun, but her name was called along with Martha's and Alex's, so the women headed outside to sit on the wooden patio that overlooked the water.

The deck was matched with wooden chairs and tables. Alex always mentioned how the stiff chairs hurt her 'bony ass.' Alex was the complainer of the group; she couldn't resist making a comment about the low-end restaurants and crammed cafes, but even she admitted that Pete's Bakery had the best cinnamon buns and pies. Her cheerful, down-to-earth side helped even her out; she would add in a compliment after her brief moment of criticism.

Scarlett and Martha brushed off Alex's snarky remarks with swallowed giggles. They both knew that she genuinely enjoyed coming to sit outside due the cabin atmosphere provided by the dark wood flooring and rails, including the rustic outdoor furniture. It made them feel like they were on vacation with a beautiful view overlooking the still blue sea that meets the September sky in union.

As Scarlett was distracted by the California sun gleaming down on her and the overwhelming smell of the Pacific Ocean, she noticed that Alex was off in another rant about how her two eldest daughters barely acknowledge her presence when she is in the room with them.

"It was Chloe's first day of high school today, can you believe it? And she didn't even want me there to drop her off," whined Alex.

"She is probably just going through that stage now where she will be trying to create a separate life from yours, or at least that is what my mother says about kids entering high school," replied Martha.

Martha's mother, Gail, was a high school teacher at Pandora High School, which was where Alex's two girls, Chloe and Eliza, attended. Gail was always telling Martha stories about how awful the children become in high school. She said they start acting like druggies, trying to sneak out of class to smoke some marijuana.

Gail loved to share her parenting, motherly, as well as teaching advice with Alex and Scarlett whenever she got a moment to speak to them; the only person genuinely listening would be Martha. She also enjoyed sharing her opinion of the kids that were in her class, telling the women how the generations were slowly getting worse. Gail's favorite thing to do was to rave about her daughter, Martha; how she was so different from the other high school children when she was younger. "She loved to hang out with her little old mother," Gail would tell Alex and Scarlett. Gail even liked to think they were best friends, which most parents cannot say about their teenagers.

"But I was involved in Eliza's life when she started high school. Now I feel invisible to both of them. Just last night I could hear Eliza telling Chloe the dos and don'ts, and what she should wear on her first day. I wanted to help her pick out an outfit. We all know I have the best fashion sense," said Alex truthfully.

"Well, at least they are getting along, right? I have twin cousins who are in their thirties and they do not even speak to each other. I believe their feud began over some stupid boy," Martha sighed.

"I guess so. What is your opinion, Scarlett?" asked Alex.

Alex and Martha often jumped to ask Scarlett's opinion on family matters. They wanted a professional to tell them that they were not crazy and that was how ordinary kids behaved, or that they would grow out of it.

"I am unsure," replied Scarlett. "Maybe it is just a phase they are going through. But I am not a 100% certain. And besides, Martha is right, at least they are getting along."

Scarlett often gave only the most basic answers in response to her friends' questions. She did not enjoy counseling unless she was at a self-help group or working, although she used to use her techniques on her family at home all the time.

"Hmm, you may be right. Enough about me," Alex enjoyed being in the spotlight, but not for too long. "I noticed that Jonathan was not there today to see Rosie off on her first day." Alex was never afraid to acknowledge the elephant in the room.

"Yeah, he said he was really busy with work and everything. I think he is having a hard time coping," replied Scarlett.

"But then why did he leave you? It's quite pathetic if you ask me," said Martha.

"You have to understand it from his point-of-view. He is struggling but he chooses not to show it. He does not like people to see his emotional side," retorted Scarlett.

"Well, if you ask me, he should be supporting you, that is what marriage is about, you know, all that for better or worse crap," Martha said sinisterly.

Martha was never the one for marriage. At the ripe age of twenty-seven, she decided she wanted to have a baby so she went and got herself a sperm donor and boom, just like that, she was giving birth to a beautiful baby girl nine months later. She liked to think of it as poetic; she wanted a child so badly that she went out and got herself pregnant without the help of any prince charming.

"Yessss," nodded Alex in agreement.

"He is still my husband, and I am willing to give him the space he needs."

"Hasn't he filed for divorce?" asked Alex boldly, already knowing the answer to her question, but needing the confirmation.

"Yes, but he just needs time," winced Scarlett.

"Scarlett, you can only give him so much time," stated Martha while sipping on her green tea.

"I can always share a little bit of Darryl," Alex laughed, "I am sure he wouldn't mind helping around your house if I asked him to."

Darryl was the same age as Alex, but looked just as young. His skin tone was a shade darker than hers, and they both shared similar dark chocolate eyes and full lips. Martha and Scarlett believed it was his amazing charm and adorable gap-toothed grin that won over Alex's hard-earned affection.

"She don't need no man," chimed Martha with the snap of her fingers, causing all of the women to laugh like teenagers.

The women focused their attention to their drinks and enjoyed their cinnamon buns until they had to part ways.

***

Later that evening, Scarlett found herself clicking through different channels while she ate her late night snack after tucking Rosie in.

With a pudding cup in the palm of Scarlett's hand and the cleanest spoon she found in the dirty dishwasher entwined between her fingers, Scarlett nuzzled herself into the nook of her worn down leather couch. The claw marks left by their old tabby cat, Toby, were still prominent down the legs of the old furniture.

She flipped to the local news station. They were broadcasting interviews done earlier today outside of Pandora Elementary School.

Scarlett recognized one of the parents being interviewed as Sandy Warner, who had a child one year older than Rosie, and lived right down the street from her.

"Do you feel safe brining your children to school given what happened in June at Pandora High School?" asked the reporter.

"Not one bit," cried Sandy. "I lost my child in that school shooting and now my little Emily is growing up without her older brother around to protect her."

"I am sorry for you loss, ma'am," said the reporter earnestly. She had probably not expected to be talking to a parent who had lost their child in the school shooting.

"I never thought this could happen to me," Sandy sniffled between sobs as her blotchy skin twitched in agony. "You always hear about shootings in the ghetto, but you never expect it to happen at a normal public school. All because some crackhead kid decided to shoot the place up. Now I... I... no longer have my Bobby... he was always such a good boy. He was about... to... graduate this year."

Then suddenly, rage flashed between Sandy's watery green eyes.

"And what has the government got to say for themselves? HMMM? Nothing, that's what!" Sandy cried hysterically before being led away with her face in her palms.

With tears in her eyes, Scarlett turned the TV off and threw the remote to the other side of the couch like it had suddenly become infectious. She decided she would have one more pudding cup before bed as she swallowed back her sobs, making her stomach turn.

Chapter 3

Since the beginning of September, once a week, the Pandora High School gym had been used as a meeting location for the parents who had lost their children in the school shooting. This support group was led and organized by Scarlett; due to her background in counseling, she felt the need to make sure everyone was getting the help they needed, with or without funds.

With the school back in session over the past week, Principal Walter claimed that the school cannot provide 'free handouts,' and that the gym must be rented out, like it was for all the other after-hours programs. Scarlett had emailed Walter, explaining that the parents needed this, this year was going to be tough for them, and some of them had probably not received the helped they needed, but had acted like couch potatoes all summer.

"The support group is a necessity for these parents who are grieving," Scarlett typed.

Walter was a stubborn little prick who would not budge when his mind was made, so the gym ended up being rented out but the adults could still meet on Tuesday nights.

Scarlett chose Tuesday hoping that there would be more parents who would show up. Once they reached the age of 40, most adults just wanted to sit at home in their robes watching their latest Netflix show on Monday nights. Then Wednesday was hump day, so everyone usually went out for drinks after work.

Whereas Thursday and Friday were just too close to the weekend that most people seemed busy. Thus Scarlett thought Tuesday was the most logical day; it also worked well for her because Rosie had dance from five to 6PM during the meeting, therefore a babysitter was not needed.

Scarlett sat in one of the twenty black fold up chairs in the gym at 4:45PM. The cheap seats were organized in a U surrounding the Panther that decorated the center of the gymnasium floor. The large cat logo was painted to appear as if it would claw at any opponent who attempted to run past it. It also gave off a multi-dimensional characteristic as it reached around and out of the thick block letter P. The Pandora symbol was also painted to appear as if it too was popping out at you with its thick black border that encased another white border before the letter itself was filled with purple.

Scarlett would have a silent chuckle when her eyes met the gymnasium floor. She thought Principal Walter probably chose to color in the big chunky letter with purple because of the color starting with the letter 'p.' He always thought he was such a clever man. To her the whole floor mural looked a bit tacky, but so did every other high school's.

The purple and gray colored bleachers were pushed all the way back, only pulled out for basketball season, which wouldn't start for another month.

Scarlett looked around to the assortment of cookies and coffee. The cheap and burnt caffeine, and the dollar-store bought cookies made for more of a depressing atmosphere. Scarlett thought it was better than nothing.

She thought if Alex were here, she would make a remark of how sad and tragic this whole scenery looked, but on the bright side, people had something to sip and nibble on. Whereas Martha would only chime in her upbeat point-of-view. Alex's more pessimistic and Martha's optimistic nature sometimes made for a nice balance.

A few parents started trudging in through the wide double doors of the gym five minutes past 5PM.

"Help yourselves to some cookies and coffee," Scarlett said with a small smile as the parents walked towards her to take a seat.

Once everyone was settled in, some parents with a coffee in hand, leaving the cookies untouched, Scarlett began.

"Hello everyone, thank you for taking the time out of your day to show support to your fellow parents." This was Scarlett's second meeting and she had picked up the flow of things very quickly. She would introduce herself, discuss a topic that she thought might help some of the parents open up, such as how it had now been a full week back at school since the summer. Then she would offer the floor to anyone who was willing or felt strong enough to share.

Scarlett noticed that she was surrounded by the same crowd of four parents, mostly women, today that had been at the first meeting. She was expecting there to be a larger audience after school was back in session; she found people mourn the most when doing the first of anything – first birthday or Christmas after the loss of a loved one. The parents scattered in front of her today were Christine, Thea and her husband Tyler, as well as Sandy Warner, who was interviewed earlier last week on the local news.

Christine was sitting on the edge of her chair leaning over Sandy, trying to comfort her while invading her personal space at the same time. Scarlett thought Christine as a follower and patron, linking on to the most distressed person, wanting to feel wanted and needed for their comfort. Scarlett quickly noticed at the first meeting Christine had spotted Sandy broken down in tears before she sat down; she quickly ran to the rescue and ushered her towards a seat beside her, giving her a quiet pep-talk to speak up first, leading the others. Today she came in trailing behind Sandy and sat obediently next to her new leader. Scarlett knew she would be rubbing Sandy's back for the rest of the meeting today, like she had done last week. Her little gesture was a form of Christine's attempt to sooth Sandy, but she also did it so that superior would know that she was there for her. Scarlett had known Sandy from living down the street from her; she was a loud woman, a born leader, and she would have appreciated to find a subordinate in this setting.

Christine was a tall, elegant women, who could not be much older than Scarlett. She had long, straight, strawberry blonde hair that reached below her fake breasts. Her nose was straight as an arrow thanks to Dr. Lee. She also dressed like Alex in high-end designer apparel, usually mixing solid black and white pieces together. Christine did not look like she belonged in the Pandora High School gym, nor did most of the parents that enrolled their children here. There was a mix of the natural California babes, the high-end mothers, and the low-key average Joe type.

On the other hand, Sandy had a petite stature that made her look more like a child undergoing a temper tantrum instead of an adult grieving over her dead son. She also looked like she had not stopped crying since her interview, her eyelids red and swollen. Her skin looked less blotchy, most likely due to the expensive makeup she used making her face seem a shade paler than her neck.

Then there was Thea, sitting awkwardly beside Sandy. Thea was a stout middle-aged women with brown hair that was often pulled back in a high ponytail. She had one dimple marking her olive skinned left cheek. It was only visible when she smiled, which had been a rare sight over the last couple of months.

Tyler, Thea's husband, placed his chair a centimeter away from his wife's; that way he could wrap his arm over her shoulders for comfort. He barely fit in the cheap seats with his broad shoulders and large hockey player thighs and gluteal muscles. Scarlett used to think of him as a brute who resembled Grizzly Adams, the type of person who believed this was a man's world. He also reminded her of a jock that she went to high school with, Chad Vincent. They both had the wide chest and muscular arms, big guys who were meant to play football or some other tackling type of sport. Scarlett was delighted to find out that Tyler was not like the typical high school quarterback; after the first time speaking with Tyler, he reminded her more of a gentle old man, a soft-spoken soul.

Thea later told Scarlett that her husband was having a rough couple of days, it being the first week they didn't have to drive their daughter to school. He may have been the old soul type, but he was old-fashioned too, not wanting to share or discuss his own experiences, refusing to cry in front of others. Scarlett knew it would probably take a few more meetings before he opened up, but she was determined to get there. For now, he remained sitting quietly beside his wife, hand on her knee for reassurance, eyes blood-shot.

Sandy, who spoke first again today, began the meeting, "I do not know if many of you saw the local news the other day, but I was interviewed."

Scarlett was a little irritated how Sandy quickly got into the habit of starting every Tuesday session with a remark about her and her life, and why she was chosen to be a victim of this heinous crime. "This couldn't be God's plan." She acted as if every other living soul on this planet was inferior to her and her loved ones.

"I was handling myself fairly well, until—" Sandy swallowed back another sob "—until that stupid reporter asked me if I was okay, okay for my kids to be going back to school when last year the termed ended with some fucking lunatic teenager shooting my poor Bobby."

Scarlett was so used to dealing with children that she nearly told Sandy to watch her language, but she thought best to refrain herself from correcting the pitiful woman.

"I understand what you are saying," Scarlett exclaimed in her soothing tone, "but you have to remember the reporter was doing her job and she seemed awfully apolo—"

"No she was not, she was probably happy to get some pretty woman crying on her station because it would give them more views," sobbed Sandy.

"Remember, Sandy, everyone gets a turn to share their opinion with respect and silence," Scarlett smiled sweetly. She was always good at hiding her emotions.

"I was thinking the same thing too," of course Christine had to agree with Sandy.

"The reporter was not the point of my story," said Sandy, glaring at Christine.

Sandy took her anger out on Christine during the first session, and it appeared this was another habit she was getting herself into. However, Christine shrugged it off without a flinch.

"My point was that B-b-obby was not there with me to drop Emily off. It was our tradition. He would always come with me to drop his younger sister off. He enjoyed saying goodbye to her in front of her classmates so that they knew she had a big brother who would protect her if any one of them tried to mess with her. He was supposed to be there. But he wasn't. He will no longer be there to protect his baby sister," Sandy said through tears as Christine handed her some Kleenex from her purse, keeping them stashed away for everyone but herself.

Sandy continued to speak for the next 30 minutes about the loss she was experiencing and how no one understood her. Scarlett reminded her that they had all experienced loss, but yes, one person cannot say they knew exactly how another person was feeling.

Christine only added to the conversation with nods of agreement when Sandy was describing the emotions she had experienced over the last week since their previous meeting.

Thea contributed her opinions and described her state of mind last, after Sandy had tired herself out from crying and talking.

"Last Wednesday was Ashley's sixteenth birthday. It would have been my baby girl's sweet sixteen. She was so bright, such a smart cookie, that we had put her a year ahead in elementary school. We were nervous about her not fitting in, but like the angel that she was, she made friends right away, winning over the class with sweetness… She always had small birthday parties, inviting only her closest friends, but this year was going to be different. We had started planning her party last May… I remember talking with her, her telling me how she wanted a hired DJ, she wanted a cake that was a meter tall, enough to feed her entire graduating class," Thea said softly. "I thought that was too much, how expensive everything was going to be… Tyler fought and argued for her sake," Thea grabbed her husband's hand that was resting on her knee, giving a gentle squeeze, "but I wouldn't budge, I planted my foot and told them no."

Scarlett imagined those arguments between Thea and Tyler; she could not picture their voices raising above a quiet inside voice.

As Thea went on talking about all of the organizing, and arguing, her and her dead child had just made in May and June before the shooting, Scarlett noticed that Tyler was holding back his own tears. She thought he was the kind of man who did not think it was 'manly' for 'real' men to cry; she was underestimating this man's fragile character once again.

Scarlett was starting to think that maybe today would be the day that Tyler would discuss the pain he was going through, he would crack earlier than when she had thought, but to Scarlett's remorse, he went on silently through the final ten minutes of the meeting.

It was always hard to get the males to talk. Even when Scarlett used to be a counselor on the Suicide Prevention Lifeline, it was mostly females who called to talk about their problems, seeking help. Scarlett thought this strange because it was males who were four times more likely die from suicide.

Scarlett hoped that it would only take a few more meetings until Tyler opened up; she believed that men were usually the most troubled ones because they never expressed their feelings, keeping everything bottled up. Baby steps, she would tell herself, baby steps.

After giving some professional counseling advice and tips as to how to communicate feelings with loved ones, Scarlett led the meeting to an end.

Chapter 4

I have had this diary for about 3 months now, I've just been so busy this summer that I haven't found the chance to write, and I kinda forgot about it.

I also feel like my life is simply just not that interesting. I don't have the kinda life that belongs in a novel or a movie, my life is not 'readable' material, it's dull and boring.

My mom tells me that I should write all of the important interesting things that happen to me, so one day I can look back at my diary, or journal (whatever you want to call it), and reminisce about the past, or I can give it to my children to read if they feel like getting bored out of their minds.

I remember being in middle school, so excited for high school, excited to meet all these new guys, excited to try different classes, and most importantly, excited to turn 16. I use to think 16 was the perfect age, the age when I could go out late with my friends, maybe I can finally go to a party and drink (or smoke a bit of weed, I am up for almost anything) (I should have written in pencil). High school is supposed to be the highlight of my life, or so I am constantly told, but I finally made it to junior year and nothing is different.

Yeah, there are more guys compared to middle school, nothing exciting though, they are just as stupid as they were back then. The girls have improved a bit, they aren't as mean, or maybe I just don't care as much. There are no longer hot-or-not lists in the bathrooms, nor notes being passed around saying who has the best BJ lips. People have finally started growing up, or maybe they have gotten better at hiding their nasty sides.

I still have my best friend Denise, it has been me and her since grade 1, with some friends coming and going. We have always had each other's backs, we even got our schedules planned out so the first half of the year we are all in the same classes! Unfortunately, the second half we don't have any classes together, but we will still have lunch together so I am not too concerned.

Okay back to the point, I get a little sidetracked when I write, I think that is why my mom gave me this diary, to practice writing. My parents think I am going to be a political author or something. I love writing, and I am very opinionated, but that doesn't mean that is what I want to be known for, or what I want to do with my life.

I actually want to be a singer. No one would see this coming, especially since I was a big Goth in middle school (my mom told me that Goth phases are very common when you are 12). I always loved singing, mostly behind closed doors or in the shower, every now and then pouring my lungs and soul into my hairbrush. My parents don't know anything. They want me to go to college, get an education, to pretend that I am living the life I've always wanted because I am so 'lucky' to have a loving family and a college fund. They act like I don't have to worry about anything because my entire life has already been planned out by them, wanting to follow in their footsteps to a certain extent.

I could tell them that I want to go to Berklee College of Music, but they would just tell me it's a waste of time, that I wouldn't be able to find a 'real job' with a degree in such an absurd field. My parents, like most, love acting like they know everything about me, that they can tell what I thinking. They would tell me, "You are just acting out because you are going through your rebellious phase," or "he's mean to you because he likes you," which is ridiculous. I don't act out, I get angry. I am not going through some 'teenage rebellion,' I have no reason to be rebellious when my parents never set any rules or limits for me, which is mostly because I don't stay out late unless I am at Denise's. Also, the whole idea that a guy is mean to a girl because he likes her, is an awful thing for parents to teach their children. Boys are mean to little girls because they are simply mean! We shouldn't be taught that if some little boy pushes you down in the sand-pit, then he likes you; that is leading us up for failure and heartbreak! It also teaches us to stay with the guys that are mean, that they are only 'acting out' because they care.

Now MOM, if you are reading this (which is an INVASION OF PRIVACY), don't worry, I love you It's not your fault you and Dad think this way, you have been brainwashed by society, being told that happiness is based on the size of your paycheck, which is determined by your education. And if that is your invalid argument, then I can tell you to look at all the singers today and you can see their grossly large net-worth! Yeah, you can say "well they are the one in a million," but I will be too! And if you think my thoughts, opinions, ideas are going to waste, you are wrong! I am going to tell the world of my stories, ideas, and theories through my lyrics, you guys just wait and see.

Sorry, I feel like this is turning into more of a rant than a diary entry…

So as I was saying, I am now in junior year. This was my first week back at school after the summer (which I spent mostly babysitting). I decided to enroll in a theater class so I can practice my singing and maybe even perform in a musical, I first need to get over my fear of performing in front of people. Fortunately for me, my fellow peers hate me, so if I can sing in front of them then I can sing in front of anyone, I just first have to get through their laughter, or their pointing fingers and judging looks.

On the first day of class, my teacher, Mrs. Cornwall, told us we were going to have 'Mug-Up Mondays.' We each have to bring a mug to school on Monday, and she said she will bring in hot chocolate, tea, and little goodies for us to have as we sit in a circle and catch up with each other. We did a demonstration that day, but since no one knew about bringing our own mugs, she gave us red solo cups, which surprisingly didn't melt in our hands when we poured scorching water in them. We went around the circle, introducing ourselves and saying something about our summer.

I am not a fan of Mrs. Cornwall's idea, I don't like sitting around wasting time, chit-chatting with people I don't even really like. I know she means well, but come on, we are no longer 5, most of us have been in the same school since elementary, we probably know each other more than we would like. I remember when Emma, one of the happy-go-lucky cheerleaders, and I use to be best friends, before Denise and I met. Emma would wet the bed every night when she slept over. I had promised her that I wouldn't tell anyone, and to this day I have still kept my promise to that kind 5-year-old, who has now turned into one of the ugliest monsters.

I know some of her darkest secrets from when we were younger, and then when we left the playful ground of elementary and were introduced to the horrors and awkward stages of middle school, that is when Emma turned on me. She made fun of me, laughed at the way I dressed, told people I was a vampire. I think that was one of the reasons why I stayed in my Goth stage for so long, to prove to them I didn't care about the nasty things they called me. One of their favorite nicknames for me was 'blood sucker' (how original). But since freshmen year, I have finally figured out myself and my style, I know what clothes flatter my body, which I have finally grown into, and I know how to style my brown hair. I also went through my acne phase in middle school, puberty hit me hard, but now my skin is soft. I learned not to wear eyeliner on my lowest eyelid, to put in on my upper instead, making my blue eyes pop. I have even noticed some of the guys take second glances at me over the past year. The girls have stopped whispering names when I walk past them in the hall, now they just ignore me, which is fine by me.

So during the first 'Mug-Up,' we all introduced ourselves, we would say "hello so-and-so" and then the person talking would say something about their summer. When it got to Denise's turn (I convinced her to take the class with me so I wouldn't be alone), everyone mumbled hello to her. Denise was like me, not very well liked for no reason, but she had left her Goth stage sooner than I did, so people seemed to be leaving her alone for a while now. She only got the odd stares and glares, it seems that people have learned that if you have nothing nice to say, don't say anything at all, or they have simply gotten bored making fun of us and have found some new victim to prey on.

When it was my turn to introduce myself, people said hello cheerfully. It was the weirdest thing, even Emma made eye contact with me and smiled. I would have thought that I would be given the same negative mumbles and grumbles Denise got. It was like they didn't recognize me, and maybe they didn't. In the past two years I did my best to sit in the back of class, hoping and praying that I would go unnoticed. Now I am starting to think it worked, that they have actually forgotten who I am! Imagine that! It's like I have been given a clean slate, a fresh start. I am starting to think that there is still hope for high school to not be such a traumatic experience, I just have to keep in the shadows. I will pray for everyone else to continue on with their fake lives while I try to create a real one for me, doing what I love, singing.

This year I have decided to finally get serious about singing, to do something to help move me forward on this path. I have made a plan to go talk to Mrs. Cornwall one-on-one. I will ask her if she could give me some extra help, or lessons on the side. I am still writing out the logistics of it all, what I am going to say, when I am going to say it. For now, I will keep my career plan a secret, I will play along for my parents' sake. I will still focus on my other classes, get good grades, start preparing for college. I will also sneak in my application for Berklee, it will all work out in the end, I know it will. Or as Ms. V likes to say, "Everything happens for a reason, if it's meant to be, it will be."

Ta Ta for now,
Love P

Chapter 5

Dear Mr. President,

It has been 120 days since the Pandora High School Shooting.

As I have told you, in one of my previous emails, that I have been counseling some of the parents who lost their children on June 8th 2018. We are currently meeting regularly in the Pandora High School gymnasium on Tuesday evenings. I may have been a counselor for troubled teens in my past but I know I am in over my head.

The parents need someone they don't know so well, a different therapist. However, with the rising prices on the basic necessities these days, parents are unable to afford to get the help they need.

Not all of the parents attend my meetings. Some must be going through this pain, stress, and heartache without any support. I know this because it is so common for people to close themselves off when they are grieving or going through loss.

Have you ever been through such a loss, Mr. President?

If there was a change to the gun laws, then maybe parents would rest easier at night. I know I would.

The change could be as simple as no longer selling automatic rifles at the local gun shop.

Everyone says they deserve the right to keep and bear arms, but why would a machine gun be needed? Are people expecting they are going to have to defend themselves against an army? But is it not our own government that we are supposed to rely on when it comes to war?

Sincerely,
Scarlett Smith

As Scarlett examined her email, she noticed that she might have been a bit repetitious, but it was hard not to be after 120 emails. She chose to ignore it, thinking it was probably helpful to repeat herself when trying to get her point across, especially when dealing with someone she thought had a thick skull.

This often made Jonathan huff and puff. He said that his adoptive mother did the same thing to him when he was a teenager.

Maybe it was just a mother thing.

Scarlett read over her message thoroughly and with a final approval, she clicks send.

Chapter 6

On Saturdays, Jonathan would pick Rosie up after breakfast. He would then take her to his rented out bachelor pad for the weekend.

Scarlett found that Rosie would get so excited Saturday mornings that she would struggle to finish her breakfast.

"Dad is picking me up soon and then he said he would take me out to the park and we could get an ice cream," Rosie said delightfully.

"Bum on your chair, honey." Scarlett put a gentle hand on her daughter's shoulder to help lean her back into her chair carefully.

Scarlett noticed that as time went on, Rosie seemed more and more pleased, maybe even happy, about this arrangement she had with her father.

After the first night at Jonathan's apartment, Rosie told her mother that she hated it. Rosie would come home with tears in her eyes, whining that she did not understand what was going on or why it was happening. Her fragile heart could not handle the idea of her parents splitting, living in separate homes.

Scarlett had not been to Jonathan's herself, but Rosie slowly told her more and more about it as the weeks passed. It was a single bedroom unit, with one poorly functioning bathroom in the entrance hallway. Rosie said that Jonathan would sleep on the pull-out couch when Rosie was over so that she could sleep in his bed. She also explained how when she would get up in the middle of the night to use the toilet, it would be smelly and clogged. Rosie would then have to wake her daddy up to fix it. She would giggle, adding more detail to the story every Monday night after supper, talking like it was her and her father's weekend routine.

Rosie's eyes would widen when she described the kitchen to her mother. It amazed her that anyone could cook in something so small. It lacked a dishwasher so the two would have to clean and dry the dishes by hand. This gave Scarlett a good chuckle. Jonathan always wanted Rosie to do more chores around the house; he thought it would make her better prepared for the workforce. Scarlett would look at him, shaking her head with a wide grin on her face, she wouldn't be surprised if he purposely did not rent out a place that did not have a dishwasher, just to teach their daughter how to do the dishes.

Jonathan was never much of a planner; therefore, Scarlett was not surprised when Rosie described his below par living conditions. He probably did not even think about finding a place that would have a separate bedroom for their daughter.

He also probably did not plan to move out, but decided one day to act on impulse and leave, staying at the cheapest hotel he could find until he found a place to live later that week. Scarlett hoped that perhaps he realized this situation was temporary, therefore he could not have been bothered to find the 'perfect' place.

When Jonathan arrived after breakfast, Scarlett opened the door, surprised by her husband's appearance. Jonathan's blond hair was shaven down on the sides leaving a small strip on the top of his head gelled to one side; it was the first time in months that he actually styled his hair. Scarlett remembered when Jonathan first got that cliché haircut, he thought it made him look stylish. Scarlett on the other hand thought it made him look like he was trying to fit in with the young business crowd. In her opinion, the only person who could pull that look off, above the age of forty, was David Beckham.

Jonathan was a well-built man who stood at 6'2" hunching over his short wife. He looked like the type of dad who enjoyed going to the gym, but not too often, saving his weekends for beer and the family. He was wearing his normal everyday attire: his favorite beige cargo shorts and simple black t-shirt, accessorizing with brown woven bracelets. Jonathan often left the house wearing the same style of clothing, no matter where he was going, to the movies or to teach his next class at the local college. It never bothered Scarlett that her husband never dressed up; she was not the type to have a sense of style, but she did try to present herself as more formal with her famous blazers. She thought she could throw them together with almost any outfit and it would immediately look more professional.

Jonathan was the relaxed surfer type of man, letting most things roll off his shoulders. Scarlett loved this about him; she thought it helped even out her crazy and uptight side. Yet, she was taken aback when she saw her husband for the first time in weeks, looking like his usual self. She would have thought maybe he would have looked lost, confused, upset, and devastated. She did not expect to see the charming, smiling man in front of her.

As Jonathan peered down at his wife, Scarlett felt a shiver crawl down her spine as her eyes met his. Jonathan's dark eyes appeared to have the ability to seek inside your soul. When they first met, Scarlett often found it difficult to make eye contact with Jonathan for longer than 30 seconds. His gaze was assertive and firm.

It was not until a year into their relationship did she find herself staring, and even losing herself in his intimidating gaze. Now, weeks after the absence of his stare, Scarlett could sense the rattling nerves and butterflies she first had when they had met. She held eye contact for as long as she could before her stomach turned, edging her to look away.

"Hello," Scarlett mustered up as cheerfully as possible, sounding like a receptionist greeting their first customer of the day.

"Hello, Scarlett," Jonathan replied looking her up and down. "You are looking well."

Jonathan was never one to call Scarlett out on her self-neglect but often did imply it when she had put on more than just a few pounds.

"I hear your new bachelor pad fits your needs quite well," Scarlett remarked with a bitter tone.

She detested it when people made remarks about the weight she had put on recently. Scarlett believed everyone dealt with loss in their own way.

"Ha, yeah I guess for the time being I will manage," he retorted. Jonathan may be the easy-breezy type, but he also had a bit of a temper when he felt like he was stuck in an uncomfortable situation, having to defend himself.

They never used to speak to each other like this, poking at one another, trying to see who would explode first. It started when Jonathan decided to move out. Scarlett was up in arms over the idea, believing her husband was being hot-headed. Eventually, she came to terms that this was how Jonathan needed to work past the feelings he was going through.

"Jonathan," Scarlett said sincerely, "it's time for you to move back home. I think it would best for everyone. Rosie misses you, I miss you. So much has changed, but we are still a fam—"

Before Scarlett could finish the word 'family,' Jonathan grimaced as if the word was a dagger. "We are no longer a family… We are broken," Jonathan replied with a hint of shimmer in his eyes.

"We will always be a family, Jonathan, nothing will change that. Please come home," Scarlett murmured.

Scarlett always made their conversations into a passive argument about Jonathan needing to return home, to her, to their family. She knew that she should let him heal, but she couldn't stand the empty space that consumed their bed. Scarlett was not ready to let Jonathan go, but she was too much of a pushover to fight for what she thought was right when it came to her husband. She wanted him to come back to her on his own accord, yet she felt the need to remind him every day that he was missed and loved. Scarlett truly believed his place was at home with her and Rosie, all together.

"We have been through this over and over again, Scarlett. I am not coming home," Jonathan said under his breath as he looked for his daughter rummaging around in the back of the hallway.

"I understand that is what you think right now, but consider giving yourself some time—" Scarlett began.

"Time? All this time bullshit again. What's with people and time? Everything has changed. That's that. No time will heal me nor fix me. I have to move on and it's about time you moved on too," Jonathan said argumentatively while jabbing his finger in the open space between himself and his wife. When he was set on something, he often was hard to persuade towards an alternative route. Jonathan was very stubborn, and Scarlett was beginning to see this side of him more and more since the summer.

"It's time for you to call the hotline and tell them to put you on desk duty or something, anything to get you out of the house and back into your schedules that you loved so much," Jonathan continued. "It's time you do something useful with yourself, something productive instead of those stupid meetings." Scarlett thought when Jonathan got into his defensive rants, he often let his sympathetic and sensitive qualities slide to the waist side.

Scarlett flinched at her husband's words. She thought how Jonathan denied her several invitations to the meetings she was holding on Tuesday evenings. He replied to each email, telling her that he thought her plan was ridiculous, that she was in no state of mind to help the parents, she needed to stop distracting herself and move on, return to the life she had, or what little of it that remained.

Scarlett wanted Jonathan there more than any one of the parents that went, she thought it would be good for him. She wanted him to see the improvement in the parents' emotional states, how far they have come since their first meeting. She knew it may take the parents a while, but she was going to help them, aid in their recovery period. Scarlett also thought it would be good for Jonathan to experience other people talking about their feelings; he was never much of a talker and it drove Scarlett up the wall. She also knew if one man spoke out in the group, such as Jonathan, then this would help the other fathers speak out as well.

"Maybe if you just came to one meeting then you would finally understand what it was like to actually grieve, to show some emotion," Scarlett explained without hesitation. She was not afraid to give her family the tough love she thought they needed.

She knew Jonathan had gone through a lot as a child, that he had experienced things that carved him into the man that was standing in front of her. His mother was an alcoholic and the father was never in the picture. He grew up with an older sister who always had his back when ever their mother had one of her 'fits,' Jonathan would call it. During these episodes, Jonathan's older sister would hide with her little brother in the closet, cradling him and telling him everything was going to be okay.

One day when Jonathan was five and his sister fourteen, Jonathan walked in on his mother and sister screaming at the top of their lungs. He didn't know what to do, so he went into his bedroom and hid in the closet, waiting for his sister to find him once the match was over. After an hour or two, and the slam of the door, Jonathan was still curled up in a little ball, trying to make himself invisible in his tiny stuffed closet. He had not moved for several hours until he heard a loud knock on the door that was not being answered. When he had gotten out of the closet, he could see a cop car parked along the side of the street of their apartment. Jonathan walked past their living room that was almost empty, except a torn couch where his mother was passed out, to answer the never-ending bang on the door. Once he opened the door, the police officers requested to speak with his parents. After acknowledging that his only guardian was passed out on the couch, the police took Jonathan into custody where he was later placed into child services and finally adopted by his new adorable parents, Fred and Doreen. Unfortunately, they passed away when Jonathan was in his mid-twenties.

It was not until he was sixteen when he found out his mother eventually died of a drug overdose only three months after he had been taken into custody. He was also informed by his adopted family that the reason for the police showing up that night was because his sister had committed suicide in the park nearest to their apartment. He told Scarlett how he had dreamt of his sister finding him and living with him after he was adopted, then the dreams slowly faded as time went on. Once he found out about her death, he felt he never really had the chance to mourn for her or his mom. He had finally reached a happy state of mind in his childhood, leaving his past behind him like it was a previous life that had been forgotten about since his reincarnation into the family he lived with now.

Jonathan was never much of a griever, nor someone who wanted to talk about his feelings. Scarlett only knew his rough childhood story because he shared it during one of the events they volunteered at for clinically depressed and suicidal teenagers. The organizers of these events thought it was best if the leaders shared one of their own personal tragic stories to make it more likely for the kids to open up to them.

Scarlett would try to get Jonathan open up more about his past as the years of their marriage flew by, but he never wanted to talk about it. She decided to leave it alone, thinking that maybe he had simply grieved and had nothing else to say about the events that set his life in motion. However, she still did try to bring it up every now and then to see if he was ready to share with her yet; the counselor in her couldn't help but try and find problems that were no longer there.

Before Jonathan could tell his wife that what she was saying was 'horse shit,' his favorite term to use over the past few years when he was starting to get riled up about something, Rosie came running up to them excited as could be.

"Daddy, Daddy," Rosie began to jump at her father like a kid on a sugar rush, then she noticed the frown growing on her father's face. "What's wrong?" Rosie asked with concern.

"Nothing, sweetie," Scarlett said to her daughter as she picked her up from her father's side, and began to kiss her goodbye.

Scarlett was a like professional now, pretending everything was fine.

"Put me down, Mommy. You are so silly!" Rosie giggled.

Rosie's current trademark was her telling someone how they were 'so silly,' repeating it at least 20 times a day, even if it was in the wrong context. Scarlett even found herself picking up her daughter's catchphrase, telling people that they were being 'so silly.'

The moment Scarlett put Rosie down, she ran to her dad's side and grabbed at him.

"Dad! This week was my first day of grade one. It was so much fun! My teacher is really nice. Her name is Miss Stewart, like Miss Stewart, not Mrs. Stewart," Rosie explained in that quick mumbling voice of a child. "Jackson and Delany are both in my class too!"

Rosie was handling the current living arrangements with such ease. She had her brief meltdowns, but for the most part she was behaving like any normal seven-year-old.

"Oh, that is very exciting," Jonathan said soothingly.

"Yeah! And, and, and yesterday Delany drew this really pretty butterfly during coloring time and one kid accidentally spilled their water on it," Rosie said as she was jumping up and down with excitement. "She was so upset she started crying. Jackson and I started telling her how beautiful her drawing was and that she was such a great artist. We told her not to cry and that sh-sh-she could draw another one!" Rosie would begin to stutter when she got very excited; it was like the words could not escape her tiny body fast enough.

"That is very kind of you, darling," Jonathan told her as he petted her hair back.

It amazed Scarlett how children would tell random stories with such glee, expecting their listener to be just as excited as they were to hear how the story ended.

"And then also Miss Stewart asked how everyone was doing. Jackson said that he was good, but I told him kindly, that it was 'I am doing well.' I told Jackson that m-m-my dad told me that is how you say it properly," Rosie said as she looked up at her father for praise, while she slowly formed the word 'properly.'

Jonathan was an English professor at the local college. He couldn't help himself when he corrected someone's grammar, it was one of the reasons that Rosie had such a large and proper vocabulary for an elementary school student. It never bothered Scarlett when her husband would tell her the correct pronunciation of a word that she had been saying wrong her entire life, she thought it was amusing. No one ever really seemed to care that much about grammar nowadays with everyone's abbreviated messages. Scarlett even heard a teenager the other day say 'LOL' out loud in the grocery store, which baffled her. She knew it literally meant laugh out loud, but she could not understand why someone would say laugh out loud while not laughing; she did find herself at a loss with a lot of the mumbo-jumbo people were speaking these days.

"That's my girl, now go grab your things," Jonathan said.

As Rosie scurried away, Jonathan turned his attention back to his wife.

"Have you signed the papers yet?" Jonathan asked.

"What papers?" Once again Scarlett was ignoring the reality of their situation.

"The divorce papers, Scarlett," Jonathan replied.

As a coping mechanism, Scarlett neglected the negative things that have been currently piling up in her life. She acknowledged that Jonathan and her have been having problems, but brushed it off her shoulders with the idea that everything would go back to normal soon.

"No," Scarlett responded lightly.

"Scarlett, I am serious about this. I think this is what is best, for you, me, and Rosie," Jonathan said quickly as his eyes darted from the ceiling to the ground.

"Jonathan," Scarlett said as she reached for her husband's hand with tears in her eyes.

He pulled away as Rosie came running up to the two of them with her pink Dora backpack hanging off one shoulder.

"Okay, I am ready to go, yo," Rosie giggled as she ran past them, racing for her father's car.

Scarlett and Jonathan had an exceptional marriage, that is before everything happened. The sex was immaculate, passionate, and vigorous. They worked well as a team, taking turns making dinner, breakfast, or packing the lunches. They had the real white-picket fence type of life, happy-go-lucky for the most part. Of course, like most couples and families, they had their disputes, but with Jonathan's usually easy-going attitude and Scarlett's attention to detail and listening skills, they were able to get over or help their family move past most arguments quickly.

Although Scarlett was mainly a suicide prevention counselor, where she mostly dealt with teens, she also did participate in some family counseling in her earlier career days. She found that the main problem with broken families resulted from the lack of love and appreciation between the parents. The scarcity and often absence of a sex life between the parents was the first sign of a crumbling relationship. This did not happen to her and Jonathan.

Scarlett thought she would have at least seen her and her husband's fiery morning, evening and even some afternoons, routine dwindle. But their affection for one another was always strong and had stayed so until Jonathan decided to move out.

"Love you, sweetie," Scarlett yelled out the door.

"Bye, Mom! Love you," Rosie hollered back with a quick wave behind her head.

"Goodbye, Scarlett," Jonathan said as he quickly turned on his heels.

Scarlett stood at the entrance to her home as her child and husband drove away. She leaned against the doorframe for several moments, watching the dust settle in her driveway. As she closed the door quietly, she slid to the floor, letting out her anguish with silent sobs.

**

***

Later that evening, Scarlett found herself once again looking at her computer screen. After seeing Jonathan, she felt a growing need to write another email, to do something, anything to prove Jonathan wrong. She wanted her husband to see that she can make a difference, that she was useful.

There was that word again – useful. Scarlett hated it when Jonathan would tell her one of her new self-help projects or counseling ideas was not useful. Scarlett thought Jonathan was nearly perfect, but he did have some major flaws, such as not being supportive about her new coping-mechanisms that she wanted to teach the parents at the Pandora High School meetings.

Now the word gave her a bitter taste in her mouth. Scarlett believed that no one should be told their time is not useful, which was the same as useless. She thought it was such a harsh word that was thrown around so effortlessly in this modern man-constructed society, and if only people knew of the type of the impact their words had on others, then maybe they would think twice before speaking.

Scarlett's clients were often struggling with their self-worth in this world, so it pained her to see people calling themselves or being called useless, worthless, stupid, unimportant, and the list goes on.

As Scarlett searched the internet for what has been trending the most in the last twenty-four hours, she decided to log onto her twitter account, *@Scarlett_smith123*. She visited the President's page with optimism, hoping to see some sort of progression with gun violence.

Scarlett feared that the changing gun laws motion would have ceased due to the short attention span of Americans, along with the most recent scandals proclaimed against the White House. To her surprise, it was still very much in the public eye.

Scarlett saw that some parents had tagged the President in posts discussing the lack of gun control. However, these threads and messages lacked the integrity required to have an impact on any government based decisions. They mostly contained improper grammar laced with threats, not helping them prove their point.

As Scarlett scrolled down the page, she noticed the endless number of vulgar terms used to describe the President. This was not what she wanted; she knew that if any type of public debate or comments from parents that were written in anger, lacking the passion and enthusiasm of an educated American, were released into the public, then it was more of a step backwards rather than forwards. If they were to speak against all of the citizens who believed that the gun laws and regulations were perfect the way they were, then they would need compelling evidence and persuasive speeches to coax them to seeing the truth, that change was needed.

Scarlett also believed everyone had the right to voice their opinion, but within reason. No one should be telling someone, the President or not, that they should go die or that they deserved miscellaneous body parts to be chopped off.

"We are real people, not barbarians," Scarlett said, thinking out loud.

Scarlett kept scrolling, hoping to find any comment that reconciled with influential, compelling, intelligent remarks. She also wanted to see people stand against the government in unison, adding in their opinions without threats or provocative language. She wanted people to use their voice of reason when commenting or regarding the government. She did not want this:

@littleRi69 tweeted: "What kind of patriotic dumbass thinks assault rifles should count as a weapon to bear arms with?"

@whosyourdaddy tweeted: "women know nothing, go back to the kitchen where you belong," in response to @littleRi69's tweet.

It amazed Scarlett that through the countless years of women fighting for equal rights, she still saw the cliché 'get back to the kitchen' response from men who felt that their opinions and ideals were being threatened.

Scarlett's frown creased her pale skin as she scrolled down the next ten replies to *@littleRi69*'s tweet, seeing either sexist remarks or agreements taking the verbal assault on the President a step further.

"At least they haven't forgotten about the school shooting," Scarlett murmured to herself, her face illuminating from the glow of her computer screen in her quiet kitchen.

Scarlett could not come to terms with the responses from the domineering parents. She never thought adults would discuss such important matters, that involved the lives of the innocent, with anything less but educated rebuttals that led to proper debates.

She believed that people were supposed to use logic and wit to defend their opinions and beliefs, not foul language and ill attempts to insult their opposition. Scarlett was starting to see the adults across the media, on the internet, acting like the children whom they were trying to defend and protect.

"We are supposed to be better than this. We have to be better than this. We must do better than this," Scarlett explained to her kitchen breeze.

Scarlett began to question the comments that were now drowning the important messages. She knew this type of bullying was unacceptable, even schools would not tolerate this, but what could she do to stop it?

In a classroom setting, all parties involved would be brought into the principal's or counselor's office for some type of resolution, making sure this type of behavior did not carry on. But who was there to step forward, to tell people enough was enough when it came to adults? Scarlett believed without doubt that it was not going to be the law that would take a stand against this, at least not in this case. The media allows these grotesque demeanors to continue.

Not one single person of the 326 million people of the United States had stated that we can longer live like this, that this type of attitude was not acceptable.

Scarlett snickered to herself at the very thought of one person, out of the hundreds of millions, acting as the voice of reason, causing people to refrain themselves from their foul language, leading to 'proper conversations' among adults.

Scarlett found this fantasy hard to believe when the leader guiding this powerful nation had the attributes of a redneck who did not know when to bite his tongue, may he be doing great for this nation or not. She knew her single voice would have no effect. People would gang up on her next, calling her an old bag, or a prune, telling her she was stuck in the polite past, but that this was the present, this was how people talk to each other now.

Scarlett also knew that these types of arguments and debates scattered across the media would not help obtain the more protected society innocent children deserve.

Wars are won with battles that have been influenced by empowering words. Therefore it should be passionate, well-constructed comments, statements, rebuttals and everything in-between that must be used for this 'advance civilization' to become actually more advanced.

Scarlett simply yearned for gun retail to meet and obtain proper requirements, so that children and ill-minded people would no longer have access to weapons of destruction.

Before she closed her laptop, Scarlett read one final tweet from *@Oprahforever*, *"I still stand by that Oprah should be voted for President."*

Scarlett signed off, her sad chuckle echoing in her empty home.

Chapter 7

On Sunday morning, Scarlett met Alex for coffee at Pete's. As Scarlett entered the coffee shop, she felt an overwhelming sense of comfort. She always felt like she was at home at Pete's. This was not just a place where her Alex and Martha would hang out, but Scarlett used to come here with her family, indulging in an afternoon snack – it was a tradition. Unfortunately, it was one of many traditions that had abruptly disappeared over the past couple of months. As the doorbell chimed, Martha appeared from the back.

"Well hello, lovely," Martha said smiling at Scarlett. "Alex is already sitting outside soaking up the sun. She has got a tea and cinnamon bun waiting for ya."

Since Jonathan left the house, Scarlett had been noticing her sweet tooth getting stronger and stronger, making it hard to resist anything bought or offered to her. She once tried to mention it to her friends, asking them if it was noticeable, but they shrugged it off and told her "you look beautiful" or "it's just stress" or even "no it's in your head." But they all knew very well it was not in Scarlett's head.

"Thanks," Scarlett said as Martha blew her a kiss and turned around back to the ovens, where she would finish her morning shift preparing strudels, cinnamon buns, and apple fritters for the rest of the day.

Scarlett's mouth began to water as she guided herself through the warm and pleasurable smell of freshly baked dough.

Thanks to Martha, not one person had ever left Pete's bakery dissatisfied. She was the best baker Scarlett had ever met, and her chocolate chip banana bread was to die for. It had the perfect amount of moisture on the inside, yet still maintained crunch along the edges. On the contrary, it was her cinnamon buns that were her signature baked good; they sold out in minutes from the quick rush of customers coming and going.

Martha took pride in her baking skills like a new mother, saying, "Yes, I created that; you are welcome, world."

Everyone enjoyed telling Martha that she was the true Martha Stewart of baking. She would put her hand up and giggle in response as if to say "oh, stop it," but Martha loved the attention and respect people had for her skills.

The only thing that seemed to bother Martha about her job was how she was in such a high demand. Pete understood, like any good boss, that family came first

36

and her being a single mother meant that she had to put some time aside for her daughter. Martha was able to work out her schedule with Pete so that she got most of the time off she needed. Martha thought he did this for her because he was very understanding, but Alex and Scarlett believed it was because he had a crush on her and simply couldn't say no like a teenage boy.

It was crazy how single thirty-year-old men acted around women that they admired and adored. It was as if puberty and the dwindling of hormone fluctuation never happened. They were just left star-gazed as the countless beautiful women walked in and out of their lives so effortlessly.

"Well hello, beautiful," Alex said as she got up to hug Scarlett hello.

Alex was always the touchy one in the group. She liked to greet friends with kisses on the cheek. However, she had tried to tone herself down when around Scarlett, who was only used to the touchy-lovey affection from her family.

"Hey, Alex. Thank you for getting me the tea and treat," Scarlett said.

Since Scarlett had left her job, and with Jonathan no longer being at home, she had had to cut back on some spending. No more late-night rented romantic comedies, no more Starbucks, no more lunch out with the ladies, and the list went on. Her and Jonathan had not yet figured out the money situation, mostly because Scarlett was just waiting for him to come home, but also because they still shared a joint account.

Alex, who was a successful businesswoman, and was quite savvy with money, noticed this lack of spending right away. She knew it would not be long until Scarlett was back on her feet, therefore she grabbed Scarlett's bills as much as possible. Alex was also the giving type; she knew she had the money to spare and was not afraid to use it.

Scarlett detested owing anyone money or favors, so she was not a fan of her friend taking care of the bill every time as if Scarlett was a charity case. Scarlett was financially okay, but when she told Alex this, her friend's face became tormented with sympathy.

When Alex was a little girl, she grew up in the rougher side of Boston, Massachusetts. Her neighborhood was struck with violence, robberies, assault, and rape. She would tell Martha and Alex that she had learned the hard facts of life at a young age; "nothing in this world is free," she would say. She did not have the same security as Scarlett nor Martha in their white privileged communities.

Alex had to start working at the young age of twelve to help pay her family's bills. She was the oldest of three children whose father walked out on them when Alex was ten. She got a job at the nearest supermarket where she was paid under the table for five dollars an hour.

"I never look back," Alex would say when talking about her adolescence. She did what she had to do to help her family; she had no regrets missing out on the childhood she never experienced.

Martha would tell Alex that "everything happens for a reason," in her philosophical tone with such pure optimism. They both enjoyed handing out one of their many inspirational quotes here and there, even Scarlett noticed herself picking up some of their spiritual cliché sayings.

Alex would dismiss any pity or sympathy she would get when telling her childhood stories. "It helped shaped me into the confident, beautiful, and highly successful woman I am today," Alex would say with a smirk. She was confident with herself, with who she was, and proud of her hard-earned story.

Now with Alex's undeniable wealth in all aspects of life – husband, children, friends, and income – she wanted to share what she could with her loved ones, helping out when needed. Therefore, it had become a race between Alex and Scarlett to see who could reach for Scarlett's bill the fastest.

"Don't mention it, honey, how are things with you?" Alex replied.

It drove Scarlett crazy how recently Alex and Martha had been treating her like a cracked little china bird, threatening to shatter any moment, even though she may have good reason to. They were constantly checking in on her, seeing where her mental state was on a fine morning, afternoon, or evening. They would call her when they had an open opportunity, telling her they just wanted to see how everything was going.

Scarlett took a seat across from Alex, as her friend slid the cinnamon bun and steaming green tea towards her end of the table.

"Good, good. Rosie has been so excited and upbeat about first grade. She was thrilled to be in the same class as Jackson and Delay," Scarlett answered, playing dumb as per usual.

She took a long sip, regretting how quickly she said "good," wondering if it made her sound as far from good as possible, teetering towards the unstable side of sanity.

"No, sweetie, I mean how are you really feeling?" Alex reached out her hand and placed it on top of Scarlett's, "I could never imagine how you must be feeling, with everything that you are going through. I still cannot get over that Jonathan left just like that." Alex snapped her fingers on the "that," as if she had ushered for a spell that took Scarlett's husband away, right from under her nose.

"Jonathan stopped by the house yesterday to pick up Rosie. He seemed… satisfied with the current living arrangements," Scarlett did not want to tell her friend that Jonathan was pressing for her to sign the divorce papers; she thought it wouldn't last, but for now will keep that to herself for a little while longer.

"He is probably just putting up a show, he is probably miserable on the inside," Alex said as she began to rub Scarlett's hand for comfort.

"I don't know, maybe he really is okay with everything that has happened. I guess everyone grieves in their own way," Scarlett remarked as she pulled her hand away to grab another sip of her tea, trying to play it off as her not to being rude.

"Scarlett's at it again, with her classic everyone grieves in their own way mumbo-jumbo," Alex chuckled as she folded her hands in prayer while leaning back into her seat.

Scarlett's friends often teased her on typical counseling advice and phrases: "it is not your fault," "you need to learn to let it go," and her most frequently used "everyone grieves in their own way." Scarlett saw herself as a healer, an adviser, and a guider of sorts. Alex, Scarlett, and Martha were, for the most part, down to earth and spiritual, but they all still had their moments of seeing things in black and white, yes or no. This was one of the many reasons Scarlett limited herself on giving her friends any professional advice if it was not needed; they would often chuckle at her typical, although correct, clichés. They may have asked her opinion on many things, but she knew she would be coming out of the conversation being laughed at by her friends, innocently and wholeheartedly.

"Well, it is true," Scarlett smiled, defending herself. It never really bothered her when Alex made a comment or fuss about her many sayings, she was able to handle one non-believer at a time, but any more than that, she would end up getting flustered. Scarlett would tell herself to just let it go, Alex does not mean any harm, before she prepared herself for more chuckles from the peanut gallery.

"Anyways, good for him for dealing with everything in such an appropriate manner," Scarlett said.

"But… there is always a but," replied Alex, as she leaned in, hoping for some juicy gossip.

"But nothing, I am just simply happy if he is happy," Scarlett remarked with the most sincere smile she could muster up. Scarlett found it hard letting anyone get more than a peek into her personal life; she liked being the only one who interrogated; however, she did acknowledge it was best to share sometimes. "Although he does think I should give up my time with the self-help group meetings at Pandora High School." Scarlett thought she should give her friend a few minor details of her conversation with Jonathan, maybe Alex would even have some insight of her own.

"Oh," said Alex with a raised eyebrow, coaxing Scarlett to continue.

Scarlett discussed how the fathers kept to themselves most of the time, and there being one parent who acted as if they were the sole victim of this heinous crime. Scarlett felt that she would be breaching client confidentiality if she were to give Alex any specific details, yet technically, they were not her clients because they did not sign any forms, nor was Scarlett getting paid, but she still refrained from mentioning any names.

"It drives me crazy when people genuinely believe that the world has decided to spite them personally, as if no one else is going through pain, as if no one else is suffering from the actions of a mentally ill person," Alex said, attempting to fire Scarlett up for more information.

Alex had always been a women who loved her 'hot juicy gossip,' Scarlett and Martha would say. She wanted to know what was happening in everyone's life all the time. But she was also a good friend, she knew what to say, she knew what to agree with, and she also knew when to drop something.

"I told that parent that they were not the only victim, we must not forget the other parents, siblings and even friends who are all experiencing so much loss. And also who cares if someone is hurting more or less, this is not supposed to be a competition about who got hurt the most, who is suffering the most," Scarlett explained.

"That is so true!" Alex agreed enthusiastically.

In the long run, Scarlett really did enjoy talking to her friends about her counseling. They would have this proud look of mothers hearing how their child scored their first goal of the season, "good job, honey" they would say in an encouraging and pleased tone. Even if it was something Scarlett thought as basic knowledge, her friends were still in awe of her guiding wisdom when it was used on anyone but themselves. They enjoyed hearing the comments and quotes she came up with on the spot, not the typical textbook verses.

Scarlett decided to dive into her personal details more deeply than she used to, she wanted her friend to feel involved in her life. "I have been occupying a lot of my time with this help group, I set up the chairs in the gymnasium and organize the cookies and coffee that have been prepared for the parents, which are surprisingly good," Scarlett lied cheerfully.

Scarlett actually thought the cheap coffee and dollar store bought cookie dough, which she used to bake the tiny cookies, made for a tragic combination.

Unfortunately, that was all the budget she could afford with having to rent out the expensive high school gymnasium.

Scarlett left out the part about baking the cookies and making the coffee herself. Her friends often told her that she dedicated too much of her own time to helping others, or that she was 'too nice,' that she needed to focus more on herself right now. This would make Scarlett laugh, she did not understand how someone could be 'too nice.' But she did not like the disapproving looks her friends gave her when Scarlett would go above and beyond, getting nothing in return.

"Well, that is good! Have the parents been making a lot of progress?" asked Alex.

"No, not yet, but they are getting there," Scarlett said hopefully. She had only one session with them, a few she had emailed here and there for emotional support, but she couldn't tell if there had been any breakthroughs or advancement in their grieving stages. Scarlett thought it was too soon to tell.

However, Scarlett was very optimistic. She looked at the world wide-eyed and full of hope. She, like her friends, also believed everything happened for a reason, or at least she used to think that. She was starting to wipe away her naïve vision, leaving only faith and a minuscule amount of confidence that the world will be just.

"Why don't you start working at the suicide helpline again, sweetie? I know how much you enjoyed doing that," Alex said, sipping on her tea.

Alex was right, Scarlett loved working with the helpline. She always felt accomplished after a long conversation with the children and adolescents that she spoke with. Scarlett rarely had adults calling seeking advice or guidance, she thought it was probably because they were too busy working and focusing on other things. It was also adults who could afford the expensive therapists, not bothering to waste their time with free counselors. Scarlett thought it was because that most adults believed the only thing to help them now was a prescription for some 'happy pills.' On the other hand, children were still optimistic enough, like how Scarlett usually was, to believe that they could recover without the aid of chemicals, that they could fix their problems with a long endearing conversation, being told they were worthy. Scarlett believed there was still hope for adolescents, that they had not been lost in the cruel wonders of this world yet.

She also enjoyed helping people who wanted to talk to her, who had made their first step in their path to a healthy mental state of being. Scarlett found it easier and more rewarding when talking to these kind of people, the ones who wanted to make and see a difference in their moods, thoughts, or behaviors. They were also the ones willing to listen.

"I did enjoy it very much, but now that I am spending my time between Rosie and the self-help group, I just find that I am still too occupied," Scarlett said.

"Fair enough, you have to make sure your little girl is okay. How has Rosie been handling this whole situation?" Alex asked, waving her hand in the air in a small circle.

"She is very brave, surprisingly brave," Scarlett uttered, picking at her cinnamon bun.

"Why is it surprising?" Alex asked.

"Well I would have thought she would have wanted to talk to me more about everything. I have tried not to pester her, tried not to ask her too many questions. I thought it would be best if I let her come to me," Scarlett paused, "But the thing is that she has not come to me yet, not even once."

"Maybe this is a good thing, sweetie. Maybe Rosie is handling everything very well. Or it could be that she is just so young she does not understand what is going on. Do you remember Margret whose kid used to be in the same preschool as Jackson, Rosie, and Delany?" Alex asked and continued on before Scarlett could answer, "Her husband passed away last year. When her boy, Josh I think it was, when him and Jackson had play-dates after his dad passed, I remember thinking, wow this is one tough kid. Margret told me she had taken Josh to a therapist, just to make sure he was coping alright, and she said that therapist told her the way

Josh was handling everything was very normal. Margret told me that it seems like some children are able to act like the world carries on after a death, that they don't hold onto anything like adults do."

"That makes sense. Some children are too young to comprehend the chaos unfolding in front of them," Scarlett remarked in her counseling tone.

"Rosie is also so quiet, she is probably more of an observer than a talker, just like her mom," Alex said, giving Scarlett a quick wink.

"Ha, that is very true," Scarlett laughed.

Scarlett loved that her little Rosie was a spitting image of her. Scarlett was more of a follower and a listener, her daughter was painfully the same way. Rosie stuck to her mom like glue when they went to school functions or parties for Rosie's fellow classmates. Scarlett had also noticed in the past year she had leaned away from her, that she was now becoming more independent, or at least as independent as a seven-year-old could be. It made Scarlett sad watching her baby grow up so fast, no longer needing her hand to hold.

"So what types of coping mechanisms have you created for yourself?" Alex asked, orienting the topic of conversation towards Scarlett herself.

Scarlett's friends were used to Scarlett holding back on her personal problems, she would show them glimpses into her life. Therefore, her friends had become very skilled at navigating conversations, trying to find out how Scarlett was really feeling, how she was handling her husband leaving her.

Scarlett was also clever at redirecting her friends. She would be able to read a situation, tell someone only a bit of information they wanted, without saying too much, and then change the conversation smoothly towards a topic the person whom she was speaking with, was more interested in.

When Scarlett first started her job as a counselor, she was terrible at redirecting questions and reading people. She could never tell if someone was crying because of sadness or frustration, which is a very important difference. Scarlett had to learn to read someone's expressions and gestures, so that she would understand what were the right questions to ask and which questions might send the client over the edge.

Scarlett also had to learn how to change the topic of conversation with ease. Some clients would try to ask Scarlett questions, as an attempt to undermine or belittle her. "Have you ever experienced such a great loss like me?" or "You have such a perfect family, don't you? Amazing husband and beautiful children?" Most of her clients where just fishing in the dark; she did not have a single family photo in her office implying her family was whole. She did this because she knew how people in pain hated seeing others happy. After years of practice, Scarlett obtained the skill set to slither through these questions very quickly; it was how she achieved great success in her line of work.

"I usually focus on some breathing exercises, like the ones you taught me. I believe you said you learned them in yoga?" asked Scarlett. "You told me to put one hand on my chest and to visualize my chest expanding as I took a deep breath in," Scarlett put her hand to her chest in demonstration.

"Yes! This is one of my favorite breathing exercises. Perfect when you have had a busy stressful day and you're lying in bed wide awake," Alex said, putting her hand to her chest, "Now move your hand to your upper abdomen, as you inhale visualize just the small section where you have placed your hand expand, as you exhale visualize it decompressing," Alex breathed out slowly and smoothly.

Alex loved talking about new yoga poses or breathing exercises she had learned. She might not look like it, but she was the type of women who meditated in her free time, believed in chakras and keeping herself 'centered.' On the other hand, Alex was not a full-blown *namaste* yogi. She was a hippy at heart, but had a fashionable fierce side like Miranda Priestly from *The Devil Wears Prada.* People usually expect hippies to be walking out of their yoga classes wearing hemp clothing, or to have Buddhist quotes posted on their mirrors or magnetized to their fridge. Alex was the perfect combination of Zen and materialistic. She believed that you should respect your body and the people that surround you, but she also wanted to be wearing high-end brands while doing it.

Alex closed her eyes, "Now repeat for your lower abdomen, inhale, exhale."

When Alex started doing her breathing exercises, talked about new yoga poses or discussed the most recent clothing she had purchased, she had this blissful look on her face. Her lips would widen across her white teeth. The only wrinkles on her face, her crow's feet, would deepen. Usually wrinkles age a person, but on Alex they seemed to make her look youthful and happy; she looked like she was thirty-five not forty-one.

"Inhale, exhale, now everyone please clasp your hand together and chant with me, ooohhhhmmm," Martha said, clasping her hands together as she walked through the open wooden door leading from the bakery to the patio.

Martha had just finished her morning shift and wanted to sit with the girls before they left to carry on with their chores and errands for the day. Scarlett noticed how stunning she looked even in her dirty clothes. Her black bakery uniform contrasted her pale skin, making her hair appear more of a darker blood red than usual.

"Hey now, I know you love this," Alex smirked as she moved her hand from her abdomen to reach for her baby blue mug.

Alex was right, Martha did love yoga, but she found great pleasure in teasing Alex when she started doing her breathing exercises.

Martha went to yoga with Alex three times a week; she said it was the only thing that helped keep her sane as she rushed from one task to the next, getting

Delany's breakfast ready, packing her lunch, dropping her off and getting ready for an eight-hour shift.

"Yeah, but you don't see me sitting in the corner ohming to myself," Martha giggled as she pulled up a chair and sat beside Scarlett. Scarlett breathed her in, once again causing her mouth to water; she smelt like baked goods.

"Well, at least I am not a woo-girl," Alex scoffed.

"What is a woo-girl?" Scarlett asked.

"It is someone who goes to spin class and woos when the teacher shouts at them," Alex explained.

"Well, that does not sound very fun," grimaced Scarlett. She never liked people shouting at her.

"It is so much fun, Scarlett, you should really join Alex and I sometime," Martha said ignoring Alex's remark. "Alex is too busy giggling as the rest of us cheer each other on." Martha also set aside her free time, when her mother baby-sat Delany, for spin classes. She believed it was also another exercise that kept her stable and upbeat in her busy life, but she also said it was a good distraction from men. She had not yet dated since she gave birth to Delany, keeping herself extremely fit in the meantime. Martha liked to mention every now and then how she was never one for dating around, she thought they were better things to do with her time.

Martha and Alex were the perfect duo when it came to working out. They both loved cardio that was 'not too hard on their joints' they'd say, as well as exercises that helped them build up their core strength.

Both of them had been going to yoga classes together now for the past year, and they did initially send out an invitation to Scarlett, but she was never one for the slow workouts. Scarlett used to enjoy getting her sweat on, which was why Alex and Martha started going to spin classes over a month ago; it was supposed to be a workout that they could do together, but Scarlett had been finding an excuse to not go every time.

"More like I am too busy checking out the hot instructor's tight butt," Alex said, grinning enthusiastically.

"Yes, he is the definition of delicious, you know he reminds me of my cinnamon buns, brown and shiny on the outside and sweet and sugary on the inside, yum!" Martha may have said she did not have time for men, but she sure did enjoy looking at them.

All three of the women laughed like they were fifteen again, gossiping about boys.

Scarlett felt that the only thing keeping her sane these days was her friends' innocent, and at times derogatory, banter.

Chapter 8

I am absolutely in love with my theater class! We are starting off with a singing unit and I can't believe how fun it is! We begin each class with this singing routine demonstrated by Mrs. Cornwall, she says it is to warm-up our voice box. She gathered us in a circle and told us to take slow easy breaths in, then exhale while saying 'hum.' With the entire class humming along, it sounds like we are in prayer. She also told us to take each other hands while we hummed, she said this would be very therapeutic and help us build a safe space, so that everyone felt like they could be their true selves in this class.

Unlike most teachers, Mrs. Cornwall was honest and open with us, she understands that theater is not meant for everyone, that not everyone can hold their head up high while singing. I remember after the first week back to school, she gave us a little speech, helping some students decide if this class was right for them. She explained how when singing we are vulnerable, and that only the brave can step forward on stage. She also said how she was going to do her best to make this a class enjoyable for every student, to make sure everyone feels welcomed.

One of her techniques she uses during the vocal warm-up, to help us feel more comfortable, is to get each of us to sing our name while the other students continued to hum. Each person sung their name once Mrs. Cornwall called upon them in alphabetical order. When it came to my turn, I could barely hear my own voice over the sound of the beehive my class was creating, it was outstanding! Even though it was only one word, or one name, that I sung, I felt like it encouraged me to continue on, that people were not laughing, or mocking me, that two people were actually holding my hand, even swaying with me to the rhythm of the chanting.

Once we finished, everyone dropped their hands with grins on their faces, even Ashley, who is only seen sneering, was smiling. The humming relaxed all of us, I really enjoyed it, and we continued to do it all of the second week. Each day we were told to stand by someone different, that way we don't stay in our 'cliques' Mrs. Cornwall said.

Yesterday I sat beside Emma and she even talked to me! She told me how she thought the humming was therapeutic too! We both giggled after I agreed.

Now don't get me wrong, I haven't forgotten all of the awful things she has said to me or about me over the years, but kids can also be mean and nasty, and sometimes you got to learn to forget and forgive, at least that is what my mom enjoys telling me.

Later in class, when we were going through some more exercises while being paired into singing groups, I was grouped with Ashley and Duncan, the two of them are literally the definition of jock & prep. If Andrew Clark and Claire Standish (from The Breakfast Club) were to have children, they would look exactly like Ashley and Duncan. The two of them aren't related or anything, just both good-looking, loved by everyone, but feared by them at the same time. Ashley can be a snarky little see you next Tuesday. Duncan is a 'macho' kinda guy, always wearing a tank top, exposing his biceps, flexing every moment he can. They are probably the two most vain people I know.

You might ask me, "How can you say you know them if you haven't talked to them in years?" I would just tell you that I don't need to talk to someone to see what kinda person they are, just by watching them, paying attention to key details, I can tell you the tiniest features about a person's character.

Duncan only flexes when he sees people walking past him, or is in a group of people. He looks in the mirror, window, any type of reflection as he passes by, just to make sure his hair is on point. Before he is about to whisper something about someone, maybe to tell his friends that I am the ugly Goth chick from middle school, he cracks and twists his neck, as if it makes him tough putting down others. He is also the vain person who is extremely afraid of what other people think, he acts like he is important, like he knows his worth, and he wants people to think he is the hero, the masculine type. I am not surprised that he is in theater, he probably tells all of his friends it's because theater chicks are crazy in bed or something absurd. I wouldn't be surprised if he actually really likes to dance, twirling around, and maybe even singing. He may have picked on me in middle school, but has since left me alone, focusing more on himself and how he has to act just to 'fit in' so that he is liked by others.

Duncan used to be a nice guy. I remember when we were in grade 1, when I use to hang out with Emma, Duncan had actually been the kid who stood up to a bully for the two of us! Can you imagine that? This older kid had pushed me down, apparently they hadn't been taught to share yet and they wanted my swing. Duncan saw me crying and took me by the hand to help me up. He turned to the bully and pushed him off the swing. Even as a kid, Duncan was always stronger, bigger than the other kids, so of course the other kid ran away crying and screaming. Now I know looking back that violence was not the best way to handle that situation, and an eye-for-an-eye makes the whole world blind, but he was my hero. I remember following him around for the rest of the year like a lovesick puppy. Then he turned on me when Emma had. It took me a while, even once he started bullying me, to get over my crush.

Now and then I forget about the person who he pretends to be, and imagine that he is still the prince charming I had once thought he was, and that maybe he has a troubled home life, which is why he acts out. I stand at my locker, catching myself gazing at him, fantasizing, thinking about him coming over to me, to tell me his darkest secrets, him apologizing for picking on me all those years. Me, being the surprisingly helpless romantic (I did go through my Twilight phase like most teens, hoping that my Edward would someday come and rescue me from this boring place), I would picture Duncan and me having our high school romance, and then I would see him do his 'flexing-thing,' and in an instant I would forget about it and realize he is just another douchebag. It's not my fault I get lost in those beautiful forest-green eyes, or how my teenage hormones make me mesmerized by his veins bulging down the side of his muscular arms. The good girls always fall for the jerks anyway, so in my defense it only makes sense that every now and then I have these thoughts. And who knows, maybe he is no longer so bad, maybe he is actually a decent human being with a reason behind his childhood cruelty.

Then there is Ashley. Her and Duncan are usually seen in a little group, surrounded by Emma, Allison, Trevor, and Brian (Duncan's cousin, not as handsome, and a little less mean). Ashley stands tall as she mockingly stares at people down the hallway, thinking she's better than everyone else, whispering about people as they pass by. She probably even pulls the same sh*t Regina George does, complementing someone on an outfit, then insulting them the minute their back is turned. She will pretend to gag behind your back, but smile when you make eye contact, which is how she gets people to like her, by acting all sweet and buttery when she is just cold in the center. She has beautiful red straight hair, natural of course, and dark brown eyes, so dark that at times I am unsure where her pupil starts and where her iris ends. She's got that girl-next-door beauty, which makes me believe my theory that the world always makes the mean people pretty.

I don't have as much history with Ashley as I do with Emma and Duncan, but I can spotty a nasty b**ch anywhere (I will try not to swear in case my kids are reading this). Ashley has always enjoyed picking on Denise and I, ever since we all got placed in the same grade 7 class, when my Goth phase was the darkest (I think I even wore a black choker, oh gawd). She didn't bother trying to pretend to like us like she did with everyone else, it was obvious that she wanted us to know that she thought the very sight of us was grotesque.

Ashley and Emma would love to whisper into each other's ears as we walked by, telling each other mean lies about Denise and I. I could almost guarantee you that is why they became so close, their combined hatred for us made their friendship, and popularity for some reason, blossom. They even enjoyed the same pathetic jokes and comments they made about us, for example Ashley loved to lean in closer to Denise and I, either when we sat near her or if she was walking past, and she would say "what an ugly pair of dikes."

This was one of her many insults that never bothered me, I was always confident with my sexuality and couldn't give a sh*t if people called me names, but back then most middle-schoolers would have cried thinking someone thought they were a lesbian. Now, no one even thinks twice when being called lesbian, gay, bisexual, transgender, or a dike, nor should they. The LGBT community stands strong in my neighborhood, not giving a rats a** about what people think about their sexuality. As Lady Gaga says, "We were born this way!" I am happy people are finally starting to accept other people's sexuality (FINALLY), but we still have a long way to go… (this is the kinda stuff I want to write music about!). Okay, but back to my point, I am unsure why she always picked on us, we never made fun of her, laughed at her, nor made her cry. To this day I am still trying to figure it out, maybe she has some repressed emotional trauma and is inflicting it on us. It's also funny though because Denise once told me her and Ashley used to be best friends in elementary school before we met, I wonder if something went down between the two of them.

So as I was saying, Ashley, Duncan, and I were all placed in a group together, they both looked at me with slight amusement and interest in their eyes, nothing like the looks I use to get from them. They both introduced themselves to me, as if we've never met, I guess no longer having braces, acne, and dyed black hair can make a difference (now it's naturally brown, like chocolate), but I was still acting in the defense, straight face, just in case they were about to pounce any minute with an attack. They never bullied me in front of the teachers, they were too smart for that, so I also felt I that I could be in the clear, but better to be safe than sorry. Ashley and Duncan sang first in our group, Mrs. Cornwall was playing background music to one of the latest top 40 songs, I think it was by Shawn Mendes.

Ashley sounded good, but nothing special. Her pitch was soft, she couldn't hit the high notes, but she was close enough that you could still listen to her. She reminded me of one of those singers who sings in a smoky bar room, good enough to not get booed off stage, but at the same time no one paid them any attention. Maybe if Mrs. Cornwall is as good as they say she is, Ashley can fine-tune her voice, practice, and become really good. Not everyone starts out amazing or talented, most people have to work on it.

Duncan was a lot better than I was expecting! Even though the song was pop, he gave a little alternative rock kick to it. His voice was high, surprisingly high, not matching his masculine stature. He sounded like Sam Harris from X Ambassadors (kids, if you don't know this band, look it up! The lead vocalist is beautifully talented! I believe he has the voice of an angel, hitting every high-pitched note). Sam Harris's singing voice is feminine, but when he talks, he just sounds like any other guy, it's incredible. However, Duncan would not be able to harmonize with Harris perfectly, but he definitely has the potential.

When it came to be my turn, I tried to remember all the time I spent practicing singing in my room, in the bathroom, in the car, etc., and I imagined I was doing just that. I closed my eyes, took a deep breath from my lower lungs, imagining a rubber ring around my waist, the way I have done so many times (I learned this trick from BBC via the internet), I breathed in and pushed the imaginary ring outwards, breathing in through my nose and out through my mouth, while all the same time remaining relaxed, letting my voice carry. As I sang, I only focused on the sound of my voice, trying to give warmth to the words that poured from my mouth. While I sang, I got lost in the melody, I forgot where I was, who I was with, I let my worries of not being accepted slide off me as I softened my shoulders and face.

Once I realized the song had stopped, I opened my eyes and saw everyone was staring at me! I thought, sh*t I have done it again, I sang too loud, probably obnoxiously loud, and now everyone is going to point and laugh. I thought that I had made a fool of myself once again, way to go champ! But then everyone applauded! They loved it, everyone told me how good I was, they even said I sounded like Adele (which was an extreme compliment, because no one truly sounded as good as Adele other than the queen herself, but I decided to take it instead of telling everyone they were wrong).

Tulip (my sister, one of few people I sung in front of) always told me that when I started to sing, it was so loud, she was surprised I didn't wake up the entire neighborhood. I guess she was right! I sang way louder then what I was expecting, I must have sung louder than the music and other students singing for the fact they had all stopped and looked at me. OOPS!

Tulip would laugh after I tell her this story, but she would probably tell me something sweet and corny like, "You sing loudly because you have a voice that needs to be heard," she is the biggest sweetheart.

After being applauded, I took a little curtsy, unsure of what to do, and then the bell rang! Literally saved by the bell! Before everyone could rush off to their next class, practically hopping with excitement for their weekend plans, Mrs. Cornwall told the class that on Monday I would be leading some of the vocal warm-ups before we got started on a new singing exercise. Then Mrs. Cornwall asked if she could meet with me at 3:00PM in the theater room to talk about the warm-ups.

When it turned 3:00 and I was standing in the theater room, waiting for Mrs. Cornwall, I realized I was so nervous that my palms were damp! (GROSS). Mrs. Cornwall arrived a little late, giving me plenty of time to freak out a bit more, she said that she had to speak with a student briefly and apologized for her tardiness.

She told me how impressed she was today, how she has never had such an aspiring student! I was so taken back I didn't know what to say, I wanted to jump up and down with glee, but I thought that would make me look very immature, so I just gave her a polite smile and nod. She asked me how long I have been taking singing lessons and when I told her I haven't taken any, and was actually planning on asking her opinion as to where I should go (hoping that she would offer to teach me herself instead, I know I can be a little manipulative at times), she looked baffled! She said how surprised she was that I was able to match the pitch of the song we sung earlier without missing a beat, and yet I've never had a lesson in my life.

I told Mrs. Cornwall that when I was younger, I looked a lot of things up online, how to sing from my diaphragm, different singing exercises and techniques, trying to perfect my own form. I explained the type of warm-ups I used, how I used to lay on the floor with a big book on my stomach, using my stomach muscles to push the book up as I drew in deep breaths. I also told her how I would practice breathing deeply into and out of my belly each night before I went to bed and before I sung, that way I was always warmed-up. I also mentioned how every day I practice my posture, I would pretend that there was a string attached to the tip of my head, like a puppet, which helped me roll my shoulders back. I believe if I manage to stay relaxed, that this perfect stance will allow me to expand and contract my ribs with my breath. (I found all of these exercises on Google).

Mrs. Cornwall told me how impressed she was by my dedication, and that a flattened diaphragm helps hold the air in the body, allowing the singer to be in control of their steady breath, necessary for singing. But then she told me that I also should learn some holistic views on singing as well, to broaden my horizon. She said that there are many beliefs and ideas of how to obtain strong vocal cords. She also said how she wants to go through some exercises with me that I haven't learned yet! She told me that she would love to give me some lessons, and that I have a lot of potential! Can you believe that? I have potential? Just to hear that from someone else makes me undeniably happy! I have always had faith in myself, but to hear someone else have faith in me too, it just feels amazing.

Mrs. Cornwall began to talk to me about the more holistic views. She got me to take a seat across from her, and it was the first time I got a really good look at her. I was not surprised by the way she dressed that she was also more of a holistic thinker/believer with her bright colorful clothes. Some kids used to call her a clown behind her back, but I personally don't see it. She did not have the short red curly hair and freckles, she didn't remind me of a Raggedy Ann doll, but her appearance made her colorful apparel look good. She was not the type of woman to wear makeup, nor did she need to, her dark brown eyes popped all on their own. She also wore her black hair down naturally most of the time, blessed by her Asian ancestry, not needing to use a straightener a single day in her life. She's probably in her 50s or 60s (I am not good at guessing older people's age), so she's got a few wrinkles, probably from frowning at the kids. But back to her clothing, it was what always grabbed my attention, she is famous for mixing and matching patterns. For example she will wear a neon yellow shirt one day with white pants, and then a neon green shirt the next day with the same white pants. I don't know how she hasn't gotten a single speck of food on them yet. Denise and I have a theory that she owns like 20 white pants, and when one gets stained, she just changes it out for a new pair. She also smells of incense, lemon, and honey, the incense she uses must be the same one Ms. V uses too (they both smell the same, except Ms. V smells like incense and lavender).

Mrs. Cornwall also told me how many people tell us to sing with our diaphragms, but that it is actually an involuntary muscle, therefore we can't control it. We are told to visualize singing with our diaphragms, or stomach, so that it helps us focus and concentrate on our breathing. She explained how the diaphragm is a muscle that reacts to us breathing, it draws the lungs down as we inhale and pushes them back up as we exhale. She said it is kinda like a placebo effect, if one thinks that they are singing through their diaphragm, to help control their breathing, and that this will help them sound better, fine-tuning their singing abilities, then it will. She doesn't usually tell students of her theories because she is told that she has to teach the students to sing with their diaphragm, that it is one part of the course requirements, and she has little authority when it comes to what things she is allowed to say that represent her opinion or beliefs (teachers are not supposed to share their opinions with the students, adults think it might influence our own decisions/beliefs).

Mrs. Cornwall explained to me how we don't sing with any part of our anatomy that doesn't belong to the larynx, which is also known as our voice box and is where our vocal cords are located. She said what we really should be doing is focusing on our vocal cords and breathing, but the focusing on the diaphragm, visualizing it, can be easier for some students. Therefore, she wants me to help the students, to try to teach them this technique of imagining their diaphragm working to their will, helping them sing. She told me to either create a new technique, or something I have used in the past to help me 'control' my diaphragm, and that I will demonstrate it to the class on Monday. She gave me her email before sending me on my way, in case I have any questions. She also said that at a later date her and I can set up a time that works best for me to come and see her to practice some new singing techniques.

So I have spent the last two hours writing and rewriting my ideas for how to visualize my breathing with my diaphragm, and I think this one is the most helpful yet, but first I will start off with introducing myself to the class, tell them how long I have been using these type of techniques for, and how helpful I find them. Then I will lead them into the exercise... "Okay class, for us to breath into our diaphragm we have to work on visualizing it. I would like everyone to put their hand in the shape of a fist between their chest and abdomen (I will do the same thing so no one is confused about what I am talking about). Now everyone please take a deep long breath in while pushing your stomach out as far as possible at the same time (I will turn to the side so they can see how big my stomach gets). But please keep the rest of your body still. I usually leave my hands at my side while doing this, but for today it's better for us to take baby steps and begin with the visualization. Now release your breath, let it all go, and on this exhale, we will pull our stomachs back in." Then I will tell the class that Mrs. Cornwall will lead the rest of the lesson, unless she wants to us to practice a few more breaths, which will also help us warm-up.

It's crazy looking back and thinking about how nervous I was to sing in front of people, and now I am about to teach the entire class a breathing exercise!

Ta Ta for now,
Love P

Chapter 9

Subject: Email #121

Dear Mr. President,

It has been **148 days** since the **Pandora High School Shooting.**

I have watched and listened to the news every single morning and night since the tragedy struck my hometown, but I have seen no progress. I have even heard that there have been two more school shootings just this month alone. You must realize this has gotten out of hand.

Fifty-six children have been shot and killed in their schools this year alone. This is a failure of us as a country, allowing this to happen, letting it get as far as it has. Something must be done, yet everyone is too hung up on us 'having the right to bear arms.' For some reason this includes our ability to defend ourselves with unnecessary means of destruction, such as automatic killing machines. The only reason we need this so-called 'mode of protection' is because of other people having the same types of weapons we keep on ourselves or under our mattress. Now tell me where the logic is in that. This is the most idiotic concept I have yet to come across when people believe the guns laws should not be changed or that they do not need to be changed. If no one was allowed an automatic rifle then no one would need one.

Now I understand that some people enjoy going to the shooting range to blow off steam, I have personally never been before, but my friends tell me how thrilling it is. And I understand that people have the right to participate in activities such as these, where no one is getting hurt. But if we were to at least give a mental health check to every American citizen wanting to purchase a gun, then at least we would know that it is a clinically sane person who has the ability to possess and carry these weapons.

This small request, or plea, would not result in that much of a drastic change, but a necessary one at the least. I also can see how this simple theory is not fool-proof on its own, I know personally that someone may be mentally well to society's standards, but they still may end up being a mass murderer, but at least this narrows it down just a smidge more. I understand that sometimes baby steps must be made before we achieve our final goal.

This simple act, or bill passing, will narrow the number of guns on the streets and in abused homes, where children can find them. It will limit the amount of possibilities for shootings in schools and in the public.

Please just consider some of my points, if not for a mother's sake, then for the sake of the children.

Sincerely,
Scarlett Smith.

Scarlett read over her email briefly then clicked send.

Chapter 10

The leaves were turning amber, orange, and red, then falling to the ground, scattering the pavement and grass. The air was crisp and fresh as the wind blew lightly.

Luckily for Californians, the temperature still sat around sixty-five Fahrenheit. The weather was pleasant and cool, a perfect time to start preparing for Homecoming.

In early October this year, Pandora High School would be holding their Homecoming dance. They chose their theme last year, so they could start preparing, which was 'A Night in Paris.' Scarlett loved the idea, but she agreed with Alex that it was very cliché.

Scarlett arrived at the Pandora High School gym the morning of Homecoming to help out with some finishing touches.

Parents of past students or current students, or any parent somewhat involved in the community, were emailed in advance to be asked to volunteer with setting up for Homecoming. Alex was emailed because her eldest daughter, Eliza, was graduating. She had been working on themes with Scarlett last year before the school shooting. Since the catastrophe that happened last June, the parent Homecoming committee had been in a frantic frenzy trying to make this the best dance yet. They hoped to raise the spirits of the teenagers who lost friends and loved ones.

It was Scarlett's task to help set up the decorations, and lend a helping hand where she was needed. Scarlett was among twenty other parents who were also involved with setting up for Homecoming. It was usually the mothers, who had daughters that were graduating, that made up this high-strung group.

Scarlett was amazed by the dedication and enthusiasm the other women had, wanting this dance to be perfect for their little girls, and boys.

It was Reanne and Isabella that really took charge this year. Reanne was one of the tall fit soccer moms, always in active wear as if she was about to be called upon to play for her daughter's team, or maybe it was because she had to be on the prowl, ready to chase one, if not all of her four sons to the car. Reanne only had one daughter who was graduating this year, Charlotte. She also could not stop talking about how she thought Charlotte was the most likely to win Homecoming Queen.

Isabella, on the other hand, was a little more toned-down than her leader Reanne. She was more of a follower, being Reanne's number one soccer mom sidekick. Alex and Scarlett loved to refer to this duo as well as their small posse as the 'tall soccer moms.' The women that made up this group all had children in the same soccer team, and none of them could be under 5'10". Isabella was one of the more fashionable mothers, always wearing a matching tracksuit. This fashion statement always made Alex laugh. "She looks like a sixty-year-old man about to go to the gym," Alex would snort. Scarlett thought she could pull it off; her tall, more curvy build could pull almost anything off. Scarlett also noticed that she seemed to prefer her light gray Adidas outfit over the other soft colored ensembles; this was also Scarlett's favorite because it was the most flattering on Isabella's tan Columbian skin.

Reanne and Isabella were nearly inseparable. Every PTA meeting, fundraiser, or other event held at the school, the two women would be found hinged to one another at the elbow. When it came to Homecoming details, Reanne was the head honcho, Isabella only pretended to be the leader when Reanne was not in the room. If Reanne commanded a task to be done, Isabella would be at her side barking orders like an obedient dog. Scarlett could not understand why Isabella had let Reanne take over the position of making all the demands, she was the louder, more enthusiastic one. Scarlett thought that it was probably her kind, easy-going side that let her slip to the sidelines while Reanne coached the team.

"Oh, Scarlett! Thank God you are here, we need you to work on the stars in the sky with Alex," Reanne shouted with a bit of surprise.

"Yes, yes, right over there in the center, above the panther logo, we need some more hung up high,"

Isabella chirped in loudly. Scarlett found it hard to understand her at times with her strong accent.

Scarlett walked over to Alex fumbling with a ladder in her six-inch heels. "Well hello there, darling, are you going to lend me a hand?" asked Alex as she tried to step onto the ladder.

"Yes, I am afraid you might fall and break something if I don't," Scarlett grimaced. Alex was graceful in her heels, making it look effortless and even comfortable, but Scarlett could picture her just toppling over any second, snapping a bone in her ankle. "Let's switch places," Scarlett said as she grabbed the ladder.

Scarlett got up on the ladder and began to hang the tiny white decorations that Alex passed to her.

One hundred Chinese paper lanterns were bought to dangle from the gymnasium's ceilings. Unfortunately for the parents, certain parts of the ceiling were too high to reach, so one parent, who was a carpenter, created a wooden patio cover with an open roof. The roof was much lower than the ceiling, so the parents made a somewhat collective decision to hang the lanterns there instead. It worked perfectly because it was still high enough so no one could jump and bang their head.

Scarlett had to hang the remaining ten lanterns from the wooden beams; once finished, a simple plugging in of a cord created the most romantic starry sky. The finishing touch to 'A Night in Paris' was completed once the gigantic picture of the Eiffel Tower was plastered onto one of the open walls.

Before Scarlett finished her task, the high school principal, Mr. Walter, spotted her and Alex standing underneath the dark brown patio covering. Mr. Walter turned to the two women and strode over to them with purpose, his loud clunky shoes thudding louder and louder as he approached. Mr. Walter's hawk eyes were set on Scarlett as he paced towards her.

"Ugh, what does he want from me now?" Scarlett mumbled to herself.

Ever since Scarlett first began her counseling sessions at the Pandora High School gym, which was offered reluctantly to the parents, Mr. Walter had been out to get her. Scarlett would get complaints from the Principal every Wednesday morning, either telling Scarlett that the floors were not properly swept, or that someone had spilled something all over the gymnasium mural. Mr. Walter complained more and more as the weeks passed, mustering up any good reason to try and kick the parents out. He was not a loved principal, had a few children of his own, but he was not good with other kids. He believed that his children were the best, more superior than any other rodent scurrying the halls. Scarlett couldn't understand why he became a teacher, and then a principal in the first place, he always seemed miserable, unless he was talking to someone who he genuinely liked.

Mr. Walter was so set on Scarlett, he hadn't noticed Alex until she spoke out.

"Hello, Chad! How are you?" Alex asked charmingly. She was one of few parents who were on the first-name basis with the Principal.

Alex was good with the men; Scarlett wished she could say the same for herself. It was Alex's beauty that often kept men staring a second too long. When she caught someone looking, she would start up a conversation with them. Most people thought Alex was a flirt. Scarlett knew that she was actually just painfully outgoing, wanting to talk to anyone who glimpsed in her direction. The men at the school loved Alex; she was attractive without being too intimidating. Scarlett thought it was her kind eyes and warm, genuine smile that made people so comfortable around her.

Chad's face softened as his gaze wandered from Scarlett's pale figure to Alex's chocolate eyes. "Good day, Alex, looking stunning as usual," Chad said with his fading Nigerian accent.

Alex had the ability to make a man behave like a teenage boy, raging with hormones, saying anything to impress her or to get her to smile.

"Chad, that is too kind of you," Alex said as she fluttered her eyelashes at the Principal, trying to soften him up before he talked to Scarlett. She also knew that he had a rough spot for her. Alex acknowledged Chad's weasel-like qualities, but she also knew her son would probably be the little trouble maker when he started high school. "Better get him on my side now when I still can," Alex would tell Scarlett and Martha.

"How are the kids?" Alex asked.

Scarlett watched the two of them talk as she remained on the ladder, hoping Mr. Walter would forget about her. Scarlett was good at standing her ground during arguments, but she hated confrontation, which was not typical of most counselors. She enjoyed watching people, finding out their secrets, reading them, finding out the reasons for their actions and behaviors. Yet, she detested being told by someone that she had done something wrong and needed to apologize, or when people would try to make her feel inferior to them.

When Scarlett was younger, she thought she was an alien sent down to Earth to make observations on the human race. She was the kid who would sit at the top of the playground, either waiting on the slide or sitting above the monkey bars, watching the other kids play, trying to understand how they enjoyed playing the silly games they loved. Scarlett never had many friends growing up, she would sit at the back of the class silently, handing her homework in on time. She would eat her lunch alone on the field, rain or sunshine. Alex and Martha were the first friends Scarlett made outside of work and volunteering. She felt that she was destined to meet them, that they were her real friends that she had been waiting for. At times, Scarlett was still reluctant to talk about herself for more than five minutes, and preferred to discuss her friends' interests and personal lives, but she was slowly improving.

"They are great, Phillip has got quite the big crush on your daughter, she sure is a spitting image of you," Mr. Walter said.

Eliza was tall like her mother, she had the long thin legs of a model. Alex told Scarlett when Eliza was younger she used to get made fun of for her legs, people would call her a giraffe. Alex would comfort her daughter, telling her that one day all of the boys, and girls, would be in awe of how her legs appear to never end. Her mother was right, everyone told Eliza that they thought she could be a model, she even had the predominant cheekbones like her mother. But Eliza lacked Alex's elegance; she was always tripping on something, even when nothing was in her way. "Yes they seem to be spending a lot of time together. Your son also looks like a little miniature version of you, well maybe more like a bigger version of you," Alex said with a grin.

Mr. Walter's son, Philip, was the captain of the football team. Most people thought he made captain because of his father. The other parents would say he was not 'leader material.' Just like Mr. Walter, Philip was a sneaky punk who thought he ran the school. Eliza told Alex one time that she was only polite to him because she didn't want to hurt his feelings. Eliza was the soft-spoken type unlike her mother. Eliza also told her how Philip often rats on his teammates who would go out partying before a big game. No one really liked him, but they just pretended to get along with him because of his father's high standing at the school.

Scarlett had only seen Philip once and she noticed right away that he must have been Mr. Walter's son. The two of them looked like twins, except Philip was twenty years younger and twice the size of his father. They both had the same dark complexion, hair, eyes, everything. They had broad shoulders and narrow hips, which came in handy for tackling or slipping past someone's grip. Their haircut was identical, a military style, nearly shaven to the scalp but their thick curls still covered their skin. Philip was only a couple inches taller than his father at the age of seventeen; he was the tallest boy in his class, standing at 6'2". Scarlett thought Philip seemed sweet, unlike his father, but it could have been because she was another parent he wanted to make a good impression on.

Mr. Walter took Alex's remark as a compliment. People were often blindsided by Alex's beauty and bubbly down-to-earth layer that they didn't realize her core was full of attitude. Eliza loved to call her mom the 'sass queen.'

"Haha, yes we are. He is good with the ladies, just like his old man too. He is going to tonight's dance with Reanne's daughter, Charlotte. Who is taking Eliza to the dance?" Mr. Walter asked.

Scarlett saw the quickest flash of rage crawl on Alex's face; she did not like it that men believed that a girl needs to be taken anywhere. She could not understand the kind of people who believed that a girl or a woman needed a man to have fun. Alex was quite the modern day feminist, but she could ignore the ignorance of some men when she knew they did not know any better. Mr. Walter was an old-fashioned type of man; he believed that it was necessary for a man to ask the father for his girlfriend's hand in marriage. He probably didn't clue in that this presumptuous expectation implied his ownership over his daughter's life and relationships. Men can often be clueless as to how their ideals impact the lives of women.

"No. Eliza is meeting up with some of her girlfriends," Alex replied, trying to soothe her tone, still wanting to coax him into a better mood.

"Oh, well I am sure she broke many hearts," Mr. Walter remarked.

Eliza was painfully shy and very dorky, very much like her father. She was the captain of the math club, which had won nationals last April. Her popularity was not affected by her intelligence, nor her quiet demeanor. She had made many friends at high school and was asked out by countless seniors, none of whom she had ever had a full conversation with. Scarlett was amazed when Eliza told her how she got invited to all of the senior parties last year; she explained how she met a lot of the older kids because she tutored them in math. "Oh how the days have changed," Scarlett would tell herself. Back in her day, boys and girls did not like the smart kids, such as herself, they would often get tormented, but now they were being invited to all the parties. Scarlett was happy for this change, and she tried to tone down her jealousy when she noticed how far high school teenagers have come from their nasty bullying days.

"Mmhmmm," murmured Alex as she turned around to pass Scarlett another lantern. You could tell when Alex felt done with a conversation, she'd flick her hair over her shoulder and turn in a different direction, or would laugh and walk away.

Now that Alex no longer had the patience for Mr. Walter, he turned to face Scarlett, his face morphing from appearing pleasant to giving off a more disapproving look.

"Fancy seeing you hear Mrs. Smith—" Mr. Walter said before he was cut off by Scarlett.

"Why would I not be here?" Scarlett knew to prepare herself for a defensive debate when talking to the principal, she was not in the mood to being throwing out unnecessary apologies just for his little power trip.

Alex turned around to face the two of them as she passed Scarlett another lantern, one hand on her hip, preparing to defend her friend if needed.

"Well, I just thought that you would no longer be assisting with the volunteering," Mr. Walter said sourly.

"She is lending a helping hand, Chad," Alex said charmingly, "We needed her help. Without her we would be hours behind schedule. We should be thanking her."

"Oh uh, well then, thank you for lending us your precious time," Mr. Walter said awkwardly and then turned on his heels to head in the opposite direction, as if someone called for him. Scarlett thought that maybe he was not willing to argue with Alex just to put her down. She didn't care though, she was simply happy he was fading out of her sight.

Scarlett's friends knew how much she hated unnecessary disputes, and like the loyal friends they are, they were always prepared to pounce to her side when needed. She was the oldest out of her mother group, but Martha and Alex babied her like the helpless fawn she was.

Alex was the most helpful when it came to deviating men's attention from Scarlett. They were hypnotized by her charming grin and found it impossible to raise their voice at such a beautiful creature. She was able to get them to apologize and change their attitude in a manner of moments. Alex never lost an argument, except when it came to her children.

After Mr. Walter was out of earshot, Alex let out a loud cackling laugh. She knew she could make a man doing anything, or almost anything at least, with a simple smile, hand touch, or batting of the eyes, and she loved it.

Alex told Martha and Scarlett once that she thought her breathing exercises helped her hypnotize people; when she began to take deep, calming breaths, she noticed the person she was talking to would do the same thing. The crazy thing was that it was true, Scarlett would notice herself take deep breaths when talking to Alex, as if she was copying her. She thought it must be some sort of sociological thing, trying to mimic the person you were socializing with, like when you were talking to someone from Scotland and you try to speak with a similar Scottish accent embarrassing yourself. Scarlett also thought it could fall under the lines with the 'monkey-see, monkey-do' saying.

"It amazes me how quickly men submit to you," Scarlett said in awe.

"It's all about the right amount of attention, honey. If you give them too much then they'll get uncomfortable and walk away, if you give them too little then they'll feel like the dominant one, but if you give 'em just the right amount then they come back, begging for more," Alex chuckled.

"I bet it's your hypnotic voodoo," Scarlett giggled as she waved her fingers at Alex like a sorceress.

"That too of course," Alex knew her friends took her breathing hypnosis theory as a joke for the most part, but it didn't seem to bother her.

"I wished I could put Mr. Walter in a spell like that," Scarlett sighed, "then maybe he will leave me alone."

Scarlett knew that it was mainly Alex's beauty that got her the attention she had, and that it was not only a blessing but a curse too. She could not imagine having multiple men in a day coming up and asking her questions, trying to talk to her, trying to pick her up or harass her for her phone number. Besides, Scarlett was confident with the way she looked; she liked her chocolate brown hair, her green-blue eyes, as well as the freckles and moles that were scattered uniquely across her body. She knew she was average, but that was good enough for her.

Scarlett's only conclusion for Mr. Walter disliking her so much was because he found her line of work distasteful. He was the type of man who said that you should walk it off, rub some dirt in it, or any other typical masculine cliché. He did not believe in counseling or therapy. He had no say in the gymnasium being rented out for the parents; the school board had thought it was a splendid idea when Scarlett brought it to them, it was mostly Mr. Walter causing the fuss. However, they probably had only agreed because it would make them look good, like they were doing whatever they could to help, even though they still expected a cheque every Tuesday night. If Mr. Walter had his way, every parent would continue on with their lives, never mentioning their deceased child's name or crying for them. Scarlett thought he was quite cold-hearted.

"Oh don't take it personally, honey, I think he is out to get almost everyone. He just has a soft spot for me, trying to talk me up all the time like I don't know his true colors. He doesn't know that we all see him as a miserable little snake," Alex sneered.

Alex had that bubbly personality, seeming like she was fond of everyone, but if someone crossed one of her friends, she was ready to fight when called upon. If you did not like someone, then that meant she did not like them either. But she never showed her true feelings towards people, she wanted everyone on her side in case of emergencies. Some people would think that's she was two-face, but Scarlett thought she was smart. She knew that you cannot get by in this world without the help of your fellow peers, she even understood this more after the shooting.

If it came down to it, Alex would reveal her opinions and beliefs to set someone straight. She was not afraid to show her true feelings, she was smarter than that. She knew that some people needed to be put in their place, but only when it was required. Alex's mother, Whitney, taught her this important life lesson; she was the reason for her two-sided personality. Whitney would tell her that she needed to kiss the white-man's ass to make it in this world, because it was a man's world after all, but more specifically a white one's. Alex knew this was not completely true, that times were changing, and that she should never have to suck up to anyone, but she also understood how important it was to have people on your support line.

"How did the blackest man in California end up with such a white guy's name anyway? What was his mother thinking?" Alex laughed.

"Alex, I don't think you're allowed to say that," Scarlett said peering down at her friend.

"No, sweetie, you are not allowed to say that," Alex retorted.

"Well maybe it's his chosen name when he came here?" Scarlett remarked.

"Then what type of black man chooses a white person's name? Chad? It just makes me think of *One Tree Hill*," Alex replied with more laughter.

"What is so bad about that? We both love us some Chad Michael Murray." Scarlett laughed.

The girls giggled like fans, fantasizing about their favorite male pop icon.

Chapter 11

In the evening on the day of the Homecoming dance, Alex and Scarlett proceeded onto their next volunteer duty, signing in students as well as selling last-minute tickets.

Standing at the entrance from the hall to the gymnasium, they got the most spectacular view of 'A Night in Paris' through the opening of the double doors. They could see the Chinese lanterns dangling from wooden planks of the patio covering, illuminating the gymnasium in the type of light people wish to have on their first dates. Closest to the gym doors was an arbor lined against a wall with a green screen hanging in front of it; this is where the students would get their photos taken. The wooden framework was painted white and entangled in fake vines – it looked like it belonged in a wedding. Scarlett thought the carpenter really outdid themself, she wanted to find them later to let them know how beautiful it all was.

The green screen was used so that the computer-whiz students could later adjust the photos and set the background as the Eiffel Tower, making it appear as the students had gone on a trip to France. Almost all of the seniors would be posing in front of the greatest symbol of romance with their friends, partners, and anyone in between, trying to catch as many memories of this night as possible. Scarlett and Alex were told that the pictures would be posted, sometime the following day, on the school website for everyone to see.

"What a pain that must have been to hang," Scarlett whispered to Alex as the women stood in awe, staring at the finishing touch, the Eiffel Tower poster hanging from the ceiling.

"It's beautiful," Alex sniffled. Alex never went to her prom, she worked most nights in high school, so like most mothers, Alex wanted to live this experience through her daughter.

Alex helped Eliza pick out a beautiful, elegant pink dress that flattered her skin tone. Her daughter was not the 'pink' type, but she wanted to make her mother happy so she played along. After setting up the lanterns, Alex had gone home to take pictures of Eliza and some of her friends on their deck, which looked over the water. She had not stopped sniffling since she got back to the school. "My daughter just looks so beautiful," Alex said with tears in her eyes when she saw Scarlett. Alex loves her children no matter what, but she takes pride in how good they have all turned out.

Scarlett admired the beauty of the night she helped create, but it all was very posh in her opinion. She knew it was not in the school budget to put on a performance as extravagant as this; there must have been some parents adding in some extra contributions. The wood looked expensive, the green screen was bought brand new, and the poster was so large and delicate looking, Scarlett thought that was probably the most expensive decorative piece.

Scarlett understood that the students needed a fun night after what happened almost four months ago. However, she did not think they needed something so decretive. She thought about all the different things the money could have been put toward instead of this, such as the debt from funerals, therapists, prescription pills, and the list goes on.

Pandora may be a public school, but there was a handful of well-off families who decided that private school was a waste of money, or that it could not teach you the same valuable lessons that a public school could. Alex and her husband belonged in this category of parents. "Private school is for the snotty, stuck-up kids, whereas in public school, you meet all kinds and types of people," Alex once explained to Scarlett. "Besides, it does not help you get ahead in life, it keeps students on a tight leash so that they can be more rebellious in their later years." Scarlett had yet to inform Alex that she went to a private school.

Alex was right though, the kids at Scarlett's school were spoiled rich kids, and they thought they could get away with anything because their parents were 'important.' Scarlett was only able to go to private school because her grandfather had set aside a sum of money specifically for Scarlett's secondary education. Scarlett's parents resented her for this reason, they could not believe that the money was set aside for her and not them. They had to sacrifice their education for her, simply because Scarlett's mom got pregnant freshman year. They were both college dropouts and had apparently little help from their own parents.

Scarlett had also missed out on her prom; she could not stand the stuck-up kids, so did not fully understand the significance of it all. Alex told her that prom meant everything to the students, especially the seniors. The boys and girls were so excited to hear about who was going to make the Homecoming Queen and King. Everyone had their own opinion of who deserved it the most, whether it was the most popular or the kindest student.

"Isn't it beautiful," Rachel said enviously with a hint of resentment, standing at the sign-in table, waiting for Alex and Scarlett to finish gawking at the gym. She was another mother who was also helping volunteer with signing in students.

"Yes, the students will love it!" Annabella chirped as she headed towards the women, jumping up and down while exiting the gym. She was one of the more cheerful parents who was honored to have been asked to chaperone this evening. Alex had told Scarlett that Annabella was only asked because Mr. Walter knew she was going to be one of few who would actually say yes.

"Everything must be perfect to a T," Reanne said in her up-tight tone.

"It is perrrfect," Isabella said, who was practically jogging behind Annabella, racing towards Reanne's side so that she could put her hand on Reanne's shoulder for reassurance.

"The kids will not even notice the hard work we have put in to make their dance so special. They will be too busy thinking about having sex and who's going to be crowned king and queen. It's all ridiculous if you ask me," Nicole announced herself as she trailed behind Annabella and Isabella, striding towards her twin sister's side. You could tell Nicole and Rachel were twins instantly; they may not have been identical, which surprised most people, but they both had the same miserable look on their face, as if they could always smell their sons' dirty socks. They were a little bit taller than Scarlett, but not by much. They also had the similar dark, wavy hair that ended at their shoulders like Alex.

Scarlett never understood why the twins had such big attitudes, they each had a son, both the same age – fancy that – who were already guaranteed full ride scholarships at a nearby college. They also both had loving husbands who owned a law firm together, which was how they both met their remarkably good-looking partners.

The two women were stay-at-home mothers who spent their time working at the gym while their cleaners made their homes spotless. They were also another set of rich parents who did not believe in private school. They had the help of nannies to raise their sons, who Scarlett thought turned out to be very kind boys, unlike their mothers.

However, Nicole and Rachel had not always been this gloomy. It was not until school started that Scarlett and Alex noticed the change in the twins' behavior. Alex had even offered to take them to yoga, but the women refused. Scarlett thought maybe it was due to the school shooting, everyone seemed to have been affected from what happened, so she emailed them, letting them know about the parent meetings. She has yet to hear, or read, a response.

Nicole's and Rachel's social lives had been quickly dwindling since September. They may be the quiet type, but they also loved to socialize together and were involved in many school activities. The parents of the graduating class found it very strange that the women were no longer attending any committee or other school-related meetings.

Alex, being the outgoing and caring woman that she was, had asked the women if something was wrong with their lives at home. Alex was also very nosy and personal, so she also confronted them for her own sake. She told Scarlett that Nicole and Rachel had admitted that they were affected by the school shooting, but they quickly brushed her off, not giving her any more details.

Alex had not been happy with the little information she had been given, but for now she was willing to back off and let the women grieve if that is what they needed. Yet, she still found it hard to not follow them around like a hound, searching for clues. Scarlett found this attribute to be amusing at times, but when it came down to Alex sniffing around Scarlett's business, she would get a little agitated.

"No need to be so vulgar," winced Isabella who was a bit of a prune, not accepting the idea of her child having sex at the ripe age of seventeen. "And the children love that tradition," Isabella said more proudly.

"Don't be so miserable, Nicole, tonight has to be wonderful and light-hearted for the children in light of the events that happened last year," remarked Reanne. The term 'school shooting' was equivalent to the use of Lord Voldemort's name in Harry Potter. The parents believed it to be a bad omen, therefore never said it out loud.

"Nicole has a point—" Rachel began before she was interrupted by Reanne.

"No, there simply is no point to be had. What matters are the kids and their happiness. Nothing about tonight is ridiculous. Two honored students will be crowned king and queen. They will represent their senior class, which is why it is so important for students to vote for the most liked, smartest, and kindest female and male representatives. If someone does not get picked, they know why, not everyone can be perfect nor well-liked," Reanne explained as her nose reached closer and closer towards the ceiling.

"You are just saying that because you think your precious Dianne will win. What about all the other kids? The dorks, geeks, and freaks? How do you think they will feel when someone who picks on them, bullies them, gets their named called so they can be crowned in front of their peers, a symbol showing they are once again more popular and superior than everyone else. It's just a popularity contest, a stupid popularity contest," Nicole retorted. Nicole was what people call the 'alpha twin,' speaking over others to make sure her voice was heard.

"That is not true, Reanne knows that there are other kids, such as Sofia for example," explained Isabella, completely missing Nicole's point.

Nicole's nostrils began to flare as Rachel reached her hand to her sister, attempting to calm her down.

"I agree with Reanne, the children want this, tonight is meant to be very special," Scarlett was surprised by the sound of her own voice. She did not even agree with Reanne, and she did believe tonight should be fun for the children, to help them forget and have a good time, but she did not believe in the idiocy of voting for a 'queen' and 'king.' Scarlett was surprised that she was starting to feel fired up from seeing Nicole and Rachel so emotional over the shooting; they did not even have children present that day, they were both skipping and going to the beach with the rest of the football team and a handful of cheerleaders.

"Hey, you guys, everyone take a few deep breaths," Alex inhaled loudly, "this night is for the kids, and don't you forget that. They are the ones who want this.

They are the ones who have suffered loss and pain." Alex loved to play the role of the peacekeeper, that is when she was not fired up herself.

"Yes, but it can be traumatic if a kid is not chosen as king or queen when they are expecting to be," Rachel pitched in while still trying to calm her sister.

Scarlett completely agreed with Rachel's remark, but decided to keep this to herself.

"Yes, but they also need to learn that they will not be the best at everything, besides nothing is wrong with a little bit of friendly competition," Alex replied, "I know Eliza is really looking forward to tonight, and she could care less about who is crowned."

Yes, but she is popular, Scarlett thought quietly. Eliza never knew what it was like to be bullied or picked on, she was always loved, just like her mother.

Scarlett, on the other hand, knew what it was like to be made a fool of by her peers. She had dreaded everyday going to her preppy high school to face the scorn of teenagers. Jonathan was the first person who was ever really nice to Scarlett, which is probably why she took an instant liking to him. She had been dying for human connection, which she had lacked growing up as an only child hated by her parents.

"I am just saying that I believe they should get rid of the whole queen and king thing, it is another useless popularity contest," said Nicole inhaling and exhaling.

Nicole's son, Duncan, was one student that Eliza had told Alex and Scarlett who she thought would win. He was constantly surrounded by people. Him being the quarterback, who had been already signed to a college football team, also helped his popularity ranking. Scarlett had been introduced to him early last year, and when she first met him, she thought that he looked like a young Tom Brady with his tall athletic build and dimpled chin.

Eliza said that Duncan may have the looks, but he lacked the brains. She had tutored him for the past two years in math and he just never seemed to get it. She was surprised that he had even made it to senior year, let alone been accepted to college. Alex came up with the theory that the coaches made up some sort of arrangement with the teachers, so that way he was not held back from the team.

Scarlett refrained herself from engaging any further in the argument about continuing the crowning tradition at Homecoming. She had enjoyed setting up for the event, but was beginning to become unhinged the more she thought about the idea behind Homecoming. She understood that the students needed this to live a little, to feel young and carefree again, but then again the crowning was unnecessary. Her counselor's voice told her: "Alex is right, a little bit of competition is good between the students. And it also helps them practice their voting rights, so that one day they can use this skill they have learned, from picking the two best people to represent their senior class, to vote for a leader whom they want to represent their country."

Scarlett also heard another voice slowly gain volume in the back of her mind: "No, students should not be choosing a boy and girl to represent their class, everyone is their own individual and therefore represents the body separately. And do not even get me started on the terms king and queen, what about the people who do not gender identify, or who are transgender? This type of setting may make them more uncomfortable or even feel insulted."

Scarlett had begun hearing this nasally voice, with a self-righteous tone, since the beginning of September. She had been able to brush it off, quiet it down, thinking it was probably nothing. But now that it had finally spoken, loud enough to be heard, over-powering her own thoughts, she was starting to get a little bit worried. *Maybe it's the lack of sleep,* she thought hopefully.

"Smiles everyone, the students are coming," sung Annabella, causing the girls to jump. She had been so silent during the dispute that they had forgotten she was standing at the table waiting till the students arrived, before she went back inside to the gym to start serving the punch, making sure no one could spike it.

As the students started flooding the halls, most of the limos arriving at the same time, the mothers listened to Annabella and stopped talking. They silently agreed that it was better to meet the children with smiles instead of their conversation regarding school politics. Even Nicole and Rachel were able to plaster on the prettiest fake smiles they could manage as they greeted the children. Nicole left her sister, after greeting some of the children she recognized, to help Annabella keep an eye on the students' intake of alcohol.

"Remember to keep them a ruler length apart," Reanne shouted to Nicole's back, needing to have the last word.

Reanne and Isabella were set up at one table, signing in students who had their last name starting with A-M. Scarlett and Alex were set up on the opposite side of the hall to sign in students whose last name began with N-Z. They were also selling last-minute tickets to students who decided to make an appearance.

Scarlett and Alex's table was still the slowest even though they had to do two separate tasks. People did not usually have their last name beginning with a letter ranging from N to Z. Scarlett did not care they only had a few students every ten minutes, she was happy to not be busy. She was also not in the mood for trying to have small talk with the students of Pandora High School. She was not like Nicole, Rachel, Jody, Reanne, Annabella, or Alex, who had a kid that was attending Homecoming.

Rachel greeted the children as they pooled in, directing them to which table to sign up at. The girls were dressed in all different shapes and sizes of dress. Most of them wore puffy, princess dresses that brushed the floor. A few also were seen wearing tuxes. The boys, who had dates, were escorting their partners through the hallway with grins on their faces, pleased with themselves for convincing someone to go to Homecoming with them. Not everyone had a date, but everyone had someone to meet them at the doorway, their face lighting up when they recognized their friends. The students all looked amazing, they looked happy, cheerful, forgetting about the afternoon that haunted most of their restless sleeps.

When Scarlett caught sight of Eliza, she began to tear up. "She looks stunning," Scarlett said as she put her hand on her friend's shoulder, assuring her that she did a good job raising a fine young woman.

Eliza approached her mom and Scarlett with a surprising grace, surrounded by friends, giggling. "Honey," Alex began.

"Stop, Mom, you already saw me, please don't start crying again," Eliza said looking down at her watery-eyed mother. Eliza was wearing the pink dress that practically screamed "ALEX PICKED ME!" It was silk and form-fitting in all the right areas. Her curly black hair was pulled to the side, pinned in an elegant bun. She didn't have a touch of makeup on, but she still looked like a model, towering over everyone in her tiny heels. Scarlett was proud that she still didn't wear eyeliner, eye shadow, highlighter, or foundation, that she was still true to some of her natural beliefs.

Scarlett got up to give Eliza a quick hug. "You look gorgeous," Scarlett said as she pulled away from Eliza to look at her from an arm's distance.

Eliza seemed a little awkward, which surprised Scarlett since her mother was the most affectionate person, but on the other hand, Scarlett did not remember ever hugging Eliza before.

"I . . ." Eliza mumbled looking down at Scarlett, who was crying quietly, "Thanks, I do not know if my mom told you, but they are having a moment of silence tonight for the students who passed away last year. I, uh, just thought you might want to know."

Scarlett was taken back how bewildered and sad Eliza looked, she was used to seeing her wide-eyed and cheerful. *She is probably upset from seeing you cry, you old fool*, Scarlett thought to herself.

"That is very nice of them," Scarlett sniffled as she regained her composure. She was beginning to regret volunteering, it hurt her seeing all of the memories she did not get the chance to experience.

"Excuse me, you're in the way," a boy protested as he tried to push through Scarlett and Eliza to sign in. "Oh, hey Eliza," he said flustered, he didn't recognize her at first while trying to move past her.

"You can go around us," Eliza proclaimed, clenching her jaw on one side, like her mother, refusing to turn around to talk to the guy who had been rude before he knew who he was talking to. *This is the Eliza I know*, Scarlett thought to herself. The sassy-ness ran in the family.

"I've got you all signed in, honey, so you are free to go," Alex said, saving Scarlett from having to talk any more as she choked back a sob when returning to her seat.

As the number of students entering the gym slowly dwindled, Alex felt the need to bring up the conversation of king and queen again. She liked to think things out loud surrounded by her friends. She also wanted what is best for her children, and if someone truly believed that the crowning ceremony was not healthy for students, then she would do everything in her power to stop it.

"At least they no longer give the whole spiel of how the students have to make their vote at the end of the night," Alex said out loud, mid thought, "Imagine being rushed liked that, the students not been given enough time to decide who is the most deserving candidate. They also no longer bring up the three most voted for students onto the stage. That would be humiliating, it would make it way more personal for the students on stage, it would be like, oh, people picked you over me. Now it's more like anyone can win, a free-for-all."

"Yes, that is true," Scarlett agreed.

"What are your thoughts?" Alex asked.

"I am not sure, I can see both sides to the debate," Scarlett did not want to tell Alex how she openly feels when she had just agreed with Reanne as if it were a matter-of-fact.

"Well, I just think that—" Alex stopped mid-sentence as two girls, who were being obnoxiously loud, headed towards their table.

The music was now blaring through the gymnasium doors, forcing the students who had not signed in yet to shout over each other.

The sound of music made Scarlett giggle; she just envisioned Annabella hopping about, telling students to keep their distance while they ignored her, grinding their hearts out. *Wow, I must be really losing my marbles*, Scarlett quietly remarked as her moods were quickly changing.

At the previous dances, Alex and Scarlett had also been guilt tripped into chaperoning. They would spend the majority of the night doubled over, laughing, as Annabella sang "keep your distance, remember boys have cooties." The students were too old to still believe in that wise tale, but everyone thought her sad attempt was humorous.

Scarlett was starting to feel more aware how delusional she looked, giggling about Annabella's quirky ways, holding back tears when thinking about how beautiful Eliza looked. Her nose was beginning to run as the two girls got closer to her, her eyes were also most likely puffy from crying. It was as if the lack of tears left in her ducts caused them to swell, making them itchy and red.

The obnoxious students started to gawk at Scarlett, trying to figure out how they recognized her.

"Is that her?" one girl whispered loudly to her friend as she stumbled over her heels.

"Who?" asked the other girl, not caring to lower her voice the tiniest amount.

"The parent that talked to the shooter before they came to school with a gun?"

"Right, what's she doing here?"

Alex's eyes darted up in a flash towards the girls, her face streaked with shock.

"Amanda! Julia!" Simone said as she walked up quietly behind the girls, "have you been drinking?"

"Only been drinking water, Ms. V," lied the girl who had been talking quietly.

"Yeah only for the past ten minutes," the other student laughed hysterically.

"My office, now, both of you," Simone said as she ushered the girls to walk ahead of her.

"Simone to the rescue," whispered Alex. "Thanks, V," she said more loudly.

Simone Vadhra, Pandora High School's Vice Principal, was a soft-spoken woman, who looked like she could not raise her voice loud enough to be heard from across a classroom. She was tall, like Alex, and had a tan complexion, representing her Indian heritage. She was also similar to Alex in her hippy attitude. She was an example of a person who agreed that plastic straws should be banned. Her theory was that hemp ones should be used instead of the paper ones too; she was very environmentally conscious.

Most recently, Simone and Alex had started attending the same yoga classes. They were quickly becoming friends, Alex had even given her a nickname, 'V.' This reminded Scarlett of teenage TV shows such as *Gossip Girl* and *Pretty Little Liars*; they all thought they were so clever by giving their 'BFF' a nickname that started with the first letter of their name, such as 'A' and 'S.' It was also starting to drive Scarlett crazy hearing them on the phone. "Oh, V, you are so right, we should get on the school's recycling system to accept soft plastics." Scarlett believed in being environmentally conscious, but they overdid it. She was also probably jealous that her friend was starting to spend more time with someone else.

"I hope they didn't cause too much trouble," Simone said winking at Alex before turning to face Scarlet, "Happy to see you here, Scarlett, your help is always wanted." She turned lightly on her feet before disappearing after the two girls.

"Was she not expecting me to come?" Scarlett asked. "And what does she mean by, your help is always wanted? She sounded sarcastic—"

"Honey, take a few deep breaths, you know V didn't mean any harm. Maybe you should go to the bathroom to freshen up."

Scarlett was not the type of person who needed or cared about 'freshening up,' she did not even remember the last time she wore makeup. It took only a few moments before she realized what she meant, and then what the two girls said finally hit her. "You're right, I am going to go to the bathroom," she mumbled.

Scarlett felt like she had just been hit by a moving vehicle, her knees were locked and she was holding her stomach as if she were about to be sick.

"Do you need help?" Alex asked as she started to get out from her chair.

"No, no, I am fine. You keep signing the students in, I will be back in a minute," Scarlett wanted to reassure Alex that she was fine, but she was finding it hard not retch. Scarlett did not handle bad news or stress well, it made her sick to her stomach. When she was a kid, she would get the same feeling when she was bullied or yelled at by her parents.

As Scarlett scurried off, she reminded herself to not let the children and parents see her cry. *What is the point anyway? They had just seen me get overly emotional about someone else's daughter going to this stupid dance and then laugh seconds later*, she thought to herself. She was feeling her marbles, one by one, roll away from her as she headed for the bathroom.

She counted her steps as she paced herself to the girls' washroom, *3 more strides, now 2.*

Chapter 12

Scarlett sat on one of the toilets in the girls' bathroom. She could feel her butt drag down the center, there was no toilet lid to sit on top of. The stall reeked of cheap cotton candy perfume, a student must have heavily sprayed her five-dollar bottle to cover up the smell of weed or alcohol. Scarlett's nostrils were on fire, but she was too occupied sobbing into her hands to care.

The students were right, she had talked to the shooters before they took their assault rifle to Pandora High, killing fifteen students.

Scarlett had worked for Suicide Prevention Lifeline for the past ten years. Before this she had volunteered with the Lifeline for five years, as well as other suicide prevention organizations. She always had a calling for helping other people who were in suffering, needing guidance, or a listening ear. When she was a little girl, Scarlett had no support group, or network from her family. Back in her day, Scarlett also did not have the option of calling a hotline or reaching out to a professional online through a suicide prevention chat.

Scarlett was a lonely child who sat in the back, watching and listening, pretending not to care, but actually waiting for someone to notice her. She had her own close encounters with suicide; she went through her depressed stages as an early teen, but she held on a little bit longer, finding comfort in novels.

After moving out of her miserable home at seventeen, Scarlett found out how beautiful life could be. She started to volunteer in youth-group organizations, she wanted to tell children it gets better. This was where she met her husband, where they made the instant connection she always wanted and got married a short four months after they had met. Scarlett had invited her estranged parents to the wedding, but they had thought she was getting married so young because she had gotten knocked up. They told her they had no intentions of having to raise her child nor helping with possible money problems. They had cut their only daughter out of their life because they had thought she was pregnant and needed money. Scarlett realized she did not need them in her life and Jonathan was going to be her family now.

Jonathan had helped support Scarlett as she graduated with a degree in Psychology, and then a masters in School Counseling. Scarlett had thought she wanted to help with children mostly, but her school counseling often resulted in conflicts with parents, who she could not force into therapy and who often did not appreciate being told they needed it either. Scarlett thought she understood kids better, which was why she switched to full-time at The National Suicide Prevention Lifeline, leaving her short-lived school counseling days behind her.

Scarlett mostly worked with young students or adolescents who needed support or advice at the Lifeline. She was being paired with mostly Americans who had mental illnesses, such as depression and/or anxiety, and apparently not only people who were wanting to inflict harm upon themselves. Scarlett had talked to these children over the phone, and she also had picked up some shifts on the weekend where she would engage in chat conversations that required her attention.

Scarlett had a few regular callers, people who needed more social contact or assistance than what can be provided in one conversation. She would tell the callers her daily advice, explaining to her best ability about what amazing things life has to offer and how life gets better, then their conversations would dive into more personal details. The callers explained their living circumstances, their friends, their families, and what life was like at school for them. Scarlett engaged in these long conversations to find minuscule details, where the caller would waver in their speech patterns, or where they would begin to cry, this helped her discover some of the real dilemmas the person was facing.

Most of the time the callers just needed someone to talk to, for someone to care, to be told they are worthy. The callers did not need to hear from loved ones, who they look up to, that they were lucky to live the life they were living, and that they had no reason to be unhappy. They also did not need to be told that there was something wrong with them because they were still upset over a breakup or something, rather they wanted to hear that they were going to be okay or what they were going through was normal.

Over the years working at the hotline, Scarlett had realized that people hated being told that they needed to get over something. She knew that everyone took their own time to grieve, either for the dead or a lost romance. Yes, there were times when a certain number of years had passed and someone had not moved on, that they should seek professional advice. However, Scarlett often would tell her clients that it was normal to grieve for a relationship longer than it lasted. This often was due to underlying circumstances or situations that people did not pick up on. For example, some people would grieve over a relationship for over a year when it had only lasted four months. Scarlett would ask the caller that maybe they are upset because the person was their first love, or because they felt they had lost a best friend. Then they would discuss how to move forward from there.

The Lifeline began as a slow part-time job for Scarlett, she had enjoyed it more than school counseling. She only started part-time initially because Jonathan's salary as English Professor at one of the more prestigious colleges in California made it possible for her to work as much as she pleased. It was not until the summer of 2017 that the Lifeline had really begun to get busy. In April 2017, the American rapper Logic released his song *1-800-273-8255* featuring Alessia Cara and Khalid. This title was the number for The National Suicide Prevention Hotline. The song helped bring awareness to the lifeline, as well as struggles associated with suicide. The more the song was featured, either on radio stations or viewed on YouTube, there was a greater increase in the number of calls to the hotline. Scarlett began working full-time in the summer of 2017 to keep up with the growing demands of the callers. She was thrilled that more people were seeking advice, and help with their struggles. She also did not want people to remain in silence, letting their problems muffle their voices. Shortly after working full-time, Scarlett began picking up extra shifts on the weekends to help keep up with the growing list of people wanting to chat online, this way she was able to work from home. Unfortunately, this took away some of her family time, but Scarlett knew that these children and adolescents needed a strong guider, a counselor, which she wished to be.

***

At 11:45AM on June 8th, Scarlett had received a call from a student who appeared in distress. She was surprised when she recognized the voice on the other end.

"Hello, thank you for reaching out. How may I help you?" Scarlett said in her enduring, sincere tone.

"I have tried and tried for years now to make friends, but I have none. No one likes me, no one listens to me, they just bully me and call me names," the caller sobbed, "They are nasty, nasty people, they make me want to end it, end everything."

"Who are they?" Scarlett asked as the caller paused to take a gasp of air.

"Them! The people out there, they are everywhere, we are surrounded by them. We see them on the sidewalks, in the mall, at school. They appear to be so busy with their lives, acting as if they are these perfect people that have perfect things to do, they are so full of themselves. They have no compassion or love for anyone else. They laugh at each other's jokes, as if their friend just said the funniest thing they have ever heard, but they just do that to make you feel bad, to make you feel like you are missing out on their perfection. And it's all bullshit! They talk behind each other's back, they act like they're BFFs but then they are willing to stab you in the back the moment you turn around."

Scarlett did not have the chance to add her opinion, or helpful quotes she often used on clients who were more distraught than most. However, she thought it would be good for them to vent, to let all of their anguish out into the open.

"I used to be one of them. We were all happy playing this make-believe game, pretending we were all perfect, that our families did not neglect us, or that we were never abused by our parents or peers. We have been taught to play all our lives; it started when we were little kids, playing house, playing the happy married couple who have a baby because that is what society wants us to do or how they want us to behave. Then we play the happy teenagers who go to school, thrilled that we are privileged enough to get an education, which is taught by none other than the idiots who believe the world should be run by imbeciles. They tell us that we need to work on helping endangered species or saving the environment, yet the people trying to force these environmentally conscious ideals down our throats are the ones who had fucked the planet up so much that it needs saving! How do they not see the irony?" The caller had paused briefly, as if they had wanted a response from Scarlett, then they continued, "They are the ones that wrecked this planet, this planet that we are supposed to cherish with our lives. They are so stupid. They believe it's on us millennials to fix all of their mistakes. Why do they put so much pressure on us? They tell us of the famine, droughts, and destruction of ecosystems, they say how there is little hope, and it's on us or we are fucked. I guess they can't help themselves, they are playing adult, pretending to be the good guys, acting as if they know everything. The magazines, the media tells us what to do, how to act like proper, sophisticated women so that the boys will like us, as if we need men to accept us into their world.

"Then they will also tell us one of their typical clichés that life gets better, but does it really? We are told that it's supposed to get better, better than this hellhole we have created. Yet, once you leave school, the protection of the adults, who are supposed to guide you, abandon you, tell you it only gets harder from here in the real world and that you are now on your own. This is where you are now on your own, you can't get away with being too young or innocent for not knowing better. The world gets tough so you better get tougher, but no one really teaches us this, or maybe they try and fail. They say grow up, but not too fast – walk, don't run. But what do they know? Is every single adult on the planet happy? HA! Yeah right, adults are too busy trying to act like the young people running around society with their heads cut off, and then there is the young trying to act like the old, like they are better, or that they know more than everyone else. I know it doesn't get better with time, maybe even worse, maybe life gets harder... There is a certain age where it's no longer appropriate for you to rely on your family financially, and if you cannot support yourself, then you end up on the streets. They tell you to hold your head, keep on moving, but what do they—" The caller paused, beginning to lose their moment of thought.

Scarlett sat in the silence, unsure how to handle or respond to the caller. She thought, *This can't be them, no way.*

"Then there is that saying that dates back to the nineteenth century," the caller started back up again, mid-thought, "Sticks and stones may break my bones, but words will never harm me. It's funny to think how long it has been around for, obviously just as relevant as it was back then as it is now, so does that mean bullying will never stop? People will never cast aside their differences and embrace one another? Instead they choose to mock the outcasts, the freaks, the weirdoes, the people who are just simply different because they don't fit the status quo… This saying is also not even accurate, which drives me crazy. Like yeah, no shit words can't physically hurt you, but they can torment you, make your life a hellhole. Then there is that other stupid saying that high school is your peak, like this is as good as it's going to get. But what if high school is a miserable fucking experience? Should I just get out now?"

"No, of course not," Scarlett began before she was interrupted by the caller – they were clearly not finished their rant.

"But like I said before, what do they know," the caller carried on as if they did not hear Scarlett, "No one knows anything in this world, at least not the really important stuff, like yeah people know science, English, math, blah, blah, blah, but what about how to stop world hunger, or how to stop destroying the planet we are living in? Or is it too late? Are we too far gone? Are we too fucked? Is that why suicide rates are drastically increasing? Are people starting to see how fucked we are?" The caller's voice changed, their tone turning less bitter and angrier. "And who is really at fault for this cruel world? The people that surround me, such as the teachers, the blue-collared people, the politicians, the kids? But why do they do it, why do they make this world shittier and shittier every day? Does it make them happy, give them a fucking orgasm every time the yell at fat people or throw trash out their window? Why do I have to suffer while they continuously taunt me and others? Why do they get to choose how I live my life, in peace or in happiness? It's all fucking stupid if you ask me. In school they say bullying has stopped, what about me? Are they pretending that I don't count, or that I don't exist? They also say only bad things happen to bad people, then does that make me a bad person?" The caller snorted. "Yeah fucking right! It's those douchebags who act like they run the school that deserve to suffer. They need to know what it's like to be in pain, or to have someone they love taken away from them. Those are the people that deserve to be hurt," the caller said before they hung up, barely letting Scarlett catch their last word.

Scarlett had never dealt with a situation like this one before. People who call the hotline were usually wanting help, they wanted to be talked off the ledge, they never discussed the harm that they wanted to inflict on others. Scarlett had begun to feel like she no longer had any control of the conversation once the caller had cut her off, like they had never heard her speak up in the first place. Callers are supposed to want help, otherwise they would not be calling, which made this conversation very frightening.

Most workers would have brushed it off, thinking this caller just needed to blow off some steam before returning to class. In contrast, Scarlett thought, due to the caller's sporadic conversation with themselves, that they were actually trying to convince themself to do something. Scarlett was not entirely sure what the caller had in mind, or how they had become so depressed in the span of several months. Scarlett thought they had always been a good kid, she couldn't see why they were so upset with the world.

Scarlett decided to take this phone conversation to her supervisor. The National Suicide Prevention Hotline may have been confidential, no numbers nor names were ever given, but this time it was different. Scarlett recognized the caller, even knew where they lived, therefore with them making threats about harming others, she thought it was best to ask her supervisor how to proceed.

"Good afternoon, Scarlett, what may I help you with?" Scarlett's supervisor, Bethany, asked.

"Hello, Ms. Day, I just received a call from a child in distraught who was threatening to harm others—" Scarlett said before being interrupted.

"Did this child specifically say they were going to harm someone or whom they are planning to harm... Did they tell you their plan like an evil villain?" Bethany joked.

Since Scarlett started working full-time, taking extra shifts on the weekend, Bethany has had it out for her. People used to tell Scarlett that she would make a better supervisor, she had more experience, that she was better at handling difficult situations, and was more educated. Most of the hotline workers majored in psychology, not furthering their education, unlike Scarlett. Scarlett also believed that maybe Bethany thought she was out to get her job, which she clearly was not, she enjoyed working directly with people, not behind closed doors dealing with all the paperwork.

Bethany took Scarlett as a joke, mostly because Scarlett was the type of worker who told their supervisor everything, insults or compliments that she received. "Ms. Day, this caller had told me I saved their life!" Scarlett exclaimed on her first call after starting full-time. It was usually the full-time workers who'd get consecutive calls, who actually made a major impact on callers' decisions to end their lives. The people who were closer to the edge called more often, they needed that extra reassurance almost every day until the medicine kicked in or their feelings subsided. It drove Bethany crazy how Scarlett would search her out to inform her that she either had a successful call or one that did not turn out so well. "Does she not understand how busy I am?" Bethany would mutter to herself before Scarlett opened the clear glass door to her office.

Bethany hated her job after her promotion, but she needed the money. She used to be happy working with the hotline, she was thinner and more relaxed when she started there. It surprised people how much weight she put on after her promotion and how the years were really starting to show on her face. Bethany's older sister had told her, "This will be good for you, no longer having to listen to people tell you about their sad lives. You will no longer have to worry about them now, you can finally focus on yourself, maybe even start dating."

Her friends and family were right, all she had to worry about now was the piling of paper in the right corner of her desk. Yet, she never did start dating, she was always content with herself and her work, not needing a companion to share her life with. She also loved helping callers, it would give her a thrill, a drive, a purpose. After having a successful day with callers, Bethany got the energy to work out, to go out, to live her life to the fullest. Her clients taught her how to appreciate her life, they showed her that anything can happen, good or bad. She loved helping people solve their problems, just like Scarlett. She wanted to give people the right answers. Bethany wanted to be the person to make them feel better. After a long day's work, she felt energized, fulfilled, but now she just wanted to go home and watch TV as she dozed off, dreaming about better days.

"No, they did not tell me this, but they did technically say…" Scarlett frowned.

"Technically? Well, technically is something we can do nothing about, so move along and get back to your station," Bethany said as she continued to write on the stack of paper in front of her. She felt too tired to deal with Scarlett's pointless comments.

"But Ms. Day, I know the caller, they sounded distraught, I always thought they were happy, carefree, I don't know what could have made them so… so… bitter."

"You know the caller? Did they tell you their name or did you ask them? We are a confidential hotline, Mrs. Smith, we are not supposed to be asking for any personal details that make callers feel uncomfortable," Bethany was infuriated. *Great, now I am going to have to write up a report about this,* she thought.

"Well no, technically they never told me their name but I recognized the voice."

"There you go again with this technically," Bethany said using air quotations as she said 'technically.' "Scarlett, I understand your concern, but we know nothing about this caller or what they had meant. So if you feel that this conversation has upset you in any way, and you are no longer able to provide counseling to others with a clear head, then return home. If you feel fine and can proceed with your work, then please return to your station." Bethany continued writing, not once glancing up to acknowledge that Scarlett was upset from their conversation, her eyes wide and bloodshot, looking like she was going to scream out in frustration at any moment.

As Scarlett turned around, a thousand thoughts raced in her mind, "What if they called to speak with me for a reason, like a warning?"; "Did they know it was me on the phone, wait no, I barely said anything, but still maybe…"; "I will go to the school first, just to see if they are—"

Scarlett was so focused on visualizing her next step that she almost did not hear Bethany yell out to her, "Oh, and Scarlett, if you are incapable to return to work, do tell Vivian so that someone else can be called to fill in your spot, and so we know how many hours you owe us."

"What a character," Scarlett whispered as she tried to not break the glass door when she shut it behind her.

***

Scarlett sat on the girls' washroom toilet thinking about that morning, how it changed her, questioning why she ever wanted to be a counselor in the first place. Then she remembered the good days, the weekends she took calls, telling people they were meaningful, explaining their purpose in the world.

Jonathan had his doubts about her being a counselor in the beginning of their relationship. It may have been her dream since she was a child, but Jonathan had told her that he thought she was too soft.

After he had told his story at the volunteer counseling event, which he had only done for school credits, he found Scarlett sitting in the washroom crying, very much like she is right now. He had knocked on the washroom stall, cracking the door open to see if the distraught girl was okay. She came out sniffling, blowing her nose, reassuring him that she was fine. "It's my allergies," she said. Jonathan didn't take her sad excuse and ended up taking her out for ice cream so they could talk about what was bothering her. She confided in him, told him that she was so moved by his story and how other children had felt comfortable enough to open up about their personal lives as well.

Later, Jonathan told her that after he found her crying in the bathroom, that he knew she wasn't going to be cut out for a counseling job. He said she felt more than most people, which was true. Scarlett may be good at hiding her own feelings, but she would feel twice as much for someone else. She would cry for others, could never finish reading an obituary, and often found herself eating ice cream in bed for the rest of the evening if she read something heartbreaking in the news. She was able to keep her emotions and feelings hidden from the outside world, but she could never fool her husband, one of few who she cried in front of. She had limited herself to reading, or watching, sad books, stories, movies, TV shows, and every-thing in between, to the confinement of her own home. However, Scarlett believed that it was her empathy that made her so good at her job. She understood people's heartaches, ups and downs, and genuinely wanted to do everything possible to fix it.

Jonathan and Scarlett's ice cream date was the beginning of their romance. It never occurred to her that maybe that night was a sign, maybe she wasn't cut out for this line of work, maybe she did feel too much. The only thing Scarlett remembered being significant about their date was how she couldn't stop her lips from moving. She found herself bringing things up from her past that she had thought she had forgotten, or buried so well that she had pretended it never happened, which she was very good at. He was, and still is, the only person she was able to reveal herself too – it was so easy with him.

It never bothered Scarlett that Jonathan doubted her in the beginning, she knew she is a good counselor, or at least was. Scarlett had loved her job; she wanted to make people feel good about themselves, and she was good at it too. She went from part-time to full-time as soon as she could, the hotline was getting busy, and she was needed, but it was her choice nonetheless. She started five days a week after Rosie went to school. For Scarlett it was never about the money, she simply loved doing what she did – it gave her purpose.

The phone call was never discussed between Scarlett and Jonathan. She didn't know if he just didn't care about it enough to mention it or if maybe he never knew about it in the first place. Scarlett didn't bother bringing it up to him either, she didn't think it was right to mention at the dinner table that she was the last person the shooter spoke with. Scarlett also didn't want to be told by the man she loves that there were fifteen deaths on her hands, that she was at fault for the victims that were murdered at Pandora High School.

Scarlett imagined every night, or when she had a moment alone, about how the conversation could have gone differently. *What if I said: 'Don't do it, whatever you are planning on doing, stop. You are loved, people love you, your parents love you, your best friend loves you, I love you.' Or maybe that is too much, I should have said: 'How about I come pick you up, we could go for a little girls lunch, you can tell me all about it in person, don't move, I will come get you.'*

Scarlett would then act out as the caller, raising the pitch of her voice, *Yes of course, Mrs. Smith, you are right, I won't do anything irrational that will destroy the lives of countless families and homes, including yours. I wouldn't want to keep you up at night replaying a conversation over and over again in your head until you feel like you've gone mad, especially when we both know there is no point, the outcome will always be the same.*

Scarlett used to believe that behind everything that happened in this world, there was a reason; maybe it was to be a life lesson, or perhaps because someone deserved it. As Scarlett sat in the high school washroom stall, wiping her eyes, she asked, "What is the purpose of this, huh? Whose genius plan was this one?" Scarlett didn't believe in God; she couldn't bear the idea that there was some higher power that would let this happen, yet still she found herself asking, questioning the vented ceiling, waiting for an answer that was not going to come.

She had thought it was fate that brought her and Jonathan together. They could start a lovely family; she could work as a counselor, helping lives, saving lives, and Jonathan would be her outlet to come home to, to hold at night and remind her she is an amazing women, a loving mother and wife. Scarlett knew she was foolish, she could so easily imagine her life, her home, being full again, with smiles, laughter, and tender happiness, but that it was all fake. Her fantasies would falter as she remembered the smile she could no longer touch, the shoulders she could no longer hug.

"Maybe if I had just said their name, let them know it was me, then maybe…" Scarlett said into her hands.

One of the rules at the hotline was that you were not allowed to call the caller by their name, unless they willingly told you who they were. You were also not allowed to ask the caller for their name; this was because they wanted the hotline to be as confidential as possible, and they knew that some callers might get scared away if the counselor they were speaking to, knew who they were.

One of the reasons the hotline was popular with teenagers was because they found it more comfortable to confide in an unrecognizable voice, someone who didn't not know their history, nor someone who would judge them based on their opinion of them as a person. It was supposed to be a safe line, a line where you could speak about the truth of what was going on in your life without judgment, which was why Scarlett never said the caller's name that morning.

Before Scarlett could murmur another word into her hands, she heard the bathroom door open.

"I see you are dancing all over Duncan! Are you planning on going to go home with him later?" one girl asked.

"No, Tiffany, I am not a slut. But, if he needs a shoulder to cry on, I am here. I can tell he is still upset about the shooting. Apparently, sometimes after school he will wait beside Ashley's old locker, waiting for her and the other cheerleaders, then he will get a sad look on his face like he had forgotten they were all dead," replied the other girl as she puckered her lips, sounding like she was reapplying lip-gloss.

"That's so sad," said Tiffany, lacking any sincerity.

"No, it's not, they were a bunch of bitches anyway," remarked a girl who had remained relatively silent since the three of them walked into the bathroom.

Scarlett bit into her hand, trying to not let her gasp be heard. She could not believe someone could speak so ill of the dead. She wanted to get off her warmed seat and walk right up to the girl and straighten her out. Scarlett would tell her, "Imagine if her mother heard you speaking this way. She would wash your mouth out with soap, young lady." Or maybe Scarlett would tell her what she actually believed, not caring how it looked – a middle-aged woman yelling at a teen in the high school washroom. Scarlett thought she probably looked and sounded deranged enough as it was, that she didn't need another outburst to add to her lost marble pile. Therefore Scarlett decided not to move, she left her butt plunked in its seat, too afraid to be looked at as the crazy old lady who had been hiding during Homecoming.

"Riley, you can't just say that," said Tiffany, who sounded like she was speaking out of habit, not actually caring what her friend just said.

"You are just jealous that they didn't accept you onto the cheerleading team. It probably saved your life you know. If you had become a cheerleader, you would have been shot just like most of 'em," chuckled the girl who had been dancing with Duncan.

"I am just saying they had it coming, they were probably targeted by that fucking lunatic," Riley sneered.

"Shhh, someone might hear you," Tiffany halfheartedly pleaded.

"Oh shut up, Tiffany, no one can hear me. Besides, I am not saying anything wrong, and I know you agree with me. They were clearly crazy, anyone who goes shooting up a school is obviously a psychopath," Riley's voice was beginning to sound slightly deranged.

"Well, I will tell you one thing, I can't wait to get out of here, I will no longer be afraid that some serial killer is going to come and try to find me with their AK-47," laughed the other girl, sounding border-line hysterical.

With no further comments to make, the girls made some final puckering noises and left.

Scarlett sat in silence for several minutes after the three students had left. She was frozen with fear but didn't know why. It was possibly because the scene that had unraveled in front of her reminded her of when she was a teenager, hiding or eating in the bathroom, trying to remain absolutely silent and still, begging to go unnoticed by any intruders. She had forgotten what it was like to be surrounded by teenagers again, how mean and insensitive they could be. They couldn't even begin to understand how or why the shooter had done what they did. Scarlett believed they would continue their lives, without knowing or caring about what happened on Pandora High School's field on June 8th, about what really went down. Scarlett also knew that teenagers were never good at placing themselves in someone else's shoes, trying to imagine what it must be like for them in their position. However, Scarlett found that she was getting better at this, seeing all sides of the story.

Scarlett tried to shake off the fear and anxiety the three girls caused her. She dug into her pocket to pull out her phone, thinking that she might as well as check her emails while she was here. When she clicked the right side of her phone, lighting up the screen, she saw the time.

"Shit," Scarlett whispered.

It had been thirty minutes since she left Alex at the sign-in table. Scarlett was surprised that no one had come to find her, she only had another twenty minutes left of her shift. They had probably known it was best to leave her, let her catch her breath before returning to the curious gazes.

Scarlett lifted herself from the toilet, thinking it would be a good idea to splash her face with some cold, refreshing water before she returned to her post, then she realized she had tucked her feet up towards her chest when the girls had come in to fix their makeup.

"I guess old habits die hard," Scarlett chuckled.

Scarlett unlocked the green stall door and moved herself slowly, clutching at her stomach. She was beginning to experience the stomach pains again, identical to the ones she got as a kid when she was really anxious.

When she finally made it to the sink, she looked up at the mirror to see a pale, blotchy woman looking back at her.

"Oh, has this last year aged you," Scarlett said to herself, remembering what she had thought about Ms. Day.

Her red lips trembled as she spoke to the mirror. Her watery-blue eyes stared back at her, beginning to close, wanting to look away from the sad sight. Scarlett was only forty-three, but right now she looked closer to fifty-three. Her eyes puffed out, looking tired and swollen, similar to an insomniac. Her pale face was blotched with red dots, making her look like she just suffered her first mid-life crisis.

Scarlett bent over, turned the tap on, cupped her hands together, and in a single swooping motion, splashed water onto her already damp face. She tried to massage the water onto her cheeks, hoping to even the blotchy-ness out. She realized it was hopeless, and began to drag her cheeks down with her palms. She was truly a mess.

"What if they saw me?" Scarlett asked, leaning closer to her reflection. "They would have been like, there goes the crazy old lady ha-ha."

Alex was right, Simone did save the day. If people saw Scarlett like this, they would begin to believe all sorts of things, things that Scarlett didn't even want to begin to think about now.

"Oh, she's a bad mother. Oh, it's all her fault. Oh, she has lost it," Scarlett began reciting a few comments that were popping into her head, not being able to help herself.

Scarlett thought that Simone may be a flakey, light-hearted, happy-go-lucky hippy, but she was a good vice principal. In an instant Ms. Vadhra could go from smiling to smoldering if a student were to step out of line.

Alex had told Scarlett and Martha that after one of her and Simone's yoga classes, Simone had confided in her about her problems at school. She said that when she started at Pandora, students walked all over her; they thought just because she was a nice, down-to-earth person, that she would also be a pushover. Students started testing her, acting like they were best friends or acting like they had similar hobbies, "Oh Simone, what was that yoga pose you told Mrs. Bernard to teach to the class?" Not even trying to pretend they were respectful teenagers by using her last name, nope, they went straight to first-name basis. She had to learn quickly how to handle the students' moments of defiance, to remind them that she was a vice principal, an adult, and deserved their respect.

After Simone began to be treated like the rest of the teachers, she soon heard her name being mentioned in the halls, the kids speaking badly about her. She felt like she was a high school student all over again. Alex said that apparently Simone was bullied in school, not having many friends. Back then it was not cool to be thought of as a hippy; most people insinuated people like this being dirty, which was not always the case.

It only took a few months for the students to stop mentioning her name in the hallways or the classrooms; they quickly moved onto the next juicy gossip. Once the students stopped acting all buddy-buddy with her, the teachers began to accept her as one of them, asking her if they wanted to meet up on the weekend to grab some drinks or grade some papers.

"I guess she is not as bad as I thought," Scarlett whispered to herself, frowning at her reflection.

Then the washroom door began to creak open in a horror-movie worthy way. Scarlett wanted to yell out to the intruder, "I am not a student! And I am sure as hell not in the mood to be chased and stabbed by Ghostface."

"Scarlett, honey, are you in here?" Alex spoke softly as she finished opening the washroom door completely.

I guess they hadn't forgotten about me completely, Scarlett thought to herself as Alex peaked around the corner to see her friend staring at her pale reflection.

"Yes!" Scarlett chimed a little too cheerfully.

"Oh thank goodness, I was beginning to get worried." Alex got a good look of Scarlett before she quickly averted eye contact, looking around to see if any of the other stalls were taken up. "Are you in here alone? I could have sworn I heard someone speaking before I came in here."

Alex loved the idea of ghosts existing. She had watched *Ghost* with Patrick Swayze, *Unsolved Mysteries*, *Ghost Hunters*, *Ghost Adventures*, *The Dead Files*, *Long Island Medium*, *Hollywood Medium with Tyler Henry*, and many more. She loved the idea that some souls had stayed behind to keep in contact with loved ones, or were trying to warn people about something bad that was about to happen. If she thought she heard voices in the girls' washroom on Homecoming night, no doubt she would have thought that it would be from some of the teenage female victims that died in June. She would probably run around telling all the parents that the girls who died were here with us tonight, celebrating, and now they can move on to their next destination, life, or wherever they might be going. Scarlett thought that Alex's heart was always in the right place, but that she would not be able to understand the type of burden that she would be giving some of these grieving parents and students, telling them that their loved ones are communicating with them, it was probably best if Scarlett were to admit that it was her talking.

"Oh no, I was actually on the phone with Rosie's babysitter. The poor thing has a terrible bug, I spoke with her, and she made the cute sick voice, which I can't say no to. She asked if I could come home early, so that I could rub some Vicks on her chest and watch *Finding Nemo* with her, that way she is more likely to fall asleep. Is it okay if I leave a little early?"

Scarlett had thought about telling Alex the truth about everything that happened the morning of the shooting, about what the girls who came into the washroom had said, about how she was truly feeling, but she also saw that look on her friend's face. Scarlett knew Alex pitied her – Scarlett's most hated emotion. Scarlett did not want anyone to mourn for her suffering, to sympathize for her, no one knew what she was going through, and besides, she had been handling herself quiet sufficiently until those two girls opened their mouths at the sign-in table. She was doing just fine all on her own. *I never needed anyone before and I doubt need anyone now,* Scarlett thought to herself as began to lie to her friend. She was surprised how quickly she came up with such a delicate story as to why she had to leave early and why she looked so distraught, it was all because her baby needed her.

"Of course! That poor thing! Does she have a fever?" Alex asked.

"Yes, a sore throat, runny nose, the whole shazam," Scarlett replied.

"Well, make sure you give her some chamomile tea with honey and lemon juice. That will help the sore throat and make her sleep more peacefully. You should also make yourself one while you're at it, you look a little pale." Alex loved giving advice when someone was sick; she thought her natural remedies could make any cold go away within a matter of hours.

"Yeah, my stomach is a little upset," Scarlett was still clutching onto her abdomen, "I will be sure to make myself a big cup. Thanks, Alex, I am sorry for leaving early."

"Don't sweat it! You get home to your girl and feel better. Love you!" Alex dragged Scarlett out of the washroom before giving her a quick peck on the cheek and headed back towards the gymnasium entrance, leaving her friend alone in the hall.

Scarlett was thrilled Alex had bought her lie so effortlessly. She was not in the right state of mind to work her way out of a conversation she didn't want to have. With a quick sigh, Scarlett paced towards her car, wishing to get out of the school as quickly as possible, hoping that another episode would not happen until she at least made it into her car.

Chapter 13

Scarlett looked around the gym, remembering how it looked with the twinkling lanterns hung in the sky several days earlier. She hadn't gone to help take down the decorations like she had originally planned. Instead, she called Alex and told her that she caught Rosie's cold. "Hey, Alex, I think I caught Rosie's flu, my throat feels like it's closing—"

Alex cut her off, "Oh, honey, you rest up today. Make sure you drink more chamomile tea with honey and lemon. Also, try and take a small shot of apple cider vinegar with a cup of warm water. It is a natural healthy remedy that I use all the time when my throat starts getting scratchy."

Scarlett felt bad lying to her friend, but she needed the weekend to recuperate for today, Tuesday, the meeting after Homecoming. She thought parents were going to be very affected by Friday's dance, thinking about all of the memories they were not going to be able to create with their children. They did not get the opportunity to go dress shopping, to hair-dressing or makeup appointments. They also did not get to give their advice to their child, telling them who they should ask out, how they should ask them, and what type of protection to use that night.

The victims of the shooting had mostly been cheerleaders, who were in their junior year, and a few victims that had unfortunately been caught in the line of fire. This meant that most of them would have been seniors this year. This was supposed to be their year, their final year. They were supposed to be applying to colleges or getting jobs, making traveling plans, focusing on their studying or partying, potentially preparing for SATs, getting boyfriends, girlfriends, and anything in between. It was their year to find themselves before they left the nest, making memories that would last a lifetime, going to the dances they decided to not go to before. But senior year was almost as important for the students as it was for their parents. They had to prepare themselves, prepare for their babies to leave, to enter the world on their own, and therefore they wanted to share and be a part of those important memories before their children left them. This was why Scarlett knew that this meeting was going to be one of the hardest ones yet.

Scarlett began her meeting like the others, introducing herself, talking about helplines and other resources that the parents could use if they felt they needed something more than these meetings.

"I would like to start today by discussing Homecoming. I know this time was very hard for most of you, expecting to see your children dress up, rent limos or tuxes, buying dresses, and taking pictures. Would any of you like to start and tell me how you felt Friday night?"

Sandy answered first, as she usually does. She began strong, holding her act together but quickly fell apart. Christine began to rub her back the moment she crumbled.

"I… I thought I was going to see Bobby, all dressed up… looking like a grown man, with a pretty girl on his arm," Sandy whimpered. She was very old-fashioned; she would have wanted her son home by midnight, but if it was her daughter who had been going to the dance, then she would want her home by ten, simply because things were apparently different for boys and girls.

"It was supposed to be his night," Sandy continued, "pictures would be taken, he probably would have been voted Homecoming King, him being such a handsome young man, very popular with ladies," Sandy smiled.

It was the first time Scarlett had seen her smile since the incident. Sandy was usually crying or looked like she had been crying for so long that her tears had run dry. Sandy was an open book, not afraid to show her emotions or tell someone when they were in the wrong. Her smile was pure, it was genuine, it had even made some of the other parents smile too, until it faltered, quivering weakly as it changed positions.

"What kinda of deranged lunatic—" *There is that word again, lunatic,* Scarlett thought. "—goes and kills a bunch of children! He was just a child!" Sandy sobbed.

Scarlett thought Sandy was contradicting herself, saying her boy was a young man and now a child; it seemed like she was using any type of noun that would give her the greatest amount of sympathy. Scarlett was not tolerating her attention-seeking ways.

"We will not use that kind of language here. Must I remind you that the shooter was a child too, and there will be people mourning for them as well," it was Scarlett's nasally voice that spoke up in defense of the shooter. "For today, I want us to focus more on our own children instead of trying to pin the blame on someone for what happened," Scarlett said in her counseling tone. "Is there someone else that would like to share?" Scarlett looked into the circle of familiar faces, avoiding eye contact with Sandy, hoping that her outburst shocked her into silence. Then, a newcomer stood up.

It was Annabella. Scarlett had been so focused on Sandy, her annoyance brewing without reason, that she hadn't noticed her, nor Gasira who had been sitting beside her quietly. Scarlett's tolerance had been shrinking away faster and faster as the days passed, and Sandy seemed to be the reason for its shortening lifespan. Christine seemed to be the only one who could actually tolerate her.

Annabella looked like she was dressed for a funeral, wearing a black dress that was hemmed just below her knee paired with a black cardigan draped over her pale arms. She didn't look like her usual, bubbly self, more solemn, paler, and even purple around her eyes. Scarlett couldn't even remember if she has ever seen her in a black outfit; she usually flaunted every imaginable color mixed with any pattern, always mixing and matching.

Scarlett didn't know Annabella had a child who was killed last year; she had seemed so happy, like her upbeat self at Homecoming. Scarlett also thought she had memorized the shooting obituary by heart, doing her best to remember the last name of every student who had passed.

She is the one who deserves a medal for saving face, no one else probably had even known, Scarlett thought as she tried to not look surprised when she introduced Annabella to the other parents. "Hello, Annabella, how are you feeling today?"

When the parents slowly began coming to the meetings one by one, starting with Sandy, Christine, Tyler, and Thea, then Mildred and Holly, Scarlett would either introduce the newcomers or get them to introduce themselves. After their introduction, Scarlett would ask the parent how they felt today; she thought it would be better to start off asking how today is or was, instead of leading up to a more general question, such as "how are you feeling?", which could easily start in a downhill spiral.

Holly and Mildred were two parents that had showed up for only a single meeting. They did not understand that Scarlett wanted everyone to sit arranged in a U-shape, that way everyone could be seen, but instead they decided to sit behind Tyler and off to the side, that way Scarlett was unable to make eye contact with them. Scarlett had decided to not mention anything about the seating arrangements and allowed them to remain silent in the back. She knew some parents found it really hard opening up to complete strangers, even if they were going through similar emotional trauma. The two women remained silent the entire meeting, and before Scarlett could speak with them after everyone had started making their way to the exit, the women were gone. Scarlett later received an email from the two mothers informing her that they were going to seek advice from a professional. Instead of taking their message as an insult, Scarlett responded wishing the two of them the best of luck, signing off with Mahatma Gandhi's classic quote, "Be the change that you want to see in the world."

Scarlett knew that her meetings were not meant for everyone, she had seen several other parents come and go over the past couple of months, which she expected and hoped for. Scarlett would get emails once in a while from a parent who used to come to the meetings, either telling them how much they had helped or that they were having a bad day and might stop in soon. Scarlett was just happy that people were getting the help they needed, or at least most of them anyway.

"Hello, um well, I don't really know where to begin, not great, I guess? I thought I had been handling everything well, or as well as can be, but I guess I just slipped off my path. You never expect to lose your child. In society today, we are all supposed to grow old, not have to worry about crazy things such as funeral arrangements for your baby girl. It's all really hard to believe…sorry… I guess that didn't really answer your question. I, ah, have never come to a meeting before so I am not sure how it all works." Scarlett thought Annabella looked cute when she got flustered, it made her cheeks become alive with color.

"That is alright, you can start with how Friday went for you if you would like, maybe talk about something that made you to come here today? Was there possibly an incident at Homecoming? Or did something happen that maybe triggered a memory of your daughter?" Scarlett didn't want to get into the specifics or detail, anything that would make Annabella feel uncomfortable, "Remember, you're in a safe place, Annabella," Scarlett smiled politely.

"Well, I guess I kinda cracked during Homecoming. My other daughter, Mary, it was her first time going to a dance, she was so excited, so when I was asked to chaperone, I felt like I had to say yes. I didn't want anything to change about my parenting style, I was always there for the girls before… before the shooting, and I still want to be there for my other girls. My youngest, Elizabeth, was in awe when she saw Mary walk down our stairs in her puffy purple dress," Annabella chuckled, "she said she looked like a princess and that Hannah would have been proud if she were there. They…they had this moment of silence while the two of them looked at each other, in an understanding way, and it was just so touching that both of them remembered their older sister so fondly. I was happy to know that… that she would be remembered in a loving way, it wasn't all the fighting and screaming matches that they had that the girls would think about when they remembered their older sister." Annabella put her black cardigan over her chair, revealing a box of tissues she had been hiding and began plucking from them. "That is not what sent me over though, it had melted my heart seeing my girls happy again, seeing them able to talk about their older sister without crying. I had left for the school early, I hate being late, so when I got there I headed into the gymnasium, and it was gorgeous. It reminded me Hannah's Homecoming dance last year, it was a Masquerade theme." Hannah was head cheerleader last year, one of the few seniors who had been on the field that afternoon – most of the seniors skipped that day and went to the beach. "Hannah was a helpless romantic like her mother, I know she would have been awe by the beautiful glowing lanterns, but once the students began arriving, and before they announced Homecoming King and Queen, Ms. Vadhra got up on stage and asked for a moment of silent for the students who couldn't make it tonight. Then they began presenting a slideshow for that minute, of the faces that couldn't be there, which we had all known would have been there otherwise. Since my little girl had already had her own Homecoming, I thought I wouldn't see my little girl up there, but I did. It was the picture from her Homecoming night, after she had been crowned queen. She was smiling her big goofy grin, wearing her tiara... and I just... couldn't pretend anymore. Pretend that everything was okay."

"How does it make you feel when you pretend everything is okay? Angry? Happy? Sad? A sense of relief?" Scarlett's typical technique was to question clients, make them reveal themselves completely, or however much they felt comfortable revealing, she wanted them to get everything off their chest.

"Sad... and lonely. I feel like I can't talk to anyone else about what happened, that I have to be the brave one. I need to be there for my girls, their shoulder to cry and lean on. And I know no daughter wants to see their mother cry. Moms are supposed to be this strong figure that children can look up to for support, guidance, and reassurance. They need me to tell them that everything is going to be alright, so that they can believe it, so that they can start to move on. I have been so focused on them, I have forgotten about my own healing process. I have become this mindless cheerful robot, going through the motion of day-to-day tasks, but forgetting to actually live. Now don't get me wrong, my kids are great, they have been handling... everything so well. My husband has been supportive and present. He seems to be coping really well, much better than me." Annabella let out a little burst of hysterical laughter. "I always thought I would handle a death in the family the best out of the two of us because I am the one who believes in a life after this one, and that we will all meet again someday. Alex is the type of man who doesn't have any beliefs, doesn't follow any type of religion, and he doesn't really have any thoughts on what was before or what could be after our lives. And yet, he is the one who keeps his smile from faltering, talking about how proud Hannah would be of her two sisters and how much she loved them and still loves them wherever she might be. He is able to tell the girls that Hannah will always be in our hearts without a quiver in his voice. Every night I can hear him tell a story about Hannah to the girls, either something that she did when she was a baby or about something thing she did out of love and kindness for her sisters, like the time she carried Elizabeth home after she broke her arm falling off her bike in the park." Annabelle's voice started to tremble along with her hands, which held the clump of tissues she kept dabbing beneath her eyes. "Alex and I barely talk about it. When he climbs into bed after tucking the girls in – Mary and Elizabeth still share a bedroom because neither of them wants to sleep in Hannah's room – I will pretend that I am asleep. I am just so exhausted, I don't want to talk about it anymore. I am constantly talking about Hannah with the girls, reminding them how much their big sister cared about them, just like Alex does, but once it's only the two of us, I shut down, not wanting to mention her name. Yet, even when I am talking to the girls about what happened, I feel like I am still not actually talking about it, not talking about how I feel. I know I am being a bad mother."

"You are being a great, supportive mother, Annabella. You are there for your children when they need you, and sometimes they do need that strong parental figure to help guide them through traumatic experiences such as this, but as I have said to the other parents that have come and gone through that door," Scarlett said pointing at the gymnasium entrance, "you need to talk to your partner, I understand that it's hard, but there is no other way of knowing what they are going through or what they are feeling."

As Annabella divided into explaining her reasoning for not talking to her husband right away, for pushing him out since the incident happened, Scarlett observed her, the way she held onto her tissues like a life support. She was a younger mother, probably in her mid-thirties, must have had Hannah in her late teens or early twenties. She may have been looking paler, sickly even, but she still looked good for her age. Her black dress may have been an attempt to fit in with the other parents; people usually dressed like they were attending a funeral instead of a meeting when it was their first time coming. Her dark outfit enhanced her pale complexion, blue eyes, and blonde hair, making her look like Lestat from *Interview with the Vampire*.

Scarlett was impressed by how much Annabella was talking. The parents that came and went would speak for maybe a minute, if even that, and then Scarlett would have to really engage in the conversation, trying to open them up without pushing them too hard. Scarlett had even been contemplating about using more forceful tactics to get the parents to start talking; she knew that it was necessary for them to begin their healing processes.

"What you have to remember, Annabella, is that no one is expecting you to be okay; what you have been through, what everyone has been through, is life-changing. Parents aren't meant to bury their children, but unfortunately it does happen. The emotions you are feeling and everything you are going through is normal. And you must not forget that you are not alone. Yes, at times you may feel lonely but you are never truly alone. Your husband is here for you, we are here for you," Scarlett made a swooping motion at the circle of parents in front of her before pointing at herself, "And I am here for you, a simple phone call away."

Scarlett felt bad about her outburst at Homecoming. She had not thought about what the other parents present might have been feeling, too busy engaging in her own temper tantrum in the bathroom. Maybe if she had maintained her composure and had been there for Annabella, she would have seen her leave upset, would have been able to comfort here then and there. Scarlett thought this would have probably saved Annabella a sleepless weekend. Maybe she would not have even needed to come to the meeting today, maybe she would have been able to continue on with her grieving process, would have had the chance to recover faster. Scarlett also thought she had been selfish, but at least now she can make amends for it by being present, engaging with the parents, reminding them they are not alone, allowing them to talk until they run out of breath, even if it was Sandy.

After Annabella sat down, Gasira stood up. The meetings before were never a stand up and then sit down type of scenario. Most people just assumed what happened in support group meetings was similar to what happened in the movies at AA meetings. Scarlett wanted to keep the meetings as non-stereotypical as possible; she thought it would help parents open up more if they were all less formal. Therefore if a parent were to start talking right away, Scarlett decided not to introduce them. She knew that most of the parents have known each other for years, having to drive their kids to either cheerleading practice, or driving them to each other's houses since most of the students had been friends. The majority of their children had also been going to the same schools or been in the same classes since grade 1, therefore everyone knew or recognized each other. Scarlett, on the other hand, didn't know many of parents personally, only recognized them.

Scarlett was taken back when Gasira stood up – she was gorgeous. She looked more like a model than a mother, having no excess or unwanted fat in uncomfortable areas. She had the slim yet muscular build of a runner, with toned arms holding onto her biceps as she stood tall like an Amazon warrior. Gasira was also wearing a black dress, similar to Annabella's, but it hugged all of her curves before flowing down her hips, resting below her knees. She was an elegant and very feminine woman with her black hair cut nearly to her scalp. Scarlett though that it was the delicate features of her dark face that abled her to pull off such a short haircut.

"Hello, my name is Gasira." Her Kenyan accent was very thick; it seemed to take some of the parents off guard. "My son, Michael, is on the football team," Gasira cleared her throat, "I mean was on the football team. On the day… of the shooting, the football team had decided to skip class that day and go to the beach. Michael had asked me if he could go; he was such a good boy, I told him of course, you go ahead. It was his senior year, and he was so close to being finished. He… had plans to go to Penn State for football, he had gotten his letter of acceptance, a full-ride scholarship and everything, I was so proud. I told him growing up that someday he would make it to the big leagues. His older sister had also accepted a full-ride scholarship from them as well, just two years before, but hers was based on her academics. Both my babies were going to be at Penn State, they would both be living in a dorm, everything had been planned out. Then, on that morning, I was watching the news while I was at home. I heard there had been a shooting at Pandora High School over an hour ago. I was frozen, I didn't know what to do. My first thought was to call my husband, to let him know that Michael was okay because he was at the beach, but mother's intuition kicked in. My throat felt tight and my stomach burned. I picked up my cell to call Michael, it rang… for what felt like an hour. So I panicked, I called the school, the line was busy, I guess I was not the only parent who was worried. I remember thinking that I should call the hospital next, maybe just in case, maybe they knew who had gotten shot, or who was injured. Before I dialed the number, the news blared, telling me that there were fifteen dead and three injured. I sat looking at the writing below the newscaster, the big numbers, I... I couldn't believe it. Then my phone rang, I looked at the caller ID; it was the Vice Principal. Apparently she had been awarded the task to call the parents of the deceased students." Gasira paused for a moment. "The minute I saw Ms. Vadhra's name on my phone, I knew, I knew that Michael... was gone. Just like that, no goodbye, no see you around, no I love you, my son was gone. And don't get me started on that 'he is right here' crap," Gasira jabbed her finger towards her heart, "I know my son, I know he will always be with me, but people act like somehow that is supposed to make it easier, but it does not. I want to be able to hold my son in my arms."

"It's not supposed to make it easier, nothing really ever does make it easier, Gasira. Sure things help, like fond memories, pictures, or knowing that he has gone to a better place and will be in your heart forever, but nothing actually makes it easier. You will always miss your son, that is a given, your heart may never feel whole again, but it will heal as much as it can. It will hurt less and less with time," Scarlett reassured her.

"You know what I found the hardest?" Gasira continued without pausing for an answer, "That he shouldn't have been there, that for a brief moment I had felt relief knowing my son was okay because he had skipped class. He should have been at the beach with his friends, laying in the sun, having a break before he gets back to practicing for his freshman year at Penn. He was supposed to come home that night, he was supposed to graduate, leave high school and start a new chapter in his life. And I... I was not supposed to make sure that they had correctly labelled my son as the deceased black kid. I was not supposed to make funeral arrangements for my son while my husband was too broken to help." Gasira slowed her voice to catch her breath; "And do you want to know why my son had not been at the beach that day? Why my son had so foolishly been killed at the age of seventeen? He apparently did not want to skip until his girlfriend was done with her cheer-meeting during lunch. She was the senior assistant cheer captain, who planned to go to Penn State with him. They were looking at getting a dorm near each other like they couldn't handle being a second apart. I had gone months without knowing my son had gone outside to meet her on the field. When I saw his girlfriend, Jessica, at his funeral, I could hardly handle the rage I felt towards her, knowing that it was somehow her fault. When she locked eyes with me, she came running over, wrapping her arms across me and told me everything. She said that he was going to drive them to the beach. Jessica explained the scene to me, how her back was to the school, that she was facing the junior cheerleaders, talking to them, and then she saw their faces change, they were stricken with fear. She explained how she remembered hearing some shooting, and then she was tackled face-first into the ground. She heard several cracks, piercing her ear, some more screams, but she was pinned to the ground by the body that lay on top of her. She couldn't move. Once the noises stopped, and she realized what happened, she screamed. She thought she was being suffocated by an attacker. The police had gotten to her quickly; she was one of few who were still able to make any sounds after the shooting. The police had rolled the body off of her and helped her get herself turned over as they checked to see if she was okay. She had been so stunned by everything that she did not speak until her parents met her at the hospital. It turns out that it was Michael's body that was on top of her. He apparently had enough time to notice what was about to happen to sprint from where he had been siting and act as a shield to protect his girlfriend." Gasira smiled sadly. "He was always known for being fast on his feet, that was one of his skills that made him such a great player."

"Your son died a hero—" Scarlett was quickly cut off.

"But I would rather he hadn't died," Gasira answered sharply, "I would rather him have gone to the beach, forgetting about all his worries, instead of being stupid, throwing his life away just to save someone else. He didn't even get the chance to live, he never had his first legal drink, got to go to the bar with his buddies, get married, have children, have a career, he was just a kid, taken away too soon. He left us here, his sister is a mess, she ended up taking this year off from Penn, she is back at home, and my husband got fired from his job, they wouldn't allow him more than a month off, he can't cope." Gasira dropped her shoulders and lifted her chin. "I have to be the strong one, I am the only one who is still capable of functioning, but it's like what Annabella said, I am just pretending, I am pretending to have my shit together... I am in so much pain, I would have thought it would have gotten better by now. People say it takes about three months to go through the grieving stages, but I am still at anger. I am angry at my husband for not being there, for being fired from his job. I am angry at my daughter for being a university dropout, for giving up on her life. I am angry at Jessica for wanting to stay behind for the stupid cheer meeting, I am angry that it was my son and not her. But the person I am angry at the most is my son for falling in love and getting his dumbass killed to protect someone he loves."

"The five stages of grief is a bunch of nonsense, pay no attention to that. Everyone grieves in their own way, every single individual is exactly that, an individual. No two people can be exactly identical in every way," Scarlett said. "With that said, it is also incorrect to say that someone should have grieved for a loss in a short time, such as three months. It can take years to fully recover from traumatic losses, such as the death of a parent, child, sibling, or partner. It even takes some people years to get over a previous relationship that only lasted months. The three-month idea was created so that people are pushed to suppress their feelings, to move on, so that they will continue pretending to be a functioning part of our society. They are just trying to get people to suppress their feelings, like they have always done, they tell you that if you see something wrong, look the other way or keep quiet about your opinions and feelings because no one likes someone who is too sensitive."

Gasira's expression changed from anger to fatigue, "I feel like a monster though, for hating an innocent girl and my dead son for being a hero."

"The hate will slowly dwindle, you may even realize that your son did a brave courageous act that will never be forgotten. Jessica will remember him as the young man that saved her life. He may have been just a young boy, but in that moment, when he acted quickly to protect the person he loved, he showed that he was a real man." Scarlett tries hard not to tell clients how they feel, or how they are going to feel; it usually causes them to react, which she doesn't like. But she thinks it is okay to assume how other people will feel, like Jessica, especially if it helps bring the client ease or peace. "Now I also believe that you should try and communicate with your family, like Annabella, maybe try and talk to your daughter and husband at the same time, but don't try to ambush them, or they might feel like they are being attacked. Sometimes it is as simple as asking how they are that day or morning. Or if they are having problems even mentioning Michael's name, then you should try to bring up a fond memory you all shared with him, this often helps people open up about their lost one," Scarlett said with her hands in her lap, left knee crossed over the right.

After Gasira sat down, Christine went next. She remained seated but had stopped rubbing Sandy's shoulders. Scarlett was surprised to hear from her; she usually remained silent, nodding along with Sandy, supporting every comment she made.

Christine spoke silently and softly, "Hi everybody, I found this weekend to be… very difficult for me. My son Garret and I had started making plans last year about what he was going to be doing for Homecoming and then Senior Prom, who he was going to ask out, what he was going to wear. My little Garret was a real fashionista," Christine said proudly. She went on to tell anecdotes about all the clothes they had to choose from.

As Christine continued to talk, Scarlett finally got a really good look at her. She usually tried to avoid looking in her and Sandy's direction. She was probably one of the oldest parents here, but she looked good for her age as well. Scarlett couldn't tell if she had a nose job or maybe Botox, either way she looked good, amazing even. She had this Hollywood style, laid back yet elegant. Her strawberry blonde hair was straightened and blown back in a sweeping appearance, her eyebrows were penciled in a dark brown, her high cheeks bones lightly blushed, while her lips glistened. Scarlett knew she was either in her mid-forties or early fifties, but she was a complete beauty queen, a real Nicole Kidman.

Christine was well put together, her soft voice stayed at an even pace. She seemed more like she wanted to talk, tell everyone about her son, his dreams, hopes and aspirations. She didn't want Scarlett's advice, she just wanted people to listen to her while she held the floor. Then she turned to Tyler.

"I just want to say from the bottom of my heart, thank you, Tyler. You made Homecoming a dream come true for those children. My daughter, Jennifer, told me how beautiful the wooden patio cover was with the fake vines entangled around the pillars. It really had added to the theme of the starry night, and I know it made it easier for some of us parents to hang the lanterns instead of on the tall gym ceiling." Christine chuckled as she looked up, knowing no practical ladder would have reached such a tremendous height.

Scarlett did not know that it was Tyler who had made the patio cover. She did remember thinking she had seen him there. He was a sight for sore eyes after all, so he was hard to miss. Scarlett had decided not to talk to him though, she thought it was best to not go out of her way to disturb any of the parents, especially the quiet ones, in a setting where they may feel uncomfortable.

"It was my pleasure. I wanted to make my little girl happy..." Tyler responded in a whisper, before he found his voice. "I, I knew that Ashley wanted it done right, she would have really loved it. I remember when it was just the three of us," he grabbed his wife's knee, "before Aubrey and Lincoln. We would go camping at the Grand Canyon; I think we would stay at the Desert View Campground and sleep under the clear sky. We would stargaze, looking at all the different constellations, really enjoying nature's wonders." Tyler chuckled, crossing his arms, which had buffalo plaid sleeves rolled past the elbow. "Then she quickly became too cool to hang out with her old man."

Thea put her hand on her husband's broad shoulder, rubbing in a circular motion. They were the most supportive couple Scarlett had seen at these meetings. Usually it would only be the mother or father, rarely did they come together.

Scarlett assumed that it was Thea who had wanted to attend these meetings. She seemed more like the sharing, and needing to talk about it type, whereas Tyler just came in support of his wife. Yet when he spoke, Scarlett was no longer so sure of herself.

"Ashley was one of the girls who had helped come up with the idea for this year's Homecoming. I thought maybe... maybe she still remembered those starry nights we used to share when she was younger, and that's why she wanted to hang lanterns for the dance. I thought that she wanted to recreate one of those nights." Tyler was beginning to get choked up. "I wanted to make my little girl proud, I wanted her to have been there, standing in awe at what I had created for her."

"She would have been so proud, my love," Thea said soothingly, continuing to rub his shoulder.

"I know, I know. But I just wish she had been there, seen it with her own eyes, danced the night away with her friends. I wanted it to be a night she wouldn't forget. I remember why senior Homecoming dance was a night I will never forget. It was the night I got to have my first dance with the love of my life," Tyler said as he turned to face his wife, "I wish I got the chance to see her all dressed up for her big night, for Senior Prom, or the talent show she had spent most of the year preparing for. I wanted to see her at her graduation, I have never been to a graduation before, not even my own, so it was something that was very important and big for our family." Tyler paused, taking a moment to collect his thoughts. "She was our first child… I remember the first time I held her in my arms, looking down at her, trying to guess what her eye color would be. Was it going to be my brown eyes staring back at me? Or my wife's blue eyes? Then when she got a little bit older, I taught her how to build her own tree house in our backyard. I loved the projects we did together, the way she would look at me with amazement and excitement in her eye. She was a good kid, always well-behaved, got good grades, and was involved with her school through cheerleading – she was my little angel. Then she grew up to become this young woman, and we started to grow apart. She became too busy for me, staying out late on weekends, partying it up, and she no longer wanted to spend quality time with me, to build things, or to work on our projects together. I felt like I was losing my daughter more and more before I actually lost her." Tyler swallowed his sobs. "In no way am I saying this is my little girl's fault, I should have tried harder, done better. I should have stayed home more often, worked a little less. She probably went out on the weekends because I was busy working in the shop, trying to finish my work before the deadline. It was also Thea who would give her rides to the cheerleading meets and practices. I took on too much extra carpentry opportunities as Ashley got older, but it was because I wanted to provide her with the best education money could buy."

Scarlett remained silent as Tyler opened up about his relationship with his daughter. She thought it was best if she kept her comments to herself; she didn't want to get in the way of him letting all of his problems, concerns, and doubts out into the open. She knew it was a bit ridiculous for him to take all of the blame for the weakening of his relationship between his daughter and himself. When someone passes away, people rarely want to say anything was the deceased person's fault, it is like everyone believes the dead should be put on a pedestal like they were saints. There were the odd ones out such as Gasira. Scarlett never understood why people talk like this, why there was a rule that no one should speak ill of the dead. But if you spoke rudely about the person when they were alive, why do you have to speak about them kindly now that they have passed on? Scarlett did believe that if you don't have anything nice to say then you should not say anything at all, but it was also unnecessary to lie about how great, caring, or nice someone was. There are more than seven billion people in this world, and Scarlett knew that not everyone could like everybody.

At the same time, Scarlett knew that Tyler should still take some of the blame. As a parent, you need to be there for your child, any second or minute of the day. Parents also rarely see it as their children's fault because they should have known better, they were the adult after all. Scarlett also realized how easy it can be for a parent to get side-tracked with work – her parents were the same way. Scarlett's parents, Bill and Loraine, had worked every weekend or during important school events. They were never able to support her at any functions, such as band practice, or swimming lessons. That is why Scarlett never joined any teams or clubs; she didn't see the point when she knew her parents were not going to be there. Yes, she wanted to remain unnoticed during her high school career, but she thought this was one of the reasons she never tried, she didn't see the point.

Bill and Loraine blamed Scarlett for them not being able to make to her teacher meetings, or other necessary school organizations. They had to pay their debts off, such as their student loans, even though they didn't finish college, which was their excuse they used for not going to anything important that involved Scarlett. As she got older, she started to believe that maybe they never were workaholics, but instead they just lied to her so they wouldn't have to be involved or pretend like they cared.

After Scarlett's parents died during a car accident, where her dad had cut someone off, resulting in an unfortunate scenario of road-rage and idiotic driving, Scarlett got their will. She found out that her grandparents had actually paid for her middle-class childhood home, including their cars – one Mercedes Benz sedan and the other Mercedes Benz convertible. It turned out that they did get help after all. They did not have any debt, nor had they been working for the past decade. Sadly, Scarlett was not surprised; she had come to the acceptance that her parents simply did not want to be there for her, because if they had then they would have made it work. Bill and Loraine were not meant to be parents.

They had made Scarlett feel like a burden her whole life, telling her that she couldn't get new clothes because they didn't have enough money, or that they had to work more than the average person to pay for her living expenses. They lied to her, treated her like she stole from them when she was given the money for her private schooling. In a way she did take their money, because if she were not born then that money would have just gone to them, but that is no way to live your life, expecting money from your parents. Once one becomes responsible enough to move out on their own, pay for their own bills, provide for themselves as well as their families, then they should no longer be expecting money from their parents. But they should still be able to rely on them for support in times of need, that is what family means after all.

Scarlett promised herself when growing up that she would be the best mother possible. She would support her children, give them love, attention, and affection, everything they needed, but without spoiling them. She would go to all their practices, team meetings, and parent-teacher nights. Scarlett wanted to be as involved with her kids' life as they would let her. She understood that some parents can overdo it, therefore she promised herself and her future children that she would never pry. Scarlett would not allow herself to turn out like Bill and Loraine; she would be there to support them, letting them know they are worth it, and they are loved.

"My little girl wanted to be an actress," Tyler smiled, "She was in theater and taking lessons. She once told me that she wanted to be considered a triple threat, so we put her in singing and dance classes as well. I think that is when she really started to drift away from me, she started making more friends in these classes, started hanging out with them. Don't get me wrong, I was happy for her, but... I just miss her. I wish I got to spend more time with her, I wish everyone got to spend time with her, she was funny—" Tyler frowned. "She shouldn't have left me, us, this early. I wanted to see her grow up, walk her down the aisle, babysit her children. I wanted to see my little girl become the star she wanted to be, the one I knew she could be. She deserved more than this, she deserved better."

Scarlett continued to sit and listen quietly as she analyzed the parents while Tyler talked about his daughter deserving a better life like the saint he thought she was. Scarlett noticed the other parents nodding along with Tyler, for they too thought their children were angels who deserved the best. Scarlett was realizing that all of the parents are the same; they felt like no one understood them, yet everyone did. They were unable to talk to anyone else, not realizing how healthy it was to communicate to your loved ones about how you are feeling and what you were going through. They were suffering, hurting over their lost children, questioning God or whatever idol they follow. They pretended to hold themselves together until it was their turn to speak. The majority of them didn't realize how good they were at pretending, fooling people. However, some of them did not even bother trying to act like proper citizens. Like Sandy; she wanted to show the world how cruel it was, what scars it had created.

As Tyler finished speaking, Scarlett realized she did not catch his last few words, too busy with her own. She saw the parents were looking at him, just the way she had been analyzing him moments ago. The parents were staring at him sympathetically, a few sitting near him offered a pat on the back while his wife looked at him. Her face filled with sorrow as she leaned in to kiss her husband on the cheek.

Scarlett thought that was enough talking for today and closed the meeting. After everyone started to collect their things and head for the door, Scarlett approached Tyler and told him how proud she was of him for speaking today, trusting the people that surround them and letting them in. And with a quick smile, the parents left Scarlett alone to clean up. After arranging the chairs, tossing the un-eaten cookies in the bin and pouring the remaining coffee down a drain, Scarlett headed home. She wanted her daughter to know that she loved her, that her love for her would never change, and she could always count on her for support.

Chapter 14

October 20TH

Sorry I haven't been able to write for a while, I've been incredibly busy!

Since I last wrote in my diary, a lot has happened. Mrs. Cornwall has continued to give me lessons where we talk about all the different notes in singing. I didn't know how to read musical symbols before this class, but now I do! I have practiced a lot on being able to match my pitch by controlling the vibrating of my vocal cords. Mrs. Cornwall says I have an amazing tessitura, she says my comfortable vocal range is incredible! She also has told me that I have a gift for tone (like Adele), which is nearly impossible to teach students!

I have also started to pick up some habits to help soothe my voice, in the hopes that this will prevent it from going raspy. I try to drink ginger tea with honey in the morning, an hour before singing, and at night. It tasted awful at first (I was never a tea person), but now I absolutely love it! I find it very soothing. One of my mom's friends said that this tea is also really good for helping people relax and staying Zen, she doesn't know the real reason why I am drinking it, but it's nice to hear that it's good for other things too!

On top of my singing lessons, I have also become quite a big leader in my theater class. Mrs. Cornwall has me start the Monday mornings with my exercises and help other students who are finding it a little more difficult to manipulate their vocal cords, like Ashley. I didn't see it before, but now that I have been working with Ashley, more I see she has great potential. Mrs. Cornwall has got me to help Ashley first, seeing what are her abilities with her singing range, and focusing in on areas that needed work.

At first I was nervous that Ashley would refuse my advice or just scowl at me, but she genuinely wanted me to help her get better. She told me how beautiful my voice was and that she would love to get tips from an expert like me (I am not an expert, but I just played along, hoping I wasn't messing up). Now Ashley and I meet every Tuesday at her house to practice singing.

She told me that singing wasn't her forte, she wants to be an actress, but she knows that if she wants to make it far in the entertainment industry, she must have many talents, such as singing and dancing.

After a few weeks of meeting up with Ashley, her and I quickly became friends. I realized that she was just an insecure kid who picked on others to make her feel better, which doesn't make up for her past mistakes, but I can at least be a bit more understanding. She has also changed so much! I think she forgets who I am and how she used to bully me, but honestly I don't even care! All that teenage angst makes us say things we don't really mean, and I would rather not hold a grudge with a 12-year-old who told me that I looked like a vampire. I now sit with her and some of her friends during lunch (even Emma!).

I was worried that Denise would get mad at me, tell me I have chosen the dark side or something, but she seemed indifferent about it all. When I first started hanging out with Ashley at lunch, I invited Denise to come along too! I told her how Ashley has changed, but she just told me to go ahead and that she had other plans. She told me that she has gotten really busy with all the clubs she has joined, I think she was talking about the LGBTQ club and the debate team. Denise has always stood for equality and loves to argue with people about it, so it doesn't surprise me that she has found some other friends who share similar interests with her at these clubs.

If I had some more spare time on my hands (too busy with signing lessons and what not), I would've joined these clubs too, and I was a little hurt Denise didn't ask me to join with her. I guess we all just need some things to ourselves. Besides, Denise is not the most fun person to have on your team, she is highly competitive and stubborn as hell. She also thinks she is always right and is willing to take anyone down who stands in her way. I know that I am also opinionated, but not to the same extent. Originally I just wanted to coast through high school, which is why I decided to not be a part of any teams or clubs, for I wanted to remain unnoticed. But now I want to be a musician, so I am going to have to step out of my comfort zone and become noticed.

Also, Denise never cared about standing out, if someone were to whisper something as she walked by, she'd turn around and say, "What's that? I can't hear you." She never turned from a fight. Now, I am not trying to say that I am a little wimp or anything, I just like to pick and choose my battles, I mean who cares if some girl I barely know is talking sh*t behind my back? It's not like I am going to let that affect me. For Denise on the other hand, that sh*t ate her up, she acts like she doesn't care what people have to say or what they think about her, but she probably cares the most. She doesn't want anyone to think she is weak by letting things go, no, she's got to let everyone knows what she thinks.

Denise can be a bit... extreme, and sometimes I wonder if she maybe brings some stuff onto herself, but at the same time I know that no one should be bullied. I used to have to beg her to not shout at kids when we were together in middle school. I would tell her that I didn't care what they thought of me or what they said about me. She cared a little too much, she would tell me I am spineless, but like most things, I would let it go and we would move on.

Now as I write this, I am starting to think maybe her and I weren't such good friends after all, maybe we were just outcasts together, that we found comfort in one another. We also don't have the same hopes and dreams that friends share, no similar goals or aspirations. Unlike Ashley and I, we both have the same career goals, or at least a similar one, she wants to act, and I want to sing. On the other hand, Emma's life plan is just to become a rich housewife, I think she's used to being given what she wants by her parents (youngest child syndrome), so she doesn't think she has to lift a finger to get the life she wants, but she's hilarious! I forgot how we used to have so much fun together when we were younger (yes we were like 6, but still). Although Emma has a different career path, she still shares similar interests with Ashley and I.

Denise and I just seem to be on different paths, or wavelengths, however you want to phrase it. Don't get me wrong, I still love her, she has been through thick and thin with me, and she is still my best friend. We have countless good memories together, playing in her fort, that her, her dad and I built in their backyard.

Their family is my second home, I feel like I can be myself around them. Her mom is absolutely lovely, a little dazed and confused at times, but a genuine sweetheart. Her dad is the tough one, he is where Denise gets all of her opinions from, looking at the two of them you can tell the apple doesn't fall far from the tree. I am actually very similar to her mom, that's probably why Denise and I work so well. I play her mother, smiling and nodding along when she plays her father going off on one of her rants.

When Denise and I were younger, we used to play all the time in our tree fort. She was the husband and I was the wife, she enjoyed taking charge and leading me around. If Denise were to look back now at how she thought how a family acted, she would be disappointed in her younger self. Now she is the typical feminist, who speaks out about how masculine and feminine roles should be kicked to the curb and how unrealistic they really are. But she would also be proud of herself to think back to how the two of us never played the damsel in distress, we never needed a man to save us.

I imagine Denise having her own children one day, her drilling it into their heads that don't have to play a particular role in their community or household just because society says so. Me on the other hand, I don't really care, I feel like what we did when we were children was more about doing the whole 'monkey-see-monkey-do' thing. We acted that way because Denise's parents acted that way. If we played at my house more, then Denise would have probably played my mother, always bossing around my father.

My parents aren't the typical masculine-feminine couple. My mom lives and breathes for her job, lately it's usually my dad who has driven me to go to the park with Tulip, or to go see a movie. My dad is probably more involved in my life than most fathers. He was always there to cheer me on during Christmas performances, where I was placed in the back because they thought I was too shy. I love my mom, but she can be difficult at times, she thinks she knows what's best, what is the right thing to do. If I were to have bullying problems, she would have wanted me to have gone to her, to ask her for advice, and how to handle the situation. She would also probably not be happy that I chose to ignore my bullies instead of standing up for what's right. But look at me now! Now I am sitting hanging out with the girls I hated in middle school, I am making more friends every day, I am even being invited to parties!

I was even asked to go to Homecoming by Duncan of all people! It totally surprised me, especially since it was only like a week before the actual dance. He said that he wasn't planning on asking anyone, most people only go with their boyfriend or girlfriend, and it was usually more important for the seniors than the juniors, but since we've been hanging out a lot, and that I seem like such a good time, he wanted to know if I would go with him. Unfortunately I had to decline his offer, more so because I am good person rather than doing it by choice.

Since freshman year, Denise and I have vowed to never go to Homecoming. Instead, we planned an annual tradition to watch movies and stay up late eating junk food. At the time, when Denise was my only friend, this sounded like the perfect night to me, but now that I have other friends, I wanted to be able to make other plans.

Anyway, Duncan said that he understood and that we will just have to go out another time, just the two of us, and then he winked at me! He is just so gorgeous, I had nearly melted away when he talked to me one-on-one. I felt so bad for saying no that I had promised him we could definitely make up for it. Now that I am thinking back to it, I realized that I probably sounded very eager, but oh well, you're only young once!

Denise and I didn't even have that much fun Homecoming night. We decided to stay at her place and watch one of her favorite movies, The Rocky Horror Picture Show. Then we watched the new IT movie to end with something that would get us wanting to stuff our faces while leaving us more prepared for Halloween. But halfway through IT, her dad came in hammering away about how he wanted to show us something that he made on the weekend, he is a very hands-on kinda guy. Denise went ballistic on him, she freaked out at him, telling him to get out and that she wanted some privacy for once. She even yelled at him saying that she hated him, which was very extreme, even for her. He left with what looked like tears in his eyes.

At the end of the movie, after she seemed to have cooled down, she whispered under her breath, "Someone's been drinking again." I didn't say anything about it because usually Denise was open about how she felt, and never had I noticed her *dad drinking too much. I thought it was probably just her over-exaggerating as usual, but I still felt very uncomfortable. The minute the credits were done, I mumbled that I had to go home and left in a rush. I even avoided eye contact with her that Monday, I just felt very awkward and uncomfortable.*

I have seen her and her dad fight before, more so just arguing, but to be so mean to him, I didn't quite understand why, maybe there is something more going on, but it's probably best if I stay out of it. She hasn't tried to talk to me either, I don't think we've actually talked since. We sit beside each other in class, smile at one another, but neither of us speak.

It has been a few weeks now, and it's beginning to grow into a very long awkward silence between the two of us, but at the same time I don't want to crack first. If she wants to talk about it, she will come to me, I shouldn't have to ask her what's going on, I am not her mom.

On a happier note, I have been invited to Duncan's party that he throws every year, this year he made quarter back position, so it's bound to be epic. His parents are rich lawyers or something, who usually go out of town on important work-related trips, leaving him and his younger brother, Stewart, to defend for themselves. I have only heard whispers about his parties, but it sounds like they have been quite legendary.

Duncan apparently lives in a mansion by the beach but still has a heated outdoor pool (I don't know why you need a pool when you have the California Ocean, but still cool though). I have also heard that there are like 5 guest bedrooms, and his house has been in a Lil Wayne music video! I've also heard that he gets kegs ordered to his house and has a fake ID so he can sign for them all! I haven't seen a keg before. I wonder if people will be doing the classic beer pong games and keg stands that you see in the movies.

As you may know (depending on who is reading this), I have never been to a party before, so I am very excited. The party still isn't for another month, he wanted to send out the invites early to make sure that everyone would be prepared for a 'total rager' he said. He also told me to not bring anyone else, so I guess that is a bonus too! He probably just means another guy, not Denise or anything.

Denise and I may not be talking right now but I am sure sometime next week one of us will probably cave, we always go out trick-or-treating with my sister (I don't care how old I am, free candy is free candy), so we've gotta talk before Halloween. Emma, Ashley, and Sasha (Duncan's cousin) invited me to their Halloween shindig, apparently every year they go out and either TP or egg someone's house before Duncan's big party that didn't start until 11PM. I told them that I have to take my little sister out around the block to get some candy so I couldn't make it. I am also not interested in anything like that, I always thought it was so mean to vandalize someone else's property and just imagine all the work they have to do to clean it up after! But I guess kids will be kids on Halloween.

Oh, and I nearly forgot, after Ashley and Emma heard that I couldn't make Homecoming this year, they told me that it's okay because it's the senior year one that really counts. They are already guessing who will be crowd queen and king, Ashley thinks that if Duncan and I end up getting together at his party, that maybe it will be the two of us up there on the stage. I never really believed in the whole crowning thing, it's just a popularity contest anyways, but I've never thought that I could win before either. Ashley also told me that Duncan and I would make a really cute couple. I giggled like a little girl after her compliment, I felt so embarrassed, but she took my hand and squealed with me (the strange things us teenagers do). Her and Emma also invited me to join the Homecoming committee to help plan for next year, which was going to be based on 'A Night in Paris.' It's cheesy, but I love it! Ashley and Emma also said that I should make a performance and sing a little song to show everyone how talented I am. I told them I was probably a little too nervous, but they assured me I would be fine by the time it came around next year. They also said that we could all perform in the talent show at the end of the year.

Since we were all in the same theater class together, it would be easy to prepare a song for us to sing at the end of this year. Ashley said her and Emma could be the backup singers, standing on stage beside me so I wouldn't feel frightened. I agreed to their plan, feeling like I didn't have much of choice, knowing Ashley would get her way somehow. But I am happy that they are so supportive of me, that they even want to help me get noticed!

Ashley also told me you never know who could be sitting in the audience at a high school talent show, maybe a producer or something! Imagine that! Me, getting discovered at the age of 16! That would be insane! I know Ashley isn't just doing it for me either, she wants to get found too, and Emma is probably more so just along for the ride. But still! That is just so nice of them to help me get over my fears!

Emma and Ashley have also introduced me to so many different people over the past month, most of them I already knew, kids that I used to think of as another bunch of preppy popular bullies. But now I am actually finally getting to know them, the real them, not just the fake people we see in the halls every day, pretending to be the happy-go-lucky kids, they are just like me, with their opinions and beliefs. They are also funny and kind. I can't believe that I had so easily grouped them all together as villains. I guess it was just easier that way for me, to play the innocent victim, but I had my moments of cruelty too, I am sure of it. I think most of us do. I also believe some of us try to hide it or do not like to admit it, but usually at one point in our life we have bullied someone (maybe accidentally or intentionally), sh*t happens. This does not make it okay, but it makes me more understanding, it makes me realize we are not all perfect.

People are used to following a superior, it happened in Hitler's time, it happens in today's government, and it is seen across the world. Yes, bullying is not as extreme as what happened to the Jews (bless those poor souls), but in a way it was a form of bullying. People followed Hitler because they feared him, not necessarily because they thought what he was doing was the right thing. Even a teacher in California, Ron Jones, proved that people could be easily influenced or persuaded by a leader to participate in certain actions that they normally wouldn't do, such as bullying, abuse, etc. This Third Wave movement really scared the kids, but it also showed them how German people could accept the actions of the Nazis, and I think it also shows how people can accept the actions of bullies.

If your friend of 5 years told you that some girl was fat as she walked by, and she was probably a bit on the heavier side (nothing wrong with that!), you would most likely agree because you wouldn't see the harm. You are not the one making the comment, just nodding your head in agreement, but at the same time that nod of approval of what your friend just said was witnessed by the passerby, the girl who you agreed was 'fat.' Now, you might think that you were just simply nodding, but in that poor girl's eyes, you are just as easily to blame about making her feel sh*tty as your friend is. You both acknowledge her as being over-weight, and neither of you had a problem of not being discrete about it as she walked by. Maybe you even frowned and nodded, because it is only a human habit to often frown when you are agreeing with an insult. Now, this frown could easily send someone over the edge, they might take it as you looking at them in disgust, not just making a simple movement of muscles to a position they are so often used to sitting in. This could also easily be how bullies are usually found in packs, the leader says something mean, and their followers/friends agree, which they look as an innocent act, yet in truth nothing of this sort behavior is innocent or kind.

Society teaches us it's not nice to agree or acknowledge someone's flaws, for example if someone were to call me a b**ch. People look at this as a rude statement, even if there is honesty to it. But at the same time, just because people associate me with this name (I am sure no one does because I've never said a mean thing in my life), does not make me an awful person, therefore I should not care. Yet, society tells us that we should care, that this was an insult, and the same things goes for being called fat or a slut. These are just a few of the greatest and most common insults girls come up with, just to put someone else down. And why? What for? For our own insecurities, usually. That is why the popular kids used to agree with Emma when she called me a freak, a geek, or a Goth, whatever name was the first one to pop up in her head.

The 'cool kids' started to agree with Emma, nodding along when I passed by as she whispered "freak." And then out of habit, when Emma was no longer around, someone else would say it as I scurried along trying to stay unnoticed. I am sure they probably eventually forgot why they started calling me these names in the first place, which is also probably why the name-calling stopped. This is also a reason as to why Ashley started to call me names, she saw me as an insinu-ator with Denise, who for some reason she had beef with. She probably went from "Here comes the psycho," to "Here come the psychos." Once one person in the group is deemed a target, the other group members quickly follow suit.

My point being is that these kids, who used to be bullies, were most likely made that way by society. We decided to take offense to their words, their name-calling, and what have you. But at the same time, why should we care? We really shouldn't, as long as we know who we are, the kind caring people that we should be, then it shouldn't matter. Yet people should also learn not to follow their undeserving lead-ers in to battle, or bullying, if they believe what is being done or said is wrong. If you think you are a good person, and if you truly are, then you should not be agreeing with someone about the poor qualities of another human being just be-cause that name-caller is your friend. You should be telling them what they are saying is not nice, that it is not acceptable to insult someone just because of the way they look or how they behave when they have done nothing to you. So I have decided to forgive Emma, Ashley, and their other friends for being nasty children, it seems like they have grown out of that stage, and maybe they are no longer the followers who I think they are. They are no longer following society, who tell us just because we are 10, 20, or even 30 pounds over the average weight this makes us pigs, or that just because we don't look like the models on magazine covers means that we are ugly. We are simply who we are, and that's that, everyone should get over their issues and embrace themselves, I know I have, and I think these girls have too.

Sorry about that little rant, I think this diary is also helpful for me getting things off my chest.

I want to express my feelings, and let either the older me, or my children, who-ever is reading this, to know that some things you just need to let go. And I know the whole 'the North Remembers,' and it is hard to forget, but maybe we should start to forgive. But at the same time, I feel like you can't actually forgive if you don't forget, otherwise you will be holding onto to your memories tightly in the back of your mind, and the slightest slip or mistake might let all of your emotions tied with those memories loose into the world.

Ta Ta for now,
Love P

P.S. I think diary sounds little childish, I think I am going to start calling you my journal.

Chapter 15

It was 6:05PM as Scarlett dressed Rosie in her Spiderman costume. They had gone shopping for the blue and red spandex outfit just several days earlier.

"No, Mom, I don't want to be a firefighter, I want to be Spiderman," Rosie chimed as they rummaged through the second store they had visited three days ago.

"Well, sweetie, I don't think they have that superhero costume. What about dressing up as an actual spider, that would be pretty cool?" Scarlett asked her daughter as she knelt down to her eye-level, she was preparing herself for a stern conversation.

"No, Mom, that's creepy!" Rosie exclaimed.

Scarlett couldn't understand how a spider was considered creepy when Spiderman had to have been bitten by a spider to get his superpowers; it didn't make any sense to her. She was ready to give up when her phone chirped loudly.

"Hello, this is Scarlett speaking."

"Hey, are you still looking for that Spiderman costume for Rosie?" Martha asked without introducing herself, she knew very well; Scarlett had caller ID.

"Yes?" Scarlett said questioningly.

"Walmart has three left! Do you want me to buy one for you?"

"Perfect! No that's okay, Rosie needs to try it on first to make sure we get the proper size."

"Okay, I will just hide the last three in the women's section, near the sweat pants."

"You are a life savior!"

With the flick of the wrist, Scarlett shut her outdated mobile phone and grabbed Rosie's hand. They hustled to the car as Scarlett told her daughter that they were not going to give up yet and were going to look at one more store. Luckily, they purchased the perfect sized Spiderman outfit for Rosie an hour later.

***

"Hold still for a moment," Scarlett told her daughter as she pinned the back of the costume; turns out in their frantic rush to purchase it, it was actually bigger than they thought.

"Mom, we are going to be late," Rosie said trying to tug away from her mother's grip.

They were supposed to be meeting with Martha and Alex in ten minutes at Venice Beach, at Alex's home, because it was supposed to be one of the best neighborhoods to go trick-or-treating in California. The only problem was that Scarlett was still wearing her sweat pants and lived at least a thirty-minute drive from there.

"Okay, let's go, grab you pillow case," Scarlett decided not to change; there wasn't enough time and she hated to keep everyone waiting.

As Scarlett and Rosie raced for the door, Rosie skipping, excited for the candy splurge waiting for her, the doorbell rang. Scarlett started to open the big white door, preparing to let down some children, telling them she didn't have any candy, but to her surprise it was Jonathan.

"DADDY! Are you coming trick-or-treating?" Rosie asked as she jumped into Jonathan's arms.

"Of course, my little Spiderman! I promised you, didn't I?" Jonathan said as he grabbed Rosie and swung her in his arms.

Scarlett stood in the doorframe with a perplexed look on her face as Jonathan put his daughter down while she grabbed at his Iron Man costume, talking in a rushed, excited voice. Jonathan looked up from his daughter's glowing face to see his wife's bewildered expression.

"Did you not get my message?" Jonathan asked in a monotone voice.

"What message?" Scarlett asked.

"The one I left you."

Scarlett thought Jonathan was being difficult for the sake of it. *It really is not that hard to fully explain yourself,* she thought.

"No I must have missed it," Scarlett smiled, she didn't want to argue tonight, not in front of Rosie.

"Oh, well I told you that I would meet you here before we all leave for Alex's," Jonathan said.

Scarlett had no recollection of telling Jonathan about their trick-or-treating plans, nor did she remember ever inviting him. She would have invited him if she thought he would have said yes. Scarlett had no intentions of splitting the family apart, unlike him.

"Okay, then let's get a move on or we will be late," Scarlett said, shutting and locking the door behind her.

"Oh how I would hate to make us late," Jonathan said as he picked up Rosie and ran for the car.

It was a running joke in the family about how Scarlett needed to be on time for everything. If she was running five minutes late, it would activate her nervous bladder and knot her stomach; this also meant she had to drive. Scarlett would laugh cynically as her family picked on her.

In contrast, Jonathan never seemed to genuinely care. He was more laid back than Scarlett was, and was someone who just went with the flow. He also did not mind not being in the driving seat if they had plans to go somewhere; he was not the kind of man who needed to be in control. People often joked that Scarlett wore the pants in their relationship, but her and Jonathan did not look at it that way. Like a good, loving couple, they balanced each other with neither of them having an ultimate say in any matter, or at least this is how the way things used to work before Jonathan left.

Scarlett clicked the unlock button on her key fob, as Jonathan reached to open the back door of Scarlett's 2009 black Ford Escape. With a few clicks and slams of the car doors, they were all buckled in, ready to go to Alex's. Scarlett reversed with ease as she had done several thousand times before and headed towards Venice Beach, only a few miles per hour above the speed limit.

On the twenty, instead of the usual thirty-minute trip, Rosie couldn't stop talking about how excited she was.

"I wonder how much candy I am gonna get this year, I hope it's more than last Halloween! I want to fill my pillow case all the way to the top!" Rosie giggled in the back seat.

"But then it's going to get too heavy, sweetie," Jonathan told his daughter, who couldn't weigh more than eighty pounds.

Scarlett wanted to tell her daughter that too much candy would give her cavities, but she decided to refrain from sounding like a 'Debby-Downer,' which happened to be her husband's favorite nickname for her, so she sat quietly and focused on the road. Scarlett was on a mission to get them to Alex's as quickly and safely as possible.

"Then you will just have to carry it," Rosie said as she giggled a little bit louder. She hadn't eaten any candy yet, but she seemed euphoric with her thoughts on the type of candy that awaited her.

"Only if you promise to share," Jonathan laughed. Him and his daughter both shared the same sweet tooth.

"I pinky-promise," Rosie said as she leaned forward holding her finger out to her father.

Jonathan turned around in his seat and wrapped his large pinky around his daughter's. Rosie was obsessed with pinky-promises; she felt as if they were the only real type of promise that anyone would actually keep; saying "I promise" was simply not enough for her.

For the remainder of the car ride, Jonathan and Rosie sang to *Thriller* by Michael Jackson, while Scarlett hummed along. The three of them were not a musically talented family – they couldn't keep up to the tempo, and kept mixing and messing up words – but it was the first time in several months they had been all together, smiling and laughing, feeling like a real family again.

As Rosie buzzed, "I'm gonna thrill you tonight," while dancing the typical moves to Thriller, Scarlett pulled into Alex's expanding driveway. She parked behind Martha's red 1987 Toyota Corolla.

Jonathan unbuckled his daughter and then the three of them walked towards Alex's wooden carved doors. Alex had recently replaced her plain entranceway for something a little more luxurious, a genuine piece of art. Her new doors were made from mahogany that had the ocean carved into it. There were waves crashing on top of one another, sea foam bubbling up. It was truly beautiful.

It took Scarlett a while to get used to this new expensive piece, she was always afraid that if she were to knock on it, or slam it too hard behind her, that it would magically chip, costing thousands of dollars to fix or replace. After a month or so, Scarlett started to see why Alex bought the new decorative piece; it really fit in with the rest of the house, extravagant, but beachy.

Alex's home was built about eight years ago when her and Darryl moved here with Eliza and Chloe. Alex had received a promotion, allowing them to buy, or rather build their dream home. Alex, picky as she was, decided it was best to look for property that they loved, and then tear down what sat on it and start fresh. They were lucky enough to find a place in Venice Beach along the waterfront. Everything was in their budget, and they knocked down the small humble home and built a cabin, a home away from home. Alex called it a cabin because of the ocean vibe, but it was more of a mansion.

The house was built with long windows, reaching from the floor to the ceiling. It was modern but had a beachy feel to it. It was big too – 3 bedrooms and 4 bathrooms, a total of 3,100 square feet. She had put in dark gray flooring throughout the house, Alex didn't believe in carpet. She also had light gray marble tiles for every countertop, making the space feel bright with the contrasting gray elements. The furniture looked like it belonged in a Water Style Cottage book or magazine. Alex had even bought driftwood to place inside and outside her home. She was a very stylish women and knew exactly what she wanted.

Scarlett had fallen in love with the house the minute she saw it; it was classic, elegant, yet warming and inviting. The kitchen and living room were open and connected, that way if someone was making food, they could still talk to whoever was in the living room sitting and waiting. The space was also well placed because nearly every room in the home got to look out at the water, the blue waves gently rolling along the shore. When Scarlett was over at Alex's, she would find it nearly impossible to pry her eyes away from the view, it was so enticing. She would imagine her friends and herself when they are older, rocking back and forth in their chairs, looking out at the beach, reminiscing about their younger days.

Rosie knocked on the beautiful wooden door without hesitation, she was eager to see her friends. After two knocks, the door opened to Jackson's gleaming face; Rosie was clearly not the only one excited for tonight. It still amazed Scarlett to see the children have so much joy for dressing up, and of course getting candy. They were practically bobbing up and down with anticipation.

"WOW. Cool costume!" Jackson said as he opened the door fully, looking down at Rosie.

"Thanks, I am Spiderman!" Rosie hopped inside. "I like your costume too!"

Jackson was dressed up as Batman, the whole shebang. He was wearing the black mask with pointed ears, covering everything above his mouth, emphasizing his adorable big gapped tooth smile. He had the black cape, black boots, and golden belt with tiny gadgets on it. He was also wearing the Batman pants and shirts, which had the outline of muscles that appeared to be popping out from under the spandex. There was also a big Batman symbol on his chest; Scarlett thought maybe they put it there just in case anyone second-guessed who this kid was trying to dress up as.

Jackson and Rosie ran off as Scarlett and Jonathan took their shoes off. It wasn't Jonathan's first time at Alex's; he had gone to all of the barbecues, date nights, movie nights, and other events Alex held at her house. But since Jonathan moved out of the house, renting out a bachelor pad by himself, he hasn't seen any of their friends. Jonathan was not as shy as Scarlett, but he was a homebody; he didn't have any friends he made at work, mostly because he worked with a handful of twenty-year-olds that he taught, but he had also liked keeping his friend group small.

Jonathan had actually gotten along with Darryl very well. They were both similar, well-educated, but dorky older men. They liked their *Lord of the Rings*, *Star Wars*, *Game of Thrones*, *Harry Potter*, and other sci-fi classics. They were also both the laid back, easy-going type. They were not sport fans fanatics, but they did enjoy going on hikes together or playing golf on the weekends. And they are great fathers, very involved in their children's lives, taking them to movies or to the park together. They were even the reason behind Jackson and Rosie dressing up as heroes; they showed the kids every Marvel and DC movie that ever existed.

Jonathan and Darryl even got Delany interested in the superhero movie franchise as well. They would always take out the three kids to the cinema, never leaving one behind. Scarlett knew, even before seeing Delany, who she would be dressed up as – Wolverine. Delany had been talking about Wolverine all year. At first Alex, Martha, and Scarlett thought that she was madly in love with him, but after a while they realized Delany wanted to be him. She would jump on tables, pouncing around like a cat, then stick her first into the air, making a grunt as she tried to release her claws between her knuckles.

Scarlett and Jonathan walked into Alex's living room to see the whole gang. Everyone was dressed up except for Scarlett. Darryl was dressed up as a Stormtrooper; his outfit looked like it had been taken from the Star Wars set itself. He held his helmet in his hand, showing off his big dimples and the similar gap-toothed smile Scarlett saw on Jackson moments ago. Him and Alex made a beautiful couple, both with the high cheekbones, dark complexion, and big pearly white grins.

Alex, like Darryl, also loved to go to the extreme with her costumes, and every year she dressed as a fashion icon. Last year she dressed up as RuPaul in drag, wearing a curly blonde wig, glamorous makeup, and a black shiny spaghetti strap dress. She may be no RuPaul, but she still looked amazing. She had spent 3 hours doing her highlighter, eye shadow, lipstick, and eyebrows, trying to get the shine and glimmer just right. This year Alex was dressed as Cruella de Vil. She wore a skintight black mini dress with red high heels and matching gloves. She also had a big, cream, faux fur coat. She looked absolutely fabulous, the best Cruella de Vil Scarlett had ever seen. Alex even had the half black and half white wig to pull the entire outfit together.

Martha had chosen a character from a newer Disney cartoon. She was dressed as Merida from *Brave*, one of Delany's favorite Disney princesses. It was a perfect fit for her, with her natural red curly hair and green eyes. She wore a green dress that hugged tightly to her chest and hips, and then flowed down the rest of her body. Martha even had a bow and arrow case hanging across her shoulder. She really looked like the real life Scottish princess.

But it was Delany who really caught Scarlett's eye. She was wearing a dirty white tank top that looked like it had some grease or oil stains on it. She wore plain jeans, a brown belt, and tiny black boots. What really tied her Wolverine outfit together, making her look ridiculously adorable, was the fake beard Martha had put onto her daughter's face an hour earlier, as well as the dog tags that hung around her neck, making her look like a war veteran. Delany also had plastic knives, which had been spray painted silver, tied around her hands to look like they were coming out between her knuckles. She also had her hair greased back and slicked up to look pointy like Wolverine's. The finishing touch was a little fake cigar dangling from Delany's lips. Some parents would probably think the cigar was going too far, but Scarlett, who had seen all of the X-Men films multiple times, thought it was absolutely perfect. She looked like Wolverine's tiny rugged child, who was picking up daddy's bad habits.

After gawking at the costumes that filled the room, Scarlett looked down at her own clothes. She realized she should have dressed up. *Better to have been late than look like a party pooper,* she thought. She was beginning to feel more self-conscious when Alex came up and hugged her.

"Hello, sweetie," Alex leaned in to hug Scarlett hello, "You made it just in time, let's get this show on the road."

After the brief hellos, Alex linked arms with Scarlett and headed for the door with the kids, husbands, and Martha trailing behind.

"What is your husband doing here?" Alex whispered in Scarlett's ear after they reached Alex's driveway while Darryl was locking up, Jonathan closely behind him.

Scarlett was about to whisper back that she didn't know, like the many other questions she did not know the answer to. She did not know why her husband had left her alone grieving, why he abandoned her, why he barely spoke to her since he left the house, and she did not know why he had shown up now. But the kids were too loud and excited for her to be heard.

"Why do you have a pillow case?" Delany giggled as she asked Rosie.

"It's to hold more candy, silly," Rosie explained as she waved her matching Spiderman pillowcase in the air.

With a burst of laughter, the children ran to begin their long trek, hunting for the best candy in the city of Los Angeles.

"No running!" Darryl and Jonathan yelled in synchronicity while chasing after the screaming children.

Darryl and Jonathan were the ones who would run after the kids, chasing them down if they were being naughty, leaving the ladies behind. Alex would tell her husband to go after them, that he was faster because he was the one with the longer legs. Then she would giggle to her friends, actually blaming it on her shoes; she would say, "No one should run in Prada, honey."

Jonathan would always start running the minute he realized the kids took off, Scarlett thought it was his fatherly instincts kicking in, needing to make sure the kids were alright, that they wouldn't get hit by a swerving car or by anything else drastic like that. Scarlett had gotten so used to him reacting so quickly that she stopped trying to chase after them when she was with him, she knew he would get there first. And most of the time the children would only run a few yards ahead of them, stopping and turning around like well-trained minions, waiting for their parents to reach them before they tested their boundaries again. Scarlett was the more uptight one between her and Jonathan, but not when it came to the kids. She thought it was because she had more faith in them, she knew they weren't going to run into the road, they were smarter than that, or at least after they reached a certain age. When she was seven, she remembered wandering her neighborhood at night, all alone, playing at the park, on the trees, or in the forest. Yet, apparently society no longer deems it acceptable for children to be wandering without adult supervision, even if there are several of them together. However, Scarlett was starting to realize they had a right to think that way with the increasing crime rates, murders, kidnappings, and all of the true scary stories your parents tell you so that you do not go out at night alone.

So Alex, Scarlett, and Martha hung back while Darryl and Jonathan reached the children in a few strides before they even arrived at the first house. Jonathan rang the doorbell of the expensive residential home, telling the children not to say "Trick-or-treat, give me something good to eat," like they did last year.

Now that there was some distance between the women and Jonathan, Martha and Alex began pouring out their questions.

"What is your husband doing here?" Alex repeated herself.

"Are you guys back together?" Martha asked. "I didn't know he was coming, did he just show up out of nowhere?" Alex asked.

"Are you okay with him just waltzing back into your life?" Martha asked.

"Does this mean he no longer wants a divorce?" Alex asked.

"Does this mean he is moving back in?" Martha asked.

Scarlett held up her hand to silence her friends from their word vomit.

"I simply don't know." Scarlett paused to make sure she had gotten their attention. "He just showed up, telling me that he had left a message saying he was coming trick-or-treating, but I had no clue. I don't listen to my messages, I never have. When I used to come home and check them, there would be nothing waiting for me on the answering machine, instead there would be little post-it notes Jonathan would have written for me if anyone left a message. I got so used to him doing that over the last eighteen years of our marriage that I just stopped checking, instead I just looked for the post-it notes."

"Oh, honey. It's not your fault you didn't check your messages," Alex said soothingly. She could always tell when Scarlett was about to get worked up over something, that is until Scarlett would try to change the conversation.

"Mmhmmm," Martha agreed. She never really knew what to say about guy troubles, she had never had any of her own since she became independent, taking on the responsibilities of a single mom with eager determination. Instead, she would usually agree with what Alex said.

Alex asked the most important question, "What do you make of all it?"

Scarlett was not sure; she didn't know if seeing her husband happy again, being the perfect father he is to his little girl, being there for her, made her upset or at ease. She felt slightly upset because he shouldn't have been there, because it was not his day, it was not his time to spend with her, but then that would make Scarlett the miserable wife in this messy situation. She also felt slightly at ease because she wanted her husband there, she wanted him back in her life, she missed him.

"I don't know. I mean I am happy that he is here for Rosie, she obviously wanted him here. But it's all very confusing. I thought he didn't want to be a part of my life which is why he moved out, why he filed for divorce, but then again why would he be here if he wanted that? He could have asked to take Rosie out after trick-or-treating, to do that family tradition without me… But he didn't, does that also mean he plans to watch a movie with us later? Or will this be too much time spent with his awful wife?" Scarlett asked dramatically. She was really beginning to lose her self-control, not even bothering trying to change the conversation to a happier, lighter topic.

"You are not an awful wife," Alex said, stopping Scarlett in her tracks, making her turn around and look at her.

"No of course not, you are amazing, Scarlett, always there, always supportive, you're a wonderful wife and mother," Martha said grabbing onto her other arm, looking down at her like a stern parent.

"Yes! You are all of that and so much more. You deserve the best, what you want, what you need. And I believe if you want and need Jonathan back in your life then you will get that, honey," Alex said, "But in my opinion, you don't need him. You have got us, we love you and we will always be here for you." Alex tried to cover any type of scenario possible, in case Jonathan left her, or he came back, she wanted to be supportive of whatever Scarlett needed.

"Amen to that, sister!" Martha sung, turning Scarlett back around, locking her arm in one of hers, Alex doing the same.

As the three women linked arms, beginning to walk with a swing in their step, they couldn't help but laugh at themselves. They reminded each other of a group of young girls, best friends, skipping to a childhood tune on their way to their next adventure, when in real life they were three women, one dressed as a Scottish princess, one as an evil fashion icon, and the other middle-aged mother wearing her clothes from yesterday, which including her sweat pants, sneakers, and a big baggy college hoodie, where she didn't even attend. They were an interesting mix of women, but best friends nonetheless.

"Speaking of your husband, I must admit he makes a pretty good Iron Man," Alex said as she nodded towards Jonathan.

Scarlett had gotten so worked up over seeing Jonathan, and then rushing to get to Alex's, that she hadn't really taken in her husband's outfit. Alex was right, Jonathan did look good. He was wearing a deluxe Iron Man costume, helmet and everything. His outfit was made of a hard plastic, painted red and gold. His joints were left exposed with a black fabric, possibly spandex, that probably lined the rest of the outfit. He even had a glowing light source in the center of his chest like Tony Stark. Jonathan was also wearing the red and gold mask, leaving it flipped up so he could see. He had really outdone himself, he never put so much effort into his outfits before, he usually just put anything on, or for Halloween he would just buy a mask from the nearest Dollar Store.

As the children scurried from door-to-door, trying to get in as many houses as they could before their bedtime, with the husbands at their heels, the women remained a few paces behind them. They didn't bother to walk up any of the long windy driveways but instead hung back, talking about what was new in their lives, while they nibbled on some candy they snuck from their children. It was mostly

Martha and Alex talking while Scarlett listened, enjoying the change in the topic of conversation.

"He is so sweet, very old fashioned. He opens the car door for me, and every single other door you can think of," Martha was talking about Pete. They had gone on a date several days ago and were even planning their second one later this week.

When Pete had finally got the courage to ask Martha out, Alex and Scarlett where thrilled while Martha had been caught off guard. She never actually believed Alex and Scarlett when they said Pete had an obvious crush on her; she thought they were just trying to encourage her to get back into the dating life. Martha had been too busy brushing them off and daydreaming about Pete to realize he had a crush on her too.

"It has been a while since I've been on a date. I think it was even my first actual good date," Martha smiled.

"I guess you focus so much of your time on work and Delany, you forget about yourself. Shame, shame, woman, you need to learn to put your happiness first sometimes. Parents get so confused with stuff like this, they think they need to focus solely on their children, that their happiness is the only thing that matters, neglecting themselves in the process. But what most people don't realize is that if you are not happy, then you won't be able to take proper care of your daughter. Think of it like the air-bag scenario in a plane that is crashing, you have to put your mask on first before helping others," Alex said in her soothing Zen voice, as she pretended to take a puff from her fake cigarette dangling from her women's 10.7"/270mm black vintage cigarette holder.

"Wiser words have never been spoken from a Cruella de Vil," laughed Scarlett.

"I never thought of it that way before. Last year I was so occupied with the bakery and Delany, making sure she fits in at school, making sure that I could satisfy the customers for Pete. But look at me now, I am the head baker and Delany has two best friends. It's crazy how much can change in a year. I use to be such a busy bee that I never got to meet any other parents, and now I have the kindest, most generous best friends. Things are really starting to turn around for me," Martha said looking at her daughter take her fake cigar out of her mouth to say 'trick-or-treat.'

"Aww, honey, you deserve it! And you guys are actually my first girlfriends. I never really got along with other women before, they always seemed to like me, but behind closed doors I just knew they were gossiping about me. It was all smiles and chuckles until my back was turned. Mothers can be very cliquey," Alex said.

"Yeah, they probably just thought of you as a hot threat!" Martha giggled, nudging Alex in the side.

"Oh hush!" Alex smiled, waving her red-gloved hand at her friend. "What I am trying to say is that I really appreciate you two, for being there for me, supporting me. I really love you guys."

"We love you with all our hearts," chirped Scarlett, wrapping her hand around Alex's waist, her biggest initiation of affection towards her best friend. Over the past year and a half since Scarlett met Alex and Martha, she had slowly grown accustomed to their touchy-feely personalities, even beginning to show more affection herself.

"Mmhmmm" Martha agreed, wrapping her own arm around Alex's waist.

The women were in semi-hugging position as their children bounded towards them, ready for the next house. They did genuinely love one another and were there to support and provide for each other if they ever needed it. They made a perfect, tight knit group, every young girl's dream, almost like they were Phoebe, Rachel, and Monica stepping onto the set of *Friends*.

None of them fit the characters perfectly, but were instead a mix of them all. Alex had the zany, spiritual qualities of Phoebe, along with her ability to talk to people about anything, lacking a filter of any kind. She was also like Rachel, caring about the latest trends and her appearance, which related to her conscious awareness of her surroundings, being able to read people's feelings and emotions.

Martha on the other hand was a mix of Monica, being more detail-oriented when it came to her life and food prepping, making her a bit of an organized maniac when it came to baking. Yet, she also had a creative side like Phoebe, finding energy in doing what she loved, in this case baking instead of songwriting. She even had the random moments of spontaneity when it came to making plans with her friends. Alex and Martha were also both like Phoebe with their high openness to experience anything, their joint motto being "don't knock it till you've tried it."

Scarlett on the other hand had an A Type personality, like Monica. In her home life, she needed to control everything, make the plans, drive the car. In public, she could be a little rough around the edges at times, feeling awkward and shy, but when she was around her friends, she felt more open to be herself. She used logic and reasoning to make her rational decisions, thinking she knew people better than they knew themselves, and she was very conscientious, which came in handy in the counseling industry. At times she could take on the qualities and traits of Rachel and Phoebe that made them fun, their humor, energy, spontaneity when surrounded by her loved ones. But everything that had happened in the past several months had toned down her enthusiastic and bubbly side, leaving the Monica in her to take over.

It was all of these qualities that made them such a good trio. They were all relatively aware of one another's feelings, Alex and Scarlett more so then Martha, but it worked to their benefit. The women knew who to go to when they needed good advice – Alex or Scarlett – or who to go to when they needed to be shown a spontaneous, good time – Alex or Martha.

The women linked arms again, this time with Alex in the middle, and they crossed one foot in front of the other as they followed Jonathan, Darryl, and the children to the next home. Scarlett was very impressed with all the costumes she had seen throughout the night, with the majority of parents dressed up as well. There were little girls and boys dressed up as some of the characters from *Recess*, *Stranger Things*, *Frozen*, *The Avengers*, *Toy Story*, *The Incredibles*, *Superman*, *Batman,* and *Wonder Woman*, just to name a few. There were also children dressed as minions, princesses, knights, wizards, witches, and animals of all sorts. Scarlett was happy to see that even some parents supported their boys to dress up as a Walt Disney princess.

"Oh look at him dressed as Belle! He is absolutely adorable!" Alex said to Martha and Scarlett. "I am so happy that some parents are able to get over gender-binary roles, supporting their kids at a young age with how they choose to dress."

"I remember if my brothers would have wanted to dress up as any female character, my mom would tell them that it was not allowed, they would be made fun of or how it is not proper. I love how the times have changed! Fewer and fewer people care about how someone dresses or how someone identifies, nor should they!" Martha explained.

"I couldn't agree with you guys more," Scarlett said smiling. She had dealt with a lot of gender identity, cross-dressing and opening up about ones sexuality during her counseling in and out of the Suicide Prevention Hotline.

Scarlett would tell her clients that they should be true to themselves, but unfortunately there will be people who are going to be hating them for who they are, but those are the miserable and idiotic people stuck in the past. The people who matter the most will love you for who you are, accept you for who you are. And it was not necessarily about them not caring who you sleep with, or how you identify, but it was that they acknowledge and appreciate the uniqueness that is you.

Then Scarlett would end their conversation by telling them they are worth love and life, that they are special and that no one should make them feel any less. It had always been difficult for her to explain to parents of children who belonged to the LGBTQ community, why their children were the way they were, that they did not choose this path to make it harder on their parents. The parents would often say that their child was acting out in spite of them, or that it was just a phase. Scarlett found it hard trying to reason with these type of people, but she did her best, fixing as many parent-child relationships as she could.

"And look at that cutie!" Alex practically shouted while pointing to a little baby dressed as a bumblebee. Their mother was holding them over her should so you could just make out the black fabric that engulfed the back of their head with antennae pointing out.

"Aw, that is so precious! I remember dressing Delany up one year as a bee, it had been one my favorite costumes," Martha said, clasping her hands together in awe.

Scarlett thought the bee was adorable, but her favorite costume that she saw that night was of one of a little three-year-old dressed as a pumpkin, it reminded her of another child with brown pigtails that had a bright red face because they had been crying so hard, refusing to walk anymore, Scarlett quickly suffocated the image of that memory.

After an hour of trick-or-treating, everyone went back to Alex's and Darryl's to watch a movie. This was a slight alteration to Scarlett's, Jonathan's, and Rosie's tradition, but they were happy to spend more time with everyone. The kids had also been too wired up on candy for them to fall asleep, which was why the parents decided a movie would be perfect to help calm them down before bed. Alex picked the *Corpse Bride* out of her Halloween collection. It was the most child-friendly one she owned, everything else belonging to either the *Freddy Krueger* or *Jason Voorhees* franchise.

Chloe and Eliza showed up halfway through the movie, around 9:30PM. They had gone to the same party but decided to come home early. They said it had been 'lame.' Alex was thrilled to have all of the children home, cuddling up to her in her big faux fur coat.

Alex later told Martha and Scarlett when they were getting Delany and Rosie ready to leave, that she texted her daughters telling them they were all at home watching a movie. She knew her girls weren't partiers, and that if they heard they were watching a movie and eating candy that they would come home early. It used to be Alex's family tradition to eat candy and watch *Corpse Bride* after a night of trick-or-treating. She tried to lay a little guilt-trip on them so she could hang out with them – she was a true mother. Martha and Scarlett shook their heads disapprovingly, but they knew that they would have done the same thing.

Scarlett drove home with Jonathan in the passenger seat and Rosie asleep in the back. The moment Jonathan clicked her in, she nodded off. The ride home was silent; neither of them bothered to turn the radio on nor attempt to begin a conversation. Scarlett wasn't sure if it was because neither of them wanted to wake Rosie up or if they simply would rather sit in silence than talk to each other.

Scarlett also didn't want to be the one to break the silence; if he didn't want to talk then neither did she. At the same time, it was nice, the quiet car reminded Scarlett of the road trips they used to go on. The passengers in the backseat would be sound asleep, and her and Jonathan would watch the trees and the road quickly pass as they drove on. They were a couple who did not need to fill every moment they had together with sounds, they could sit in silence for hours, just enjoying each other's company.

When they got home, Jonathan unbuckled Rosie, picked her up, and carried her to bed as Scarlett unlocked the front door for them. Scarlett and Jonathan both knew Rosie was pretending to be asleep, she had woken when the car parked, opening her eyes quickly, giving herself away. She also let out a silent giggle as her dad picked her up as he had done thousands of times before. Rosie played this act so she could be carried; she would tell her parents "I am too tired to walk, carry me," with a spur of giggles.

After Jonathan put Rosie down in her bed, Rosie opened her eyes. "Will you please read me a bedtime story, Daddy and Mommy," Rosie said in her best puppy-dog voice.

Her parents sat down on the bed next to her, grabbing and opening her favorite bedtime story, *Goodnight Moon* by Margaret Wise Brown and Clement Hurd. They took turns reading page after page, in their best soothing story time voice.

"Goodnight room," whispered Scarlett.

"Goodnight moon," whispered Jonathan.

"Goodnight cow jumping over the moon."

"Goodnight light."

Before they got halfway through the book, Rosie was sound asleep. Out of habit, Jonathan and Scarlett finished the remaining pages.

"Goodnight air," whispered Scarlett, planting a kiss on Rosie's forehead.

"Goodnight noises everywhere," whispered Jonathan, who also kissed his daughter.

Seeing Jonathan being such a good father to Rosie made Scarlett remember how much she missed him, how she wanted him home. Scarlett wanted her husband more and more each day, trying to think about how she could get him back, but then she remembered she had done nothing wrong. She would start to feel rage for her husband time and time again, until she saw him, heard him talk, and then all of her anger slowly melted away.

Scarlett would complete her daily tasks, making breakfast, lunch and dinner for her and Rosie, thinking about how Jonathan used to make them food in the morning. Now they usually eat toast with jam to make sure they leave on time for school. Jonathan had always been there for Scarlett, even though he often did not have the patience to talk about someone's problem for hours. He was always what Scarlett needed, just another human being to accept her, to love her, and to spend time with her.

Their parenting skills were also better when they were together. Jonathan was the cool level-headed parent; he evened Scarlett out. She acted like she didn't pry, but she would ask too many questions, and tried to get too involved. Since she started working at the hotline more, Scarlett realized she had stopped nagging as much, and was finally letting go a little bit.

Also, since Scarlett started to recover from her dazed and confused state that lasted several months after the school shooting, she was beginning to realize that it felt like she hadn't seen her husband in over four months, like this whole time he had been in an unreachable location.

"Would you like a cup of tea before you go?" Scarlett asked.

"No," Jonathan said abruptly, heading for the front door.

"Why do you hate me?" Scarlett asked, already starting to feel the tears daring to be released. This was the only reason she could come up with on the spot for the reason her husband had left her.

"What do you mean, Scarlett?" Jonathan asked in a monotone voice, trying to hide his emotions.

"You have barely spoken to me since you moved out. Everything has just been happening so quickly, I don't know how to describe it. You act like you hate me, wanting a divorce, not talking to me. You won't even communicate with me about anything, you haven't even opened up to me about everything that has happened!" Scarlett was beginning to raise her voice out of frustration, saying her feelings out loud for the first time.

"Why won't I talk? Are you kidding me? Scarlett, you didn't talk to me for two months, you weren't there for me, or for Rosie. I know you had your reasons, we all had our reasons, but in no way was that an acceptable way to handle… handle everything."

Scarlett wasn't sure if her husband was right or wrong. Like she said, the first two months after the shooting were a blur for her. It was like she was trying to forget something, maybe even everything, to make the pain a little more bearable.

"Why did you even bother coming tonight?" Scarlett finally asked the question she'd been dreading the answer to.

"Because I want to keep our family traditions alive. I want Rosie to grow up with a normal as possible childhood. And I knew you were going to be a mess, Rosie should at least have one functioning parent present."

"I am not a mess!" Scarlett said ignorantly.

"Scarlett, look at yourself! You've gained weight, have bags under your eyes, you are not even wearing clean clothes." Scarlett looked down at her toothpaste-stained hoodie and muddy pants. "You are not even trying to keep yourself to-gether, I know you think you have everyone fooled, that you are under control, but we all see through it, we all know you are in denial. But I guess that is just one of your stages of grief," Jonathan said with a sad smile. "I will be here to pick Rosie up at 10 tomorrow," Jonathan said as he shut the entrance doorway behind him.

Scarlett's little voice in her head snapped, "You have no patience!" it screamed.

Scarlett refused to cry; she didn't think Jonathan deserved her tears anymore. He was bitter, not thinking clearly, and she was too tired to waste another second on her marriage, which she was starting to realize was falling apart.

Later that night, sometime after 12:00AM, after Scarlett gave up on sleep, she went downstairs and clicked on the TV. She opened up the freezer and grabbed the Ben & Jerry's Moose Tracks ice cream she bought last night, and plopped herself on the couch. As she lay there, ice cream in her lap, flipping through channels, she looked down at herself.

"Oh God, he is right, I have put on weight," Scarlett whispered as she rubbed her tummy like she was pregnant. Scarlett had always been confident about her size and body shape since she turned twenty-two. She had always been active and enjoyed eating vegetables, salads, all the healthy food you can think of. She actually hadn't weighed herself since she had been pregnant with Rosie, and even then it was because it was mandatory. She had a bit of natural athletic build to her, but still had the curves of a woman.

Now it was a little more than a few love handles here and there. She must have put on at least twenty pounds in the last three months, which was a lot for her. She had stopped working out and began eating more, treating herself to fun food more often than she should. Scarlett didn't care that she had become a bit bigger, a more bodacious women, but she did care why she was putting on the weight; it was the grief. She had gone to food as her comfort and support when Jonathan was nowhere to be found. She had created this emotional connection that she had never had before, and she did not like it.

Scarlett had turned on the news before she got up from the couch, about to throw away the ice cream, and what she heard made her freeze in her tracks. The news reporter was announcing that there had been another shooting at a middle school this afternoon, thirteen dead, and the only lead for the suspect was that they were an adult wearing a clown costume, reaching approximately 6'2". They were asking for any information that might be helpful in the investigation and to call the number displayed on the screen. Before Scarlett realized, she had already plunked her butt back into the dent of her cushion, and had finished what remained in her ice-cream tub.

"I guess I will start tomorrow," Scarlett whispered as she wiped the tears off her cheeks, turning the TV off and heading for bed. She knew she would probably just lay in bed for the remainder of the early morning, checking to see if there has been any new information on the clown culprit, or maybe she'd get started on her email for tomorrow.

Chapter 16

After Halloween, the next morning Jonathan came to pick Rosie up. He waited in the car, giving two quick honks to indicate that he was there. Scarlett guessed he wasn't over their fight from last night. *If you could even call it a fight,* she thought.

In their eighteen years of marriage, they never fought, maybe bickered, but never raised their voices at one another. Last night was probably the first time Scarlett ever raised her voice at Jonathan. Usually they were able to discuss their problems, eventually see eye-to-eye after Scarlett explained herself; she was the one that would have to open up if they were to get over their predicaments.

They had worked as a couple, Scarlett with her planning, schedules, organization, Jonathan with his more easy-breezy, going-with-the-flow personality. It was also their harsh qualities that brought out the best in each other, one person stepping up to the plate when needed. If Jonathan was really agitated, or starting to finally get riled up over something, he would make a big scene, go over the top, acting irrationally. It was his spontaneity that made him act out, but Scarlett also loved this about him because it meant that he could also be passionate and romantic, which Scarlett had troubles being. Scarlett could also be calm, cool and collected, listening to everything someone has to say, helping them work through their problems with a clear and level-headed mind, making her shine in the workplace and with children who needed an adult to hear them out.

Unfortunately, over the past couple of months, Scarlett had begun to see herself lose control. She was no longer organized, forgetting things she had planned several months earlier. She was also only seeing Jonathan's irrational side, if any side of him at all.

For the rest of November, she didn't see him, only a few phone calls and honks at the front door, letting her know he was there. Scarlett could tell that their conversation had irked him. He had not even turned around to talk to her during their conversation on Halloween night. Like every man, Jonathan had his tells, and one of them was that when he was upset or something was really getting to him, he would look in the other direction, not daring to show anyone his emotions.

Jonathan had always been a good husband, a good man, kind, caring, and passionate. But he always had a problem with opening up, letting anyone in. He was a good listener for a short period of time, but not a good talker, which was one of the reasons why he never became a counselor himself and decided to follow his passion and became an English professor instead. He loved reading, talking about the metaphors he could find in novels, what authors actually meant, and the definite meanings of every story.

Jonathan also didn't have the patience to deal with someone's problems for several sessions. He thought people should be able to get over their problems after talking about it once. He couldn't understand why people needed to keep repeating the same things over and over again, to finally move on from what they were going through. Jonathan was a clean-cut type of person. He was able to just accept things and work through it on his own, unlike Scarlett.

Scarlett would go through life-changing experiences, death, heart-ache and never bring it up, not wanting to talk about herself because she would rather talk about someone else's problems. It was almost her way of healing, helping a client grieve helped her grieve. And then there were times where she would bottle something up for too long, before exploding, needing to talk to her husband about it at once, getting the advice she needed. Then she would go to her friends and share the story she had been trying so hard to ignore.

Scarlett liked how her husband was clean-cut, revealing everything at once, and saying what needs to be said and then moving on. She didn't like to repeat herself to the same person, talking about the same problem for days and days when she would rather be talking about someone other than herself. It made it easier for her to open up to her husband about anything and everything because she knew it would be dropped, not being used against her in the future.

However, Scarlett also knew that Jonathan's cut and dry ideology wasn't always a good thing; he could be irrational, making up his mind quickly with no hesitation. Like how he wanted a divorce, something Scarlett thought was so final. Scarlett couldn't understand his reasoning behind this. It was one of the many thoughts that raced through her head, keeping her up at night.

Scarlett and her husband were a team, and like all teams they had their struggles, but they had never given up, especially so quickly. But now, Jonathan was ready to throw their eighteen years together down the drain, Scarlett could not begin to fathom his logic behind his decision. It had maybe been only two rough months after the shooting that lead him out. Before June 8th, everything between them was good, they were happy, they were a full family.

The more she thought about her husband that month, the more Scarlett wanted to call him, let hell loose on him. She wanted to tell him that him filing for divorce was his form of a temper tantrum. She wanted to also explain how he was not being supportive, or how he was not there for her or Rosie. Well, she knew that last bit was a lie, but she still wanted to let him know how he was being irrational. When Scarlett got fired up, she wanted to say hurtful things that she knew were not completely accurate, but it was her way of getting her husband to show some emotion.

The nasally voice that had been coming and going in Scarlett's head told her that her husband was acting like a brat. "He is huff and puff, storming around, stomping his feet," that saying was familiar but she could not place it. And it did have a point, her husband was acting like a child.

Scarlett chose to ignore the voice in her head, along with her desire to call Jonathan. Instead, she put her mind on decorating her house. Rosie loved Christmas, the decorations, the lights, the food, the family dinners, and cookie nights – it was her favorite holiday. Scarlett decided to outdo herself this year. She knew it would be hard for her family to get together, but she thought if she turned the house into a winter wonderland, even though it never really got cold in Cali, that it would help turn some frowns upside down.

Scarlett bought Christmas pillows to stuff the couch and Christmas stockings to line the fireplace. There were faux red poinsettias placed randomly throughout the house alongside red and green ball ornaments. Scarlett wrapped Christmas garlands along the railings, intertwined in red and green lights. She bought a long thin strip of white faux fur, which she laid lengthwise across her dining room table, putting candles and a velvet poinsettia centerpiece on top of the soft material. Her dark wooden dining table contrasted the white fur, making the decorations really stand out.

The finishing piece was Rosie's favorite snow globe that Scarlett had bought with her when she was six, but Scarlett could have sworn that this was the tenth year she was putting it out. She didn't think about it too hard, and instead, out of habit, she shook it and then turned the snow people counter-clockwise, one full spin, making the snow globe come to life. This was a very unique decoration, which had the typical Santa Claus and snow people decorating a white and green Christmas tree. They looked jolly and merry as Santa was frozen in place acting as if he were placing his gifts from his sack under the tree and one snow person was adding finishing touches to the snowman, wrapping him in a red and green scarf. The globe was encased in a blue and white Christmas scene. There were trees, snow, tinsel, red ribbons, woodland critters, igloo homes, lights, reeves and snow people dressed in mittens, Christmas hats, and big jackets to keep their snow hands warm. At the bottom of the big globe, there was a little cave between the globe itself and its blue and white surroundings. In this cave, there was a hollowing where two snow people sat by a fire, waving at the other snow people who circled them. If you pulled the snow people back counter-clockwise, then you would see rabbits, a snow person in a sleigh being led by two reindeer, and a snow person in skies trying to keep up with their friends in front of them. There was also two other snow people, each pushing a friend, who was either on top of a cut tree or sitting in a chair. It was the most delicate snow globe Rosie had ever seen, which was why she had been so fascinated by it. Scarlett was also amazed when she saw the decoration, so much time was put into it, so much detail, and each year she found a new element that she had previously missed.

By December 1st, Scarlett had finished decorating her home, making it a beautiful red and green Christmas themed wonderland. She was even able to put up the green and red lights on the porch this year; usually Jonathan did it, but Scarlett had no intentions on asking for his help when he refused to behave like an adult.

Scarlett had been so satisfied with herself while decorating, she was able to tune out most of the negative news, only half listening when she heard that the clown killer, who had killed the thirteen middle-schoolers on Halloween day, had been found three days later. It turned out to be a middle-aged man who had been experiencing a mental breakdown.

The killer's mom had turned him in after she heard on the news about the information of what the culprit was wearing and what type of weapon they used. The clown and his mother lived a block away from school, so she knew that he had time to run there and back without his mother expecting anything strange. She also knew her son had dressed as a clown that year, and the missing piece was the information about the weapon used, which happened to be the same gun her late husband left hanging on a mantle in the living room. After the son had been brought in for questioning, he apparently pleaded insanity before his lawyers showed up. Due to his easy cooperation and using the defense by excuse in this criminal case, he sounded like he was going to get a light sentencing with several years of counseling and being placed in a psychiatric facility for an indeterminate amount of time.

Scarlett had also only been half listening when she heard about two more school shootings in the United States, which was made a mockery of by a politician. He said, "Bad things come in threes," as if this has never happened before, or that it was something that could be laughed at so lightly. Scarlett was starting to feel like a normal parent again, focusing on the circumstances that lay ahead, and only thinking about the people in her life.

Chapter 17

It was the first day of Christmas break. Jonathan had picked Rosie up early that morning, so Scarlett made plans with Martha and Alex, one last hurrah before Alex left for her holiday.

"We are going to miss you!" Martha said frowning, sipping her green tea.

Alex, Martha, and Scarlett were sitting on the porch outside of Pete's bakery. They were taking in the crisp, cold ocean breeze and were lightly bundled in their sweaters. It was California after all and the lowest it usually dropped during December was 46 °F, therefore they did not have to wear outfits made of fleece like their further-up northern neighbors. Nonetheless, the girls were still acting as if it had dropped below 32 °F, ordering warm drinks, wearing the classic Christmas themed beanies with infinity scarves wrapped around their necks.

"I will be back before you know it!" Alex glowed as she drank her Red Eye, preparing herself for the packing that awaited her at home.

"Make sure you bring your scarves, snow jackets, snow pants, beanies, and gloves," Scarlett always had to vocalize her mothering voice, not being able to resist. "Oh, and pack sunscreen, it would be awful to get a burn!"

"How is she going to get a burn in Canada?" Martha asked doubtfully. She thought Canada was all cloud and snow year round, that every neighborhood had to own a plow truck so that people could get their driveways cleared.

"Because when the sun hits the snow, it can reflect, burning your face," Scarlett explained as she grabbed her face, feeling the non-existent burn already.

"Don't worry, I am always careful with my beautiful skin," Alex giggled touching her flawless face, "I don't think I have gotten a burn before."

"Is it because you are African American?" Martha asked innocently, making Scarlett laugh.

"No, honey, that is just an old wise tale. Black people can get sunburnt too. I am just very careful, and I don't usually go places where the sun is strong enough to burn me," Alex said soothingly. "Besides, I will probably be bundled up, wearing my goggles and ski mask, covering most of my face, and I may even wear a scarf on top of all that! It's going to be freezing so I had to buy a few new things to accommodate."

"Didn't you buy clothes last year when you went up to Whistler?" Martha asked skeptically.

"Well, yes, but this year it's supposed to be even colder."

Martha and Scarlett looked at one another, chuckling silently so as not to be heard by their fashion-conscious friend.

"For this trip, I purchased the Moncler Hellodore, which is this beautiful dark blue quilted jacket, made with Japanese fabric, fitted at the waist to accentuate my curves. It is absolutely gorgeous."

"And overly priced," Scarlett's nasally voiced whispered to her. Scarlett cleared her throat, "What is it you're doing up there again?" Scarlett said, trying to change the subject to silence her pubescent conscious.

"We are renting a cabin up at Whistler again, that way we can go skiing and maybe one night snowmobiling if the girls feel up for it." Alex enjoyed to over-explain herself, she could easily talk about herself for hours. "This will be our fifth time going, we started this tradition after Jackson turned two. Back then, I just cozied up with him by the fire, snuggling all day and night until he got bored, then we would go to the Coca-Cola Tube Park in Blackcomb. It was close enough to the Fairmont to walk if it wasn't too cold outside," Alex continued to explain every detail about her stay in the beautiful British Columbia ski resort over the past several years. She talked about how she thought the snow was absolutely beautiful, making Christmas feel more traditional, the way it is supposed to be. She also mentioned how they are getting Jackson skiing lessons this year, so it will be his first going down the mountain.

Alex explained why she never took Jackson out before, that she didn't want to be one of those parents skiing around with their baby on their back. She couldn't help but think of all the things that could go wrong if she fell, if she crushed him, if they got chased by wolves. When it came to her children, Alex was the most concerned mother you ever met. She would try to play it off, act cool in front of them, but the moment they were out of earshot, she would call up her friends about all the possible scenarios that could happen if they were to go surfing, biking, or were to participate in any other outdoor sport. She loved being active but preferred the more gentle sports, like walking or yoga, nothing that involved going somewhere where she might be mauled by an animal. Skiing was the only sport she allowed for her family to do together that involved "pressure on her joints," as she would like to say as her excuse for not participating in the adrenaline seeking adventures that her husband enjoyed so much.

As Alex began to explain to the girls about how Darryl wanted to go on a zip line expedition with the whole family, and she would simply not allow it, Pete came out from his warm bakery, holding three plates of freshly baked cinnamon buns. Scarlett had told herself that she was going to cut back on the fun food, but she simply could not resist Pete's pastries.

"Here you go, lovelies," Pete said in his charming accent, eyes holding onto Martha's, "Now let me know what you think, I have added something new."

Things must have been going really well between the two of them for him to change Martha's recipe. She was very possessive of her recipes, not thinking anything should or needed to be altered. And if someone were to dare make a comment, she would tell them she had spent her life baking, perfecting, sweating, and bleeding over these recipes to make them flawless – every pastry coming out divine. Either Martha encouraged Pete to try something new with her recipes, or that he had no clue what he had gotten himself into – Scarlett hoped it was the first one.

Alex and Scarlett gave each other a questioning look as Martha took a bite from her steaming roll. Martha had once told the girls that she didn't think she could ever get mad at Pete, he was just too cute and sweet, but a Scottish accent could only save a guy so much.

"It is delicious," Martha exclaimed, whipping the cream cheese frosting off her ruby lips, "The flavor seems more enhanced, a little bit sweeter, but without being too sweet, I also feel like I can really taste the cinnamon."

With Martha's approval, Alex and Scarlett took two delicate bites of their pastry. They both thought it tasted amazing, but just as amazing as it always had, nothing seemed different.

"I used unsalted butter and added fine grain kosher salt instead of salted butter. I thought it might really help heighten the taste of the cinnamon. I am really glad you like it." Pete was glowing; it even looked like he relaxed his shoulders after receiving Martha's approval.

Everyone went to Pete's because of his pastries; he was a pure genius when it came to flavors. His tea and coffee were good but nothing special. It was the rolls, buns, pies, donuts, sweets, and everything in between that brought in the herd of customers. Even before Martha worked there, he had delicious baked goods, everyone knew about his coffee shop, even celebrities had been reported to stop by now and then. When Martha started, there was an average of 50 customers a day, which was really good for a locally owned coffee shop, more so a bakery, but Scarlett couldn't deny the wooden sign posted on top of Pete's shop door. Now there were about 80 customers a day and the number was still increasing. Most people came and went quickly, while Alex, Scarlett, and Martha appeared to be some of the few who knew that the patio had a small table looking over the water. People were too busy rushing around during their busy lives to notice the side door leading to the welcoming deck.

Scarlett thought that she had been possibly missing something regarding the new and improved cinnamon bun. Perhaps her taste buds had weakened, because she couldn't taste the difference Martha was now raving about. Yet, when she looked over to Alex, she noticed that she had been chewing very slowly, as if she was also trying to decide if there was anything unique about this cinnamon bun compared to the countless ones she had eaten this past year.

I guess it's a baker thing, Scarlett thought, *Maybe that is what makes them good, what brings in the customers, the tiny details that bring out the flavors, things us regular people wouldn't even think of or notice.*

As Pete said his goodbyes, leaving the girls chewing in silence, Scarlett noticed that him and Martha were really two peas in a pod. They were both outgoing but had their shy moments, shared their ancestry with the Scottish – Pete was actually from Scotland, not looking the part, while Martha was not from Scotland, but looked the part. They were natural leaders, well-liked, easy-going, charismatic, charming, bold, and had sociability, self-confidence, and assertiveness. They also were funny and genuinely happy people, always wearing a smile. And their attention to detail was immaculate, Pete and Martha were always the first to notice a haircut, a new shirt, and apparently the tiniest change in a recipe. The only thing Scarlett didn't know about was if Pete was as unorganized as Martha. She really hoped not, she could only handle one person running late for everything in her life, she didn't think she would be able to take on two.

"Damn! Look at that tush!" Alex practically screamed once he was inside. She was always faithful to her husband, but she still enjoyed to appreciate a good-looking man when she saw one. "Is he going to be keeping you warm this holiday season?" Alex asked in her best news reporter voice.

Scarlett and Martha erupted into laughter. Sometimes Alex's free and sensual spirit became a bit much for Scarlett, making her laugh and blush, but Martha was always down on the same level as her friend, making sexual and even slightly crude comments. Either way, both women would end up laughing like they were teenagers who just made a sexual joke about their newest hot substitute teacher.

"Oh, he will be keeping me very warm. He has actually decided to close down the bakery from the 22nd to the 3rd of January."

"Shouldn't he be going home to visit his family?" Scarlett asked dumbfounded, assuming that every other person in this world has a stable relationship with their parents, or that their parents would be guilt-tripping them into visiting.

"No, he decided to stay here this year. He said he saw them last year and that was enough family time for him for the next couple of years." Martha laughed. "He is the youngest of 4 boys, or men I guess. He says he doesn't get along with his brothers, he was always the shortest and smallest one of them all, so they would pick on him the most. Even his parents don't seem to mind that he is not going out there this December, their hands are full with all their grandchildren. Pete is the only one who doesn't have any children."

"Not yet at least," Alex said, nudging Martha.

"Slow down, you naughty reindeer." Martha enjoyed getting festive with her name calling. "We are taking things slow. Yes, he will be spending a lot of time with me and Delany this holiday, but no sleeping over or anything, at least not when Delany is home. I don't want her to get too attached, just in case." Martha had still been putting her daughter first, but she has gotten better since their conversation on Halloween.

Baby steps, Scarlett thought.

"But don't you worry," Martha began to explain as she saw Alex's face turn at the very idea of abstinence at the young age of thirty-four, "we will have plenty of date-nights just the two of us, if you know what I mean," Martha said winking. "Scarlett offered to take Delany on playdates so we can get some alone time."

Martha had called Scarlett three days ago, asking her what her plans were for the holiday. She had been treading lightly during their conversation, as if she were walking on eggshells. Scarlett had decided to not make of a fuss of it and bring it up, so she let it go, allowing her friend to dance around her questions, buttering her up slowly before asking her if she would be interested in taking Delany for a few days here and there.

"It will only be one night at a time, and I would have my phone on me so you can call in case of emergencies or if she becomes too much to handle," Martha said over the phone. Scarlett told her that she was being ridiculous; it would be no trouble at all and Delany was never too much to handle. Scarlett had started noticing over the past couple of months her friends acting like she was fragile, telling her not to take on too much or that she should never feel obligated to take care of all the three kids by herself, which she had done countless times before.

With a quick dismissal, Scarlett reassured Martha that she would be happy to take care of Delany for as many days as she wanted. She even joked that she would be happy to adopt her as her second daughter, which caused a bit of awkward tension on the phone that was quickly brushed off once Scarlett changed the direction of that conversation.

"Things are going really well," Martha said as she plucked another piece of cinnamon bun into her mouth. "He is kind and sweet. Honestly, the nicest person I have ever dated, which is not saying much, but still," Martha chuckled, "And he is absolutely amazing with Delany. They adore each other and it's the cutest thing I have ever seen. The three of us have only hung out a couple of times, like gone on dates together and stuff like that, but he was also a big part of her life before we even started dating. When I would come in for my short shifts on the weekends, I would bring Delany and he would help her with her homework." Martha paused as she took another sip of her tea and unraveled the cinnamon bun just a touch more. "I am just unsure of how it will all play out, him being my boss and everything. If things turn for the worst and we do end things, I won't be just losing someone I… really like, but my job too."

"Oh, honey, don't you worry about that," Alex said while she put her hand on top of Martha's. "When Darryl and I started dating, I am sure he was nervous about all that too." Darryl had originally began working under Alex at a fancy law firm until he later joined her side-by-side, now both of them running the firm together.

"But I also think that is what makes it more exciting and thrilling. You are both willing to throw the lives you live up in the air, willing to give what you have a chance, while acknowledging that it might change everything. You may lose your job, him his best baker, money-maker, and a lot of his clientele, and he would probably even have to move away, afraid of me and Scarlett coming after him." Alex was not the violent type, but she was like a momma bear when it came to her friends and family.

"But, honey, it is honestly so worth it. To start a family with someone you love, to be part of someone else's family. I had put everything on the line, if I were found out then I would have lost my job, it doesn't look good when the boss sleeps with the intern, but for Darryl I would do it all again, even though he may be a little shit at times," Alex laughed.

Alex began talking about her and Darryl, and the most recent and ridiculous battle they have had at home. Alex could only talk about someone else's love-life before quickly switching the conversation to her own. Scarlett was not sure if she did it on purpose, but she never minded, nor did Martha. They both would become so entertained about her talking about her and her husband's disagreements. Her friends thought it was hilarious seeing her get so riled up, when most of the time she put on her Buddhist persona.

The most recent debate Alex had with her soul mate was about whether or not they should be buying any more straws. With the new bill in act, Alex believed it was best to make their contribution for the cause and simply stop purchasing them. She said, "That way they will stop producing them all together, no more straws in our ocean and one less thing polluting our streets." Darryl on the other hand thought it was absolutely ridiculous, and that they shouldn't be trying to get rid of something small and insignificant, but instead they should be focusing on bigger things like carbon monoxide poisoning in the atmosphere and decreasing green-house gas emissions. "He just doesn't see the big picture, that every small thing counts," Alex argued.

As Scarlett's friend discussed the most recent ecological trend, Scarlett thought about Christmas. She thought about all the presents she still had to buy, what to get for who, who wants what, trying to decide what she should plan for her, Delany, and Rosie to do during their playdates and so on. Jonathan had told her this morning, instead of waiting in the car like he had done for the past month, that he was coming early Christmas morning to make breakfast and to spend the day with Rosie; he hadn't plan on missing it because "It wasn't the weekend," he had said. Scarlett was glad that he was going to be there but hurt when he went straight for the defense mode. She tried to let it go and focus on what lay ahead of her – the frantic shopping. She actually only had Jonathan left, forgetting how small her family was.

Trying to distract her own reeling thoughts, Scarlett brought herself back to the conversation Martha and Alex were having about plastic straws.

"Darryl believes it's the animals' fault if they eat the plastic," Alex said, "but I think they just don't know any better. They are used to a world where they can eat whatever they find on the ground, and if it was too hard then they would spit it out. Now there are thousands of different plastics that make it back into the environment, like straws. And an animal isn't going to know any better; it's going to think, hey what's this, and then put it in its mouth. Then it will die because of the poison in the plastic."

"The animals are actually attracted to the smell of plastic. The biofouling of microplastics produces smells that attract seabirds, because it smells like DMS-producing algae, which is why they eat it, they think it's food." It was Scarlett's nasally voice speaking out again, but this time it gained an audience. "It is the PCBs in the plastic that attract the animals. And it is what causes them to die. The PCBs disrupt endocrine systems, such as the thyroid, which is critical for the brain and body development and can cause immunotoxicity, reproductive impairment, and affect animal health like lipid metabolism and energetics."

Alex and Martha look up at Scarlett with surprised, questioning faces. Scarlett was never the one to pull knowledge out of thin air, that was what Alex did, but she also was never the one for knowing science facts, such as the reason why animals ate plastic. Scarlett was not the type of person who you would find reading a peer-reviewed science article while sipping her coffee in the morning.

"Where did you learn that?" Alex sounded a little hurt, she was the one who was the most informed out of the group, giving the answers to everything and anything.

"I learned it from the Nature Channel, I think they were talking about it a few days ago. Rosie just loves that show," Scarlett lied. She couldn't remember where she heard it from, just that she had been reading it over someone's shoulders as they read it out loud off of a science article about PCBs affecting the endocrine system, leading to the decrease of many animals, especially ocean mammals.

Scarlett didn't know why she didn't just tell her friends the truth, maybe it was because the way they had been treating her lately, as a fragile delicate bird. She didn't want to encourage their behavior, letting them know that she had started hearing a voice in her head, telling her things for about several months now. Or maybe it was the way they looked at her right now, gawking at her, doubting her credibility. Scarlett had the urge to prove them wrong, to tell them all the other things about the particles in plastics mimicking hormones, causing animals to become sick or die. Her urge to lash out was childish; it felt like her teen angst was coming back alive after all these years, but it seemed to be brought on more by the voice than by her own feelings, she didn't really care if her friends believed her. She also didn't really care about why the plastic was affecting animals, more so that they were simply affecting animals and that should be enough to limit the use of plastic in society.

Scarlett began to feel more uncomfortable after her little outburst and attempted to change the conversation back to Martha and Pete, unfortunately not as smoothly as she thought. "When was it that you were needing me to take care of Delany again? Sorry I have been so forgetful lately, I am going to write them down in my phone."

Martha told her the dates questioningly but happily that the conversation had returned to her love life. Now she was able to dive into the details about what they planned on doing during each date.

Scarlett was surprised that her sad attempt to transition the conversation away from her worked so effortlessly. Martha had begun to glow again quickly after talking about Pete's first date that he planned for her over the holidays, which also distracted Alex in the process. They both were suckers for a good love story, even Scarlett felt herself get lost in Martha's genuine joy about the new and only man in her life.

I guess him and Martha are getting along really well after all, Scarlett thought, *It is truly adorable how they look at one another, with such love in their eyes.* Scarlett was not sure if they had said those three life-changing words, but she knew that they did feel that way about one another, you could tell by the way they acted around each other, how they looked at one another. They were in love and it was beginning to make Scarlett feel emotional. *You should leave, you don't want them to see you like this, they will get the wrong idea, thinking you're upset about that stupid plastic conversation, or how your love-life is slowly being drained empty*, Scarlett encouraged herself to tell her friends goodbye and head home. There was probably something important on the news about upcoming politician meetings for gun rules and regulations, or maybe she had a pile of laundry to do while she flicked through the channels, trying to find something proclaiming any movement in changing the Second Amendment to the United States Constitution relating to guns.

Chapter 18

I can't believe it's already been 2 months since I wrote last! So much has happened.

I guess I should get started where I left off. I had gone to Duncan's party, sometime in November. It was the best night of my life, it was what I had imagined a high school party to be like and so much more! There were drinking games, chugging contests (which I was surprisingly good at), and all the free booze a kid could ask for!

His house is a complete mansion! It has 5 bedrooms (not as many as I had thought but still!), 6 bathrooms (each bedroom had its own bathroom and then there was one downstairs), a heated out-door pool, which also illuminated different colors at night due to the effect of the lights built inside it. His place is absolutely gorgeous! He has a foosball table, a ping pong table, and a karaoke machine all in his games room, which is like the size of half my house! There was also Rock Band for his PlayStation, which I definitely spent most of the night drunkenly singing to, still managing to kill every note.

All in all, it was great night full of laughs and giggles, leading to my first hangover the next morning. I spent the night at Ashley's so I wouldn't have to explain to my parents why I got home so late reeking of booze. Ashley told me her parents don't really care, she says her older sisters were such rebels that she is able to get away with almost anything.

Also, Duncan's and my relationship had progressed really quickly once I started attending his games. After he would score a touchdown, he would blow me a kiss to where I sat in the bleachers, he drove me wild! When I came to his party, he grabbed my hand the second I stepped through his door, introducing me as his 'girlfriend' to everyone he walked by. I would have thought he would have asked first or that there had to be an official first date, but there had already been a first kiss (after he won a really important game, I don't remember who it was against because I never paid attention, just more interested in catching up with my new friends who weren't on the football team or on the field cheering). I didn't really care, I was just so excited to have finally got my first boyfriend, even though I am sure I had probably called him my boyfriend in elementary school when he wasn't around.

Unfortunately, our young love didn't last. We had been dating for about a month, I guess you could say he had hit every base, but lacked the home run, and it seemed to be getting to him. He would pull the whole "come on baby, it will be quick," or "I will barely put it in" acts, but each time getting denied with "I am not ready," or "mine/his parents will be home soon." No way I am going to lose my V card and have either one of our parents walk in on us! At my house you never know, especially since I am the one who usually has to babysit Tulip. And I just simply don't know if I want to lose it to him. To be honest, he doesn't have much going for him.

He hasn't been offered any position to one of the college for football teams, I don't think he is good enough to make it, and frankly that's all he's got. Yes, he is devilishly good looking, and yes, he does come from a wealthy family, but his personality really doesn't do much for me. I had no desire to tell him I loved him, and he didn't seem bothered enough to try and pretend like I was the one for him either. I was also starting to get annoyed with his constant begging, pleading, just to put it in once. Do you guys not understand no means no? He didn't even want to use a condom! I am not stupid, I know that he's gotten around at school and I've got no clue what kind of STD he could be carrying. I just think I could do better for my first time, even if Duncan is really good looking, I need a little bit more than that.

I know I am talking all this smack about him, but he was surprisingly the one who dumped me! I was just along for the ride and I felt like there was no need to end it if we were both having fun, which we were. I am still confused as to why he broke up with me, it's not like I did anything wrong, or at least nothing I can remember.

We were at one of his parties, the first one and the last one that I brought Denise too. It took me a while to convince her that these people were no longer the bullies they used to be. So that night I happened to have too many drinks, and like the good boyfriend Duncan was, he was carrying me to his bed, that way I could sleep it off. Next thing I know, Denise comes running up the stairs yelling at him. She completely went nuts, practically dragging me out of there. Duncan yelled at her, calling her names and stuff, and I don't really remember the exact details, but I do remember him yelling at me, saying it was over. But I didn't really believe him, like why would he break up with me because Denise was acting bat sh*t crazy? So after Denise practically carried me to her house and I sobered up, I texted him the next morning, asking if it really was over, and he told me yes! I really don't know why he did it, and maybe I will never know, guys are crazy.

Oh well, there are plenty of fish in the sea, right? Besides, I have a growing list of potential suitors Ashley and Emma are trying to set me up with, but I think I am going to stay single for a little while longer before I dive back into the dating pool.

I was originally really bummed out about Duncan and I, because this also means I no longer had a prospect date for Homecoming and all of the other exciting events that really matter for seniors. But that stuff is still a year away and so much can happen in a year.

I also didn't really start getting over the whole breakup until Eliza and I recently started hanging out more. She showed me that I don't need some arm candy to have fun and go to parties. And yeah, I might say that there is plenty of fish in the sea, but Eliza has taught me to say screw the sea, hang out with your besties instead.

Eliza and I just met for the first time last week, and we have been inseparable ever since. She is on the math team, a real brainiac, and people love her for it! She is always herself, cool, smart, and confident. It's hard to not like her. She is also very kind and has even hung out with Denise and I during a class we all have together. Denise was hesitant at first, she automatically hates all the popular kids without trying to get to know them, but I think she will warm up.

Also, Denise and I still have not been really talking since Duncan's party, she looks at me differently or something, so it's nice to have Eliza there to fill in some of the gaps during our class. Denise seems to be getting weirder and weirder as the days go by, but I don't really care, if she doesn't want to talk about it then I am not going to force her to. It's strange though because we used to tell each other everything, but since I started hanging out with the popular kids, Denise acts like I have changed, when I know I haven't. But oh well, I am making new friends and if she wants to stay, great, but if she wants to go then I am not stopping her.

Back to Eliza's and my new friendship: we have started to hang out almost every single day after class, now that Denise hasn't been asking me to go to her place. I am still seeing Ashley and Emma a lot, but Eliza is more friends with the kids who are part of the academic teams, not the sport ones, so she doesn't talk to them as much. I would say Eliza is more so an acquaintance of theirs, even though they still sit at the same lunch table but on different ends. And with Eliza's impressive academics, she is more so a part of the smart popular kids group, whereas Emma and Ashley are a part of the athletic popular kids group.

But they still all go to the same parties and sometimes hang out in big groups on the weekend.

I know Eliza and I have only just begun being friends, but I think she is probably my best friend right now, I trust her more than most people, including Denise. Ashley and Emma are great, but I guess I still haven't forgotten everything they put me through, even though I do try. With Eliza, it's like a fresh, clean slate, no beef between us, which makes it easier for us to share things. I am not sure if she feels the same way though, she is well liked by everyone, constantly surrounded by people, and it's hard to read her at times. I am just happy that we are getting along!

Oh, and as I was saying, Eliza helped me really get over Duncan by showing me how I can have such a good time without him. I hung out with her and all her girlfriends one Friday night instead of going to Duncan's football game which became sort of a routine over the last month or so, we all went to her friend, Olivia's house. Olivia is also a super nice girl! She is a cheerleader (a smart one though), but she sprained her ankle, so she couldn't make it to the game and decided not to sit outside freezing her a** off (which the cheer captain was not happy about). So we went to Olivia's house, it was me, Olivia, Eliza, Claudia, and Tiffany. I had a blast! We just ate Twizzlers, Salt-N-Vin Kettle Chips (my favorite), Pop Tarts, and even had some Dunkin Donuts. We really pigged as you can see. And then we binge watched Parks and Recreation*, which I have never seen before. I can now tell you it's my all-time favorite show! Eliza told me when everyone gets back from their vacation, before school starts, we can continue where we left off, I think we are on the 3rd season now.*

Eliza also told me how her and the other girls that were at Olivia's house that night, had made a pact for their senior year to not go to Homecoming with any guy, but instead to rent a limo together. She had this idea after the whole #MeToo movement that is going on with the celebrities, she said it's the time of women, that we don't need men to show us a good time, and that we can have fun on our own! She even invited me to join her and her friends! Of course I said yes, I knew I would have guys asking me out, but as the saying goes 'hoes before bros.' I am also so excited for Homecoming, I know it's still like a year away, but to have friends that want to go with me and make plans with me that far in advance, it just feels nice! They make me feel important.

I also realize now that Denise actually held me back from a lot of things, it was never me who didn't want to go to the parties or to Homecoming, it was her, it was always her. I just followed her around like a lost puppy, just wanting to stay 'unnoticed.' And boy have I been living the past 15 years of my life wrong! I now want to be noticed, I want to make a musical career, I will make a musical career, and I want to finally be heard! I want to tell people, not just my family, but my friends, and anyone else who is willing to listen, about my views and opinions, my stories that will help them through heartaches, breakups, and bad days.

I know it's not Denise's fault that I didn't get invited to any parties or dances when we were younger, she didn't hold me down against my will, telling me I couldn't go, but still, I think she can share some blame for it. I mean, if I had gone to parties and left her alone on Friday nights, without anyone else (she was an only child after all), she would have gotten lonely, gotten mad at me for 'ditching' her, which would have been completely unfair. But whatever, now I can move on to bigger and better things. I feel like if Denise doesn't try with me, then I am not going to try with her. I have new friends, ones that are kind and caring, not selfish and self-centered like her.

Now another aside, I just want to say that I absolutely love writing in my journal! It's so helpful when I just need to rant to someone and I feel like no one would understand. But at the same time, it would be the end of the world if Denise were to see this, she would think I am talking sh*t behind her back. And Denise, if you are reading this, just remember I still care about you, girl! You are still one of my best friends, and sometimes I say things I don't mean, but I need to say it to get everything off my back. And whatever happens between us, remember we have all those fond memories from our childhood, I will never forget how you were there for me when no one else was! You also helped teach me how to be strong and not care about what other people have to say because I had you, my 'ride-or-die' partner. But if we are drifting apart, that is okay too, we no longer share similar interests and goals. We are going to enter the real world soon, and we will most likely go our separate ways. Remember, I still love you! And you will always have a place in my heart.

Hm, that actually sounded pretty good! Maybe I will write something like that in her yearbook next year or something. What I said was true, I do love her, and she will always have a special place in my heart, but she still is driving me crazy lately. And you never know what could happen, or what the future holds, like I said I am learning to go along for the ride.

Oh and I nearly forgot, now that theater class is close to being finished, I am heartbroken! BUT, Mrs. Cornwall told me that she would like me to help her with the grade 9 students that will be taking theater for the first time next semester, she said I will be titled as the 'Teacher's Assistant,' and that it will be an easy A. She also said that it would look good on my application to Berklee. I said yes of course, and I am a little nervous but I think it will also help me get over talking to strangers and singing in front of unfamiliar faces even more.

I am completely over my fears of singing in my theater class now, but these are all faces I recognize. There is Josh sitting in the back with his dark hair covering his eyes, and there is also Emma, Ashley, Denise, Sasha, Chantal, Janette, Erica, Michele, Kyle, Mike, Jack, Phil, Britt, just to name a few. Most of the students are football players and cheerleaders, I think they all want to be famous, but we have created such a special bond with our 'Mug-Up' days, always learning about people's plans and some of the exciting things they have done recently. They are the faces that I now picture when I sing at home, I guess out of habit. It will be sad parting ways with them, but I think I will try to convince some of them to take theater again next year, just because it was so fun!

Mrs. Cornwall also told me that she would like to continue giving me singing lessons for the rest of the year, and that she would help Emma, Ashley, and I pick a song to sing at the end of the year talent show! She said that I have picked up everything she has taught me so quickly that she thinks I have a natural talent, and she said that she has never seen a student like me before. I nearly cried when she told me all of this good news! Everything is going exactly how I wanted it to, and so much better at the same time. For once in my life I feel complete joy! Yes, there have been hiccups here and there, but I am just so… I don't know, maybe fulfilled that I will be able to do what I love most in this world, that I will able to sing and show people how good I am.

Oh and I nearly forgot, something very strange happened on the last day of school before the break. Denise and I still were not talking that much, like something nasty was still in the air between us. So I decided that I would at least try to say something nice to her, at least before the holidays. Yet, when I tried to talk to her, she had shushed me. Who f**king does that? It's so rude. Yes, I was whispering because the teacher was talking, but I was trying to be nice! And that has never stopped either of us from talking to each other during class before. I was beginning to think that she was purposefully ignoring me. It had just been over two weeks after Duncan's party and she was still acting this strange, I don't understand what I could have done to upset her so much.

Things had gotten so awkward between us after Halloween, regarding her practically calling her dad an alcoholic, but I thought after I invited her to Duncan's party that everything was going to be normal between us again. I highly doubt I did anything wrong, but then again maybe there is something else going on. Maybe she was having some family problems or something. But she could also ask me for help instead of bloody shushing me! And then when the bell rang, she got out of her seat immediately, practically raced for the door to get away from me.

I didn't see her in the next period, which made me nervous for some reason. I just had a feeling that something was actually wrong, I thought that maybe if I didn't see her for the rest of the day, I would stop by her house (so much for letting her come to me), but I was really nervous. Then lunch time came, I was sitting with Ashley and Emma as per usual, then I saw Denise out of the corner of my eye walking towards us. I thought maybe she was finally going to apologize for acting so strange. When Denise approached, I could barely hear Ashley whisper something to Emma, but didn't think it was anything important. Emma hadn't whispered anything back and instead just nodded the second Denise approached our table. Ashley told her the table was full even before Denise opened her mouth, and she was right, the table was full, but Denise looked at me with utter shock and surprise.

I agreed with Ashley that the table was full, because it was, and she stood there, staring at me, like I was the lunatic! I don't even get what I said was wrong! I was just agreeing with Ashley that the table was in fact full. It's not like I was telling her it was the end of the world or anything, more so I was just agreeing with a statement my friend made. Denise smacked her hand down in front of me, giving me a big, cold, brown-eyed stare. She just looked at me in silence for what felt like an hour, it was the creepiest thing. Then someone laughed and with a quick look at the table she stormed out. So much for her apology!

I really don't understand her sometimes, she just gets so worked up over the tiniest things in life. If someone were to look at her the wrong way, the rest of her day would be ruined. Things just get to her like nobody else, I guess you could say she feels more than most people, over-analyzing every situation, trying to figure out why the world was so cruel to her. But it's also her best quality because she cares about you and if you're mad at someone, then she will stick it out with you, being mad at your side. She is the definition of sympathetic, maybe to an extreme at times, for example when I cry she does too, as if she can feel my pain. However, she will also do anything in her power to fix your tears, trying to turn that frown upside down. And some of the funniest moments I have experienced have been with her, if you laugh, she will laugh harder, even if a joke is not funny, and shortly there will be milk running out of your nose from howling so hard.

This was probably just another thing she is dramatizing, blowing it out of proportion, now I will for sure let her come to me first before I try and say anything again. I had tried after all, and I can't really say she did the same, she more so just walked up to me and freaked out. I don't have the time or desire to stress about it either, I am too happy right now and I don't need someone brining me down for God knows why.

And another weird thing about the whole event was that I noticed I was smiling as she walked away. I think I was even laughing at someone's joke, but I didn't hear anyone say anything... That girl is making me lose my marbles!

I later asked everyone that I remembered being at Duncan's party what had happened, thinking that maybe I said something to Denise which set her off. Maybe I do need to apologize, but I just can't remember what I did. But if I do need to apologize, she could at least tell me what I did wrong. Now she may not seem that interested in talking to me right now, but I am still curious what happened. I don't even remember how I got to Denise's house or even what time I got there at. I just remember thinking I wasn't going to drink that much, I had one sip of some big glass bottle of Vodka, and then lights out. I may not remember specific details, but I can recall glimpses here and there, like Duncan brining me to bed so I could rest, and I think I had vomited on him too (poor guy).

I first asked Ashley and Emma what had happened that night. I didn't want to ask anyone right away because I was also nervous that I made a fool of myself in front of everyone and that is why Duncan broke up with me. I also didn't want to sound desperate either, I didn't want people to think I was just asking what happened to try and fix what was going on between Duncan and I. When I asked Emma and Ashley about it after Denise had stormed off, and it seemed like everyone forgot about her for the most part, they both looked at each other and then glanced away, as if they were being asked about a secret, neither one of them being sure if they should share. Ashley told me that she was so drunk she barely remembers what happened, then Emma stammered right after her, avoiding eye contact, saying the same thing happened to her. I asked them if anyone put drugs in our drink or something because I was pretty sure we all drank from the same Vodka, and it was weird that none of us remember the night. Ashley and Emma were more classy drunks, they would only have only a few shots, staying away from beer or fruity drinks (they said there was either too much sugar or calories in them). They never blacked out or forgot things they had seen or said the night of a party, which is why it made the night even more strange.

They both looked at me baffled, offended that I would make such an accusation. They told me that it was only our friends at the party, no one was slipping drugs into our drinks just for sh*ts and giggles. Ashley got up from the table and Emma followed her, they were obviously hurt by what I said, so I apologized later and they seemed like they had forgotten all about it. They told me that they both just needed to go to the bathroom before class which is why they got up. I guess I am used to Denise storming off when I say something wrong that I now assume I have hurt someone's feelings if they walk away all of a sudden.

After school, before everyone left for their family vacations, I decided to ask one more person about the party. I know I couldn't ask Duncan himself, he would probably just tell me nothing happened and that things were just not working out between us, then stammer off about his football career or something, he is very self-obsessed (good riddance I say). So I decided to talk to his right-hand man, Sasha. Sasha and Duncan are almost inseparable, their moms are identical twins, who happened to get pregnant at the same time, so the two of them grew up like brothers. Unfortunately, Sasha got the short end of the straw, he was not good at athletics, and not very bright nor pretty. I mean he is still a good-looking guy, just no Duncan, no super model, simply average. He is also very shy, timid even. I also rarely see him talking to the girls the way Duncan does, now that I think of it he usually is either sitting beside Duncan or sitting alone. I bet he probably just coasted on by, getting help from his cousin, kinda similar to what Denise and I had going on.

I found Sasha sitting at the front doors after the bell rang, freeing us from our prison. He was sitting on the grass near the front doors, so that he could see all the cars, probably waiting for his mother. When I came up beside Sasha and sat right beside him, he seemed very flustered, not charming and charismatic like Duncan at all. I said hi to him and tried to warm him up with some small chit-chat about plans for the holidays. I didn't want to go straight into asking him about the party because that would be rude, and he would think that I had gone over there just to ask him that question (even though that was all I was interested in). After a couple of minutes, when I felt like it was the right moment to strike, I asked my question.

He didn't look around, avoiding eye contact like Ashley and Emma, he actually looked a little angry. He turned to face me and asked what I remembered about the night. I told him, a little embarrassed, that I didn't even know how I got to my friend's place nor how many drinks I had, I had only assumed that Denise hauled my drunk a** to her place. He had put his arm on my shoulder, smiling, before taking it off very quickly, the smile vanishing with it. I hadn't pegged him for the touchy-feely type. Then he told me how some things were best not to be remembered.

I had thought for sure I must have made a big fool of myself! And I must have looked terrified because he quickly assured me I hadn't done anything to embarrass myself. He said that he actually saw Denise struggling with me, trying to carry me, but mostly drag me down the stairs. He actually even had helped her bring me back to her place! He said he hadn't been drinking so offered to give the two of us a ride home. Denise was apparently reluctant (no surprise there), but she probably realized that she wouldn't be able to carry me and all of my love handles home.

Sasha then tried to transition the conversation towards Denise! He asked me how she was doing, and what her plans where for the holidays (he didn't even ask me about my own plans). I could tell that he is totally into her! Denise has never had a boyfriend and is not the typical girl who would believe in cheesy romance, but this could be good for her! Her first boyfriend! I even teased him about being into her, and he didn't even deny it! I totally see it now too.

Denise is loud, not very shy, more so unsocial, while Sasha is quiet, very shy, but super social. Yeah, he is only seen at school with either Duncan, who is usually surround by a flock of people, or alone, but he attends all the parties, all the dances. Sasha probably enjoys going out, being around people, but enjoys listening more than talking. They are total opposites, which is why I think it would work so well between the two of them! I would love to play the love guru here, but Denise still hasn't talked to me, so I am not going to mention it until she apologizes. And who knows if she would actually have the courage to even go on a date with Sasha, but I hope she would! It would help her soften up towards Ashley and Emma, and maybe she will finally see what I see in them, good people.

After saying my goodbyes to Sasha, he grabbed my hand before I walked away. He told me it was probably for the best that Duncan and I broke up. He said that Duncan is a narcissistic prick, who usually gets what he wants. I was shocked, I thought they loved each other like brothers.

Since I started hanging out with them more, and when I was dating Duncan, I saw Sasha a lot, never actually talked to him, but he was always there. He would laugh when Duncan made a joke, whisper things into his ear when no one was looking. They seemed like best friends. Duncan had actually even told me that Sasha was a quiet guy, but a great dude, a true best friend. It was probably the nicest thing he ever said to me, even though it wasn't about me. I think it was the only time he had actually complemented someone else.

I thought Sasha felt the same way about Duncan, but I guess not. Come to think of it, since the party I haven't really seen Sasha. I no longer see him eating lunch with us. I haven't seen him in the halls, leaning on his locker, laughing about something Duncan said. Maybe something happened between the two of them at the party too.

I nodded and agreed with Sasha before turning away, I was free of any responsibilities for the next couple of weeks and I didn't feel like listening to someone telling me what not to do. Besides, I had other plans.

Ashley, Emma, and I got together later that day to start making some song covers that we are going to post on YouTube. It was Mrs. Cornwall's idea, she thought it might help me get discovered, just like Justin Bieber! She said to post a video at least once a week of my favorite songs. She thinks it's best when I sing with my emotions, to sing to music I understand, and can relate to. Mrs. Cornwall also meant for me to be doing it alone, but once I told Ashley and Emma about her idea, they wanted to help me, and I couldn't say no to extra help!

The first song we posted was Female by Keith Urban. The second song was Bodak Yellow by Cardi B, which was Ashley's choice. She told me that I shouldn't be selfish, and her and Emma get to have a say on the songs we sing together. I don't think she understood what Mrs. Cornwall was wanting from me. Now don't get me wrong, I love their song choice, but I can't rap! I am no Nicki Minaj or Cardi B! I am more of a soul singer. I sing from the heart, mentioning issues in today's society, such as inequality, and maybe mentioning a bit of romance here and there.

On the other hand, the girls were right. I shouldn't be selfish, everyone deserves a chance to pick a song that they want to sing to. It would also be good practice for me to try singing different songs or along with other tunes, such as ones I am not used to. It's also a good idea to sing different songs so we have a wide selection to choose from when we pick what we would like to perform at the year-end talent show. We also need to pick a name for our talent show group, we were thinking maybe something catchy like 'California Girls.'

Oh, and Christmas and New Year's just happened! Ashley, Emma, and Eliza had gone somewhere where there is snow with their families, like Whistler or the Alps (depending how much their parents' make). And in the meantime, I have just been stuck at home babysitting. I could have called Olivia, or one of the other girls I have been hanging out with, who are a part of Eliza's crew, but none of us have ever hung out alone, which makes me think that it would be kinda awkward. Besides, I am such a homebody, I think it will be hard for me when I start going on world tours, performing at concerts. Luckily there is Skype and FaceTime! It's just *a matter of showing my dad how to work it, he is the not the tech-savvy one, whereas my mom can't seem to put her phone down.*

I have enjoyed my Christmas and New Year's at home with the family, partaking in the classic traditions such as Cookie Night (where we bake cookies, make gingerbread men/women with ginger bread houses), having Eggs Benny on Christmas, and the banging of pots and pans on New Year's. But my mom has been on her phone the entire break!

My mom has been telling me that I need to spend more time at home with the family, as if I am the one has been missing dinners and game nights. I think she is just bitter because I am starting to get an actual life, and it's involving her less and less. And I still make it to all of the important family events! She's putting all of her flaws on me, as if I was the one who interrupted Christmas dinner to take a work call, because god forbid someone else's life was on the line (I don't mean to sound harsh, but you would understand if you knew my mom).

It's not like she has changed or anything, she is still my mom (I love you), but she has just been so busy! I have barely seen her this Christmas break. It has been mostly Dad, Tulip, and I home together for the past two weeks. We've indulged in board games, card games, a little bit of Xbox, and have even gone for strolls on the beach. Where has my mom been during all of this you might ask, she has been on the phone or computer, or at work, always working. I liked it better when she worked less, driving me and Tulip to all of our practices, team meetings, and school. Tulip has all the practices, she is a little social butterfly with her close-knit friend group. What I am trying to say is that my mom used to make time for us, now it's work first, the typical cliché daughter-parent problem.

I was even hoping that this year for the holiday we could go away somewhere. I know my parents could afford it, and I have never experienced a white Christmas before! There is just something so magical about the white powder on the ground, reflecting the bright shining light, as you stay warm and cozy by the fire, sipping hot chocolate and opening gifts. That sounds like the perfect holiday to me!

I think my mom just feels like she is needed here more, close to work, where she can answer any important phone call or urgent messages. Maybe when I get the money from selling my albums, I will take my family on a real vacation, to somewhere we have never been before, where there will be 3 feet of fluffy snow, as if it was just for us. I will buy plane tickets for my dad and sister, but then tell my mom she is only allowed to come if she can leave her phone behind. She would be livid! But it would be worth it! Maybe she will finally realize how big of a workaholic she has become.

On a more cheerful note, now that I have mostly caught up, it's still Christmas break and I have only a few days left! We are going to finish Parks and Recreation *tomorrow (everyone calls it* Parks N Rec, *but I feel like it sounds funny if I don't say it's full name). We are going to start early in the morning and stay up late for as long as we need to. Olivia said the only break we can have will be for the bath-room or grabbing more food. She also explained how she had run to the grocery store earlier this week and is stocked up on all of the necessities. I will let you know how it ends! Or maybe I shouldn't in case someone else is reading this, I wouldn't want to ruin it for them...*

Ta Ta for now,
Love P

Chapter 19

Dear Mr. President,

It's Christmas morning, the sun is shining on the West Coast and it is absolutely beautiful. I am hoping to get outside with Rosie, to go for a brisk walk along the beach, taking in that crisp air.

Right now it's 5:08 AM, too early for Rosie to be awake. The house is silent, too silent. It feels like any moment I am going to hear the sound of a gun crack, forcing multiple bullets into the air. Did I mention that I still hear the awful screams and cries that occurred that warm June afternoon? Did I ever tell you that if my house is quiet enough, I can make out the echo that the gun made as it shot its final victim?

I am usually not the only one up right now. My house used to be warm and cozy on Christmas morning, filled with laughter as we stuffed presents under the Christmas tree, completing the finishing touches. I guess I am still trying to get used to all the important things missing in my life, trying to adapt to the changes as best as I can for my little girl. I need to do what is necessary to make Rosie happy, to make sure she is not affected, or as little as possible considering all the circumstances.

But I also need to make sure I don't lose her too. I need those gun laws changed. I need this to happen to feel safe, to feel like my child can go to school, grow up, have a family, or not, it's her choice, but I need to make sure she gets the chance to live. I am sure that I am not the only parent who thinks this way. I am sure there have been countless lives altered from the creation of guns, and the brining of guns into homes and schools, letting them out into the world to destroy innocent lives.

Like most people, I am praying for a Christmas miracle. I need you to take the first step, the step to recovery for our nation. We need to salvage what we have left, the remaining lives, the remaining innocent children who have not yet been corrupted or affected by guns.

For one moment, can you think about what it would be like to be them? To be the teens, hiding in the library, terrified for their lives. To be the elementary students undergoing lockdown, crying in front of their classmates, or having to go to the washroom in garbage bins in front of their peers. To be the teachers, wondering if they will have to put their lives on the line to protect their students, or a single student. To be the parents who have lost a child from a bullet that never should have been shot, or to be the children recovering from PTSD, wondering if they will ever be able to live a normal life again, or if they will forever be in fear. We could also start more simple, imagine yourself being a friend of someone who had lost their friend or child, imagine what they are going through, what they are trying to say to comfort their loved ones.

You are supposed to be our leader, our guider, our counselor, we have chosen you. And what have you done? Nothing. I see no improvement or changes in gun laws, no reduction in the number of gun violence seen on the streets. There has even been an increase in the number of school shootings since you have been in office. Is that a coincidence? Or correlation?

I have heard the promises you had made after the massacre at Stoneman Douglas High School, leaving 17 people dead. You promised immediate action, as well as changes to a number of bills. But what happened? Nothing. Simply nothing. Your promises have become meaningless to the public, we need a response, we need you to take action.

You are smarter than what most people think. I can tell that you have played us from the beginning, like most politicians, giving us promise of change, of hope. And then when it really matters, you turn your shoulder and brush us off, telling us you never guaranteed anything. You have manipulated us since day one, and I am afraid how much further you will take it, how much further the public will allow you to take it, or take us.

We need change for the better, an improvement, but all I see is us going back in time. We are becoming more righteous about our prized possessions, our guns, ammunition, and killing machines. It seems like we are taking steps back even on other manners, such as equality, accepting African Americans, Hispanics, differing sexuality, people part of the LGBTQ community, practically anyone who does not belong to the upper class of a white male.

I am not trying to pin all the blame on you, like I said we are allowing it to happen too. We were the ones who voted you in, or maybe we didn't, but either way we must rise together to protest what is right and wrong. We must defend the children, the innocent people of the United States, and we must do it as a team. No person in history has ever single-handedly done something themselves. Humans rely on each other, if we like to accept this or not, we are a part of a social species.

It is on all of us to make a change, but why haven't we yet? Where are the other parents of this great nation? Where are the people who have not been affected? Are they ignoring us, ignoring what our society is becoming, more interested in social media, about what some famous celebrity did? Are they focused more on wealth and greed?

Am I the only parent who still cares? Or are there others bombarding you with emails, trying to do their part to help make a change?

Then it comes back to you again. I wonder if you care about the shootings, or is it something you pay little attention to. Are you too busy with other "political business," or updating your Twitter page? I may be a silly mother to you, but try to imagine if it was your child who was shot, your friend who was killed, what would you do?

Sincerely,
Scarlett Smith

Scarlett briefly skimmed her message, checking for spelling mistakes before hitting send. After 198 emails, she no longer cared if she was redundant, inconsistent, or simply rambling, she just needed to write something, anything.

Chapter 20

After Scarlett sent her daily email, she sat on the couch, sipping her coffee out of her white and black 'Best Mom Ever' mug that her daughter bought her several years ago. She was still wearing her red and green stripped pajamas she bought from Nordstrom Rack last year specifically for Christmas. Scarlett was cuddled up to her big white, soft fluffy pillow, staring at the presents under the tree.

She found it crazy to think that ten hours ago Martha had come over to wrap gifts, while her mother watched Delany. It was the first time Martha and Scarlett saw each other since the two of them and Alex met at Pete's bakery, before Alex left for Whistler. They had only seen each other in passing as Martha picked up or dropped off Delany. Martha had been so busy either working, Christmas shopping, going on dates with Pete, and doing Christmas events with her parents and her daughter, that she didn't get the chance to catch up with Scarlett until last night.

***

"He is genuinely amazing. He is chivalrous, funny, intelligent, kind, empathetic, an active listener, interesting, giving, and very committed, but yet not too committed that he makes me want to run away. He gives me the right amount of attention, without being too clingy. And I can't get over how good he is with Delany." Martha paused to collect her thoughts. "I was always nervous about dating, being a single mother with no dad in the picture and no time off from my kid. I also thought that some guys might find it hard to handle Delany being a part of the whole package. I thought if a man in my age range was single and had no children, then that meant he wouldn't want any, or that he didn't like them. I think that is why I didn't date for so long. I was afraid of falling in love, telling the man of my dreams I had a kid, and then him backing out."

"He wouldn't be the man of your dreams if he ran away just because you said you have a child," Scarlett reminded her.

"I know, but back then, when I was younger and naïve, I didn't know that. I also didn't know how to tell someone I was a single mother. Was there a rule I hadn't been told that I have to wait so many dates before I tell the poor chump I've got a kid, or was I supposed to tell them on the first date, or even before we start dating. And what if they couldn't see how amazing Delany was, or maybe she would hate them and then I would have to break their heart, telling them that it wouldn't work out. I love my daughter and would do anything for her, so if she didn't like someone then he would have to go. It has always been her and I against the world. I know my parents have been really supportive, but it had still felt like it was just the two of us, until I met Pete."

Scarlett always thought that Martha was the type of single, independent women who didn't need nor want a man. She knew that Martha could get nearly any guy she wanted; she was good looking, funny, charming, witty, intelligent, loud at times, but with a good heart. Martha had everything you would want in a partner. Scarlett never realized how lonely Martha had been. She had been the only single one out of their friend group – Scarlett refuses to think of herself as a single mother. Martha had gone to all the family barbeques at Alex's with the kids running around, husbands chatting, and not once did Scarlett think about how Martha felt being the odd one out.

Martha had embraced the single mother attributes so well that she was able to mask her loneliness and her desire for a boyfriend. Alex and Scarlett had even talked about how good of a job Martha did, all alone, working, taking care of Delany, making it to all of the school meetings, events and organizations, mind you she looked like a mess at times and was always late, but that seemed more like a part of her personality instead of it being because she had to do everything alone. Well, not completely alone, like she said, she had her parents, her over-supportive mother Gail. But she also had Alex and Scarlett, who would do anything for her. However, just because someone could manage being alone, did not mean that they wanted to be alone. Like most people in this world, Martha wanted the love, admiration, and support that only a lover could provide, and she had finally gotten it.

"He has been supportive since the beginning. He always catered to my needs, giving me flexible hours to drive and pick up Delany from school, or giving me time off to make it to the parent-teacher meetings or school plays." Martha was beginning to really glow with excitement as she talked about her new love-interest. "He has also been so encouraging with my baking. I thought that with me starting at a new bakery, where I was no longer head baker, that I wouldn't be able to explore my creative side, that I would be held back my someone else's recipes, and I thought my bossiness and ideas would get in the way. But not with Pete; he inspires me to be artistic and imaginative with my creations. He even has told me that I am not demanding or bossy, but that I have the qualities of a true leader, that I am inspirational."

Martha told Scarlett how her relationship was continuing to progress, and that she was learning things about Pete that she had not known before, such as the crazy habits that he had. One such habit being how he liked to tap the roof of his truck when he drove through a yellow light. Martha also told Scarlett about all of the things she was learning about that Pete hates, such as when everyone assumes that he loves soccer just because he is from the UK, or even how when there is a rainbow outside the bakery, people would come in doing their best impersonation of a Scottish accent asking "Where is me lucky charms?"

Martha also delved into the details of the dates she had been on in the last two weeks with Pete. They had done picnics, walks on the beach, and watched the latest movie with Leonardo DiCaprio. She talked about how they stopped at Pete's bakery to make some cinnamon buns before going to Martha's parents' house. Scarlett was a bit surprised to find out that he had already met the parents, but then again the way her friend was glowing, it looked like this was more than just a crush. Martha reassured Scarlett, reminding her that they were taking it slow and it was only for a quick visit. Scarlett thought it was best to let her friend figure out her feelings in her own way, better to realize yourself that you have fallen madly in love instead of being told by someone else.

"When I brought him to my parents' house the other night, Gail asked what his plans where for Christmas day. When he told her that his family was all back home and he did not have any plans, her face lit up in instantly," Martha chuckled, as she wrapped her last gift at the dining room table. "You should have seen it, she had been so quickly charmed by him, taking him by the arm, showing him around, it was like she had never seen a man before. And where was my dad during all of this you might ask, stuffing his face with the cinnamon buns, nodding in agreement with my mother. I felt so embarrassed, like a teenager who brought over their boyfriend for the first time. I was sure he had plans with friends or something else, but to my surprise he said he would be delighted to come. He is actually going to come over tomorrow before lunch and make me and Delany a surprise meal. Pete said he is not only an excellent baker but a chef too."

With all of this talk of taking it slow, not wanting to put too much pressure on the relationship for their sake and Delany's, Scarlett couldn't help but laugh at her friend who was diving into this relationship head first, as she wrapped her last gift, which was a book of all of Pete's favorite recipes, ones that he already had and others that Martha never shared with anyone. With a quick tie of a bow, Martha was out the door, practically jumping with excitement at 2:00AM.

**

Scarlett had been awake since Martha left, sitting and thinking. She felt like something was missing from her Christmas, family maybe? Rosie was sound asleep upstairs, but her empty house didn't feel right, it felt sad and lonely, but Scarlett thought maybe she was just projecting her own feelings into the quiet open space.

Scarlett and Jonathan both no longer had extended families; their parents were dead – well Jonathan actually never knew about his father but presumed him dead. Scarlett hoped that when Jonathan showed up, her house would feel right again, but she knew that wouldn't be the case.

Scarlett and Jonathan decided a month ago that they would try to keep as many Christmas traditions as normal as they possible could this year. Jonathan would come home to make breakfast, open gifts and then they would spend the remainder of the day together like a proper, functioning family. Scarlett was happy that Jonathan was coming home, she couldn't imagine Christmas without him and just assumed he would be there. It wasn't until he told her that he was coming, did she realize he had thought that he was not welcomed. She still didn't understand why he was not back home yet, she still missed him, wanting him back in bed, but she was also no longer in the mood for begging or questioning his actions. She thought if this was going to be how her husband coped, then she would let him grieve in peace, no more pestering, no asking why he left her, or why he won't come back.

Scarlett sat in silence only for a more few hours until Rosie got up. She came running down the stairs, shouting at everyone to wake up because it was Christmas, sadly forgetting the house was empty. Luckily, Jonathan arrived shortly after his daughter bombarded down the stairs, not giving her enough time to soak in the quietness and the reasoning behind it, unlike her mother who had been bathing in it all morning.

Jonathan began to unpack his groceries into the fridge. When Rosie ran towards him, he picked her up and threw her into the air. "Good morning, sunshine, are you excited to open presents?"

Rosie nodded and giggled as her dad carried her towards the living room.

"Me too, so what gift would you like to open first?"

"No, Dad, we need make Eggs Benny first, remember? It's a tradition!"

Making Eggs Benedict was a tradition Jonathan started after being shown by his college roommate, who was from Victoria, British Columbia. They had shared this tradition for four years until Jonathan built a home and a family, who he now makes Eggs Benny for every Christmas breakfast, with a little bit of help of course.

"Oh how could I forget, I will get right on it, but you can open one gift before we eat if you like," Jonathan said wiggling Rosie around, trying to distract her from his attempt to change the subject. "It will be a new tradition," he said.

Rosie freaked out, fussing in her dad's arms,

"No I want to keep all the old traditions, everything, I want to keep it!" she practically screamed.

"Okay, love, how about you and I take some pictures in front of the Christmas tree dressed in your PJs? Alex and Martha told me that Jackson and Delany would be doing the same thing," Scarlett said as she went to grab her baby from her husband's arms. "Wow you've gotten bigger or has Mommy just gotten weaker." Scarlett huffed and puffed, exaggerating just a little bit, as she cradled Rosie in her arms like an infant. "My baby," she said as she nuzzled her nose into her daughter's neck.

"MOM! You are being so silly," Rosie giggled, quickly changing her temper.

With a quick glance in Jonathan's direction, Scarlett and Jonathan went separate ways to carry on their tradition as best as possible, leaving only one major part missing.

Jonathan unpacked his groceries to get breakfast ready as Rosie took a quick photo in front of the tree before racing into the kitchen.

"Dad, can I crack the eggs?" Rosie asked as her father began prepping for breakfast.

"Of course, sweetie," Jonathan passed his daughter the eggs while Rosie dragged one of the black bar-stools to the kitchen counter.

Scarlett leaned against the kitchen doorway watching her husband and baby girl waiting for the water to boil in their pot before cracking the eggs. Her husband started to show Rosie his technique to limit as many shells as possible when breaking the eggs against the counter before pouring them into the pot. Jonathan told Rosie to use the countertop instead because it had a harder edge than the side of the bowl, making it easier for a clean break.

Scarlett was beginning to think that everything was feeling normal, or as normal as it could be. It felt like Jonathan had never left, the way he was making his way through the kitchen effortlessly like it was his own home, because it was after all.

Scarlett had grown tired of questioning her husband's actions, but there was that nagging voice in the back of her head again, not willing to give it a rest. "Why is he willing to throw your marriage of eighteen years down the drain?" She agreed that it did not make sense, she still loved her husband, supported him, and cared for him even though she was certain most women in her position would not let their husband back in the house after abandoning them like the way Jonathan had done to her.

Scarlett still couldn't understand why he left. She always thought she could read him, know where he was coming from, but this was something she never expected. "Maybe you had gone delusional, hadn't seen the marriage fall apart? You have to stop pretending like you know everything." Scarlett wasn't sure if she agreed with that reasoning.

Was it possible that her subconscious understood why he left and has even already forgiven him, which is why she still looks at him with loving eyes?

"Maybe if you actually listened to him, instead of shoving your beliefs and ideas down his throat then he could explain himself." Scarlett's nasally voice was getting fired up today.

The idea of divorce was what really threw her for a loop. She could possibly understand him moving out, needing some space, or possibly marriage counseling if things were not going the way they should be, but to actually file for divorce is a whole other dilemma.

Jonathan had moved out of the house in August, filing for divorce in September. He had told her about it only once he handed her the fresh, crisp papers, asking her to sign them. He acted like it was supposed to be something simple and easy for her to do, as if she was not signing away part of her life she had spent the last eighteen years planning.

They had talked about the renovations they were going to make to the house, or the idea of another baby had also popped in their minds over year ago when Scarlett started to feel her clock ticking away. They were going to move to a smaller house once the children and/or grandchildren moved away. They were supposed to be a family, which would get bigger and bigger with time.

What could cause someone to file for divorce after living out of the house for only several weeks? Had Jonathan finally had the last straw with her?

"Maybe he met someone new? Has been getting his needs met somewhere else," the voice interrupted her thoughts, sounding like a teenager who just found out their parent was having an affair.

Scarlett had never been the jealous type, she had always known her husband loved her and would never leave her, or at least she used to think that way. But she also could see how women looked at him, giving him that second glance as they walked down the street.

Jonathan looked more like a high-class businessman, who was well-educated, born from a good-looking family, and had the time to take care of himself, working out and staying active, he only lacked the business attire. His blonde hair and dark brown eyes drove the mothers crazy, along with his sharp jaw line that suited his straight nose. He had thin lips that nearly disappeared when he smiled, which Scarlett thought as humorously adorable.

He also kept a little stubble on his face at all times, refusing to be perfectly shaven. He did not resemble the average English college professor, except maybe one of the ones in the movie who is extremely gorgeous and for some reason decides to get with one of his students, even though he can clearly get a good-looking women his own age.

It was not only Jonathan's ravishing good looks that made him such a catch, but his personality as well. He was outgoing when he needed to be, charming and sophisticated. He never gave away too many of his personal details, keeping himself intriguing and mysterious. When he decided to shine some light on his personal life, it made you feel special, unique, like you were the only person he has ever trusted to share this type of information with. Jonathan was good at making Scarlett feel special, the way he looked at her, the way he talked to her. She would feel his eyes meet hers in a crowd, or his fingers easily interlocking with hers.

Scarlett had known they made a good couple. They were both kind, educated, caring, passionate, optimistic, and shared all the qualities that make a well-rounded person, but they also shared hobbies, tastes, desires, and they wanted the same things in life. Scarlett had never seen any flaws in their relationship in the past, sure they had their squabbles here and there, but nothing major, and most definitely nothing to get a divorce over.

Then Scarlett remembered the women over the past several years who had shown a slight interest in her adorable husband. She knew there would be many contestants lining up at Jonathan's door after finding out he had left his wife.

There was Joana from work; she was younger than Scarlett, just as pretty, but smarter. She had her PhD in molecular biology and taught during the same times as Jonathan, leaving their lunch breaks open at the same time, which was how they ended up meeting. Scarlett had met Joana several times. She always seemed nice, but the way she looked at Jonathan made her feel a little territorial.

Then there was Xana from next store. She was a single mother who had everything planned out. She had her calendar planned years in advance, making Scarlett feel a little spooked out when she would go to her place for playdates, seeing all of her post-it notes across her multiple calendars. She was a lovely woman, an amazing mother of two children, but she had her obsessive compulsion about certain things, such as planning, and being on time, just like Scarlett, but was more of an extremist. Scarlett didn't think Xana seemed like much of a threat, but Scarlett also knew that she had a big crush on Jonathan. At all the parent teacher meetings and school functions or events, Scarlett would see Xana go straight for Jonathan and start a long and deep conversation with him.

"Maybe he is gay?" the voice asked excitedly.

Maybe they're right. He hadn't found someone new, but had realized he was gay. He constantly had men hitting on him too, either at Pete's bakery, out for dinner, or at the local pub. Alex always did say, "He dresses like a fashionable gay man." Scarlett imagined her spending all night talking about clothes and the latest fashion trends with her husband, or talking about the attractive men in their most recent binge-watched TV show. Would they become the cool hip couple who created a family before the husband realized he was gay?

"That is so stereotypical," Scarlet's voice sneered.

No it's not, I am just joking, and besides it's a compliment.

"That is not the point."

Hush, Scarlett silenced the voice as she had done so many times the past couple of months.

Scarlett continued thinking, trying to decide if it would be better or worse finding out Jonathan was gay vs. him having found a new girl. If he was gay, she would still love him, but slowly over time it would probably turn into a loving friendship. If he found someone knew, she would still love him but grow to hate him, or at least that is what she thought because that is how it worked for most people.

Scarlett also knew her husband the best. She knew he wasn't gay, nor had he found someone else. She knew she would be able to see her husband differently if he thought that way, or notice him look at her differently. She knew he still loves her, he still had that look in his eyes when he spots her in a crowd. It may only be slight glimpses she catches, but it is there nonetheless.

Scarlett knew there must be some other reason why he left and some stupid reason why he was filing for divorce, which was why she had not signed the papers yet. Jonathan may not be good at diving into the details about his feelings and emotions, but Scarlett believed if there was someone new or that he realized he was gay, then he would tell her.

Scarlett also didn't care for his reasoning, she just wanted her husband home. Jonathan may be behaving like a child, acting in a tantrum, over-reacting about something she did wrong, but she didn't care. She wanted him home.

"Mom, why are you frowning? It's Christmas, everyone has to be happy on Christmas," Rosie pleaded as she grabbed her mother's hand, directing her back towards the Christmas tree.

Scarlett didn't notice her facial muscles acting without permission, or that Rosie had finished helping with her dad so now it was time to get the plates set up.

"Sorry, love, Mom is just being… silly," Scarlett said as Jonathan raised his eyebrows at his wife's back, as if he was thinking to himself, *Is she really going to break down here.*

Rosie and Scarlett went to the dining room to place the plates and cutlery at their designated spots as Jonathan brought in breakfast from the kitchen.

After breakfast, Scarlett washed the dishes as Rosie dried and put them away, she didn't see the point using the dishwasher when it was just three of their plates. Then the three of them sat in front of the Christmas tree, grabbing their gifts to hand to one another from the huge pile.

Scarlett handed Jonathan an oddly shaped gift-wrapped in Iron Man wrapping, she thought it would be funny after he dressed up as Tony Stark in his full plastic costume on Halloween.

Jonathan smiled with pure sincerity when Scarlett handed him his gift, Scarlett thought that smile alone was enough of a sign to indicate that he still loved her. He unwrapped his gift slowly, as he has and will always do with all the presents he received. This was his way of building up the anticipation, making Rosie giggle as he slowly and delicately peeled off the tape, then the strings. Finally, Jonathan pulled his gift free, revealing to his family what he had received, which looked more like a child's toy then a grown adult's. It was a wolf golf cover; it was gray and fluffy, resembling something out of a cartoon.

"Thank you," Jonathan said with an earnest face of appreciation as he held Scarlett's gaze, the first time he had looked at her in months for more than just a few seconds.

"You're welcome," Scarlett replied. She knew that Jonathan would like it; she couldn't remember why, but when she saw the picture of wolf on the internet when she had spent hours searching for something golf related for her husband. Scarlett handed Rosie the next gift.

Rosie unwrapped her present with all the might and speed a seven-year-old could muster. She was delighted when she reached the end of her maze, turning her prize over in her hands again and again. It was as if she was memorizing the detail of the diary her mother had given her.

It was a brown leather bound journal, decorated with a big tree on either side. It looked like something that belonged in a fairytale, something for an adult to write in during their traveling years, or maybe someone who had sophisticated thoughts that had to be written and remembered. It also did not look like something a young pre-teen would enjoy.

Scarlett explained her gift to her daughter as she ran her fingers across the engraved tree. "This is the exact same journal I had when I was growing up, and I thought you might like one too. You can either write in it every day or when something important or interesting happens in your life, that way one day you can look back at the journal and reminisce about your past. Or you can give it to your children to read. And I know you might think it's boring to write or that it feels like homework, but I know one day you will really enjoy—"

"I love it, it's beautiful," Rosie said fascinated.

Chapter 21

It's me again!

Sorry was that a little cheesy? I still am not sure how to start off my journal, maybe I should begin with a simple "hi" or "hello," kinda like how you begin an email.

Anyways, once again I have been busy, busy, busy! All of last month, Ashley, Emma, and I have been getting together three times a week to rehearse for the talent show or post a new video on YouTube. One day we will pick a song, for some reason it takes like 3 hours for us each to agree on a song, and we usually end up with something in the top 40s.

I would prefer to sing something from the '90s' acoustic genre, or a little bit of soul, anything with emotion and feeling! But Ashley keeps telling me how those songs are no longer relevant, which is totally absurd! I tell her how these classic oldies have metaphors, or have actual meaning, unlike so many pop-culture stuff played today. And the songs with meaning are usually just trying to sell sex and drugs, lacking the heart-to-heart experience.

Ashley and Emma both agreed that no one in today's society wants to listen to a song that needs to be deciphered just to be understood. I am starting to realize they don't know much about music or its recent history. Not every song needs to be understood for what it says word-for-word, it's the sound of the beat, with the instruments playing in the background, along with the lullaby sung by the singer that brings meaning to the song.

If you are wanting a song that means exactly what it says, then you can just look at Bitter Sweet Symphony *by The Verve. It has no subliminal messages, nor hidden meanings, what they sing is what they mean. They sing how life is a bitter-sweet symphony, because we grow up trying to make ends meet by becoming a slave to money, something that has no real value, but is only artificially profitable due to society deeming it so. This is something that people still struggle with in today's society, what the meaning of life is, how we should live our lives, and how we can change, or if we even can change. It is just such a classic!*

But Ashley and Emma would rather sing about some random guy's big dick, or how we just want the party to never stop. I can't relate to any of that, it's just people singing about their sex lives, or artists who just want people to get up and dance. And don't get me wrong, I do love the majority of these partying songs! But I want to sing about something relevant, like child slavery, human trafficking, the corrupt political systems, or the recent struggles with school shootings (that one really hits home for me).

Ashley and Emma would probably just find my taste in music too depressing. I guess I just need to find some current music that speaks to me, something that is discussing today's relevant issues. Something that we actually all agree on!

I keep saying yes to their ideas because I don't want to be bossy or come off as a b**ch, and they sometimes do have a good point. They said that if we play current music, music that is being looked up on the internet, then our music videos are more likely to pop up and therefore we are more likely to be discovered, which is true. So they are technically not wrong, and they are my friends. They are probably just trying to look out for me, doing what they think is best and will help me get discovered sooner rather than later.

Besides, the music videos have been coming along great! We already have 300 views on the first cover we posted! Ashley and Emma think it's a little low, but I think it's wonderful! A year ago I never would have imagined the progression I have gone through and how far I have come! I am so proud of myself!

On our second and third days of meetings, we either write the song that we have chosen down at least 15 times, making sure we have it memorized. Then we sing at least 10 times to practice all together, figuring out who will sing which line and who will come in at which part.

We still haven't chosen what song we will sing for the talent show, but we were thinking something maybe like Girls Like You by Maroon 5 ft. Cardi B, which I think is a pretty good choice. Yes, it's not in my favorite genre to sing, but it has great meaning! It is also something that Emma and Ashley can't stop listening to, they say it's impossible to over play it, so by the time the talent show is here, they know that no one will be sick of it because it's just too catchy. I hope this is true, but we still haven't made a decision yet.

Mrs. Cornwall is also still giving me lessons. She thinks that I should do my own solo act for the talent show. She said that I am someone who can carry myself and that it would be a waste for me to downplay my talent just so my friends can sing with me on stage. She also explained to me how friends in high school come and go, and that I shouldn't change myself or who I am just to fit in. Mrs. Cornwall and I have gotten very close over this past year, her opinion matters to me, so I wanted to reassure her that no one is changing me, and I am definitely not changing myself to fit in with the crowd.

I told Mrs. Cornwall that I do not plan on downplaying my talent, but the opposite, I want to shine!

And to do so, I need a lot of practice, so I am practicing with Ashley and Emma, but I am also doing it because I enjoy it and I think it will help me get over my stage fright!

I do not plan on performing in a band or anything like that, I want to be my own artist, with no one holding me back, no one telling me which song to play or what to write about. I want to do my own thing, be my own person, and I plan to show this through my music, which is why I want to be on my own.

Don't worry, I know I can't be completely on my own. Of course I will need a band performing with me, playing the instruments in the back. They will be people that I trust and have grown a connection with, people who understand that they are part of my music career, but that they are not people who are in charge of me and cannot tell me what to do. We will have an appreciation for each other, and we will also understand one another.

Mrs. Cornwall also said that I am just overthinking the whole stage fright thing. She believes it's all in my head. She explained to me how I am able to speak in front of the younger students, even teach them singing techniques without a stutter or my face going beet red, therefore I will be fine performing. Maybe she is right, maybe I am just overthinking.

I am constantly told by my parents how shy I am or how I was such a shy child. Maybe part of me is playing up this whole timid persona. I now have new friends, even had my first boyfriend, my first kiss, all this year, and I am only 15! I have probably grown out of my cute, quiet phase. It's like what my mom says, if someone is told constantly who they are, then they are probably going to act like the person everyone believes them to be. And like all parents, mine love to act like they know who I am, my every thought, my hopes and dreams. But also like most parent, they are wrong. They haven't seen this outgoing side of me yet, this new person I am becoming, just like they haven't seen, or heard, my singing abilities.

I still haven't told my parents about the singing lessons or the talent show. At this point I want to surprise them, show them how good I am before they start judging about my future career choice. I also want to show them that I am not who they think I am, my mom can't categorize me like she does with everyone else.

I want to make this happen and it will happen. I just hope that it happens with their approval. I think I have said this before, but my parents are just so old-fashioned sometimes. They believe that you should get to college, get a degree, then get a 'real' job, where you can make enough money to support your family. I understand that you should be able to support your family, but at the same time not everyone needs to get an education to do that. Some people are talented or smart enough to work their way up in this world so that they can pay for food, shelter, and other necessities.

I am not saying that I don't want to go to school, I do, I want to go to Berklee College of Music, where I can practice my singing, song writing, and become talented in other musical areas, such as learning to play other instruments (I have always wanted to play the guitar). I am just trying to say that I don't need to get a business or some science degree to go far in life. I want to be happy, I want to do what I love, I want to sing.

I plan to do the whole touching speech after the talent show, we will probably go out for dinner as a family to celebrate my great performance. I will tell them how much I love them, giving them some compliments, plumping them up just a little bit without being too obvious, and then I dive right in. I will tell them how singing has become such a big part of my life, how I have been filming videos with Ashley and Emma once a week and posting them on the internet, and how many compliments we have gotten. I will also tell them how I have been singing in my own videos as well, some of my own songs and some covers by artists that I actually like. I will also explain how I have been getting lessons from Mrs. Cornwall, who has commented on my improvement and has told me that I am and will be a rising talented singer.

Then I will slowly progress to my conclusion, how I still plan to further my education, but in music instead of law or economics, whatever they had been planning for me before. I will say how I am different, and they have always known that, I was meant for something greater than following society's plan for its citizens to go to school, then get a higher education, get a mediocre job where you get paid enough but not at a satisfactory level, therefore you are always working harder to improve your income, then get a house, a mortgage, but all everyone is doing is dying without living.

I know their plan for me was to eventually end up in court, or write a book, or become a politician, doing something where I am making a difference, where my voice is being heard, but I want it to be heard somewhere else. I want it to be heard on the radio, the TV, the internet, on someone's iPod, or at a concert, giving my heart and soul for my fans, telling them of pain and happiness, how life should be lived, how people should be treated.

If my poetic story does not convince my parents, then I will just have to show them the videos, introduce them to Mrs. Cornwall and get her to convince my parents how I must carry on with my singing career.

I know that adults are usually not good at understanding kids, God knows why, but maybe they will at least listen to my teacher with reason.

Now my parents have always thought that Denise and I would be friends for life (I guess I did tell them this when I was younger), and that we had planned to go to college or university together. Therefore I could also see them trying to play the guilt trip card, asking what about Denise, and telling me that I am bailing on our plans. But life happens, people grow up and move on, and I think I have moved on. Yes, when we were 10 we had planned our entire lives together, how we were both going to get married at 30 after we had gone to school and established our careers, and then we were going to have babies by age 35. Society tells us that we should put a limit, or an age on everything, what age we can drive, drink, have sex, or get married in some states! And Denise and I, being young and naïve, sometimes believed in our society's rules, theories, ideas, and proclamations.

It has been a month since Denise and I have talked. Our classes have changed over, so I don't think we are going to see each other much. After she freaked out at me during lunch that day before Christmas break, maybe freaking out is an exaggeration, but she still acted really weird, she hasn't tried to sit beside me in our classes, nor talk to me. I think she even turned her head when I looked her way. Maybe she realized we are just on separate paths now, me moving on towards a singing career, and her wanting to a be politician, or lawyer, whatever profession she was wanting to do. Don't get me wrong, I still miss her and our Fridays nights, but I have also just gotten so busy with all my lessons, practices, and meetings with Ashley and Emma.

Also, now I am starting to hang out with Eliza and Olivia a lot more. I really enjoy hanging out with Ashley and Emma, but they are just so cliquey. Whenever I am around them, I feel like I always have to be on, I can't just sit and enjoy their company, I have to contribute to their sometimes pointless conversations. Don't get me wrong, they are great to hang out with, a great time, we have so many laughs, and they have really helped me figure out how to make music videos and to post them online, but sometimes I wonder what kinda people they really are.

At first I thought that I was seeing the real Ashley and Emma for the first time in a long time, but now I am starting to second-guess myself. I think I thought I was seeing what type of people they actually are because they were telling me some of their darkest secrets, their hopes and dreams, their ideas about life, stuff that is personal. But since those philosophical conversations (as philosophical as it can get for 15-year-olds), I can see their personalities change. They haven't progressed since I have started hanging out with them, I think it's more so like I am actually seeing them, really seeing them for the first time. Before, I was flummoxed by the idea that these pretty, popular girls, who are loved by everyone, were talking to me, a living shadow, someone who tries to stay in the darkness whenever possible. I was mesmerized by their lives, how important they seemed to be, as well as kind. But now that I have experienced their way of living, going to parties, kissing boys (only one for me, everyone says I am a prune, but I think I just have good taste), I can see through their fake personalities. They will be kind and all innocent seeming in front of everyone, but when it's just the three of us, they will make their judgmental comments as people walk by.

It took me a while to notice it at first, I think it's because they mostly said it under their breaths, but now that they are comfortable in front of me, they say exactly what their thinking openly, and loudly I might add. But not everyone is perfect! I have to keep reminding myself that, and maybe it's just me being paranoid, afraid that they are going to turn on me like they did when we were younger. I guess even after these last couple of months of hanging out, I still haven't gotten over it, even though I keep acting like I have. Maybe Denise hasn't either, which could by why she is ignoring me.

I guess it would make sense that Denise would be mad at me for hanging out with Ashley and Emma, because if you become associated with the devil (Ashley), then you are technically just as bad as the devil himself, or herself. I don't think Ashley or Emma were ever that bad though, they just glared and made comments under their breath here and there. It's not like they never made us a laughing stock in public, like the popular kids did to the geeks in the movies.

I would also never do that! I would never scowl or talk about Denise behind her back. Even the other day, Ashley and Emma had mentioned how fun it was now that we have become friends and have moved on to bigger and better things, leaving that weird chick behind. I had told them that Denise wasn't weird, she was special, and besides, her and I were still friends (which is not entirely true, can you even count someone as your friend when they just all of a sudden stop talking to you?). They got this weird look on their faces, and looked at each other as if they were thinking the same thing, but then they dropped it and changed the subject. It really put me off what they said, I know once again I am probably just overreacting, but it was so rude! Like you don't insult someone's friend who had been there through thick and thin with them over the past 8 years.

There was also that time that they had acted really weird about what happened at Duncan's party the night he broke up with me. The more and more I think about it, the more it bothers me. Denise never talked about it with me either, since for some reason we had stopped talking after it.

I almost felt like Denise wanted to tell me something, maybe I am the one who made a mistake that night, maybe I did something and that is why she isn't talking to me. But if that's her reasoning then that is pretty pathetic! Like you can't hold something against someone who is drunk! Same thing goes for Duncan, if I had done something to embarrass him and he got upset enough to break up with me, then that is also pathetic.

Sasha also never mentioned anything to me again, but for some reason I have been listening to him, I have stayed away from Duncan, he doesn't do anything for me now anyways. I no longer see Duncan as the ultimate hottie, but just some guy I dated. I did really like him, but he didn't break my heart or anything. He was fun to be around, is great looking, and that's about it, I have moved on.

Yet, there is still something about that night that bothers me, maybe the reason why I had left? I remember Sasha said that Denise had gone upstairs to get me when Duncan was putting me to sleep, I just thought maybe she wasn't having fun anymore, but maybe something else happened. I know I shouldn't bring anything up, especially since it has been over for a couple of months, and people would probably think I am still not over him yet, which I am! I would also just rather people not spread any rumors about me, or for anyone to get the wrong idea. I am sure it's nothing, probably just the paranoid voice in my head.

It's getting late, I better head to bed before my mom starts hammering on my door, telling me that I got to go to bed because it's a school night, when we all know that she will be up till 2AM (at least), answering calls from work.

Ta Ta for now,
Love P

Chapter 22

Subject: Email #250

Dear Mr. President,

The other day I was on YouTube, looking up some previous news reports and other clips about gun violence. I was looking for something new, something I have not talked to you about before. And then I came across the song by Childish Gambino, it is called "This is America." Have you listened to this song before? Have you seen it in the media after its release date? If you haven't, then I think you should.

This musician speaks of the truth that is seen but ignored across America. It explains how we treat guns with more respect than lives, how we use them as entertainment, but also as part of our national conversation. Citizens are either fighting, adding to the destruction, or observing, dancing, watching, recording, without trying to help.

The music video opens up with a guitar leaning against a chair in what appears to be an abandoned building or warehouse. Then an African American man sits down on the chair and strums along to a beautiful melody on the guitar. The camera leaves this man, focusing on Childish Gambino standing in the distance, his back facing the viewer. He slowly turns around and starts dancing, making his way to the guitarist, who is now hooded. He positions himself in an odd, dramatic way before pulling out a gun and shooting the man playing the guitar. Children drag the man away as Gambino hands his gun to a teenager holding out a red cloth. People begin to run across the screen and the camera captures more people sitting outside cheap car windows while someone else is driving the car inside the building.

Gambino begins to dance with children, who are dressed in their school clothing. Their moves are sharp and fast, while they maintain happy, smiling faces. The dancers distract you from the fighting and people standing on top of cars in the background.

Next, Gambino enters another room where there is an African American choir singing, reminding me of music from South America. Gambino gets an automatic gun tossed to him and he begins to shoot the entire group of singers. The same teenage boys come up with a red cloth to retrieve Gambino's gun from him. Again Gambino walks away from his violent crimes, a stampede of people following his violent actions with weapons in hand. There is also an empty cop car seen in the background, sirens illuminating the abandoned building.

Then it goes back to Gambino dancing with the children, once again distracting you from the violence in the background. The camera shows a man being pushed off a balcony, while people are running around chaotically for other reasons. Then the screen moves, focusing in on the children watching, filming, and recording the mayhem that is going on around them. The kid, who is filming with his phone, is wearing a mask to cover his mouth and lower face.

In the next scene, there is car on fire, another empty cop car, and more dancing. A person crosses the screen while riding a white horse, dressed in black, and once again hooded. There are more people running in the background. It appears that every person in the music video is an African American, or at least most of them are. Gambino is dancing with the kids still, then he poses, as if to shoot a fake gun, which is represented by his hands clasped together and pointing. This causes the children to run away, and for a moment there is finally silence.

Gambino goes up to the same man who was hooded and shot playing the guitar, and who has also magically reappeared alive, but his face is still covered. Gambino gets on top of one of the dozens of cheap cars and begins to dance in his white gray pants while shirtless. There is one women sitting on the hood of one of the vehicles, having her long, black hair curl pass her mid-back.

The screen then goes black for a moment. Next is the final scene which shows Gambino running, where you can barely make out his gold chain and white teeth. I thought it was the white in his eyes that really stuck out, giving off this terrified expression. Slowly, lights begin to illuminate Gambino running from a crowd of people, who appear to be white; once again it is hard to tell with the faces blurred. But it is also possible that Gambino is running in front of them instead of being chased by them.

I hope from this brief summary that you are able to see the elegant symbolism that was created by this musician and the people that surround him. The guns are handled with care and delicacy, being placed in red cloth as they are passed from the shooter to a child. This illustrates how we treat guns, with the carefulness and respect that is neglected with humans, who are being shot, ignored, or dragged away from the scene. The children in this scene, either having the gun being passed down to them or dragging the body away, could represent how adults are showing children to treat others and how to take care of their weapons, illustrating their beliefs that lives are not as important as this materialistic stuff that surrounds us.

I also see the dancing as a representation of the entertainment Gambino sings of, distracting people from the violent actions that surround them. Some of their moves I recognize from either my kid or her friends dancing, others I am not sure if I have seen them before. But it is Gambino's facial expression that really grabs my attention.

Then the shooting of the choir could represent exactly that, how an African American choir was shot in a church. Unfortunately, this has happened multiple times in the past, such as the Charleston Church shooting. It sickens me that people would perform such heinous crimes out of pure anger because someone was simply born with different pigmentation.

I believe there is so much more to this music video and song then just about being an African American in America, or how our pop culture mixes with violence, slavery, the changing and being able to accept our violent culture and history, and the famous contradictions existing in our society. This brilliant, artistic creation is also about how people treat guns and violence, as well as how we are distracted by the media, our screens, and our society by what is going on all around us. It is also about what we are teaching our children, what they are learning from our actions, or how our society is growing and what it is becoming.

I can also understand that some distraction in this world may be needed to cope with the mess we have made. Our planet is dying while we are still trying to live. One person can only do so much while they still try to enjoy their life. I reduce, reuse, recycle, but I also own a car, my husband owns a car, I rarely carpool, and some days I will go for a drive with my windows down, headed nowhere in particular. This doesn't mean I hate the planet, or that I am the sole purpose for its destruction, I can only do so much. But at the same time, everything that I do counts, including everything that I don't do. What I am trying to do right now is help save our human population or help salvage what we still have left.

We should not be selling these weapons of mass destruction so easily. There must be rules and regulations, like with everything in this world. I understand that people want to use them as their entertainment, to go out and go hunting, or to go to the shooting range and let out some steam, but this is enough.

Numbers are constantly rising. The innocent lives of children, the young, and the old are continuing to be taken by these guns that we hold with delicate care, close to our hearts. We need to start thinking about the well-being of others before we start thinking about what we want for our own entertainment and leisure.

Now, for the people like you that are out there, letting the entertainment drown out the background noise of the violence occurring in our country, you need to listen. Listen to what is happening at schools, on the streets, in your neighborhood, well maybe not your neighborhood, but the cities and towns of the less fortunate. Listen to the people that need you, not the people that don't. Listen to me, to the other pleading parents out there, and stop getting wrapped up in your own drama.

I heard today on the news about you cheating on your wife. It's like hell broke loose. "Is it true, Mr. President?" "Why would you cheat on your wife, Mr. President?" I thought the President would be too busy to find himself a mistress.

Over the last couple of months, there have been less and less conversations and discussions about gun laws. Yet, there has been more mass shootings since you have been in office compared to any other Presidents before you. But the media has dived right into your infidelity and continues to question your decision making while still ignoring the real problem at hand.

No one is talking about the five elementary students who were killed just last week. No one is talking about the hundreds who were and are still affected from their children being killed by a gun. No one is talking about the thousands of innocent people who have died due to the actions of people too young, old, or who were not in the right state of mind to be able to possess weapons, machines that can end tens of lives in an instant.

Everyone chooses to focus on the dramatic lives of others, such as celebrities. They want to listen and watch information about their hookups, their breakups, their past lovers, and their current ones. People have become obsessed with the lives of people they don't even know while, like I said before, ignoring all the negativity around them. There is *People, Us Weekly, Entertainment Weekly, Star Magazine, People Style Watch, OK! Weekly, In Touch Weekly*, and countless other magazines. People are busy either hating celebrities or loving them, treating them like they are royalty. But why can't we look at the lives of everyone as if they were just as important? Why can't every single individual life be treated as if it was something special, like they are one of those celebrities who we mourn the death of, even though we have never met them?

Can we change our ways? Can we make America great again? That is to say that it was even great in the first place. There was, and has always been the stealing of land, then there was slavery, then inequality, and we are still working through our past mistakes. We have had civil rights movements, the American Revolution, the Abolition Movement, the Women's Rights Movement, the Anti-War Movement, and the Environmental Movement. We have been working on some of the wrongs we have done, but what about everything else? The violence, the crimes, the guns, and everything in between.

What is it that holds us back? A document that was written over 200 years ago. Nearly 100 years before slavery ended, or before women began their work towards equal rights. It was written during a period of sexism and racism. People argue that we have the right to bear arms, but do we not have the right to live as well? The right to live in a society where everyone gets the chance to a fair life? Have we not evolved from thinking beyond these words written so long ago? Should we not be continuing to evolve?
Scarlet Smith

Scarlet acknowledged this was the greatest rant she had been on yet, but she was not bothered enough to change her email. Maybe if there was someone actually reading this then they will take her more seriously, or maybe they will just laugh, saying "Here goes another mom on one of her rampages."

Chapter 23

This was the second year Scarlett decided to attend March for Our Lives. Last year at this student-led demonstration, Scarlett had gone with Martha and Alex. They decided that they wanted to show their support for the parents, children, staff, and anyone else who has been affected by school shootings. They had brought all of their children and husbands, making it a family and friend event. Martha had also brought her mother Gail willingly, even though Scarlett and Alex were convinced that she had played one of her classic 'guilt-trips' to get the invite. The children had made their own posters and signs, with some help from the parents.

It may have been held due to the many lives lost during school shootings, but everyone enjoyed themselves. The children were happy to shout, to participate, and get involved. The parents had a few looks of disapproval from other adults, questioning their reasoning for bringing kids that were so young, but they were not bothered. They thought it was a good way to show them at a young age how demonstrations are held, organized, and worked. They also thought it was a good way to show them how people all across the country could get together, unite, and fight for what they believe is right.

March for Our Lives was also so much more than a simple demonstration held in the streets across the world; it had grown into this expanding organization that seeks to abolish gun violence, enforce stricter gun control laws and stand up for school safety, for no one should be going to school worrying about if there was going to be one angry, disturbed, or distraught child, parent, student, teacher, or adult that was going to be carrying or shooting a gun.

This organization had also expanded its horizon past marches, but now were also doing bus tours to register young people to vote. On these tours, they also educated people about corrupt elected officials who refused to stand up for students, for gun violence, and to the National Rifle Association (NRA). They also discussed how some corrupt political people accept and were bribed with money from such organizations.

The student survivors of the shooting at Marjory Stoneman Douglas High School in Parkland Florida, had helped create and get this organization rolling. Now, with the help of parents, adults, teachers, and other students, there was a website for the March for Our Lives organization, where people could also vote. People could reach out to this site and make a difference, to help bring change to the laws and restrictions, or lack thereof, that surround guns and their distribution, sales, and accessibility.

They were educating people about what was going on – no 'fake news' here, nothing but what was seen happening on the streets, in our homes, and on school grounds. They helped illustrate the government's lack of involvement that they continued to falsely promise.

The website provided all of this and so much more. It provided people with the ability to organize a voter drive, informed them how and where they can volunteer, or how they can get involved by starting a local action club. People were also able to sign the petition and find information telling them how they can vote and fight for our lives.

The website said: "Not one more. We cannot allow one more child to be shot at school. We cannot allow one more teacher to make a choice to jump in front of a gun to save the lives of their students. We cannot allow one more family to wait for a call or text that never comes. Our children and teachers are dying. We must make it our top priority to save these lives." They were not completely focused on the students, but also for the adults, every innocent life lost that could have been prevented if we had the rules necessary to stop gun violence from entering schools and public areas. This website was accessible to help prevent and spread the knowledge of gun violence, and how there should be no more shootings at nightclubs, churches, concerts, movie theaters, and airports to name a few. No one, child or adult, should fear a bullet blasting from a barrel, coming for them, promising them the end, the only agreement that is being kept.

Scarlett often found herself reading, and re-reading, the website, trying to find comments, points, or anything worth adding to her emails to the President. She appreciated how the website explained its points accurately and simplistically, even allowing the young to understand what was being said, for knowledge is power. Her favorite arguments or requests that she made to the government, which she gathered from the website were: performing universal, comprehensive background checks; bringing the ATF (Bureau of Alcohol, Tobacco, Firearms, and Explosives) into the twenty-first century with a digitized, searchable database; creating and distributing funds for the CDC (Center for Disease Control) to research the gun violence epidemic in America; having a high-capacity magazine ban; making a ban on semi-automatic assault rifles, which Scarlett believed to be the most important requirement needed to be met.

Even after a year of having the website up and running, a year after the first March for Our Lives, nothing was being met. No government official was being held accountable while they sat back sipping their expensive drinks, enjoying the breeze, and whispering, maybe even shouting fake promises into the ears of the naïve.

Shooting after shooting, and still nothing, not a single piece of paper signed. Nothing but empty promises, but people were not willing to give up hope, which was why they organized another March for Our Lives. Some people wanted to show the government they were not giving up, that they needed to be heard, and that they will be heard.

This year, Scarlett and the girls decided to stay in Los Angeles, that way they didn't have to make a big trip again. Scarlett thought it was also better that they didn't bring the kids this time because of what happened at Pandora; it might affect them too much, bring back traumatic experiences. So they decided to meet up this year right at the beginning of the march before it led to the big stage, where it was rumored that Amy Schumer, Gal Gadot, Reese Witherspoon, Jessica Alba, Anne Hathaway, Mark Ruffalo, Bill Murray, and even Oprah Winfrey were going to speak out about gun violence. It has also been said some musicians such as John Legend and Macklemore, who are against gun violence, will be performing live for the audience. Scarlett thought it was best that she take her own car, in case anything happened at home requiring her attention.

The women met outside of Evoke Yoga, just before 7th street on South Spring Street; it was where Alex often goes to her yoga classes.

Alex was dressed head to toe in black. She wore black high-waisted pants with a black blazer, making the white words 'WE CAN END GUN VIOLENCE' on her black shirt stick out. It was a simple outfit that she made look flawless. Her black ensemble also brought attention to her white sign that proclaimed 'Enough is Enough' in big black block letters.

Alex, being her mostly peaceful self, even had a rainbow peace sign sticker on the top right corner of her cardboard cut-out, adding in some color. She may be the chic modern-day hippy, but she was a woman with great power nonetheless. She rolled her shoulders back, adding to her height, walked with the grace of a model, but had a stern face of a queen who had been wrongfully crossed. If you were to threaten her, her family, loved ones, or the lives of innocent people, she would be ready to attack like a rabid dog, white teeth shining behind her snarled lips.

Martha was wearing black leggings and her gray and red #MSDStrong sweater that she got last year. To Scarlett's surprise, Martha's outfit was perfectly clean, probably the only thing in her wardrobe that didn't have any flour or baking ingredients on it. She had her scarlet locks pulled back in a ponytail, wearing a bit of mascara, making her emerald eyes pop. Every time Scarlett saw Martha, she thought about how the song *Jolene* by Dolly Parton was written for Martha. She was the spitting image of what Dolly described, including her ability to get any man she wanted, if she were to have tried.

Martha being the most brave, bold, and daring out of the three, she held her black sign with big block letters high. It stuck out in the crowd like a red tulip in a field of yellow flowers, telling the government to stop spending the payouts they get from gun companies on strippers, and where they can go shove their heads.

When Scarlett saw Martha and Alex standing outside of the yoga studio, she immediately regretted not wearing the same outfit from last year. For the last March for Our Lives, the three women wore matching red and gray #MSDStrong sweaters, but Scarlett couldn't find hers and had spent an hour looking for it this morning in her messy closet before she gave up. She would have rather been wearing the same clothes she did yesterday than have arrived late.

Scarlett did however miss the big ice cream stain on the front of her white shirt. Although she promised herself to cut back on the desserts, she treated herself to a little splurge last night while she was busy stressing about today. When she rushed out of the front door, she had also did not notice the pair of shoes she had slipped onto her tiny feet, which happened to be her daughter's yellow crocs. Luckily enough, she had her black blazer that she wore to Tuesday parent meetings in the back of her car, which she put on and buttoned up to cover most of the stain. At least she had remembered to do her hair this morning; she put her brown waves into a tight bun. Scarlett thought it would be the most efficient way to look professional, as well as to help get her rat's nest out of her eyes.

Scarlett was usually laid back like a wallflower, being more of an observer, blending in quietly to the background noise that surrounded Alex and Martha. Unfortunately, today she realized she was sticking out more than the other two women in her unique attire of bright yellow shoes, sweatpants, a dirty white shirt, and a blazer to top it all off. Her outfit was not the only thing that caught a passerby's gaze, but her sign, which was not as enthusiastic, creative, or simple as Martha's and Alex's, but more so upsetting and sad. It said: 'YOU ARE NOT ONLY LETTING THE CHILDREN DIE, BUT THEIR PARENTS TOO.' Some people thought it would be too brute, but she thought it was a good way to get her opinion across.

The women said their quick hellos as they began to follow the crowd towards Grand Park in front of L.A City Hall. They didn't really talk, but they didn't need to either, they were there to show their support, yell and shout what needed to be heard, and besides they had met last night to make their signs and discuss the latest news on Pete's and Martha's relationship, how they have said I love you, and anything Alex thought was worth mentioning about her life, which was a lot.

They started chanting with the crowd, proclaiming that the gods, politicians, anyone who could make a difference must listen, that 'Our Lives Matter.'

After marching and reciting with the crowd for half an hour, the girls' voices began to break and crack, their pace slowed, and their fists were getting too tired to be continuously held in the air. Now they mustered a 'yeah' and pointed every time they saw a good poster. They eventually fell in line with a group of older women, maybe ten years older than Scarlett, who Alex quickly began to talk to.

In the group, there were three spunky gray-haired women who wore matching blue and white sweaters that said 'MARCH FOR OUR LIVES.' They looked like they belonged in Hollywood with their designed lips, blonde hair, which was worn in different styles, wrinkle-free foreheads, and caked-on faces. Scarlett was in awe of their Hollywood glamor; she felt like she had never seen anyone so done up before, making her feel more insecure about her outfit choice, hoping the women wouldn't notice her youth crocs.

Scarlett was so busy sizing them up, watching them and their celebrity-like glow, that she only barely heard them ask Alex if she had known anyone who passed away in the eleven school shootings that have occurred since the last March for Our Lives. Alex and Martha looked at the ground, for once remaining silent.

After Scarlett processed what the women so bluntly asked, she said, "Yes, we have all lost someone important in our lives from a bullet that shouldn't have been fired." Alex and Martha raised their chins in unison to look at Scarlett, surprised how she answered their question with great ease as if it was not a topic they had been dancing around all year.

"We all lost our grandchildren over a year ago," said the woman who introduced herself as Carol. Carol was the only one out of the women who had her flat blonde hair falling past her shoulders. Scarlett thought the women must be over a decade older than her, their makeup and surgery making it hard to tell how old they were.

"That is actually how we all met," chirped the woman in the middle, who introduced herself as Leanne to Alex earlier. Leanne looked like she had the least amount of work done out of the other two women, and she styled her blonde hair in a half up and half down bun, revealing some of her gray roots.

"It's crazy the things that bring people together," finished the woman farthest from Scarlett, who wore her hair in a side ponytail and introduced herself as Jewels, which Scarlett couldn't tell if that was her nickname or her given name.

The women began diving into their personal details about how they were really there for each other when no one else was, how they handled losing not only a grandchild but dealing with their own child's broken heart, how they had to be so strong for their family.

It amazed Scarlett how such a horrific accident could bring three women together, how they could bond over their loss, share with one another, and confide in complete strangers. Scarlett was finding it hard enough to get some of the people in her parent meetings to speak up to the other parents that they have known for years. These women prove that it can be and should be an effortless thing to disclose to others, how good it was for them, and how much it benefits them.

Alex and Martha asked all of the right questions as the women continued to discuss all of the emotions they have felt build up during the first year after the shooting. They also mentioned how they were finally able to release some of their heartache once they opened up to one another.

"How were you able to be supportive for one another when you were grieving yourself?" Alex asked.

"How were you able to get the other person to open up when it felt like they didn't want to talk about it? Should you be pushing them to talk about their feelings?" Martha asked.

"Or should you be letting them come to you?" Alex added on.

Scarlett also added in her counseling advice, and mentioned what she was doing for some of the parents who had lost their children during a high school shooting. She told the women how a support system is so important, and it seemed to her that they made a great team. The women thanked her.

"We wouldn't have been able to make it through that first year without each other," Carol said. She was the most extravagant out of the three grandmothers. Carol's long blond hair was tossed over the side of one shoulder, exposing her left dangling, expensive earring which matched her heavy diamond necklace.

"And it really hit us even after the first March. After all that effort to make things right, to get our voices out there, to be heard, and nothing in return," Leanne added.

"Even though it's not people we know that are dying, it still hurts, especially when it hits close to home, or when so many lives are lost, like Pandora. We all found that a tough one, we couldn't believe fifteen kids were killed. And this was the highest number of deaths since the Sandy Hook Elementary School shooting that happened in 2012." Jewels frowned while she wiped at the quiet tears that were beginning to smudge her makeup.

The women nodded in agreement, except for Scarlett. It was beginning to get too close to home for her; she could see where this conversation was leading and she did not like it. She was starting to feel her walls build back up as the liquid collected in the corner of her eyes.

Scarlett had thought she was doing so well, but being reminded of how many children were killed was a sensitive subject. It made her think about all of the lives, all of the people she would no longer be able to see, who were no longer going to be a part of her life. It also reminded her about what she could have and should have done to stop her life from being torn apart.

Then the song, *Big Girls Don't Cry* by Fergie, played in Scarlett's head, making her want to curl up into a little ball. She was unsure where it came from, but it made her stomach turn. She decided to get out of there as quickly as possible. *No one needs to see this, they will just think I am another grieving parent who is a big mess,* Scarlett thought as she reached for her phone as if it was vibrating in her pocket.

"Hello," she paused, "Okay, I am on my way." Scarlett flipped her phone shut, letting her friends know that the babysitter called her, saying that Rosie was sick and Scarlett was needed back at home. She quickly waved her friends goodbye and walked up towards the sidewalk and back from where they came.

Scarlett's thoughts began to race as she headed for the car, thinking about how many children have died during her life span alone. "There was the Virginia Tech Shooting where 33 people were killed; Sandy Hook Elementary School shooting where 28 people were killed; University of Texas tower shooting where 18 people were killed; Stoneman Douglas High School shooting where also 17 people were killed," Scarlett whimpered as she continued to count and name all of the mass school shootings she could think of.

"These unstable people should not have the weapons or accessibility to school grounds making them an unsafe place," Scarlett murmured out loud as she paced towards her car.

Scarlett began to read the signs as she passed, choking back her tears that were forming into quiet sobs. She agreed with each and every poster, thinking about what they are saying, what they mean, what they are proclaiming must be done.

"Why have these simple things not been met? We need to see movement with these policies, they are simple demands, he needs to fulfill his promises, take action, stop being the brute that people think he is." She pauses for a moment, taking into consideration other factors. "I know he is not the only one to blame, a President can't pass or make a bill or ban something without the vote from the people, his republican allies, the libertarians, and everyone in between who says they are all for gun control but have not proven it," Scarlett explained as she finally reached her car door.

Scarlett took a deep breath, attempting to steady her breathing as she puts her car in drive. "What if one of their loved ones got shot from a bullet that should have never been fired due to gun restrictions? Would that then make a difference? Or would it just cause panic and mayhem? Would they try to cover it up as a terrorist attack or have they used that one too many times?"

"You cannot be implying that you are going to shoot one of the government officials, or someone they love. You are losing it, you have officially gone insane," the juvenile voice was trying to reason with Scarlett.

She didn't mean that she wanted anyone to get shot, she knew that someone else losing their loved one was not the way to make things progress, to get a movement on creating and establishing bans on gun. This was a plan that every widower, murderer, or grieving parent in a story tried to muster. They all wanted to know how they could get revenge, to commit a crime and get away with it. Scarlett believed that these delusional villains or troubled heroes had never heard of the saying that two wrongs don't make a right, or simply chose not to listen to it.

This act of violence and contribution to mayhem was not something Scarlett saw in her future. She didn't believe in violence, or guns for that matter, which was why she told the voice in her head, "That is not what I meant and you know it. It's just something needs to be done, and I am tired of sitting around waiting for things to change. I see nothing, nothing is different, people have been fighting this cause for more than a year, people have died since the invention of guns due to their stupid laws not existing. How long will this continue?"

The adolescent voice remained silent, probably because it was exactly that, an adolescent. Scarlett thought that it was maybe her inner child or youth speaking out, but she was not sure. She did know that this voice of reasoning, or whatever it was, knew nothing about the pain she was experiencing. It did not know all of the life lessons she has faced, and it did not know how to handle situations such as this. Therefore, it stayed silent, listening to Scarlett rant about what needed to be done, what must be done for her to continue in this life, and about what she could do to make a difference. Scarlett knew she had to keep doing something, she needed to help, to make a difference.

After two hours alone with her thoughts, she finally drove into her driveway, cutting the engine, making slow movements towards the front door. She was glad that Rosie wasn't home, that Jonathan had taken her for the day so she could attend the march. They had both agreed it was pointless to pay for a babysitter when Jonathan was available to take care of his own daughter.

Since Christmas, Jonathan had slowly started making more of an appearance back into Scarlett's life. He either stopped by to say goodnight to his Rosie or called to see how her day was going, and wanting to speak with Scarlett after. He even had long conversations with Scarlett here and there, always warning her when he was about to head over. Therefore, Scarlett was able to get her act together in time for her husband's appearance. She always cleaned the bedroom in case things escalated. But right now Scarlett was happy to be alone, happy that no one was at home waiting for her, needing her attention. Scarlett decided she was going to slowly make her way up the stairs and into her fluffy white bed where she would wait, in a semi-dazed state, until her husband called her, letting her know that he was coming home with Rosie. Until then, Scarlett could let out her anger, sadness, and fear into the covers of her bed, screaming into her pillowcase when necessary.

Chapter 24

I went to the March for Our Lives this year! It was absolutely incredible! To see all those people band together, fighting for a cause they believe in. It's stuff like this that makes me want to write meaningful lyrics, to show the world what needs to change for the better, to help the cause.

I also loved how many A-listers where there showing their support. I saw Arianna Grande, Miley Cyrus, Jennifer Hudson, Demi Lovato and many more artists perform. They were all so powerful, holding their heads high, some with tears in their eyes. It was all very moving, but it was Arianna that really blew me away. It was her first performance since the bombing at her Manchester concert. For her to have the courage to get back up on stage is inspiring, she is a true leader.

I don't know if celebrities realize the power they have over their fans. They make us laugh, love, cry, and live. Some people will live for people in the limelight, but for me, I laugh, love, and cry with and for them. They have such great power over us, telling us their opinions, beliefs, what is right and wrong in their eyes. Fans look at them as if they are gods, or queens and kings. Some people will follow their every word, agree without hesitation to every statement. I don't think they realize they have this ability to influence other people's lives so intensely.

This is why when I become a singer, song writer, the musician of my dreams, I will remember these days, the day of the March for Our Lives and every important event that has changed me. I will sing about my beliefs, my opinions, telling everyone what I believe is right and wrong, influencing the masses.

Maybe I will be able to help make this world a better place. I will tell people to not fear or hate one another, and that it is okay to dislike someone, or to start separating ways from an old friend. And that I understand we cannot all love one another, and that is okay, but at least we can respect each other, ourselves, and the planet we live on.

We need to stop being rude and disrespectful towards others. If we don't have something nice to say then don't say anything at all, has no one else heard this motto? Leave your negative thoughts for yourself, or maybe write it down, just like what I am doing.

Speaking of negativity, Denise finally talked to me, well messaged me over Facebook actually. She told me that the reason why she didn't talk to me after Duncan's party is because she didn't know what to say, she wasn't sure how she should comfort me, and what words would make me feel better. She messaged me saying that she should have called the cops, or my parents at least.

I had no clue what she was talking about. She then told me that on the night of the party, after I had one drink, she noticed I was acting funny, like I had already gotten drunk. She thought that I was just acting like that to be a part of the 'cool kids crowd' (as if I wasn't apart of them already), so she didn't really think anything of it.

Then as the night progressed, she said she noticed Duncan was very grabby with me, trying to feel me up in public. I was grossed out that I would act so sloppy in front of people, letting him touch me like that, but I decided that I should read everything before I replied to her message. She said that at some point she noticed I went missing, and Duncan wasn't in sight either. She said she spent ten minutes looking for me, she started with outside and then downstairs before making her way upstairs. The first room she checked was Duncan's, where he had me laying on the bed with my shirt off, laying on top of me fully clothed. I had thought Denise grabbed me before Duncan put me to bed so I was completely shocked!

Apparently I was unconscious while Duncan was trying to drunkenly take off my bra while making out with me. She said she freaked out at him, screaming at him to get off while she shoved his drunken a** off of me. She had dressed me before half carrying, half dragging me down the stairs where she ran into Sasha. The two of them had been speaking to each other most of the night, I guess it makes sense that the quiet ones would somehow mingle, finding one another. When he offered his help after she had freaked out at him, telling him his cousin was a per-vert, she accepted because she knew she wouldn't be able to carry me home alone, and he hadn't been drinking so would also be able to drive us.

She thought I knew this whole time that my ex-boyfriend, boyfriend at the time, had allegedly attempted to rape me. She said that I had been avoiding her in class and that she thought I must have been mad at her for letting me out of her sight, letting him take me upstairs. I lost it on her.

How could she think that Duncan was going to rape me? He was my boyfriend, by choice! I don't have bad taste in guys, I don't f**king like rapists. It's not like he had me undressed, trying to stuff it in! I knew she knew that I was still a virgin, but when I chose to have sex with my boyfriend was none of her business! For all she knew, I could have wanted it.

It makes sense now why Duncan broke up with me. My best friend of 7 years freaked out at him, looking like a deranged lunatic, which by insinuation made me look like one too, because who can be friends with a lunatic unless they are one too?

I also understand now why Sasha told me to stay away from Duncan. I have noticed over the past couple of months that Sasha still has not been seen standing at Duncan's side, or at his locker, waiting for him like the quiet lost puppy. He probably thinks the worst about his cousin! How could Denise get him involved?! I will have to tell him next time I see him (I have to tell him face-to-face because he doesn't have social media), that Duncan isn't a rapist, and that Denise is a mentally unstable psycho.

So on Facebook, I told Denise exactly what I thought of her and how she is f**king deranged! Not only about the Duncan thing, but also about avoiding her! It was her avoiding me!

I guess it kinda makes sense now, she was probably just too afraid to speak to me, thinking I was mad at her for almost letting me get 'raped.' But f**king still!

If she did think that was what was going to happen, then she should have been there for me, she should have tried harder than just that one day at lunch. She shouldn't have let Ashley and Emma scare her off from talking to me or whatever her reason was for getting pissed at me and walking away. She should have seen if I was okay. A good friend would have said something, tried to comfort me, to make me feel better, I know I would have done that for her.

When I messaged her back, explaining that Duncan was not the bad guy she thought he was, she completely freaked out! She said that I have no clue what I am talking about, that he had probably given me some drug to knock me out so he could take me upstairs. I told her that her theory was ridiculous, Duncan doesn't do drugs because of football and he would never give drugs to someone else.

Then she started calling me naïve and that ever since I started hanging out with Ashley and Emma, something has changed about me, I had become distant. Our conversation was starting to go all over the place, but I guess that can happen when you keep everything bottled up for so long. So I released all of the thoughts I have had about her that I have been keeping to myself since October.

I told her she was the one who has changed, that she has started acting like a complete cow! I explained to her how she is bitter all the time now because I have friends and she doesn't. I said that I thought it was good that she joined the debate team, maybe she could finally become independent, grow up and make some new friends. She did not like what I had to say.

Denise said I was the one who was so dependent. As if! I would have been happy on my own, Denise was the one who always asked me to hang out, was the one who was always making the plans. And now she says that I needed grow up, that I was becoming this fake person, pretending to be perfect, just like the people I surround myself with, to hide my insecurities and flaws. I told her that I actually don't have any insecurities or flaws like she does, but that I am sure her 'new friends' probably won't notice them for a couple years so she will be fine for now. She literally said 'LOL.' Who even says that anymore? Then she added that how she doesn't have any friends (I am not surprised), and that she actually stopped going to the debate team.

Pathetic, Denise always needed me to get by, to have any social life, and I am realizing this now for the first time. I thought people were just afraid of her because she has the resting b**ch face. But I guess it's more like she hates everyone else. She couldn't even stand to be a part of a team for a couple of months, that is just sad. I told her my opinion on her sad lonely life, and there was no reply, at least not until the next day.

She called me a b**ch. Never has she ever called me a mean name, even when we have had tiny fights when we were younger, but I guess I never called her a lunatic before either, things change.

But no way am I a b**ch! I am probably the nicest person she knows! She's just getting her panties in a knot because she knows I am right, she is living a sad life. It's not my fault, it's not like I told her to stop talking to me, to stop trying with me. She is the one to blame for her own misery, and I won't let her drag me down with her, so I decided just not to reply. Emma and Ashley are right, she is a freaking weirdo.

P

Chapter 25

Since March for Our Lives, Scarlett's days have come and gone in a blur. She has been present for her daughter, her friends, even Jonathan when he calls and stops by, but the days seem to melt together. Before she noticed, it was Mother's Day.

It being on Sunday, Scarlett thought maybe Jonathan was going to join her and Rosie, but he left the two of them alone to do mother-daughter things; apparently him and Darryl had an early tee time. Scarlett was not sure what to do, how to keep her daughter occupied without giving herself away, without losing herself in public. She decided to take her for pizza and see a comedy playing at the local movie theater, Pandora Cinema – it was one of their family traditions after all.

Rosie had been excited to go to the movie; they hadn't gone to the cinema for almost a year, and she had missed her popcorn and M&M's combo.

"Mom, it makes it taste sooooo much better," Rosie would tell Scarlett every time she combined the mix. Scarlett was more of the fuzzy peaches or Twizzlers type of movie-goer.

After the movies, Scarlett dropped Rosie back at Jonathan's one-bedroom apartment. Rosie told Scarlett that he slept on the pull-out couch when she came over and his bed smelt like boy farts. It amazed her how her daughter kept such a brave face about everything going on, or maybe it was that she didn't care. Scarlett couldn't tell which one it was, but she was just happy that Rosie had the joyful twinkle back in her eyes.

Scarlett remembered going to Jonathan's on Mother's Day, and even having tea with him after they tucked Rosie in together. She was surprised how they were starting to build this new routine. They were slipping into this lifestyle a little too easily for her liking, but she no longer had the energy to fuss about it, or to tell Jonathan to come home, that he was needed there with her.

Instead, Scarlett put on her best smile, cleaned her clothes, and acted like the mother she needed to be while she started to feel more and more empty inside. Jonathan had also started being more and more friendly since Christmas, which could have been one of the reasons why Scarlett no longer made a fuss about him needing to come home; deep down, she knew it wouldn't be too much longer before he caved.

Everything from the outside seemed normal for her, or normal as possible. Her life looked like it was beginning to piece itself back together. Scarlett appeared to be returning to her normal, organized self. She felt love when she looked at her daughter, husband, or friends, but something was still missing. There was a hole in her heart that was slowly collapsing.

"I only have to pretend a little bit longer," Scarlett told herself every night, "I have to do it for them."

Then she would roll over and stare at the big red numbers on her digital clock slowly change, minute by minute, while she counted away the hours until she had to get up and change.

Scarlett could also see herself getting lost in the parent meetings, agreeing with the unheard statements the parents made. She was no longer giving advice, and they were no longer accepting it. It felt like the meetings were becoming more like a therapist session, being able to complain, grumble, and be as negative as they would like without any comment or regard, just to get everything off their chests.

Scarlett had realized over the past thirty or so meetings that no one really knew how to deal with death. Everyone thought they did, but they were all just pretending. People thought there was the grieving stages, which is what everyone went through, not missing a single process or step, but that was inaccurate too.

Sure, maybe for some people their ability to handle loss can be defined by sociologists and psychologists, but Scarlett did not believe that the mental processes of an adult are similar or unique. She was starting to lose faith in her counseling abilities. "What if it's all bullshit like they say?" Scarlett has dealt with many negative non-believers throughout her career, her defense being, "Everyone has their own beliefs and opinions, and I accept yours for what it is."

She could not get over how passive aggressive she used to be, or still is. She had always stepped around eggshells for people, and she was starting to lose her patience. Her husband told her after she had worked for the Suicide Prevention Hotline for over five years, that he had been surprised she was still doing it, still dealing with people's problems, their negativity, their lack of faith in her, and that she was able to put a positive spin on everything. Scarlett was the type of person who would back down from a fight smiling, thinking every loss was someone else's gain.

She got over the non-believers quickly. If people didn't want to listen to her advice, that was fine by her, but she could at least put it out into the world, hoping it would be received and would help someone. That was one of the reasons she started the parent meetings; she needed to focus her energy, or harness her "healing power" as Alex would like to call it.

However, Scarlett was now slowly feeling the energy being sucked out of her. She was paying more and more attention to the negative news, the only news that really mattered to her nowadays. Scarlett even found herself looking towards the extremists, people who have theories on every reason why something has gone wrong, or has become corrupt in the American government.

Scarlett was starting to lose respect for her government, and for what she used to believe in. She was starting to lose sight of her purpose in this world. She was becoming the cheerful robot she had always tried to help over the phone, or who she would see walking down the streets, in magazines, in movies, or posting things on social media.

Scarlett could see herself change, she saw the weight gain was going away, slowly dwindling. Her hair was gaining color, her skin was glowing, thanks to her moving her computer time outside, as well as her new obsession with organizing the gardening. She looks the healthiest she has been all year, but she didn't feel that way. Yet, she carried on; she kept the meetings going, thinking *maybe this will be the one that helps me*, or maybe *I can really help someone today*. It was like Scarlett was a broken porcelain doll that she had nearly completed gluing back together, without realizing the inside was still hollow.

Scarlett thought the meeting after Mother's Day was going to be one of the busiest ones yet. Mothers were going to be devastated to not have their child there to celebrate with them; they too would feel that ache in their chest that Scarlett was experiencing. But to Scarlett's surprise, only four people made it to that meeting.

It was only a few months ago that her group sizes really started to dwindle. Gasira and Annabella were not there, but they had not come since their first meeting either. They had emailed Scarlett letting her know that their meeting had been a big breakthrough for them, that they had needed people to listen to them and support them, which had been enough to encourage them through their hard times.

Christine had also emailed Scarlett a month ago that she no longer planned on attending any more meetings. She had observed enough, listened enough, soaking in all the information she needed to process what had happened to her child and how to come to terms with what that meant. Scarlett thought it was probably more likely Christine had just gotten sick of listening and supporting Sandy, looking for any way out.

Scarlett felt that everyone was getting over the shooting, moving on with their lives, leaving her alone with a few stragglers. There was still Sandy, who had not missed a single meeting yet. Scarlett did not think she was getting anywhere with Sandy, but at least she could count on her to show up. Scarlett knew that she did not have to worry about going to these meetings, waiting for the hour until it was over, watching every minute pass by, wondering if someone was going to pop their head in through gymnasium door any second.

At the last meeting, Tyler and Thea had come up to Scarlett and thanked her for all of her help. They told her that they also had finally accepted what had happened, that their little girl was not coming back, that she did not deserve this, but nonetheless it still happened. They said how Scarlett taught them how to cope, how to continue on living to their best ability. The little voice in Scarlett's head told her to tell them the truth, that their kid was not as innocent as they thought, but she was able to silence it, thinking that these parents had suffered enough.

At today's meeting, it was Sandy and a newcomer, Hayley, who were sitting across from Scarlett, surrounded by empty chairs in that taunting U-shape. Scarlett had never met Hayley before, but she recognized her the instant she entered the gymnasium. Since Scarlett was taken by Annabella's appearance at one of the meetings, not knowing she had lost a child in the shooting, Scarlett had started to familiarize herself with the faces of the parents who had lost their children that June, so that she wouldn't be taken off guard again.

Hayley was a petite gorgeous women, with big glittering lips, kind brown eyes, and black wavy hair. She reminded Scarlett of Lucy Liu, minus the adorable freckles. She was wearing a slim fitting black dress, reaching just past her knees, paired with black 6-inch heels that were laced in the back, crossing over the front of her feet. Hayley looked like she belonged in a high-end business magazine, pointing at colorful pie charts, informing her colleagues that prices are continuing to rise in the States.

Scarlett welcomed Hayley as she introduces herself to the two women. Scarlett knew her daughter was Tiffany, who was with the cheerleading team outside practicing when she had been shot and killed.

Sandy began the meeting, enjoying a pair of new ears to explain her broken story to. "It seems like what happened has been completely forgotten. Like everyone has moved on except for the people that were actually affected. The President, the government, the political leaders, the reporters, newscasters, they all no longer care. They think that they have run this sob story dry, and people are tired of hearing about what happened at Pandora, tired of hearing about what I have to say," Sandy spoke strongly as she looked at Hayley, almost ignoring Scarlett who has heard this story nearly ten times now.

However, each time Sandy re-told this story, her voice gained strength, a certain amount of sternness that was lacking before. Her shoulders slowly rolled back over each time. Now she was beginning to look more like herself, the type of mother who would tell her daughter to stand straight, that no one liked someone who slouched.

"Even my sisters are tired of hearing what I have to say," Sandy continued, "They listen to me, but have nothing to add in to the conversation. They are not sympathetic, just happy it didn't happen to them. I can feel their eyes roll back when I tell them I had a bad day." Sandy paused to add in some dramatic effect. "Their children are no better. They continue on their days without a care in the world, as if they didn't lose their favorite cousin. I also feel like it is having a bad effect on Emily. I am afraid they are going to forget, forget all the good memories they shared – Bobby's laughter, his fierceness cheering on the field, everything about him. I feel like I need to remind them every day what happened."

When Scarlett first heard Sandy tell this story, she would tell her that some children dealt with loss by acting like it was no longer there, or that they handled death differently than adults. She would tell her that just because they do not seem upset does not mean they are not upset. Scarlett also explained how it was okay to grieve and then accept the circumstances that had occurred.

Then Sandy would go on a rampage about him liking cheerleading, how good he was, and how far he would have gone. She would let out a timid whimper, transitioning to how she still has not returned to work, but instead she lays in bed all day. Sandy would mention how people act like she should be over it by now, that it was old news. She explained how people think she is a loose cannon, that she needs to get her act together, for her children, for her family.

Sandy would end her sad story by explaining how messed up the world is, how people expect the parents to take care of their children, drive them to school, feed them, make sure they don't die, and if by some chance they do, and it's not your fault, then you need to get over it quickly, start functioning like a proper person, adding in your daily contributions. At this point, if there were other parents at the meeting, they would nod in agreement, adding in their own opinion about how messed up the world is.

These meetings used to be more positive, Scarlett used to try to direct and lead the conversations to a more enthusiastic outlook or perspective. Unfortunately, the negative energy slowly grew. The meetings allowed the parents to release their toxic thoughts and opinions out into the safe space of the gymnasium. They talked about some of their opinions and beliefs that were not allowed to be said out loud, using crude words to explain how the government was letting them down. Scarlett thought she had led this meeting to this darker, yet more helpful path. She had truly given up on adding in her constructive quotes, opinions, or beliefs, silently agreeing with the other parents.

Today, Sandy had stopped her conversation there, not diving into further details about the shootings, or who could have, and should have prevented it. Instead, she asked, "Now what brings you in here today?"

"Well, I guess I am here because of what happened on Mother's Day. My partner and I were out on a picnic with our daughter and son, Riley and Josh."

Scarlett was waiting to hear Sandy snicker at Hayley's use of the term to describe her significant other. She had thought Sandy was the old-fashion homophobic type, but to her bewilderment, Sandy had simply nodded encouragingly.

"We got on to the topic about Tiffany, my daughter who passed away, and it made me emotional, more than I would have liked. I try very hard to not cry in front of the children. I have been the tough one out of Shawna and I, she took it a lot harder than I did… She has always been the more emotional one." Hayley sighed. "But I was still in pain, trying to cover it up like a good parent, not letting my children see my weak side. Then Josh turns to me and asks me why I am crying.

When I told him it was because of how much I missed his older sister, he looked surprised, even skeptical, and it infuriated me." Hayley baled her fists at her side as she frowned. "I have been dealing with this bullshit since people found out Tiffany was not my biological daughter, as if I do not have the right to be upset because she was not my child because I did not give birth to her. People will tell me that they feel bad for Shawna, as if she is the only one suffering, as if I have not lost my daughter. I never thought my son felt the same way."

Scarlett stopped Hayley there; she had seen many adoptive parents, or children, get upset about this type of thing before. They all assumed the world was ganging up on them, saying that losing someone who was not technically your dad, sister, mother, or brother, was supposed to be easier, or how people believed they had no right to be distraught because they were not blood.

Scarlett cut right to the chase, "Hayley, that is not what your son meant and you know that. You said it yourself that you have been the tough one out of this situation, you have been the strong one in your family, therefore when your son saw the moment you finally revealed your true feelings, not a moment of weakness either, it caught him off guard. I have a feeling your son and you have not talked about what has happened after Tiffany passed away. It is usually the more emotional parent that speaks with their children, telling them the truth of what is going on. Josh had probably thought you handled her death with a stern and clear judgment because that was the type of person you are." Scarlett had never been so bold to make accusations and assumptions about her clients before, but she did not stop herself there. "That does not mean he does not think you did not love her, or that you do not feel an ache in your heart for her loss. You need to talk to your son, and daughter too, tell them what you have felt, what you have been going through. Let them in, show them how brave you are, how you have been holding yourself together for the sake of the family, but that you have experienced loss just as much as they have. Tiffany was your daughter, and will always been your daughter, you know that, so screw the people who question the facts."

Scarlett had not realized she had put her hand up, pointing her finger at Hayley like she was scolding her own teenage daughter. Scarlett always understood where people were coming from, why they were upset, and that they were fragile when it came to them searching for help. She knew they needed to be slowly coaxed into making the right decisions that were best for them. Scarlett never told her clients what they should and should not do to get over their grief, she simply made passive suggestions, and she definitely never castigated them.

Before Scarlett realized she should apologize for her outburst, and break off character, Sandy broke the awkward silence, "Well you really nipped that one in the butt, didn't you," she said.

Scarlett looked towards Hayley as she sat there thinking, and then with quick movements, Hayley gathered her bag at the side of her chair, stood up, and left.

Scarlett received no goodbye, no thank you, no cursing, nothing. Scarlett knew she should get up, chase after her, let Hayley know she was in the wrong and what she did was unprofessional. Yet, Scarlett didn't get up, didn't apologize, but remained in her seat.

Scarlett was tired, tired of listening to everyone else complain, tired of being polite to people she didn't like, tired of giving advice without stepping on anyone's toes, tired of her passive-aggressive attitude, tired of never sharing her own grievances.

Scarlett got up from her black plastic fold-up chair and told Sandy the meeting was over and that this had been their last one they would have. Scarlett quickly collected her things as Sandy sat watching her, slowly getting up and making her way towards Scarlett who had begun throwing out the stale cookies and week old coffee.

"Thank you for everything you have done," Sandy said as she reached towards Scarlett, forcing her into a comforting embrace.

Scarlett had always pictured Sandy as the ungrateful type, the person who needed everyone to listen to them, the type of person who would not accept something being taken away from them. Scarlett thought that when the day would come for her to tell Sandy the meetings were going to stop, that she would go down kicking and screaming.

Sandy left with a quick goodbye, leaving Scarlett to clean up her mess, alone with her thoughts as she tried to process the brief and strange meeting that just happened.

Chapter 26

June 7TH

It turns out I have been wrong about everything. My life has gone downhill quickly since the last time I wrote in my journal. I realized that Ashley and Emma are conniving, manipulative bullies who only care about themselves. I also now know that Duncan is an ignorant prick, and that Denise was right about everything, poor Denise.

I was so pissed at her, for thinking that I would date such a creep, that I had gone completely ballistic on her. She was trying to be a supportive friend and I ignored her, I realize that now.

I thought long and hard after my conversation with Denise. Her getting mad at Duncan was still not a good enough excuse for him to dump me, unless he was actually taking advantage of me and therefore dumped me to make it look like I was a drunk mess, or something like that. So after thinking about it for a few weeks, I decided to finally confront him. I asked him when he was alone, I thought he would probably be more likely to tell me the truth as to what happened that night.

I tried to bring the night of the party up like it was no big deal, first introducing the idea that maybe someone had put drugs in my drink. He kinda laughed at that, not thinking I was trying to see if he did it (he would be too stupid to figure that out), and he said that he heard that some of the guys were sharing MDMA with Ashley and Emma, who had put it in their drinks. So I guess I probably picked up one of their drinks accidentally.

I explained to Duncan that I was so drunk that night, trying to laugh about it like it was funny. I then asked if he was drunk too. He told me that we were both smashed out of minds (no sh*t, I couldn't remember anything). So I asked if he brought me up to bed so I could rest, and he said he planned on doing more than just resting with me! What a f**king pig!

I told him that I hadn't given him my consent to do that, that I was clearly too intoxicated, and that he should have known that! His faced changed, before he had this dumb goofy smirk, like he was so satisfied with what he said, then his brow furrowed, and the lines on his cheeks deepened. He looked enraged. But it was his eyes that really caught me off guard, they had seemed to widen, his pupils dilating with hatred, as he realized what I had been implying.

Duncan took a step closer to me as I inched back without even realizing. He pointed his finger at me as he stood aggressively, hovering over me. He said that he didn't have any intentions on having sex with me, and will never in his life, and that I am a crazy lunatic just like my friend for thinking that he had planned to rape me.

Then he regained his composure in a heartbeat, slumping his shoulders, leaning back, no longer on the defense. He licked his lips and said that I was enjoying myself anyways, even moaning his name, begging for more. He looked me up and down, his eyes staying on me for longer than I would have preferred.

Duncan was beginning to make me feel uncomfortable, I guess my instincts were kicking in, telling me to run or scream. He leaned over and whispered: "No one would believe you anyway." I felt a knot turning in my stomach, gaining fire and momentum as it tried to reach for my throat. My eyes burned as I turned away, refusing to let him see me cry.

I walked as quickly as I could to the girls' washroom before throwing up my breakfast I had prepared in a hurry that morning.

What a f**king scum!

I can't believe I actually dated him! That I had actually wanted to lose my virginity to him! I was so wrapped up in this idea of dating the 'school hottie,' becoming the perfect couple, and then making my way to win Homecoming Queen.

I thought that I had enjoyed hiding in the shadows, watching people instead of interacting with them.

Then when I had my chance for popularity, I lunged at it blindly, sacrificing my beliefs, my friends, and who I am as a person. I had become what I despised, a bully.

I started laughing at Duncan's, Emma's, and Ashley's jokes, usually at the expense of other people. I think once I had even laughed at a comment Ashley and Emma made about Denise, I think that is why she had freaked out at me during lunch instead of seeing if I was okay after the night at Duncan's party, poor Denise.

I pretended like I hadn't heard what they had said, so I had just laughed with them, because what was the harm in that? It was just another lie I was feeding myself to make me feel better, that I couldn't be cruel like these popular beautiful people. I pretended to see the kindness in their eyes, or see the sincerity in their compliments, but that too was all just a lie.

I had fed myself another lie, that I had liked Duncan, that I had found him interesting, that I wanted to date him. I know now that I didn't find him interesting, but thought that he was just a cute a**hole. I so badly wanted to fit in for once in my life, to get a taste of popularity that I was willing to date the dumb jock, simply because that is what I thought other people wanted. I was willing to stoop down to their level just to have a social life!

And Duncan was right. No one would believe me, and maybe Duncan would have just passed out beside me instead of trying to take my virginity, but I guess we will never know. He may not think he did anything wrong, and maybe technically speaking he didn't, but I still feel violated. Your boyfriend is meant to protect you, not use and abuse you when you are semi-conscious. And just because I was willing to do stuff when I was awake, does not mean that I was willing to do it when I was no longer coherent, that is just disturbing!

It was wrong what Duncan did. He will have to face the consequences for his actions. He must learn how f**king messed up that was! He simply doesn't get it probably because he is a guy, he has never been afraid about someone dominating, overpowering him, doing what they like with him. I will have to tell a teacher or something.

Yet, I feel like so much has happened since then, to be honest it's the least of my worries. I will make sure though that he will never do that to anyone again, by either telling a teacher, maybe Ms. V, who would definitely handle it better than Mr. Walter. He needs more than a slap on the wrists, and he is not the only one who should get in trouble about what happened that night either!

I thought it was very strange that Duncan had thought Ashley and Emma were putting MDMA in their drinks. It made sense that I had probably just picked up one of their drinks throughout the night, and me being the goody-goody that I am, having never taken drugs before, I would assume that the first time would have probably affected me a lot. But I was still confused as to why they would put it in their drinks instead of just taking it normally, like what was the point? So I decided to confront Emma and Ashley about this the next day, after talking to Duncan.

I asked Emma and Ashley about Duncan's party and they had given me vague answers, just telling me that they were too drunk to remember much. I didn't care about Duncan, so I ratted him out quickly, telling them that I heard they were putting MDMA in everyone's drinks. I thought if I dramatized the story, making it sound, hopefully, worse than it was, then they would tell me the truth. Luckily, it worked.

Ashley and Emma laughed when I first told them that Duncan said they had put MDMA in everyone's drinks because they wanted the party to be a wild one that no one would ever forget. As you can see, I am pretty good at making things up on the spot. Ashley began first, telling me that no they didn't put an MDMA pill in everyone's drink, that would be so f**king expensive. Emma laughed with her agreeing, saying they had actually only bought one pill off some stoner.

My first thoughts were, did they give me an MDMA pill as a f**king joke? Did they think it was funny to make their friend blackout? To make their friend an easy target for perverts? Was it supposed to be one of those clichéd mean girl schemes, where they pretend to be friends with the loner and then build it up over a short *period of time, just so that they could make them into a total embarrassment, like their entire friendship was all a joke? What were they thinking?*

They must have seen my face change as I began to wonder about all of the possible f**ked up excuses they had for doing such a terrible thing because they quickly told me to relax. They said they had put it in Denise's drink, but after they saw her leave with Sasha, the two of them dragging me out the front door, then they realized that I must have taken her drink accidentally. They thought it was hilarious! I couldn't believe it, they had tried to drug someone at a party, and while revealing their plan to me, they told me to relax?!

WHO DOES THAT?!

I was also confused as to why they had tried to drug Denise, it's not like they were planning on taking advantage of her or anything. While my brain struggled to process everything they were telling me, I was able to stammer out the only question that really mattered: Why did they drug Denise? They looked at each other in that way that they do when they are about to laugh at a girl down the hall for wearing an ugly skirt, they snorted and belled over, laughing so hard that they actually had to put their hands on their knees to balance themselves. As Ashley wiped away a tear from her reddening face, she said, "Well, why the hell not?" Emma stammered in next, "Yeah! She is so boring, we were just trying to spice things up a bit for her, make her let loose."

These two girls, who I had thought as my really good friends at one point, were absolute monsters. They planned to drug my best friend, just so she would let loose? YEAH RIGHT! They probably were going to make a fool out of her. Turns out, I wasn't their target, she was.

I looked both of them dead in the eye and finally spoke the truth that I had been hiding from them, as well as myself over the past 8 months. I told them that they were miserable cows, who feed on the joy of destroying other people's lives. They were bullies, who acted as if they were the innocent, nice girl that you would want to bring home to impress your parents, "Hey Mom and Dad, look at how pretty, smart, kind, and popular my friends are!" What a joke! They are two insecure teens, who need to pick on people, to tell people how ugly their outfit, hair, or face is, just to make them feel better about themselves.

Mrs. Cornwall was right, these girls were just using me to make themselves look like better singers, they were downplaying me to improve their quality of worth. They probably just kept me around because it made them look good. I had blossomed into the young female my mom promised I always would, and they were F**KING using me! They didn't care about me, just like they didn't about anyone else except for themselves.

I ended my rant by elaborating on the future details of how their lives would turn out, explaining to them that they would become the leathered skin old bags, telling everyone who they met how they used to be a cheerleader or how they were so popular back in high school. I told them how they would gain weight in all the wrong areas as their tits began to drag and their skin began to make crevasses along their flesh, accentuating their frown lines. Their hopes and dreams would soon come crashing down after high school, because this was their peak after all. People in the real world wouldn't fall for their act, they would be able to see right through it, as they have seen through the other countless mean, nasty people they have encountered.

I also explained to them how they wouldn't make it in showbiz. They would be lucky if they could hold down a job as a clerk at the mall or gas station. They would have failed marriages, with children who no longer loved them, and husbands who no longer wanted to touch them because they finally could see through their fake girl-next-door mirage. And that it would be the actual cool kids, like Denise, who would end up putting their sorry asses behind bars due to their DUIs or being found in possession with drugs. I also added in how they would probably die too young due to heroin overdose, forgotten about by their family. They also would probably not even end up having a nice funeral, and there would most definitely not be a single tear shed for them. They would end up as the miserable b**ches they were meant to be and have always been!

When I finally took a gulp of air, having rushed my words before I could be interrupted, I noticed that both of their faces had gone bright red! Emma was even crying! HA! Who would have thought? I guess no one had ever put these girls in their place before. I was even beginning to feel bad, but I had to remind myself that these girls needed to hear how awful they were being. Then Ashley opened her big mouth.

Ashley started by saying that I was just as cruel and awful as they were. I guess they both already knew that they were bullies, maybe had even accepted it, not caring enough to change. She said that I pretend to be 'little miss perfect' who has a great voice, is pretty, well-liked, kind, and innocent, but I have dirt on my hands too. Apparently I had been laughing at all their jokes, that were made at the expense of others, all year, and now that I am finally realizing how awful I am, that I need to put them down too.

Then Ashley went into a fit about how I was actually worse than the two of them combined! I realized she was just reaching for anything at that point.

I raised my hand to stop her before she embarrassed herself any further. I told her to grow up and to enjoy the rest of the time they have at high school before they end up in the sh*tter where they belong, then I turned around and walked away! I have never been the type of person for confrontation, but I was on fire! Ashley had made some valid points, but nothing I didn't know already.

I figured out over the past couple of months I had become a bad friend to Denise, (poor Denise), and I finally realized it was my fault for our falling out, not hers. I had been acting pretentious, like I was going to be some important singer one day, which I will be, but that doesn't mean I should neglect my friend who had always had my back, or at least tried to! Just because we no longer share similar career interests doesn't mean we no longer enjoy each other's company, or that we don't have other similar hobbies. I still love hanging out with her, watching movies and pigging out on all the Tootsie Rolls we could buy.

Yes, I realized things were starting to change when we hung out, but I think it was actually me who was changing, not us. I was starting to pretend I was something I am not just so I could hang out with the popular girls. I guess I had gotten tired of being unseen, which I thought I enjoyed, and I wanted to be known for once in my life. The price I paid for this popularity is not worth it! I just want my friend back!

I want Denise to be a part of my life, for us to plan our class schedule together like we did last year, for us to hang out on Friday nights together while the rest of the junior class was busy filling themselves with liquid courage, just to have a good time. Her and I didn't need that, we could be ourselves in front of one another. And who knows, maybe even Eliza, Olivia and some of their girlfriends could join us some nights. They were never really a part of Ashley and Emma's clique, never a part of the bullies, they are more so seen as the confident girls who know their worth. I think that would be really good for Denise and I, I know we have always struggled with our self-confidence, which is why I quickly hung to Ashley, Emma and even Duncan, just to be told that I have a pretty voice, or that I have grown out of my awkward stage.

I also think that is why Denise also has never been able to make other friends, she doesn't have the confidence to approach other people without her borders up. She is a fun, loving, kind, caring, charismatic person, but unfortunately she is able to hide that side of herself so well. She needs to learn to be able to let others in, to open up. I think Eliza and her friend group would be perfect for helping Denise learn to let go. We all share or have similar ideas, theories, and opinions about the world. We may not all want to go to the same college, or may not even want to go to college (Olivia), but we can still be friends and have a good time together in the meanwhile!

When I realized how I had acted like such an a** to Denise, it was too late. I had texted her and after a few days of no replies, I messaged her on Facebook to find out she had blocked me. I spent the rest of the week looking for her during lunch, but no luck! I didn't know what classes she had, even though I am sure she had told me at the beginning of the year, but like the bad friend I was, I had forgotten.

She lived too far away for me to walk to her house. My mom and dad had always given me a ride, but I didn't want to involve either of them with my dilemma. I know my parents would be disappointed in the way I have been acting, and they would probably find some way to blame it on singing, banning me from learning music at Berklee (which wouldn't stop me), which is why I left them out of it.

I decided to log onto her Facebook, that way I could unblock myself and send her a message. I know what you are thinking, if Denise blocked me then she probably would have changed her password if she knew I had known it. But Denise didn't work like that, she was hot-headed. When she blocked me, she probably did it in a blind rage, not even thinking clearly, forgetting that our passwords were the same: 'donnie.' Her and I both started Facebook when we had just watched Donnie Darko *with Jake Gyllenhaal, we were obsessed with the movie so it only made sense that we would both remember our password if we shared it and it was related to one our favorite cinematic character. One year we even compiled all of our Christmas and birthday money to buy a Frank the Rabbit costume, just because. We didn't really have any intentions to wear it for Halloween, or to a party, we thought it might scare people too much, and we didn't really see ourselves at any parties in the near future.*

As I was saying... When I typed in her password, my heart raced, I couldn't help think what if I was wrong? What if she had thought about deleting me from her life for good? What if it wasn't an irrational decision like I hoped it was? As I pressed Enter, my heart continued on, and I was right. She hadn't changed her password. Hallelujah!

As I was about to type my name into the search engine to unblock myself, I noticed she had 3 unread messages in her inbox. I know I was prying, but I didn't think she had any friends on Facebook other than me, her mom, and those random people you just accept to bump up the number of friends you had. No one else had ever sent her messages before, so I couldn't imagine who would now.

When I looked at who sent her messages, I could feel that tight knot in my stomach again, burning its way up my throat. I pushed it down as I read the names of the people who wrote to her and I just had to see what Duncan, Ashley, and Emma said.

I looked at Duncan's message first. They had been talking since the night of his party. She had messaged him to let him know that I had gotten home safe, no thanks to him, and that she was planning on telling me everything the next morning. He had told her there was nothing to tell and said pretty much the same stuff he had said to me when I confronted him. He told her how I wanted it, that she was a dumb b**ch, a c*ckblock, and some other nasty names.

I would have thought it stopped there, but after I confronted him a week before, I guess it lit another fire inside of him. Denise hadn't replied to his first insults he said to her several months earlier, she probably thought it wasn't worth it after the way I acted towards her. But after I confronted Duncan, he must have gone home and messaged her more, he said how we were both so stupid, that no one would believe us, and how he didn't do anything wrong. I guess he was starting to get *paranoid that we were going to tell someone about what he did, maybe his coach, his parents, or Ms. V. He stopped calling her names and started defending himself, trying to play the smug cool guy, saying how blessed I was for even getting the chance to date him.*

Denise never replied to any of his most recent comments, possibly because she no longer cared since she didn't see me as a friend anymore, or she had more important things to deal with, Ashley and Emma. She had Duncan where she wanted him, he had admitted that night that he had done things with me, while I was clearly too drunk to remember, thus taking advantage of me. At any point in time she could show these messages to anyone, for sure getting him in trouble, if the world decided to be fair for once.

I moved onto Emma's messages next, I was assuming that I would be saving the worst for last. Emma had been messaging Denise since September! I had no idea! Denise never told me, she always acted like the tough one out of the two of us, like she could defend us against the world. I wish I knew, maybe then I would never have even bothered becoming friends with her, or Ashley.

Emma started off saying only a few things here and there. She would begin by writing something like, "Hey I notice in theater class today that you were wearing the same outfit you did last week! Looks like you can't afford to buy something else!" Who makes fun of someone for being poor?!

Denise didn't reply to Emma's first few comments, she was often hot-headed and would defend herself, but if it was something she thought as a pathetic insult, she just shrugged her shoulders and looked the other way. Their conversation progressed quickly.

When Emma and I began to hang out more, she began to say nastier and nastier things. She told Denise that I no longer wanted to hang out with her, and that I thought she was a stupid little freak. Denise still didn't reply because she knew that I never would call anyone stupid, I just hate that word! It's so rude. But as the insults and comments continued and became more frequent, it appeared that Denise started to doubt herself and our friendship. Denise would say: "No, Penelope doesn't think that way about me," or "You are a hopeless, rude, manipulative little girl."

Emma's insults weren't getting any more intelligent or well-thought out, they were just simple things that implied Denise was worthless, ugly, unintelligent, and the list goes on. Usually that type of stuff wouldn't get to Denise, but I guess with me no longer by her side to reassure her of her self-worth, she began to crack.

I could see some of Denise's comments becoming less and less thought out but more abrupt as she was starting to lose her temper. Then I got to the day where I had confronted Emma and Ashley. It appeared that Emma also went home after I exploded at her and took her anger out on Denise, I guess I also really started a fire in her. She told Denise that her and I were worthless, pathetic, and should go kill ourselves! Once again, WHO SAYS THAT!! That is so messed up. If my mom taught me anything, it was that you should never, ever tell someone to go kill themself. Everyone deserves a chance to live a happy life on this planet, and that not one soul was better than another!

Denise hadn't read Emma's last message. I was thinking about deleting it, to save her from the pain that it would cause her. However, I decided that it was best to leave the message. I planned to find her the next day, for us to decide together what would be the best action to do, take it to the school counselor, principal, or vice principal (Ms. V would make sure it would get handled fairly, without thinking about school politics getting in the way, unlike Mr. Walter).

I was about to log out, sickened from what I had read, but I needed to know the extent of the bullying, I needed to know what Ashley, the cruelest one, had said. I tried to scroll to the beginning, but never seemed to be able to reach it. It seemed that Ashley had been sending Denise messages for years!

I always thought that Emma and Ashley's bullying was only kept to the whispers in the halls, or maybe some nasty words written here or there on bathroom stalls or locker rooms. I never could have imagined that Denise would put up with Ashley saying awful things over Facebook for years, literally YEARS! Why would she keep the messages? I have no clue! Maybe she wanted to keep her messages around as a reminder how much of b**ch she was, or that she was planning on outing her to the school, a parent, or teacher. I am not sure what her intentions were, but that is not the point, the point is that Ashley went out of her way to continue saying things over Facebook, not caring if she got a reply or not, just wanting to put Denise down!

Ashley's messages were by far the worst. She would some days just say, "hey ugly," not requiring a reply before she messaged her again, "freak." Ashley really enjoyed calling Denise a freak, I had counted her say it at least 56 times. I spent 3 hours just reading her messages alone. She told Denise that she was dumb, hated, ugly, fat, the list goes on. But what really got me was when she called her a lunatic about a month ago. She said, "Everyone thinks you are a lunatic." That is probably why she got so upset when I called her one, I have been such an awful friend and it's taken me too long to realize.

Ashley had told Denise multiple times that she should go kill herself or that she just wished she would die already. Not once in the past 2 years of messages had Denise replied, feeding into Ashley's insults, until the night of Duncan's party. Denise actually messaged Ashley first, saying: "I know you saw Duncan take Penelope upstairs, you were with her last. How could you let that happen? What awful person lets someone, who is practically unconscious, get taken upstairs by a guy, who obviously had no good intentions!"

That is when things really escalated. They had been sending each other para-graphs, back and forth, for the past 6 months. As the days drew nearer, the mes-sages got longer. Denise was putting her heart and soul into these messages, tell-ing Ashley that she better stop, better come clean, better stop writing mean things about her in the bathroom stall, better stop laughing at her during class, better stop tripping her during lunch.

I knew nothing about all these things Ashley has been doing to Denise this entire year! Why did she never tell me? Did she really think that I was that low to have joined them? To have agreed with their insults? To have been in on it? I felt and feel awful, I couldn't even finish reading Ashley's replies before I shut my lap-top, throwing it to the side as I raced for the toilet, my anxiety finally bubbled up from my stomach reaching my throat.

The next day I had promised myself that I would find Denise, tell her how sorry I am, and that I would do whatever was necessary to make things right between us. Unfortunately, things didn't go as planned.

I found out the following day that her dad had committed suicide a couple of days ago. Rumor has it that him and Denise had gotten in a huge fight, and he ended up hanging himself from the ceiling in their shed. This happened over a month ago and I am still finding it hard to comprehend.

Terrance was like a second father to me. We would have barbeques at their house every Saturday in the summer, it would be Denise, Terrance, her mom (Daphne), and I, just the four of us. Denise was like me, she didn't have any aunts, uncles, cousin, grandparents, just a small knit family, composed of people that really loved each other. They were like the three musketeers before I got into the picture.

Terrance was the typical burley dad, a real handyman. Daphne would always call out to him when some electrical appliance or plumbing went haywire. He would tell her to just give him a minute, no matter how difficult the task at hand was. It always made Denise and I giggle when we were younger, we use to time him to see if he actually could fix everything under a minute, and he proved himself each time.

On the other hand, he wasn't the macho type who thought it was only the mom's duty to take care of his daughter. He was at every Christmas show, graduation ceremony, orientation day, parent-teacher interview that there was. Terrance was always there for his little girl.

One year, the three of us built the tree house that sits in the lone, gigantic tree in their backyard. He even let us use the hammer to nail things together. Everything was supervised of course, but he never thought us as being incapable of doing anything. I remember the summer that we finished it, spending our afternoons at make-believe tea parties, with our pretend friends, as well Denise's parents up in our pink and blue castle in the sky.

We also played war games with water guns, where the tree was our shelter and the grass was lava. Terrance would always win, each of us in one of his arms, giggling and screaming as he plucked us from our hiding spot, shooting us with his Super Soaker. Some days he would tell us, when Denise's mother wasn't around, that when we got older, as long as we promised to behave, that he would take us to the shooting range where we could fire his real guns, the ones that are powerful enough to shoot 15 rounds per minute. I always forgot about that promise, I think as we got older, we wanted to play less and less in the backyard, and as Denise got fussier, more opinionated, she wanted less to do with her parents. Denise so badly wanted to be a mature, responsible young adult, who didn't rely on her parents at too young of an age.

I think that is why over the years her relationship with her parents crumbled. She wanted to be independent too much, and maybe that is why she also didn't have any friends, she didn't want to need or rely on anyone else. She wanted to be self-sufficient, but I think she didn't realize that humans are such social creatures, that we need one another to live, to interact, to communicate, or we will go insane and become depressed from loneliness. She was so busy focusing on acting like a mature adult, telling her parents off when it was unnecessary, reminding them she no longer needed them, which was all clearly just an act that sadly grew more and more convincing.

I don't think her parents ever realized how much she actually did need them. There were times when we would go to my house, every day after school, for an entire week, and then Denise would make up an excuse as to why she wouldn't be able to hang out the next day, like she needed to do some chores or something. I knew it was just because she was homesick and needed to spend time with her parents. She likes to act more independent than she is.

I also know that her and her dad had not been getting along lately. The last time I had gone to her house she had made a comment when he had come in just to talk to us. She said something about his drinking, I had brushed it off, thinking nothing about it, because I knew that if I asked, it would turn into this big thing, something she would blow out of proportion. I knew her dad wasn't an alcoholic or abusive, or anything like that, and that he was actually the opposite, a very supportive parent. I think Denise would sometimes look for flaws in people even when they weren't there, as if it was a reason as to why she didn't need to rely on them, or couldn't rely on them. She would make up these false problems in her life, probably because everything was going along too well, and you know how teen angst can just act up sometimes.

At the same time, I don't know what to say, or how I am supposed to feel. I haven't seen him in over 7 months, and now he is gone, poof, just like that. This is also the first death I have ever experienced. I never had any grandparents, aunts, uncles, cousins, or anyone close to me that I had to mourn for before. I have also never known anyone to committee suicide, someone to leave this life and their loved ones behind because the world was getting unbearable.

How selfish!

How could he have just given up? Just left us? Oh poor Denise! I couldn't imagine what her and her mother must be feeling right now! My heart aches, but what about theirs? I still have a dad who I can run into his arms when a boy breaks my heart, a dad who will tell me that he will always be the man who will be in my life forever, no matter what. I have someone to walk me down the aisle, to go to my graduation, to see me live, to see me sing, and to meet my children. Denise has lost a huge part of her life, a part of her home, and I want to be there for her, I need to be there for her.

I found out about the news a couple weeks ago, but still hadn't heard anything from Denise. I called their home phone countless times, as well as her and her mom's cell. I have memorized all of their numbers since I was in middle school, even her dad's. I don't know what else to do. I don't want to pry, because if she needs time then I will have to give her time. But she also needs to know that I am here for her. She probably still thinks that I am hanging out with Ashley and Emma, making fun of her behind her back. She needs to know she can still count on me, and that I will do anything she needs me to do.

The past weeks have dreaded on slowly, I still haven't told my parents about what has happened either. I know that they will be upset too, we used to have family brunches when we were younger, all of us together. My dad used to call Terrance when he had a problem that he couldn't fix. Terrance used to even come over when my dad couldn't figure out how to stop the downstairs bathroom sink from leaking. They will be devastated, but I don't want to say anything. They have the right to know, he was their friend too. Yet the words can't seem to come out of my mouth. I have been trying to busy myself with singing, writing some songs, putting my heart and soul into words that can be heard by anyone else experiencing pain, letting them know they are not alone. I think when I find out when the funeral will be held, I will tell them then, otherwise they don't need to know something that will crush them, especially my mom, considering her line of work.

Denise also hasn't been at school once in the past couple of weeks. I asked Ms. V about it, I thought it would be better to go to her than the school counselor, she just seemed wiser. She told me that she has spoken with Denise's mom and that Denise still needs some time away to grieve. I asked her if she knew anything about the funeral, but she said that she was not informed about anything yet, and if I needed to speak with a counselor, or her, for any reason, that she would make time for me, whatever suited me the best. She hugged me before I could turn around and head to my next class. It was the first time I had been hugged in a long time, I got a big whiff of incense and lavender, it was surprisingly very comforting and exactly what I needed. I embraced her for a moment too long before she pulled me away at arms' reach to look at me, I felt like she was peering into my soul with her big brown eyes. She made sure that I was alright and that I didn't need to talk to her before sending me off to my next class. I must remember to thank her in my senior quote for the yearbook, she has always been there for Denise and I since grade 9, making sure that we were alright, and that no one had been bullying us. I wonder now if she ever saw anything but didn't want to pry, and wanted us to go to her for help, or maybe she was letting us know she was always there, either way she is one of my favorite teachers (same as Mrs. Cornwell).

Ms. V had comforted me, but it didn't last long. After a week of countless phone calls, and voice messages, I had to see Denise, to comfort her, to tell her how I feel, and how sorry I am about everything that happened. I decided that I was going to go yesterday after school, I would figure out what busses I had to take to get there, but then she actually showed up to school! I saw her right after the morning bell went off, people were running to their classes, and she was too far ahead of me for me to reach her before she ducked into a class. I was just happy to see her, to see that she was still breathing! I planned to find her during lunch, to talk to her, and maybe cut the rest of our classes and go get some junk food while I listened to her, or if she didn't want to talk then we could bus to the beach and just watch the waves roll in. I wanted her to have the opportunity to get everything off her chest, about how she feels about me, what happened, and what happened with her dad, I know she does not have anyone else to talk to.

My plan didn't work out so great. When I found her at lunch, she was surrounded by Ashley, Emma and a few other girls from the cheerleading team on the field. My stomach turned faster than it had before, I had to choke back my anxiety, there was no time for such nonsense when I knew she was in trouble.

I ran to the crowd, pushing through the girls laughing and sneering to reach Denise. I heard Ashley first, she was talking about Denise's dad. She said that it was a coward's way out to take their life, and that he must have really been miserable, but she understood why, it was because he had a little b**ch for a daughter. I was frozen, I had never not been able to move until that day, I guess my flight or fight senses where trying to kick in, but even they did not know what to do.

Then Emma quickly chimed in, saying how she heard that Denise's no good of a mother was a mess, hadn't come out of the house since she found out about her husband, and hadn't looked Denise in the eyes since she told her. Everyone was saying how it was Denise's fault that her dad committed suicide. Ashley snorted and asked: "Was it your fault, Denise? Did daddy kill himself because he's got a f**king freak for a daughter?" Those words burned my eyes, I felt them repeating, over and over in my head, like a child's taunt, "na-na, na-na, boo-boo." Emma answered for her, it was as if they had rehearsed what they were going to say to her. She said probably or he most likely had taken his life because his daughter was such an evil b**ch.

As my best friend of 8 years got tormented from half of the cheerleading squad, I stood there. I just f**king stood there! I have never been more disappointed in myself. Then Denise looked at me and her face changed, it was blank before, and then in a flash you could see how she was actually feeling, how broken she was. I saw the rage and sadness in her eyes, she actually looked deranged. I could tell that she thought I was with them, the crowd, there to gawk and sneer at her. I tried to reach out to her, stumbling on my feet. Ashley and Emma jumped out of my way, they must not have noticed me either.

When I got into touching distance from Denise, she recoiled back and spat at me. She looked me in the eyes, hers tearing up, and asked if I was there to make fun of her too, or better yet to ask if it was true, if it was her fault that her dad committed suicide, or was I just sick in the brain and wanted to know what the body looked like when she found him hanging in their shelter, dangling from a ceiling pillar he had fixed a month ago.

I had no idea she had found her dad's body. I couldn't begin to imagine how hard that must have been, all of the questions, thoughts, theories running through her head at top speed, which would have resulted in a migraine before she broke down. I also couldn't begin to imagine what the body must have looked like, had it gone blue from the lack of oxygen? Had it been a day since he had done it, had it begun to smell of rotting flesh? Were there flies? Were his lifeless eyes open, looking back at her, taunting her too?

A million things ran through my head. I had to tell her I was not with these nasty people, and that I was on her side. I wanted to defend her, tell her how beautiful she is, how smart, kind, and caring she is. I needed to say how talented and bright she is, how she has such a great future, that she is still loved. I had to let her know that her mother loved her, and never in a million years would blame her for such a tragedy. I wanted to say how sorry I was, about this, about everything. I have been an awful friend, but I need to make it up, I have to. I had to tell her not to listen to these idiotic people, that her and I can leave, go anywhere she wants and just talk, talk about everything, or nothing, whatever she needed. But I had remained silent, looking at her, trying to gather the courage to say what needed to be said, to tell her I love her.

She turned away too quickly, she left without any room for me to release my word vomit. With the sharp turn of her heels, she was off running, pumping her arms. I didn't know where she planned on going, but I knew I had to go after her, I had to, but I couldn't. My knees wanted to buckle, I felt wobbly in my legs. I remember putting my hands onto my thighs to catch myself from falling over, and then I saw in my peripheral vision that feet were beginning to move around me, circling me.

I had become the next prey in an instant. Ashley and Emma circled to my front, laughing, looking down at me as I tried helplessly not to fall over. Ashley said:

"Look everyone, it's Denise's lesbian lover, here to comfort her, but it's a little too late." I guess people still tried to bully someone about their sexuality, I had been so hopeful that today's modern bullies had at least matured a little bit, but once again I am disappointed. The girls roared with laughter and someone said something else, but I was too frantic to hear, I had to get to Denise. They continued on speaking, saying things I couldn't understand, but it didn't matter, I knew what they were trying to get at.

They probably said something along the lines of me being pathetic, how I am an awful excuse for a human being. They probably mentioned some of the nasty things that they said on Denise's messages. However, I didn't, and don't care what they were saying. I knew I had to straighten up, regain my backbone! I had to see her, to let her know everything was going to be okay.

So I moved, well I think I actually ran, but I ended up at home! I had no recollection how I got here. I wanted to follow Denise, but I also had no clue where she ran off to. I had probably run for at least 30 minutes, with backpack and everything, probably looking bewildered and frantic.

Now I am here, I have been up in my room all night, my family has come and knocked on the door checking in on me, asking me why I left school early. I pretended that I had felt sick, which wasn't a complete lie, but I thought that would be easier to explain. I want to talk to Denise before I tell them about everything that has happened, I know my parents will just stress about what is going on and right now they both have enough on their plates. I need to fix this on my own.

Before my mom went to bed, she came in and sat on my bed, petting my hair back. She said I did look sick, and that I should rest up because tomorrow was going to be a big day, it was going to be my big 16 after all.

I had completely forgotten my own birthday!! So much has been going on in the past couple of months that I hadn't even thought about it at all!

My mom had made me invitations for 10 of my closest friends, me not being the partier that I am, had decided to rent out a community center, where we were going to play a movie and have a huge arrangement of junk food such as pastries from Pete's bakery, candies, chocolates, and several varieties of pop tarts. I think the invitations were still in my backpack...

Just checked and yes they are... Sorry Mom!

It's now 2AM, and I am supposed to throw a party in three days but haven't invited anyone and my best friend's dad killed himself, and she thinks I am evil monster who is in cahoots with Emma and Ashley. I have to talk to Denise, maybe it can be just the two of us Friday night at my sweet 16. I never really had a birthday party before, this was supposed to be the year that I actually had more than just Denise show up, but then again 'friends come and go,' as the old saying likes to inform us.

Maybe I can use the whole birthday thing to my advantage. Denise and I have always hung out on my birthday at my place, she loved my family dinners, I think it was because she really enjoyed being around Tulip, she is like a younger sister to her, she is also the only other person who calls my sister by her nickname. I know that she might not want to come over, but she at least has to hear me out now!

I think I will make her favorite cinnamon buns. Martha gave me the recipe from Pete's bakery early this year, I am sure it's around here somewhere...

Found it!

If I show up with food in hand, a big smile, or maybe I will go more for a weak smile, and try not to look like a psychopath for once, she will have to listen to me! I will find her at lunch and tell her everything! I just need to take some deep breaths and remind myself that everything is going to be fine, her and I will get through this together.

I will let you know how it goes!

Chapter 27

Subject: Email #365

Dear Mr. President,

It has been 365 days since the Pandora High School shooting, exactly one year since I lost my beautiful baby girl, my sweet Penelope.

Did I ever tell you the shooting took place on her 16th birthday? I told her to stay home, it was a celebration; we could both call in sick that day, me from work and her from school. I knew I had been really busy with work lately, so I thought I could plan a whole day just for the two of us, and we could do anything she wanted. Unfortunately, she had told me she needed to go to school. She had baked her friend cinnamon buns the night before and was wanting to give them to her. I didn't even hesitate when she told me no, as if it was a normal thing for a teenager to miss out on the opportunity to ditch school.

I guess I had been missing a lot of things going on in her life that past year. I didn't know anything about her beautiful talent show that she had planned, the singing lessons, or the videos she created. If it was not for Mrs. Cornwall, I would not have known my beautiful daughter had the voice of an angel.

I thought she wanted to be a politician, or a lawyer, to do something where her voice would be heard. She was always soft spoken to strangers, but when you got to know her, you saw her opinionated, fiery side.

Penelope was actually the one who gave me the idea about emailing you. I remember when she was twelve years old, she wrote to the President at that time, telling him there had been a shooting at a school in Florida, killing three students and a teacher. She said how gun laws should be changed, that we needed change, and that no child should be afraid in the halls of their own schools. She understood that it was part of our history, but like everything else, it needed to be updated. She was one bright kid.

If she had told me that she wanted to be a singer, I would have been supportive, and I would have paid for the lessons. I would have done anything to see my little girl happy.

I had also missed all her friends, coming and going. I had been so wrapped up with work, I didn't even notice that Denise was no longer coming over, or that we were no longer having family brunches. I thought it was because of me being too busy, taking on too many extra shifts. I somehow managed to miss my daughter having a falling out with her best friend. What type of mother am I?

All of that confusion and stress in the past year of her life, and I was nowhere to be found. Well I could actually be found at work, or in my home office. I would have told her that some friends come and go, but best friends are meant for forever, and that if her and Denise were genuinely best friends, then she would come back to her, but if she didn't then everything would be okay.

Penelope was more understanding of my actions then I would have been. She never got angry or mad that I was not there as much as I should have been. She never told me that I was losing touch with my daughters, spending too much time with someone else's kid over the phone. She saw it from my perspective, but she also saw how naïve I was by thinking that what I was doing was better than spending quality time with my family, putting my love and effort where it mattered to me, where it hit close to home. I loved my job just a little too much. I loved feeling wanted and needed, saving lives, but I didn't realize how much I was loved and needed somewhere else.

Did I also tell you that I was there that day? How after I got off the phone, finished talking with my boss, I got out of the office as quickly as possible. I drove like a mad woman to the school; I think maybe part of me knew what was going to happen, or what had happened.

Maybe it was that mother's intuition, I am not sure, but either way I was still not prepared to see my daughter's dead body in the hands of her friend that had just shot herself, as well as fourteen other students.

I couldn't handle it, seeing all those lifeless bodies being pulled away and zipped into bags by the cops who had arrived moments earlier. The next couple of months I felt like I had gone into a comatose state, I was a walking zombie. It was not until my husband moved out of the house that I started waking up, realizing what I had to do to get everything back in order. I acted like it never happened, never mentioning her name, nor talking about her. I even started imagining her voice in my head as if she was still there. It sounded the same just before she died, nasally and high pitched from the lack of sleep she had the night before. I also started these parent meetings with Penelope's college fund. I thought I was trying to do some good, but I realized I was just trying to distract myself from what happened.

I changed the subject when my friends tried to talk to me about what happened, growing quietly resentful that they didn't ask more, didn't push me further. But I was the one pushing them away, acting like everything was fine and dandy. I acted normal, and tried to be normal, or fine, whatever you want to call it. What I really was acting like was a cheerful robot, listening, watching, going through the motion of living without actually living, while a smile was plastered on my face.

I feel like I have been in a suspended liquid state, present enough to take care of my daughter, without actually being there for her at the same time. I have been able to make her laugh, smile, and enjoy herself, trying to make her forget or not realize what had happened. However, I now know this was not the right thing to do, I should have asked her once how she was, or how she is feeling. People don't usually think about asking eight-year-olds how they are, or how they are handling everything. They expect that children will come to them, crying, fists balled up, with any problem they might have. But what about the quiet ones?

My little Tulip, which is what Penelope use to call Rosie, is the quiet type, just like her older sister. She doesn't talk much. She is more like the giggling, adorable kind of kid, but still, I have no clue what's going on in that precious head of hers. And for the fact I was not really present for the first two months, I wonder how she got by. I only remember getting up out of bed to wash my face, eat, or go to the bathroom, otherwise I was laying around on my computer, looking at the news, watching, listening and waiting. My husband must have stepped up his A-game when he needed his wife the most, I can't blame him for filing for divorce.

When I got into the routine, acting like the robot I was with my meetings, emails, driving my daughter to school, talking to friends, avoiding any discussions about how I was feeling, or how I was handling my situation, I think I was slowly getting better, making myself feel like everything was normal. But that was also just an act, simply make-believe. I was letting myself crack away slowly, while my metal shell rusted and chipped away.

It was all the major days that helped me realize I was not doing well, not handling everything. It was my husband leaving me, moving out, that first got my butt in gear. Then there was Homecoming, pretending like everything was fine. I even heard two students talking about me, gossiping, saying that I was the last person to speak with the shooter. I found it really hard coming to terms with this, accepting that I took some blame in the matter, not all, but some. Then there was Christmas, the first major holiday without my baby girl, the entire holiday I had been ignoring what was missing.

Next there was March for Our Lives, which was harder than I was anticipating. I was surprised how easily I was able to say that I had lost someone I loved dearly in a school shooting, or I at least implied it. Then Mother's Day crept on me quickly, and I believe it was my real cracking point. I realized that morning that I was going to be fine, I was going to be able to adjust as much as I could to the new life I had to live. I had not acknowledged that this was what I was experiencing, I just thought I was getting better at acting, that

I was starting to fool myself. I had gone to one of my meetings expecting people to be broken; to my surprise, it was the opposite. I think Sandy, one of the parents, had finally turned a new leaf, introducing herself to the newer-comer briefly and efficiently, stronger than ever. It was also this new-comer that made me realize I was done. I was done pretending to be the nice parent, the parent who gave passive opinions and suggestions. I told her exactly how I felt and how to handle her situation. Yes, I was in the wrong, I should not have freaked out at her the way I did, but I believe it will all work itself out in the end, and if it doesn't, then I tried my best. After my conversation with this parent, Hayley, I understood that I had to spend more time with my daughter, to follow my own advice that I had been giving to some of the parents over the past year. I was going to have a talk with Rosie about everything that happened, which I have decided to do today.

As I have also said, I can see why my husband left me. I forgot he ran away from his problems, and then slowly warmed up after a while, which is why he started softening up to me too. He probably remembered the type of person that I am. We both know I lost myself, but I was starting to find my way back home, and he is too. He loves me, I love him, and he may not be home now but we will get there, we still have a lot to work on, I know that, but love is worth it. I am once again going to take my own advice and speak to my husband about everything that has happened, how I wasn't there, and then he wasn't. I have written down some points that I need to bring up during our conversation. I can also see that I am starting to return to my normal self as I am slowly becoming more organized! We both have done some wrong, but marriage is all about working on our problems, working as a team.

I also decided to book a meeting for today. I thought it would be good if today I shared my story, or maybe give the parents who have not come yet another chance to talk about their problems with everyone. It also gives everyone a chance to see how different we all are, how people handle grief, death, and loss in similar or peculiar ways. It also being the first anniversary, I thought it would be a good idea if parents had the option of not being alone today. Now I know the parents' well-being is not my responsibility, but I still feel like I owe it to them, to give them what I can, yet also keeping my own well-being in mind.

I also finished reading my daughter's journal. I know that makes me sound snoopy, but I needed to know what was going on in her life before she died, and I needed to feel close to her again. It also made me realize that everyone is to blame. The teachers should have noticed something, the students shouldn't have bullied one another, parents should have noticed something, I should have notice something, and you should not make it possible for mentally ill people, adolescents, or children to be able to purchase or possess such weapons of destruction, automatic rifle or not.

I am tired of pointing a finger, trying to figure out who is to blame, who I should be yelling at for the death of my baby girl. I am also tired of pretending that this didn't happen to me, that I didn't lose one of the most precious things in my life. Finally, I am tired of realizing all the mistakes I have made over this past year, how I pushed my husband out of my house, how I was not there for my little girl, and how I tried to occupy my time with helping others when I needed to focus on myself.

I don't want a parent, sibling, grandparent, friend, aunt, uncle, cousin, or other loved one to experience what I have gone through over this past year. We need change and we need it now.

I know people are protective over their 'things,' these materialistic objects that give them power. I also know people love to hear that ting of metal, smell of gunpowder, and to feel the recoil of their toy. But it is guns that kill people. Yes, you can say people kill people, but one teenager is not humanly capable of killing fifteen students in a matter of seconds, milliseconds even. By stripping away people's ability to cause such damage in such a short amount of time, we could save hundreds of innocent lives.

I have also decided that I will leave you alone for now. If 365 emails have not helped this cause, then I do not believe another year of writing will have any effect. I will change my pro-active steps, toning down my obsession and instead I will continue to reach out to parents and students when I can. I will return to work eventually, but only as part-time, making sure my family comes first.

My last thoughts and prayers are for you to finally take part of the blame for what had happened at Pandora High School, and continues to happen at other schools, dance clubs, concerts, movie theaters, and everything in between. Take charge and be the man you say you are, make America great again, make guns limited in accessibility, unobtainable to the young, unwise, mentally ill, and other people who are not capable of making proper decisions. Please do not let this happen again, we cannot take any more losses.

Ta Ta for now,
Scarlett

Chapter 28

One Year Ago

On June 8th, 2018, Penelope slowly got up from her bed, groggy from staying up late baking cinnamon buns for Denise. When she finally made her way downstairs, dressed for school with her gray Herschel backpack slung over one shoulder, she found her mother in the kitchen, surprisingly not taking a work call but making breakfast.

"Good morning, birthday girl!" Scarlett chimed as she attempted to flip a chocolate chip pancake. Jonathan was the one who usually made breakfast, but this morning Scarlett had insisted, proclaiming her novice flipping skills to be better than what they were.

"Morning," Penelope croaked, all the stress and late nights had really hit her immune system hard. "So I was thinking, since it is your big sweet sixteen, that you could stay home from school today. I could get off work early, come pick you up, and we can go shopping, just the two of us." Scarlett was still stuck trying to flip over her tiny circular pancake, bubbles popping all around its side, quietly shouting at her.

Penelope felt like her mom was trying to make up for some lost time they had not shared over this past year. Penelope had gotten so wrapped up in the drama of her own life that she forgot about her mother, how she had spent her free hours on her computer or on the phone, working in every single text, call, or message possible, "saving lives" she liked to call it, as if she was a doctor performing open heart surgery.

Penelope missed her mother's happy expression change to guilt as she told her that she had to go to school today, she needed to talk to a friend, and then with a quick wave goodbye and a nasally "love ya." Scarlett was left alone in her big kitchen, with her deformed pancakes questioning her parenting skills before Rosie came bombarding down the stairs towards the smell of her chocolaty breakfast.

***

Penelope waited until lunch time to find Denise. She had left her freshly baked goods stuffed in her locker all morning; she did not want anyone questioning her for walking around with her big pink Tupperware filled with what looked like white icing. Denise's favorite part about cinnamon buns was the cream cheese icing, so Penelope made sure to add extra, making her twelve rolls look more like an iced cake.

With her pink container in hand, Penelope searched for her friend, first checking the excluded places, the washrooms, the library, and then she made her way to the cafeteria. She was beginning to lose hope.

Maybe she didn't come today, maybe she is still at home... I could call her house, but she knows my number and would probably just hang up, Penelope thought as she headed towards her final destination, the field.

Penelope could not imagine Denise in a million years hanging out where the cheerleaders and jocks slowly migrated to after eating, especially when there is a cheer meeting or practice going on, but Penelope's body led her there while her thoughts raced a thousand miles a second. *What if she kills herself, it would be my fault. I should have been there for her. I should have seen through Ashley's and Emma's bullshit, their lies, their fake personalities. All I did was help make Denise's life miserable, I pushed her away... I still can't believe it, that Terrance is gone. I never thought her dad would kill himself, he was always so nice, so supportive... What if it is hereditary, what if Denise is actually suicidal? What if she plans to harm herself? I couldn't live without my best friend. It would be all my fault. I have to tell someone, I can't handle this on my own. Ashley and Emma need to be told what they are doing is wrong, what they have done is wrong, and that they must stop. I will tell Ms. Vadhra.*

Penelope no longer cared if she was going to lose the respect of her fellow students, or that people were probably going to make fun of her until she graduated, calling her a tattletale like they were in middle school, or whatever immature terms and names they could muster up. She finally realized she needed to get help from a teacher or an adult, that she had taken on too much responsibility all alone, but it was too late.

As Penelope devised a plan of when and what she was going to tell the Vice Principal, she saw Denise. Denise was standing in the field, her back to Penelope, facing the cheerleaders and anyone who dared to be associated with them. She had a duffel bag that Penelope didn't recognize, which Denise removed from her shoulder, laying it down beside her as she knelt over it, unzipping it quickly. She removed what looked like a long black bulky thing of plastic, which Penelope's brain slowly began to recognize, then it dawned on her as she became aware what Denise planned on doing to the girls who had bullied and tormented her for the majority of her life.

Denise fired into the crowd of young boys and girls that were grouped closest to her, sending Penelope's reflexes into fast action, her muscles pushed her to the ground, while she clutched onto her obnoxiously bright container as if it where her life support.

"No," Penelope whispered to herself, trying to gain the courage to stop her friend, to plea for mercy, to beg for forgiveness. Penelope's instincts told her to run, to get away from here as fast as possible.

It was the quick rupture of screams that got Penelope running. She was the closest person to Denise, and the only person that was behind her. She was the only person that had the ability to get a jump on her without entering her line of fire.

After letting out her sad attempt of a plea, muffled by the adolescent screams, Penelope jumped to her feet sprinting towards her friend as fast as her skinny jeans would let her. She used the cinnamon rolls as weight, digging the glass into Denise's back, while she leaped into her, knocking Denise to the ground. There was brief moment of struggle, but Penelope was too shaky to hold Denise down. Denise managed to kick and rear Penelope off her back, getting up quickly with her new shiny toy in her hand.

Penelope remained on the ground, elbows on the freshly cut grass, the pink Tupperware laid awkwardly on her small stomach. Her chest sunk towards the ground, trying to inch away from her friend. Denise gained her balance back instantly, standing and leaning over Penelope, pointing her gun directly at her friend's young shaken face.

"Denise, what have you done?" Penelope whispered, barely being heard over the roar of the shouts of the children who had now made it to the gymnasium doors, warning their peers what fate awaits them.

"They fucking deserved it. They have all been fucking bitches, Penelope, pretending to be great, amazing, beautiful people, putting others down just to make themselves feel better. They had everyone fooled, even you, but not me, no, I saw them for the monsters they really are. I did the world a favor."

"How can you think you have done the world a favor? They were just stupid kids like you and me." Penelope paused, looking at the wasteland that surrounded her. "Some of these people were kind, genuinely good people, Denise." Penelope choked up after she saw Olivia's lifeless, twisted body reaching for her help from the girl that laid still next to her. "They didn't deserve this." Tears were beginning to burn Penelope's rapidly blinking eyes. "No one deserves this."

Denise refused to look around, to see what she had done. Her eyes remained focus on Penelope's pink container laying on her stomach, refusing to meet her friend's face.

"What is in the container?" Denise asked questioningly as she pointed the rifle towards her friend's stomach.

"Denise, you are sick, let me get you help," Penelope let out one last attempt to find her friend in this disturbed person that stood aggressively above her, reaching her hand out for help so that she could stand. Denise's eyes began to dart from side to side slowly, before again steading on her stomach.

"No, I don't need your help!" Denise let out a tormented cry, firing at the pink glass container.

There was a silent sigh as Penelope's outstretch arm fell to the side along with her body, collapsing on her left elbow. Denise knelt down towards the container, chuckling to herself, thinking, *What dumb bitch brings a bomb to a gun fight?*

To her reckless surprise, as she peeled back the lid forcefully, she saw no red and blue wires, no big clock ticking away the fleeting seconds, no water bottle filled with a homemade explosive. Denise's senses were traumatized by the overpowering, mouth-watering smell of freshly baked rolls. Through her blotchy vision, all she saw was white, ignoring the splattered imperfect red dots.

Denise picked up one cinnamon bun delicately with her dirty fingers. As she lifted the big roll, she saw red drip from the bottom. At first, Denise thought it was weird that they would have red food coloring on them, and that maybe they had been poisoned with some red toxin, but then with a quick shove, her senses came back crashing into her.

Denise pushed the Tupperware away to see red tiny holes freckled across the body that lay in front of her. It was as if she had forgotten everything that had happened moments earlier, forgetting what or who the box of rolls laid on. Denise's eyes slowly made their way to the face of the body that she was now rocking back and forth, gently in her arms.

It felt like torture for Denise seeing the life drain from Penelope's pale blue eyes. The first dead body Denise had seen was her dad's, but she couldn't stand the sight of him dangling so she ran for her mother after finding him hanging from the pillar. She never got a second look at his lifeless body, but now she had her chance to experience it all again.

Denise held Penelope's unreachable gaze after the short, shallow breaths finally drained from her chest. She finally understood why in the movies actors would close the eyes of their loved ones; she felt like it was as if something was missing in them. The longer she stared, the more she noticed that they had no movement, that they looked like they were no longer staring at anything, but just set on a point, not visible to the living.

Denise was finally coming to, as if she was in comatose state, acting without acknowledgment, as if she was possessed. She had been blinded by rage, hatred, but now she was beginning to see, see what she had done. Denise could hear the sirens, beckoning closer and closer. She closed her friend's eyes with shaky, frosted finger tips. Then Denise grabbed the rifle one last time and let out her final shot as the cop cars and a single black Ford Escape pulled up to the back of the field, unleashing a crowd of uniforms rushing towards her.